GREATER OCEANS THAN THINE

Greater Oceans Than Thine

Nelson McKeeby

CONTENTS

Chapter I

The Fallen One

It was a sandy beach with a deep blue sky upon which some mystical artist had painted roiling clouds of pregnant white and featherings of gray streaks lit with carmine filaments of sunshine. She opened her eyes to the sight and was overwhelmed by the bursting colors and the reverse horizon line. The things she was seeing were hypotheticals from a visidrama, not anything that should exist. It was unlike anything that should be seen by anyone, an impossibility, but it was real indeed.

She made an initial effort, levering herself onto one arm.

The world was one of chaos. A murmur of white noise came from the water rolling onto the beach from the endless sea. Wind blew trees to rub their green-plated leaves, scraping against each other in a concert of rasping stipules and shaggy fronds, the tiny sounds of chaos forming an organized concert that a philosopher might call a natural orchestra. It was a popping turmoil, distracting, and hit Adjeness with a weight of confusion as she sat up from the sand.

There was one hope. This sort of resolution would only happen in a tank, and that tank needed a physical connection. She used her hand to pull any unseen primary bud from behind her ears and thought the words, "programmer mode," to end the simulation. It was no simulation though. She sat up and looked at both hands, opening and closing alternate eyes, trying to force a parallax error to invade the captive reality simulator or to disturb the visualization. No application, no matter how sophisticated, could completely account for the stochastic randomness of human synapsis found in finger motions against a reality lens. But if it was a lens, then it was the best one ever created.

Thus, it was no lens. She was here. She felt sick.

If the cacophony of noise was not damaging enough to her sense of well-being. Adjeness was also attacked by vertigo caused by an endless visual horizon. The sky was large and curved in the wrong direction, like her head was in a great bowl. Instinctively, she tried to orient to gravity but realized too late that it was a fool's errand. She fell on her face into the sand and had to recover her balance and position again.

You do not expose yourself to the primary, she thought. It was a scary experience to see in the corner of her eyes that indeed, the blasting radiance of a naked star was just a glance from her eyes. The naked radiation of the primary, Tau Ceti, rained on her face and body, threatening to blot her from existence, or else that was what her body told her. Her skin screamed under the assault of the light that poured onto her. She had to will herself not to look into the cascade of visual radiation that likely had a passel of cosmic radiation riding in its wake. The assault nearly overwhelmed her.

There was no use denying it. She was down a well, ten meters per second with an escape of thirty kilometers per second, thrown into a primitive world. The figures for escape ran through her head and then were erased as useless. She doubted she could generate even ten kilometers an hour thrust perpendicular to the center of mass of the planet, let alone what would be needed in opposition to return to orbit.

She fell into the sand again and started to cry. "Sky-borne!" She screamed, "*Jebu-Se! Vržem se dol, jebci!*" Her brain did not process standard for a second, which was scary, but her cortex snapped into place. So many people learned standard Galax through technology that being removed from the matrix of modern living, they could actually lose the ability to communicate, but the academy required her to have actual fluency in the language. But the need to actually think in the language was disturbing in its implications.

She had to get standing and see what she had to work with. Adjeness rolled onto her back and thrust her fist to the sky. "Damn you!" She yelled. Then she turned over again and pushed herself to standing.

"Grimora, rescue protocol," she subvocalized. There was no response. The aether was silent to her. "Grimora, respond," she said verbally and realized that the lack of a carrier indicated the worst. She could not connect to the mesh at all.

Her skin was exposed to the sun because someone had dressed her in a single-suit, and good to its name, it was delaminating. She pulled the suit off and looked at it curl up in the sun. One-use suits were convenient unless you happened to be cast onto a beach under the heat of Tau Ceti. Then Adjeness would have preferred an expedition carapace.

However, there was something in the suit's pochette that was not delaminating. She tossed aside the dross of the suit and pulled the bag that had ridden on its hip belt. Someone, in dressing her, had given her a gift. It was a wänd.

She pulled it out and inspected it. Like most wänds, it was a truncated dodecahedron, milky white, with four sides colored in pastel colors: one in green, one in blue, one in red, and one black. It was about the size of a number ten bolt, able to fit in the hand with the fingers closed around it. The dodecahedron was quiet, cold, dead. That made some sense. An active wänd could be detected as it communicated with the grid and called on services for its owner. Leaving an active wänd about was dangerous, especially if an untrained user was able to connect to it in some meaningful way. The joke was that wänds were smart in a very dumb way. They wanted to help their user and they had access to great power in a properly prepared environment, but that power could bite people around the user. Planetside would be worse as there was likely no safety net in place to detect misuse and no one who would audit the wänd's actions. If she could activate it, it would be a powerful aid to her survival. Nowhere on the planet was devoid of access to the mesh with an amplifier like a wänd, and she was an expert in their use.

Adjeness looked at the blue sky, then the green chaos of what she decided to call a "forest," if that was what it was, and then down to the sands of the beach. Her mind was in turmoil, just like the land she had found herself on. She ripped off the rest of the clinging suit and tossed it to the sand, then stood watching it delaminate completely into a welter of primary silicoids and burbling polymer protease, just as they were supposed to do. Single-use really meant once and done, and photo-disposal took on a new meaning for speed when it was attacked by a thousand watts of energy per square meter. The creator of the things probably never intended them to be used on a planet with a direct and unblocked line of sight to a primary.

Now, she had only a basic pair of station-made undershorts, rubberoid ship's slippers, and the cold, dead wänd.

She looked over her most important item of survival. It was a Mark IV, so the finger pad had 4,096 different input combinations. It would accept three chances to wake it from its sleep, then it would never be useable again. Her own code was green, green, black, blue, red, black, but activating it using that code would mean that one of her captors knew her security protocols and had put them into the Mark IV before giving it to her.

That was too much to believe.

The factory reset on a wänd straight from the box was never supposed to be left unchanged. Most wand-wrights would use their own private reset code to make sure that the device was safe to handle and could not be used by the unskilled. The factory code, though, was black, red, blue, green, red, red, red. She entered that combination.

The wänd vibrated a little, the haptic response that indicated it was working, and then sat quietly.

Kidnappers. She was remembering what happened, if not who and why. A dark corridor and a door that expanded without command. Dozens of hands grabbed her as she fought for her life. She was not large, but she had the power of her mesh authorization. Yet they must have blocked it. Darkness swallowed her as someone used an old-fashioned trank on her neck.

Adjeness was stupefied. One of her kidnappers had put into her hands an unlocked wänd after going to all the effort to separate her from the mesh and assaulting her like some common criminal. It made no sense. Why strand her, then hand her the tools to rescue herself? She could enter any combination when concentrating on the wänd now and it would wake up and call for help from CentCom. She would not have to identify herself to her rescuers. They would get her just because she was a castaway with a wänd. Then her kidnappers could be exposed and defeated.

She paused. That could be an issue. If she started calling for help, her kidnappers could know. They could track her through the wänd. The purpose of leaving her the wänd could be to trap her as she sought to escape the well and find support. Adjeness had ideas on why and who would target her for stranding, but they were not fully sketched out in her mind, and that created a level of paranoia that was not helped by the chaotic chiaroscuro of weather and life on this hellish beach.

Luckily, she was an expert in using wänds. A Warden needed no other tool to protect their charges if they had a wänd and access to the aether and an active mesh. Dwimmer-kind was trained into them at the academy. Where most people dabbled in dwimmer for their daily affairs, relying mostly on frames and frellons to conduct business, a Warden could never trust that a frellon was not arrogated, that a frame could be hiding secret code-stuff that would surprise them in some moment of weakness. A wänd might be designed so that simple and unskilled users could conduct tasks using it with only a passing thought, but a true master of wänd-dwimmer could literally move mountains if they desired to do so.

She closed her hand around the device and connected with it. After a few seconds, she released it. There was no time to fully tune the wänd to her own psyche. That could take hours. However, it would slowly integrate to her as she used it. All she had to do was set it for propitiation and keep it in her possession for a few hours. Trying to ignore the wind, the waves, and the scratching of leaves on each other in the virulent forest that hummed next to her was distracting her from being able to make a good connection. That confusion would be gone in a score of hours and that would be when she needed to get comfortable with her new wänd and figure out how to proceed next. Still, she could protect herself from having the device arrogated.

She constructed a command code for the wänd that built privacy into it. It was an empty tool without any structure that had formed, so the process was easy. Still, it was a perilous command because she could forget the wänd if she left it someplace for too long, but it would constantly be guarding its signature and forcing unskilled and unprotected minds to ignore its existence. Those who handled it would be see it as a plain object of no real significance, a bobble to be toyed with. But unless the person had the right training, or at least a mind that was strong and open to the dwimmer of the wänd, they would forget it in due course. And like all forgotten pieces of pocket nothing, soon handed on, lost, or simply misplaced. That would protect her until she could get the unit operating.

Better yet, even a skilled search for the wänd would be an exacting and difficult task for an expert. It would now draw only small powers and effects from the grid. It might be able to move a mountain in theory, but when set for privacy, it would not be able to take the command to try. Instead, it would put most of its effort into information, local protection, mind ghosting, and simple tricks of shifting mass and weight. The wänd was still an important tool, but it was now unable to reveal her position unless she changed the basic setting. She entered the program and set it running.

Now for survival. In the woods, there stood a mobile denizen, a sophont, if one were to stretch the definition. A creature of the well, a dirt-born. Adjeness regarded the creature. She was a woman who looked impossibly old, with a craggy face, white hair, and deep red-brown skin, dressed in vegetable rags and strips of leather. She had a stick in her hand that she leaned on, and a fur-covered companion who, if it was possible, possessed less intelligence than their seeming master. Adjeness walked over to the person and said, "Speak to me in your language. I must learn your speech."

The personage replied, "*Aljawu barid 'iilaa hadin ma eind aliastihmami, walan yakun alqawm al'aqwia' sueada'a.*"

Adjeness considered the speech. It was not any of the tongues she knew or could decipher. She made a mental modification to the Mark IV to increase its language processing capacity and, in essence, teach her the tongue as fast as it could. It was a shortcut because if she left the wänd behind, the language could fade without practice. It was a sloppy way to really learn a language, but she had no desire to communicate more than was needed with this woman. "Good," she said, "keep talking if you may. Water, food, clothing, shelter." She stopped for a second, then walked to the water that was lapping the sand shore, scooped a handful, and held it to her mouth. "Water."

"*Tilk hi amra'at almiah almalihati!*" The women said, "*La yumkinuk shurb dhalika.*"

Adjeness frowned. "Water," she said again.

"*Ma',*" the woman replied and motioned with her hands to follow.

Adjeness followed the women into the woods, while the fur-covered creature followed, making a "yap-yap-yap" sound. Each time she said something, the woman responded with a torrent of language. Each word was useful in getting the Mark IV to provide her fluency.

The green-leaved objects with sturdy, wide stems were indeed trees, which the woman called "*shajara.*" As a group, they were "*ashjar*" or "*ghaba,*" which meant forest. "*Al ghaba*" was the forest they were in, but was not a proper noun, just "the forest."

Her stick was part of a tree named "*taqsus.*" She called it "*easa almashy alkhasat bi.*" "*Easani,*" meant staff. It would take a while since the Mark IV did not have the language in its library, but it would learn it while teaching Adjeness how to communicate in the tongue.

The trees were closely spaced, and the ground was covered with other plants, but the woman seemed to have the trick of traversing the terrain, and Adjeness duplicated her moves. Despite this, her feet were soon cut and blistered. The wänd made a real effort to protect her, but the ground was too broken with wooden debris, small rocks, and plants that did not easily yield to being stepped on as if some quirk of their development had actually added this to their very nature. After ten minutes, they arrived at a cabin made from vegetable matter and her feet were torn up. The woman went into the cabin and returned with a wooden container with a stopper. She looked down at Adjeness and her feet and said, "*Lays ladayk qadamayn litamshi hafi alqadamayni.*" She handed the container to her and said, "*Ma'—vodo.*" The last word was close to the word for water in Galax.

Adjeness took the container and opened its top. It was water inside, so she drank it down as far as she could. She noticed that the woman was staring at her feet. "Shoes," Adjeness said. Her own slippers were a torn mess, defeated by the chaotic ground. "Shoes," she said again.

"*Čevlji?*" the woman said, making a hash of the Galax word. Then she said, "*Ahdhia,*" and touched the sandals she wore. She went back into her hut and returned with sandals and a length of white cloth. "*Ajlis,*" she said, pointing at the ground. That meant "sit," either based on context clues or because the wänd had caught enough of the tongue to start making sense of it compared to other languages spoken by humans.

Adjeness sat and stretched her feet out. The woman took a small jar from a pouch around her waist and kneeled, applying the material to first her right foot, then her left. Her danger-sense did not indicate this was problematic so she let her, and the lotion turned out to be soothing. She then swaddled both feet in the long, narrow lengths of cloth she had. Finally, she put a sandal on each foot. The whole time she nattered on to herself like a telltale set to automatic, a constant fluid wash of words. In any other situation, Adjeness would have ordered the woman to shut up, but the constant stream of speech was in effect helping her wänd implant the language into the psyche of Adjeness.

"Do you understand me?" Adjeness asked in the language, letting the wänd lead her in her speech.

"Limadha not say lugha Eurabani, you know?" The woman asked.

"I am learning it," Adjensss replied, pulling one foot, then the other up and checking them tenderly for the fit of the new shoes.

"*Ana atiealam,*" the woman corrected her, "*Ana atiealam.*" Then she thought for a second. "*Yataealam, tellum, taealamt.*" Adjeness started to hear the woman saying "learn, learning, learned," as if teaching a child the basics of the tongue.

"Do not correct me," she said, knowing the Mark IV already probably was working the language into her head without real learning. "Just speak."

The native woman nodded, "As you say, high born. What service may I give you?" That at least was clear in her mind,

Adjeness thought to herself. It was probable the language had a known analog in the human universe and that analog was helping the Mark IV implant grammar into her mind, only having to seek a solution to the dialect the ignorant woman spoke.

The words sounded wrong, poorly ordered, but Adjeness was unlikely to be speaking with good grammar yet either. It would come. "I need you to lead me to a place where food, transportation, clothing, and service may be purchased."

"I am not to leave my watch of the coast," she replied. "It is my duty."

Adjeness stood. "You have a new duty person. Lead me now, I am a … *Glavni Paznik… wôrdn…*"

"You are a Warden?" The woman asked. The word was "haris" in her tongue.

"That is so, a Warden. Do you know what this is?" Adjeness asked.

"I am not apostolical, high born. However, if you are a Warden, then I am your servant … *'eabd.'* She stopped, then said, "Naked?"

Adjeness understood. She would ordinarily be disturbed at being disrobed in public, but she tried to say to herself that it was not a matter. She had no need to earn this creature's admiration, and the weather was actually warm, even under the trees. She shrugged and said, "No matter."

"*Alsaaqitun yafealun ma yuridun,*" the woman said.

The words made no sense to Adjeness, but it did not matter. The wänd had quickly caught the trick of the language, and random natters from the old woman were not important enough to bother with. It was even possible that the statement was an aphorism that was like an Earth-Born quoting some memetic statement from their past. A meaningless little clip of language. "Then take me to the place where I can have my needs met," she told the woman.

"'*Ana amtathalat*," the woman said, bowing a little. "Follow me."

Adjeness tried her feet and was relieved that the pain was under control. She could feel the wänd's automatic routines making adjustments to her blood chemistry, muscle learning, circulatory system, and breathing, to protect her from the worst damage. Properly tuned, the wänd would allow her to walk through a raging fire protected by a thin layer of sweat, to turn away physical impacts, and to move gracefully in variable gravity. That would take weeks unless she worked with the device, but it would come if she needed it.

The woman's camp was primitive, but it fit the world she was embedded in. As they walked into the forest, the world seemed to close in on Adjeness with its wild and unpredictable spirals of vegetable matter. The dappled light of the sun played games with perspective in the tree-filled woods. Despite being bent and seemingly frail, the old woman was nimble. At times, Adjeness had to trot or even run to follow.

It was exhausting, even with the wänd tuning her for the effort. Hour-on-hour the woman spoke of nonsense, and they traveled for five kilometers or more with a slew of crazy speech discussing children Adjeness could not care about, weather that did not matter, useless accomplishments, and victories that were hollow and lacked importance. If anyone had dared talk such a stream of crazy to Adjeness before, she would have backhanded them and reported them to their dorm manager, but again, she thought that the nonsense had a practical purpose even though it wore on her nerves.

They broke into a clearing where a small building was positioned by a stream of water that was crashing out of the forest. Sitting out front of the stone structure were three well-dwellers dressed as the older creature. Their clothing was better repaired but still crude and random, as if each stitch was placed by hand. Adjeness realized that indeed, that was likely why all the structures and clothing looked so odd. It was all built with primitive tools by creatures who suffered constantly from horrible diseases and stifling ignorance. The trio had a fire built from broken pieces of wood and were simmering water in a stone urn. They looked up and then stood as one.

"Perga, you have brought us an *eahira*, and my birthday has not even passed!" the tallest of the creatures, a male, said.

The old woman they called Perga, Adjeness's guide, said, "She is a high-born Warden."

"Courtesan then," the dark-haired female creature replied, picking up a long chunk of wood in her hand.

The second male creature laughed and leaped to his feet, "Damn if her hair is not red like an Emporian! I would give some silver for that."

"Shut up!" came a yell from the stone house. The loud voice proved to be owned by a larger and better-dressed male who wore a large curved sword of bright metal on his side. He had to duck to leave his structure. "What is this, Perga? Why are you here, and why bring this woman here?"

Perga cackled. "A fiery rock fell from the sky, then she swam ashore just meters away from where I and my dog were sitting. You say I should yell if trouble lands on the coast, but I think she may be trouble."

Adjeness stepped forward. "I am trouble if you do not do as I say. Now let us discuss how you can serve my needs." She may have stumbled a little on the words and they did not have their intended effect. But then again, the wänd was not active and could not aid her commands with psychological effects projection.

The three laughed. The first male picked up a chunk of wood matching what the female had in her hand and said, "Civil tongue '*qariban liakun eabdan.*' Taste my *qadib!*" And he swung the wooden object at Adjeness's shoulder.

Adjeness knew how to fight, but no one who faced a surprise attack could defend from a sudden blow. The wand, though, could. Adjeness stepped forward onto the male's instep and grabbed his arm, sending him flying forward into a low stone wall with a thud. There was a second when the whole group stood, mouths agape. But then the young female was charging her, running past the one called Perga with the intent to tackle her or beat her with her wooden tool. It was simple to step into her run and clothes-line her neck with a straight arm, though she smelled of what Adjeness associated with bad fish product that had been left in a cafeteria too long.

She was stunned then, with a blow to the back of her head and the wänd dropped from her hand. She fell forward into the dirt. The male she had almost maimed came after her, but the large, loud-voiced personage pushed him away.

"Let me stamp her, Zamüg!" The first one screamed.

The large man, named Zamüg, said, "You do not do anything to this one. Look at her!"

The old woman with the dog laughed. "Just so, dimwitted fisher. Look at her! A thousand if you tame her and get her to sale in the capital. If you stamp her, you are throwing the catch back before it can be sent to market, Hamk!"

Adjeness tried to get to her feet but was given a swat with the wooden staff carried by the old woman, Perga. The third male, though, was contemplative. He kneeled down by Adjeness's face and said, "Is this not why the First Citizen pays us to watch the coast, to tell him of odd happenings and things of import?" He put his hand in the dirt to help him stand but yelped in pain. He came up with his fists around Adjeness's wänd and said, "Is this a die?"

"Is what a die, Bailjos?" the one called Zamüg asked. "Pay attention. If we tell the First Citizen we caught this one, then she will take the treasure from us! What harm is she, and why would anyone care?"

The one called Bailjos looked at the wänd and said, "It has no numbers."

Hank yelled, "Shut up, Bailjos. Of course, Zamüg, we can tenderize her here, then send her on to Borglie. He will know her worth and be able to seek out some silver for her.

The man with the wänd took a sack from near the fire and shoved the tool in. "A die with no numbers is worth something, maybe."

Adjeness tried to say something, but the woman who she had thrown pushed a sack over her head and she could not stay conscious anymore.

Chapter II

A Surgeon's Daughter

S etchi woke up when Sir Ordell Brastingwell slapped her. She opened her eyes and saw that the disgraced noble was dressed and had his two remaining retainers, Midhges and Prout, standing like sacks of onions in the corner, sketching evil looks on their faces.

"Get out of bed," Ordell said. "Change your camisole."

The knight had no interest in her nudity. The interest in her as a meal ticket so far outweighed his desire for a young woman that it made his request simply a demand for action. His two retainers were different, but as long as Ordell was present, they would do nothing. He had killed two men who had tried.

She got up, removed her old camisole, and replaced it with one that the servants of the merchant had laundered. When she had done so, she said, "You are a fool if you think my father wants me or will pay any money for me."

Ordell took out a small leather folder and removed an odd canvas tube. The tube was small, split down the middle, and seemed to be stiffened by something that ran down its middle. "Well, that may be so, but a father might not want you and can still pay for your comfort." The knight turned her about physically and wrapped the canvas around her neck and down around her body.

"Why were you given the death sentence on Emporia?" she asked as he worked.

"Same question, same answer, none of your business." He finished his work then added, "I was paid to bring you here, and now I will be paid to hand you over ... enough that I need never see Emporia again."

He turned her around, then reached into her travel chest and took a pair of worsted trousers. "Step into these, carefully though," he said.

She did so and wished he had given her leggings first. The trousers were newly bought apparently, and not previously laundered. However, he then offered her a naval jacket and no shirt or waist wrap. She wanted to complain, but it was easier to let him slide the garment on.

"Now listen closely," he said, grabbing her face roughly. She tried to struggle, but he made it plain that he would twist her head if need be. "That canvas work is a minder. Inside of the canvas is a strong, thin, cutting wire. If I take the canvas end and pull, it will leave the sharp wire around your neck. If I pull the end for that wire then, it will cut your head off."

She gasped. Midhges and Prout laughed until Ordell silenced them with a look.

"Your father is not poor. He is the surgeon on what is reputed to be the richest tea merchant in the northern Halo. The captain is married to the new Dominar of Cycus. The docks are abuzz. I am going to meet with your father and see he pays me every silver he has ... and steals more on top of that. Then I will give you to him and that is that." Ordell was sweating in anticipation despite the cool weather. He took her shoulder and then guided her to the door.

She tried to struggle a little, but the knight knew his business and she could feel the canvas around her neck and what seemed to be a metal, grating wire inside of the canvas. "Feel that?" he said.

"Yes," Setchi replied.

"I have longed to toss you and your pretensions and sense of wealth overboard since we left Emporian waters. If I am frustrated in any way on this matter, you will find your head by your feet, and your last vision will be your neck pumping out all the blood from your little body." He put his finger on her neck-crease. "Knowing that this is the last sight you will see." He pulled the canvas wrap a little more to emphasize how her death would be accomplished.

She nodded, promising herself not to cry. If her last sight was to be of blood fountain from her body, his last sight of her would be her contempt for his very existence.

The rooming house was of the lowest possible quality and led into a bar that served more than tea in it. Reprobates and low men and women were drinking what looked to be spirits from wooden glasses. Some were eating pickled eggs and sour cabbage on slices of toasted bread. The smell was like a fist to the stomach. Ordell guided her to a table in the middle of the room, sat her down, then waved off his minions to corners of the tavern. A woman detached herself from one of the early-morning revelers and approached.

"Are you Circum-Valus?" he asked her.

She nodded. "Not sure I like this deal you proposed to Latif last night."

"Who is Latif?" Ordell asked.

"The man who you asked for aid of the Circum-Valus. He is my liege," the woman said.

"Fake nobility and wispy fears do not impress me, gang mistress. If you are here, you must have heard of my request from the man I spoke to last night. If he is Latif, good enough. Did he explain the job?" Ordell motioned with his head to Setchi.

"Muscle for an exchange, my lord," the ganger said.

"Watch your tone," Ordell said.

"What of pay, my lord?" the woman asked.

Ordell laughed. "Pay on completion, or do you expect a man such as me to trust people such as you?"

Setchi could see that Ordell was not as impressive to this woman as he seemed to think, but the Circum-Valus nodded. "Our people are here, and you will have the service your pay rate deserves." The woman then looked at a man at the tavern window and added, "Your mark approaches."

"The surgeon?" Ordell asked.

"You really expect the surgeon to appear from a ship like the *Remarker*? Two of her crew though," she said.

Ordell took a seat. "Good enough."

Setchi felt calmer as he adjusted the tails of the canvas and metal wraps that sketched a deadly trail around her neck. She was concentrating on this when the door to the tavern opened and two people walked in, both wearing merchant uniforms. One was a long, dark-haired Lurian man, and the other was an aggressively bald woman. They approached the table and the merchant-woman said, "Are you Sir Ordell Brastingwell?"

"I am. Be seated. The lovely, young, healthy woman next to me is Setchi Darrell. I believe your surgeon is her father," he said.

They took a seat opposite Setchi and Ordell but said nothing. Ordell grew nervous and said, "Come, this is a business deal, not a deck fight. Order something to drink, and give us your names!"

The woman said, "My name is Commander Sunstar Nine. I am First Officer of the *Remarker*. My companion is Lieutenant Igor Bosanac, Third Officer. We are here to discuss this woman who may or may not be related to one of our crew."

Ordell laughed and drew a leather folder from his jacket. "Can either of you read?" he asked.

"Yes," came the reply from the hairless woman.

He passed the leather folder over and she opened it up, pulling out a sheaf of documents. Reading carefully, she passed each sheet to Bosanac, who glanced them over and returned them. When Sunstar Nine finished reading, she put the papers back into the leather document folder and said, "Captain needs to see this to hand over that much silver." She moved the folder in her hand. "This is not the business of her father. The captain does not permit his crew to screw around on deck like this."

Setchi almost laughed when Ordell took a worldly air. "Of course, you may carry the proposal to your captain, but only one of you. The other stays here where I can watch them. You cannot expect me to let your captain scheme. He should have left this to the girl's father anyway. Safer for his ship."

Sunstar Nine looked at Igor Bosanac, who nodded, got up from the table, and left for the door. The officer watched until he was gone and said, "Twenty minutes for him to get those documents in front of the captain."

Ordell nodded and rotated his hand in the air. "That seems fine. Very fine, in fact. The captain has the money, no?"

Setchi watched quietly as Ordell tried to control the situation that he had no skills to control. The hairless woman was trouble. She scared Setchi. Flowers of the Sun they were called in the core, fanatic worshippers of a false Sun God by many people's accounts. In the lands of her birth, they were known for their touchy pride and sudden violence. Ordell had to know their reputation. The officer's visage screamed that she was not to be trifled with. Her clenched jaw and severe head with its tattoos promised terrible vengeance if she felt misused. And her "third officer" was no less serious business. How could her captor not know these people were not to be trifled with?

The woman named Sunstar Nine addressed Setchi. "Has this man mistreated you?" She asked in a deceptively soft voice.

Setchi felt the canvas minder tighten. "No," she said.

"You really should take that rig off her," Nine said to Ordell. She indicated with a nod that she knew exactly what type of horror her captor had equipped her with.

He laughed. "You foolish tea merchants. All that wealth and it clouds your eyes for the quality. Well, I was born to quality. I am not some fanatic worshipper of a false god. I do not need to snuffle around for silver to be quality. This 'rig,' as you call it, is just one of the dominoes I have in my hand. You remember that I hold the cubes and a mere flick of my fingers will cause them to crash down around you, your ship, and this little girl. The game pieces are mine and I decide when they turn up, and when they turn down. Do you understand?"

Setchi yelped as she felt the canvas slide against her skin. She would not cry, she said again to herself. Not in front of Lord Ordell, the shit. She could see he was smiling as he rubbed her back, and each rub caused the canvas garrote to be felt, not a pain, but a reminder of her being on a leash of death.

"You hired the Circum-Valus. That was an expensive move considering we might not give you a brass zot for this girl," Sunstar Nine said, waving her hand in the air for service. A bar-master came by, and the officer said, "Pot oh the shanty, Dighles." The servant nodded and went to the bar.

Setchi gasped. The blind, blind man Ordell did not see what she had displayed for him. He was blind to the obvious! The absolute idiot. Ordering tea in the gutter speak of the docks, knowing the name of the server of the tea and having it served with alacrity? She looked intently at the merchant officer. The officer glanced at her then looked away, a feral smile on her lips.

The clay pot came with three wooden cups, religiously proper for a place that served beer and rum-spirits to the worst the dock had to offer. Even the most el dari person could not complain of metal taint in the drinks. Nine took a cup and poured tea into it. "Some for you?" she asked Ordell.

"Shanty … might as well piss in my mouth and call it the best porter-grape. No, the pot is yours," Ordell said.

Sunstar Nine poured the stiff dockside tea into a second cup and pushed it in front of Setchi. She then drank her own portion hot from the cup. "Lord Ordell, consider tea."

"Let us consider the silver tea buys and how much will be in my pockets in an hour," he suggested instead.

Nine ignored him. "When I first came out in the sun temple they served temple tea. Strong smokey stuff, dried in the sun and grown on a hillside by the temple. The most amazing drink, made by the priestesses who pulverized it to a powdered essence, filtered clear water through it, heated it for a precise time, strained it out and again dried the paste, and rubbed it on a screen, and when it had aged, served in it small wooden cups. What an amazing experience. Yet, tea never grows old. The captain favors this horrid brew, Junebug, boiled over paraffin. Nasty. But in a cold storm with the northward wind pushing us off the tolan, ice rimming the sheets, and everyone a minute from being taken by the next huge wave, it is that old, acrid, acrimonious Junebug that shakes you awake. And everyone sharing the same miserable tea, in the same horrible storm, it makes us brothers. You can say the act of drinking tea together is what makes the Halo a society, not simply a hundred tribes, ten thousand kiths, spread across a hundred thousand spits of land. We all sit to tea together each day."

Setchi was fascinated that this rough commoner with her shaved head screaming religious suppuration or even madness, was so calm-spoken and intellectual. She had no truck with the sun struck and their idiot religion, but was forced in this time to make a different calculation. She said, "May I have the tea?" She looked at the cup in front of her.

Nine looked at Ordell. "May she?"

Ordell laughed. "Why not?"

Sunstar Nine motioned to the cup cooling in front of Setchi. "Mind the crash of that, my child. It is real."

Setchi reached for the tea and nodded. Indeed, the tea was a bruiser, a crash, as this woman said in her Eurabanni cant. Even on the various ships that they had taken passage on to reach from Emporia to Cycus, the tea had not been this common. However, the truth of Sunstar Nine's comments came through as she brought the beverage to her lips. It was the ritual that here, at what could be the end of her life, mattered. Indeed, here at this horrible tableaux, tea was a connecting thing between the ship's officer and herself, so far apart otherwise in class and candor.

"Why are you crying, my dear?" Sunstar asked.

Setchi did not realize she was crying. "Because my mother died," she said, though it was more than just that.

Sunstar Nine nodded. "*Alalihat tadeu alsalam* my child. That is the best reason to cry. If I had tears left, I would cry myself."

The merchant turned to Ordell. "Leave now, my lord. You have the girl in a chinchad of razors, but if you make a false step, the captain will see your body to *Chakroun-Denal.*"

Setchi, crying harder, said under her breath, "The place of bones." She looked up and saw Bosanac with a sword drawn entering the tavern with a grim visage.

Ordell pinched the garrote but stopped as the officer moved, placing the blade of his sword on his throat.

Suddenly the bar was in motion as reprobate drinkers drew weapons, and sailors in uniforms crashed in behind the third officer. She felt the canvas drag as Ordell tried to pull it loose and expose the razor wire to her neck, but big men and women were around her, some grabbing the rig, some grabbing Ordell's hands, and one with a wicked sailor's hook reaching under her jacket and attacking the deadly device that was embracing her neck, holding it clear of her skin.

"Tabarik, cut the damn thing!" an angry, curly-hair man yelled.

"Doing it, gunner," came a reply. "Ain't exactly a sheet caught in the findings," and with a grunt, the man named Tabarik had the deadly rig cut away. Two giant hands pulled her away from the table, while more hands subdued the struggling Ordell.

"Get her to the side," yelled Sunstar Nine at the mass of humanity, which seemed to all obey her orders. She watched through the melee as Ordell's servants, Midhges and Prout, were stripped of their arms by a group of ruddy-faced gangers with the Circum-Valus sigil on their lapels, the same ones that had ignored her the night before in their dissipations.

Ordell screamed at a woman in the crowd, "I paid you, you thief!"

The woman detached from the struggle and walked up to Ordell. "You promised silver to Latiff, my henchman, but no silver reached the hands of myself, Yadira, mistress of the Circum-Valus. Daniella would say, half down or none at all."

"Who the Hades is Daniella?" Ordell yelled.

One of the gangers said, "Blown up." It was just loud enough to be heard, causing riotous laughter.

Sunstar Nine yelled, "A little quiet." The room hushed except for Piran Wearn, a *Remarker* marine in dock clothing, harrying Ordell's henchman Prout. "Wearn, control your captive."

Wearn nodded, then clouted the man a heavy, meaty blow. If by chance or design, the man fell silent, supported from hitting the ground by the large marine.

Sunstar Nine waited a few seconds, then said, "Hate, Nanda, Balchandra, take the child to the ship. She does not need to see this."

"I want to see it," Setchi said, shrugging off the men and women who had pulled her from Ordell's grasp.

Sunstar nodded. "Mr. Ordell, as the lady Yadira says, you did not hire a gang, but we, in fact, did. You could say they are on retainer. You now get some dockside justice. Take the next ship from this port, and if the *Remarker* ever warps into a port you are in, you will hide from us or vacate the port. Take your gutter trash with you."

The Emporian noble looked like he would argue, but he stopped as he finally gauged the crowd.

Mistress Yadira said, "You sure you do not want us to take a tour of the swamp with this lot? That was a terrible thing that had wrapped around that lass of a girl."

Sunstar shook her head. "This lot did not even make for an interesting workout for our marines. No matter how dry it could have turned out, it did not." She turned to Setchi and said, "You have seen justice girl, now the captain wants to speak to you."

Setchi looked to Ordell, beaten and looking defeated, then to the man who held her, one of the so-called marines. Were they lying to her? A man took her arm and said, "Gunner Hate, my name, that is, let us get you to the ship." He was dressed in dock gear and looked disreputable, but his forearm had a tattoo of a firelock and the letter "R" in a formalized script. She nodded and the three marines fell in around her, one leading, and two following.

They walked out of the tavern, down a side street, then turned to a boulevard along the high walls of the port city's defenses. After a few hundred meters, there was a rampart down to the main docks. They passed through a guard point where a pair of uniformed women checked their identification, then onto a masonry dock lined with warehouses. Drays and pottles ran from side to side and up and down the docks, loading wooden crates and bags from the great storage buildings, and dragging them to ships. They turned onto another dock, this one a wooden affair with cranes and pathway unloaders, and she saw the trade flag of the *Remarker* on the middle ship of three. It matched the tattoo on the third officer's chest that she had seen in the tavern. She stopped and gazed at the three ships, then said, "*Remarker* has cranes."

The man they called "gunner" stopped and nodded to the two other marines. "Nanda, Balchandra, fore and aft guard. Give mistress Darrell time to take in the sight of the proud lady, *Remarker*." The two marines silently nodded and moved off to give her some room. The gunner stood nearby though.

"Why are the three ships so different?" She asked.

The gunner said, "They do very different things. The captain says we all have to learn and teach as we can. I am not the greatest teacher, but I can answer this question. Behold the grainger, *Best Lad*; the tea merchant, *Remarker*; and the clipper, *Hustle Harry*. And, as you observed, only *Remarker* has cranes."

She looked on at the three ships, but had a different question. "Why does the captain insist on all this learning, Gunner?"

The gunner said, "Call me Sergeant Banji off ship, as my brother is sergeant as well. It is easier. I am a gunner, but it does not matter here. The captain is an odd one—argues with the spoons, so to speak. Never know who he is. They say that is over with, but to tell the truth, this is the best lash of my life. So who cares why he wants his spoons shined with olive oil, just shine them and smile. Makes life easier 'cause the spoons work just as well as if you dipped them in vinegar."

She nodded. Any conversation that was not about her father was just fine with her.

Sergeant Banji pointed to the first ship. "*Best Lad* is a grainger. She is a big ship but has a small crew and not much for sail meterage. She runs the tolan between two ports, Cycus and Dartia. All she carries is grain one way, fruit and sour cabbage the other way. They have cranes on each side, so she does not need to have them or the crew to on-load without them. How much is keena grain a gram?" he asked her.

"I could not imagine," Setchi replied.

"They sell it in the market in twenty-kilo bags, and the common folk, like my parents were, use the bags for clothing. If commoners can afford twenty-kilo bags, it cannot be that dear. No pirate will waste their time with a slow grainger because it is a lot of hassle and not much money."

She nodded. Despite telling herself it was useless stuff to know, she felt that feeling for simply knowing things that she had fed all her life. Why did this plant make you sick, or this plant calm the nerves...

"The ship on the other side is *Hustle Harry*, a clipper. Lots of sail. She is long and fast, but she has more staterooms than cargo and mostly carries diplomats, mail, that sort of stuff. No pirate can catch her, but only things that cost a lot or must be delivered fast go on her," the gunner said.

She had been on a clipper before. Wealthy people took clippers in the core. It was how she went to and from school—a private stateroom and a clear deck to study on.

Finally, the gunner pointed at the *Remarker*. "Yet neither ship can hold a candle to *Remarker*. She was a pirate ship for some of her life. Two large drivers and two maneuver sails make her nimble in the water. She is as long as the clipper, but as wide as the grainger. She can easily carry more than a hundred crew and, in fact, has berthing for five score without crowding. And her cranes, the cranes you noticed, means she can take in cargo and leave cargo behind without relying on local staff to shift the goods. Twenty kilos of keena is five silver, to answer the question I posed, but twenty kilos of the finest tea is five hundred. That wealth means every jackrabbit in the grassy field wants a nip at us. But we are big enough to make them think twice. That is why all the marines."

Setchi stood silently and pondered the ship. "That is why she has you," she said quietly.

Sergeant Hate nodded. "Better believe it."

"Do I see my father now? I do not want to see him," she said.

Banji smiled. "Captain is who you see first, and what he orders, happens. Take my advice on this: if he is loony as a bug or stern as a chanter, you answer truthfully and do not try and shine him. He will see through you in a second, and someday, ask some of the crew about Buskus or Cosh. Poor souls did not understand a ship like this."

They approached the ship and climbed the gangway. The *Remarker* was a bustle of activity with cargo being taken on, marines exercising on deck, sails draped about being inspected and repaired, smoke coming from the galley house on deck telling of food being made, yellow bricks of sandstone being rubbed against wood to clean it, while other wood was being pulled from its place or being replaced with wooden pegs. A thousand acts a minute seemed to be taking place, an organized chaos of human power being applied to just this one ship, in just this one port, in this place so far from home. The marines guided her aft through the chaos, into a deckhouse and up a gangway to a small room where a woman and a man went over paper charts and canvas-bound books. Finally, they deposited her at a doorway and knocked twice. A man said, "Come in." It was not her father.

She entered and saw that the man was rather young. He had unkempt, long hair; a half beard; shining, intelligent eyes; and was in an undress uniform of a hook-and-tail sweater and simple canvas pants. His hat, a cockade with the letter "R" stylized on it, hung on a hook.

The meeting room had ten chairs crammed chock-a-block around a table with clips and graspers to hold food or books steady on high seas. One wall had scientific instruments racked and ready to use, and another had dozens of charts. On the table, though, Setchi noted her papers out and arranged around the captain, the leather folder pushed far to the side. He looked up from them immediately and said, "Have a seat, Ms. Durrell. Can I have tea brought for you?"

Setchi looked past the captain. He had a tea service that steamed with tea. "Why send for what you already have?" she asked.

The captain looked back. "Yes, my tea may not suit a woman of letters such as yourself," he explained.

"You can serve your Junebug, I am not scared of tea," she said.

He nodded and laid out a pair of copper tea mugs, which clasped neatly onto the table. "My name is Javier al-Rasheed," he said.

"What do I call you?" she replied.

He looked up from serving the tea. "Good question, one that we will explore here. For now, as the daughter of a valued and valiant crew member, you may call me Javier, and I will call you Ms. Durrell."

"Seems like I should call you Captain al-Rasheed and you may call me Setchi," she said.

Javier finished pouring the tea and said, "Hmmm." He clipped the teapot back on the paraffin and returned to his seat.

Setchi was put off by the lack of argument. It was a game, an adult game with bizarre rules that no one explained to you. She reached for the tea and sipped from the hot mug. It was vile stuff, a dreggy sharp tea with a bitter aftertaste. Just what a sad-sack captain like this would drink when better could be had. She grimaced but forced herself to take another sip.

The captain sipped his as well but seemed to not notice the horrid flavor or biting texture of the inferior tea. He watched as she sipped, then reached back and pulled a rope that dangled from the wooden ceiling. A man in a neat uniform ducked in and waited silently. Captain al-Rasheed said, "Urimaris, my compliments to Mister Sloan, have a tureen of Faraway, a jug of fresh water, and something fresh off the dock sent up."

The man named Urimaris replied, "Captain willing, there are some fresh cockles and white beans."

The captain looked at Setchi. "Do you have a religious or a personal preference? You won't find any swine in the northern seas, but anything else can be acquired on this dock if you have a preference."

Setchi shrugged. "Cockles and white beans seem a bit fancy."

Javier shrugged. "The crew throw in, and they get some fancy cull from what we haul. Nature of the beast, you cannot bind the mouth of the beast that threshes your grain."

"Dried fish and tomatoes on rice?" Setchi asked hopefully.

"See what I can do," the yeoman, Urimaris replied and ducked out.

"May I drink your tea?" the captain asked.

Setchi looked at him oddly but passed her cup to him. He combined his cup with hers and took another drink. "I could tell you did not like it," he said. "There is no need to stand on ceremony here and now. As I said, nothing is settled."

"What is there to be settled?" Setchi asked.

The captain drank more of his tea and looked at her with a jaded eye. He glanced at the papers on his desk, then back at her. "Your mother passed, and your family, who I take it are not related to you by blood, paid to send you here to your father. Is that common in Emporia?"

Setchi felt like crying again, but she had done enough of that in front of older, uncaring men and women. "It makes things easier for settling property and title."

Javier nodded. "Believe me, my wife and I have dealt with that. So they paid this Sir Ordell Brastingwell to take you out here. He is an odd sort, is he not? Takes you here when he could have dropped you in a current and been done with you, then tries his hand against us for silver on the assumption that we would pay a mint for you?"

"He is a foolish person," she replied.

Javier laughed. "Not as much as he seems. If he had played the game right, he would have left with silver and goodwill. Your father is indeed a person whom I value. All of my crew are."

She could not believe her father was valued by anyone, but she remained silent on the subject.

The yeoman, Urimaris, returned with a plate. "No rice, but keena in a nice pot, and the fish is goby tench. It was dockside and quite reasonable. The food carts are quite nice on the docks. Oh, and the tomatoes were cut and fried right in front of me. Done savory."

Setchi teared up again. "Thank you," she said, looking down at the food. Out of the corner of her eyes, she saw the captain nod and the yeoman withdraw.

The food was toothsome and hot. The tea was world class, the best she had ever had. She was so hungry she ate and cried at the same time, all in silence as the captain did not break into her misery.

After she had finished her meal, she looked at the captain. He poured her water from a bottle and said, "Like your father, you are educated in the finest schools of the core. In fact, you graduated seven years before your peers in medicine, same as your father. Like your father though, more than you can guess, you grew up in a world of stories where four people on stage solve the world's problems in two hours of poetry-filled, logical discourse. Stories, though, have hundreds of people. If this ship was a stage and our lives a chorus, then each person's story would be sung by a unique singer, all singing together, but while the audience would see the mass, each person in the chorus would be the most important person, to themselves."

He stopped for a second, then said, "It seems to you right now that no one cares, or at least the wrong people care. But right now, I care, your father cares, and this ship could find its way to care. But you have to make some choices quickly, and those choices are forever choices."

"I do not understand," she replied.

"I am being too long-winded. I lost my parents many years back." He stopped and looked out the verge window of his cabin. After a few seconds, he returned his gaze to Setchi. "Perhaps I am speaking to myself and my own wounds, and not to you. You have three choices and a day to select one. And if the choice turns out wrong, then neither myself nor your father can further help you. Oh, he would destroy himself to help you, but he would fail," the captain said.

"What are these choices?" Setchi cleared her tears and looked at the captain with serious eyes.

"The first is the easiest. You get off this ship now, and maybe I have some silver for you. You live your life with dry feet in a foreign land where you can be whatever you want to be. With your education and intelligence, I am sure you would find work and a life that would be suitable for anyone's needs. You may not ever see your father again, as ships do not always connect I have found, but the universe is likely to treat you with a fair hand." Javier took some more of his tea and then turned to refresh his cup. He then poured more of the exquisite tea from her pot into the mug they had provided.

She caught up the mug and drank it down to half in one deep drink. The restorative power of tea was legendary, and she was feeling its full force today, the additive effect of the horrible dock tea, the few sips of Junebug she had consumed, and now two cups of the finest brew. It made her head spin and her eyes click. "What is the second choice?"

Javier said, "Like the first, only we take you to Kemaya or Dartia, and the same option applies. Those ports are known to us, but they may be easier for a person of your intellect to handle than the current politics of Cycus." He then waved his hand in the air. "Oh, they, like this port, have ships leaving every day for the far ends of the Halo. I would give you enough to engage a craft from any of the three ports and have gelt to rest on while you made your way. We even have a clipper docked ahead of us whose captain is known to me. The Halo is open to someone with silver and intelligence."

She looked at him again but chose to remain silent.

"The third option is you join the crew. You are no younger than many of our valued staff, you have an extensive education at a young age, and you even have some experience with the world. Your documents say you ran a healing clinic successfully. For a person who has only seventeen years, you have shown yourself your father's equal at the same age, and he is a substantial talent."

The captain drank more tea and looked at her before continuing. "Every crew person can come to me and ask for us to take on a person, either as a short-term passenger, or a crew that meets our staffing needs. It is like having one die to roll in a game. If they roll well, then they can roll again.

But if they roll badly, they never get that die back again. Your father has asked to roll this die and to spend that roll on you. And many people, I might add, wish they could join the crew of a successful tea merchant. So there are your three choices, and you have until we leave dock on the morrow to decide."

Setchi looked down at the food the yeoman had brought. She had asked for a simple dish she figured they would not be able to find cooked in short order, but the crew, in the face of the yeoman, had been successful—mostly. "Can I leave the crew if I join?"

"Yes," the captain said. "All crew have to give notice to their gang leader and then to the first officer before port is reached, and if the crew member is essential for the operation of the ship, and if the ship provides passage to a destination of their choice by merchant ship, then they may be required to continue for five additional legs of the voyage, or two months."

"The contract says this?" she asked.

Javier smiled. "You can spend an hour reading it. Two if you want. Then five days in shakedown, and if you and the crew do not accept each other, we will put you off at Kemaya or Dartia anyway, both ports with traffic into the core and to the edges of the Halo."

"What about Buskus and Cosh?" she asked.

Captain al-Rasheed looked at her without an expression. "Do you plan to bully and almost maim a junior crew member, or threaten to kill your captain in a drunken rage?"

"No," Setchi replied. "Is that what they did?"

"What they did and what happened to them is an issue for the decks to discuss. I ask again, are you a shark in the fishery?"

"No, Captain," Setchi said.

"I hardly see how that is an issue in that case," the captain replied.

"Then I will join the crew," she replied. Damn her father if he would think this was a climb down. He would have to treat her as crew.

The captain tugged the cable again. The steward entered, and he said, "Hand Mistress Durrell over for shakedown to the second officer and tell him that she will be the second healer and is assigned to the medical bay."

The steward nodded and motioned for her to follow him.

Chapter III

Tajir al'Amir

The Merchant Prince of Kemaya was large in every way. Two meters and maybe 115 kg mass, with a slight paunch, great silky cloaks, curl-toed shoes, a fez, and a surcoat of brocade, he sat at a magnificent table filled with brew pots and samples of tea leaves in small bowls. Guards and servants surrounded the room. They were dressed in puce and pale orange livery, each with a campaign hat, a brace of small dragoon firelocks, and a yataghan at their side. The only difference, in fact. between the servants and the soldiers was a golden enameled wooden cup that the servants carried on a red jute rope around their necks. The servants used these cups to take turns tasting everything the prince was ready to consume, from tiny sweetmeats and dainty morsels of shellfish and candied carrots to the tea itself, some of which sold for many silvers a gram. It seemed to al-Rasheed an easy life, being the taster to a noble lord. Of course, it was not much of a life if you consumed a horrible poison. He wondered if the servants were up for a game of dice, considering they lived such a life of gambling with each swallow of tea.

This was the first and most important stop outbound and inbound from Cycus, a cluster of rich islands that were sometimes called the southern Cyclonidees and were under the protection of the Camellia Fleet. Kemaya was the homeland of the Dominars, the lands from which they launched their invasions of Cycus, and thus this wealthy noble was some sort of cross-cousin to his wife, Nazira. He called himself uncle, which might be accurate enough if it really mattered.

A thin nervous man sat next to the prince. His name was Lipscomb Fernando, and he was the guild banker who handled the escrow for the Dominar, Javier's wife, and also served as a speaker to allow the prince to remain detached from the negotiations. If he wished, that is.

"Captain al-Rasheed, may I greet you on behalf of my prince, of the family al-Nabeel," Lipscomb said with an over-stuffed dignity. Javier had met the man once, before he had risen to command a merchant, and did not like him then. But the tea business created strange bedfellows. The banker looked at his prince, then back to Javier. "Will you introduce your entourage?" he asked, his voice like an adder.

"I have with me to my right," Javier gestured at the first person in ship's livery, "my Quartermaine, Syid Samedi Darkfather." Darkfather was an odd duck, Javier thought. He wore a black oilcloth sea coat, cotton pants like those of a soldier, and a black flowing shirt made of soft corduroy. His ship's livery was a sash in blue and red. Despite his role as an accountant, he wore an age-blackened yataghan; a pair of expensive hammer-forged, falling-block, firelock pistols; a cross belt with cartridges slid into loops; and a straight blade at his shoulder in a wooden sheaf. When introduced, he stood, bowed at the merchant prince and his mouthpiece, removed his hat with a flourish, then sat back down at his seat. The move seemed to endear the prince, who smiled and softly clapped.

Javier looked at Darkfather as he sat down. The idea of the man made Javier nervous. Not because there was anything unusual in any single aspect of the man's affect. Well, that was a misstatement. Everything was odd about him, which made him no odder than the rest of the crew. Instead, there was the creeping knowledge that Darkfather had replaced Sedrick Devious, and no one cared. Of course, that was as it should be, because no one had known Devious had been aboard, being an imagined alter ego of his own dark persona. The crew had assumed that he had gone a bit mad, doing two difficult jobs on the *Remarker*, but he had only awoken to his crisis of sanity when he had visited the "Island of Silence" where he had grown up, a memory that was lost on the currents of his mind. Darkfather had done nothing to earn Javier's worry, but the worry came nonetheless. It seemed like a betrayal not to look over and see Devious taking in the conversion with a practiced ear, offering advice in his ear. Still, his wife has insisted on the Darkfather as the quartermaine.

Yet, there were times when it was quiet that he could hear the sinuous and careful speech of his lost companion asking him if now was the time he was needed. It disturbed him.

In fact, he had every reason to be thankful for the Darkfather. He had protected Nazira during her procession, and his efforts had assured her victory during the revolt. That time was cloudy for Javier, he had spent it in a haze. Yet Nazira had presented the man as an educated and important partisan of hers, who not only should be rewarded but also would be a key member of the crew in the next voyage.

"Next to Syid Darkfather is Sayida Eversail, our Tea Master." Eversail stood, bowed her head, and returned to her seat. She wore a lesser veil and headscarf as a polite gesture to the prince of Kemaya. It was not strictly required for commoners, but it was a gesture. One was better off taking old traditions seriously, where possible, with their mercurial host.

Lipscomb gestured at the Tea Master. "Eversail is a scholar's scholar, who has just confirmed her master's dissertation, and now, truly is a master. An *Ealim jalil,* if you will. Is this not a fine accomplishment?" He was simpering in a way that Javier found hard to take, but he had to take it. He bowed his head to Lipscomb, trying not to act as if Lipscomb was just an expensive piece of furniture that happened to have the unusual capacity of speech. "As a tea buyer, she now only has to spend a few weeks with a teacher to earn the title officially. However, she has already proven herself. She has made a number of shrewd bets on our last voyage and has won the praise of our crew by making them a tidy profit. In fact, she and the crew have bet on a cargo fifth, my lord of Kemaya."

Lipscomb clapped his hands and said, "What is this fifth you speak of, my lord would like to know."

Javier ignored Lipscomb this time and addressed the merchant prince. "A 'cargo fifth' is a tradition of the tea traders. The crew get a share, but that share is finite. The captain and the owner get most of the wealth for most of the risks financially." He reached for his tea and drank some. "Yet each of us has but one cup of life to fill with the fruits of our risks. The crew thus shares in the cost of the ship and takes cargo space on the *Remarker* for trade as they wish."

"You are partners with your crew?" Lipscomb asked.

"It is a form of *'shuraka' alshurafa'*." Javier turned to Lipscomb and pointedly translated the old tongue to him. "As the prince knows but you may not, it means 'honorable trade partner.' It means more than being a partner in the sense of being an investor. It is equality, in fact, in that the cargo they carry is theirs to decide. They bet their trading skills against a significant portion of their pay and the crew's tithe. All crew make small trades off of their personal cargo. It cannot be stopped, and I would not if I could. Yet this crew is special. Their partnership assigns Master Eversail as their trading factor, believing her skills will make money for them. That tells you, and likely is already known by my lord prince, these are the signs of a unique crew."

Lipscomb gestured at Eversail. "Such a responsibility to lay upon this young set of shoulders. If she cost me my hard pay, I would heave her over the side. Yet if she is worried about that this voyage, she does not show this mortality on her face. She gives the air of one who is a tough, calculating, knowledgeable practitioner, who seems like she can turn information into money with a practiced ease."

Eversail interrupted. "Before *Remarker*, I was on a ship that was hellish in hate and misery. It was hellish, if the hell of the Southerns exists."

Lipscomb simpered again, but the prince of Kemaya looked at the scholar's darkened face and seemed to be collecting it all in, even the subtle conflict in which they had joined, the crew of the *Remarker* and his own mouthpiece.

"Splendid, Captain, very splendid." Lipscomb clapped his hands and squeezed them a little. "I believe Master Eversail was the person who brought us the many kilograms of King's Cup! I hope the Jalosie Tea we are pouring today is good enough for your pallets despite not reaching the superlative heights of 'the Cup.' Of course, we have porcelain kiln-ware, water bottle gourds, fillion baskets, all at a good price to trade if you are interested."

Javier looked at the prince, again ignoring Lipscomb. "We are not loading that much outbound. Perfume, some gypsum paints, and tiles. Enough, though, to make you happy for the silver in your treasure chests. But I understand you are seeking something special that we can find in the far edges of the Halo. Is this true, honorable banker Lipscomb?"

"First, Captain al-Rasheed. My prince, Kemaya, wishes to know of his cousin, the father of your wife, the now Dominar of our ally Cycus. What became of the great one? Is the former Dominar, how do your people say, feeding the crabs for breakfast?" Lipscomb asked, while his prince turned his face away from the table.

A servant came by and refilled a steaming cup of tea in front of each of the guests. Javier looked at the silent prince, hulking in his resplendent clothing. "You are the son of the brother of Nawaz, first Dominar. I would expect you would worry over your cousin. My wife, Nazira, is of course your family as well, with a heart from the land of Kemaya. *Aldam yahki alhikaya.*"

Lipscomb retorted, "Technically, the prince of Kemaya has no route to the rulership of the Dominion. Yet he is closer, in fact, than your wife, is he not?"

"The brother of my lord prince's father, known as Nawaz, indeed took Cycus by the force of his spear carriers, but he had the wisdom to sign the Cycus' dustari. It is what allowed Nawaz to rule, a compromise with the great noble families on how the land would be ruled. Even when his grand-daughter has overthrown his son, she has done so in a way that respected this document, or else would see the islands fall into endless civil war."

"That is an interesting dissertation," Lipscomb said.

Javier reached for the tea before him and took another sip. It was indeed Jalosie, he thought, with peach and bergamot added; a touch he did not prefer, but was common in some lands. "The oils in this tea cover its flavor," he said, directing his attention to Lipscomb. "I have had tea that is tainted, and while I do not prefer it, I do not mind it. What does the trade call it, Eversail?"

"Cheater's taint, Captain, though there should be no derogatory meaning attached to this," Master Eversail responded.

"Exactly," Javier said. "It was used to cover up inferior tea, but now even the best tea is adulterated with it. I prefer the acrid bitterness of Junebug, my dear Lipscomb, because it does not pretend to be what it is not. I do not have to expect a great tea and be disappointed when it is not what I expected."

"My dear captain, you are a font, truly a font," Lipscomb purred.

Javier looked into his tea. His soul was tired, and his body seemed more tired. Tea was bracing on the coldest day and could keep you awake on the longest night. The prince remained silent but watched Javier closely as his tasters tested the tea that would be given to him, agreeing it was theoretically free of adulterants before giving it to a small girl who drank it down deep. Javier pointedly moved his gaze to the girl who was thirty kg in weight and under 110 cm in height, hardly grown past child age.

Determined safe, the cup tasted by the child was filled again and handed to the prince, who blew on it, then drank it deeply.

Turning his attention to the prince and ignoring the banker, Javier said, "Abelard has abdicated and moved to a private residence in the leading islands. He is unharmed and is glad for the rest. Do you want to send him a letter?"

Lipscomb waved his cup in the air and was rewarded with another portion of the tea. "Of course we believe you, my dear Captain, although we understood that your wife was to be, well, shall we say, tossed from the southern rocks as soon as the heir was born. I am to understand Nazira was quite hasty with some monetary transactions?" Lipscomb simpered.

"Seems to me that you, as a representative of the bank, are completely 'read in' to this so-called 'hasty monetary transaction,' and that you, yourself, were part of the group who earned quite a nice fee from the process that led to your prince's cousin being removed from the throne," Javier said.

"One finds your tone objectionable," Lipscomb replied.

Javier looked into his tea again, then braced the prince's lickspittle. "I am not a representative of the Dominar in diplomatic matters, nor do I know the details of the change of policy or leadership of the Domain of Cycus. I will point out she is no queen though. She is Dominar. And as for my tone, it is not for you to complain. If your prince needs to rebuke me, I will hear it from his own mouth."

Lipscomb's face screwed up in anger. "Come now, I know each detail of the Great Bank's backing your princess, as you say. Yet you call the princess the Dominar and are at least her consort and father of the young prince, Jamil of the al-Youseffi I believe. So it beggars belief that you would not have more intelligence for us. Now young man, speak, the prince demands it."

Javier scowled. What would Devious do with this bank man? Arrange for him to run into a knife? Something clever and violent, no doubt. He just could not muster up the hate his alter ego had once kept for him. He remembered the darkness, the rain, and his father and mother on their knees. He remembered … nothing more. Devious had known what happened next. With Devious gone, his history was gone. He looked at the Darkfather, then to the Tea Master and his crew members standing guard. They expected him to be a captain, but he could also sense their searching for something in himself that he no longer had. This was the first stop of the voyage, and this negotiation counted for so much. To fail would be horrible. "I am the captain of a tea trader. My marriage and son have nothing to do with my powers or inclinations. I have no intelligence, as you say, to offer, except on the issue of acquiring your master the tea he desires at a price he wishes to pay."

"Not acceptable, son. Not acceptable at all. Look at me when I am speaking, not at my master. It is rude. You are not so addle-minded to feel that the occupation of a tea merchant is one that is exclusively about the trading of tea. The 'queen' is the protector of the Cyclonidees, though not grasping the nettle. And we are ourselves technically in the trailing Cyclonidees. You are technically a lord, are you not? Thus the interest of my prince in what you have to say on the, well, bloodshed that has rocked the greater of the lands of the Cyclonics." The banker simpered, cleaned his conical, the signet of the bank, and then replaced it on his award rack affixed to his chest. It was a way, Javier felt, of emphasizing that there were money games being played as well, not just political issues of certain noble families who lost esteemed and ancient heads in the revolution.

Darkfather suddenly coughed, expressing outwardly the inner boiling of Javier's nerves. He suddenly stood and faced Lipscomb down. "I should pay your gild, brother Lipscomb, if not for my respect for your prince and my captain. And if I pay your gild, it will be paid in hard money." He touched his darkened yataghan and then said, "There is no queen. My mistress, Nazira, is Dominar."

Javier carefully slid his own hand onto his talwar and nodded to his guards, Gunner Hate and Grenadier Wearn, who came to the balls of their feet from the indolence that was their normal self-array. The merchants were outnumbered five-to-one, but if Javier had to bet, he would have given three to two for a wipeout of the prince's henchmen by his two marines, followed shortly by the end of Nazira's uncle and the banker who held their debts. Hate nodded at Javier, saying in a silent communication that if the Darkfather jumped, he would personally clear the room with his sword. Wearn looked to the Tea Master and the door, then at Hate. There was no way to tell what the marine was thinking, but he was ready to fight as well, it seemed.

The prince suddenly spoke, breaking the tension. "My good Lipscomb, please relax a small bit." His voice was squeaky and high. Not what one would expect from such a large man. "I will contact my cousin through my brother, the ambassador, though I do not fault you for bringing up these troubling questions." He took a sip of cooling tea and said, "Indeed, there are questions that I would hope the captain would learn the answers to when he has the opportunity, and someday share these answers with my royal self, your wife's cousin. The story of how your Dominar and wife-consort went from prisoner on procession doomed for the strangling post to the mistress of the greatest power in the Northeast Halo is one I wish to hear. However, there is no reason it has to happen now. Instead, let us consider tea."

Javier looked up at Darkfather and said, "Samedi, be seated." The Darkfather nodded, bowed, and sat. Javier glanced over at Lipscomb and was surprised: the man was terrified. His face had flushed the color of sandy mud, and he was sweating like he had eaten some horrible brand of hot pepper directly from the jar. Seeing that the prince's mouthpiece was frozen in fright gave Javier a second of grim satisfaction, though the cost might be high. The Great Bank held the loans that had paid for a revolution, and if those loans were called in, a new revolution could unseat his wife and queen with terrible results. Nazira's money was more notional and did not clink when it was placed in a chest.

Javier considered the words that the prince had said, "greatest power." Cycus was not on anyone's list of greatest powers that Javier knew. It was a power in the Cyclonic Islands and had a growing trading fleet as well as a good Navy that kept lines of trade open and pirates suppressed, but the prince knew well that they were not one of the great powers of the Halo and treaded lightly on the stage of Ocean lest one of the sleeping giants of the core ward islands should awaken and notice they existed. Come to that, more than one island had died when the pirates of the extents had come to understand there was weakness and treasure to be had. The Great Bank had paid mercenaries like these before to ensure a loan was repaid in treasure taken from the burning docks and slaughtered ruling families.

If Javier was to be an ambassador, he had much to learn, and the first thing would have to be to see through the subtle world of language that princes essayed. Was the prince of Kemaya's words the offer of a shield, a sword, or a glaive held to his neck? He did not know. Instead, he sipped his tea, looked closely at the prince, and said, "Your desire is our command, Sayid-Musharaf, Prince. We ask no reward. Please tell me what treasure you desire of the trader, given I am so poor of a servant in the realm of stories."

The prince drank a draught of his tea in return, seeming to savor it, and then looked into the sky above the presence chamber with a smirk of delight. "King's Cup is said to be the greatest attainable tea of creation. You drink it once in your lifetime and you need never explore for a greater tea. Your wife gifted me with a kilogram and sold me another ten. That has meaning to me—the loyalty of family to reward an old 'uncle' with such an amazing prize. And the Galatian you hold monopoly on is certainly a near equal; its origin found on no charts. Its existence proven only by a few songs and rumors. Even if you were not my niece's husband, I should have you here before me and bestow upon you a mission."

He drank another draught of his tea. "Yet I do not require you do this for me without reward. You have brought me the greatest tea any tea merchant can find, and you have given me a tea of quality that does not exist on our charts. Now I want the greatest tea that no one can find, and I task you to deliver it to me." He reached over to his side and rang a small bell.

A heavy-set, serious-faced woman in her late fifties came into the prince's presence chamber carrying a box of sandalwood. She bowed in front of Javier and presented it to him. He reached out and took the box and opened it carefully, finding it contained a small, old, wood-covered book. He looked up at the prince with a quizzical face. "What is this, my Prince?" he asked.

The prince laughed. "Oh, we know of the library you have formed at Cycus City from the books of your travels. This is another book for you. While we would normally have no use for such frivolities, in this case, one of my readers found this ancient tome and assures me it is real, not just the product of a forger."

The prince motioned and the woman who had given Javier the book took a page-comb of alabaster and looked to Javier for permission. He nodded, and she inserted it into the book, flipping it open carefully to a page marked with a slender strand of silk. The words were in Eurabaa, the language of Cycus and the most common trade tongue of the Halo, but written in an archaic form. It was an ink script with a blocky flow rather than the fluid strokes normally associated with the language of Cycus.

Wafi madinat alqumash, kan hunak burj mutasil bialsama', damarath nar allah alati ainshaqat hjran wezman mhtrqan. Ti hadha almakan namat shay aleawalim alkubraa, alati tajlib alshabab wal-farah iilaa aleizam alqadimati.

The prince read the passage from memory, taking the archaic words and translating them into modern parsing. "And in the city of cloth, there stood a tower which connected to the sky, ruined by God's fire that split stone and burned bone. In this place grew the tea of the greater worlds, which brings youth and joy to old bones."

Javier read it silently as the prince said it out loud. When the prince stopped reading, Javier read the key passage out loud to show he had understood what the prince was after. *"Shay Aleawalim Alkubraa."*

The prince nodded. "Your understanding of the tongue of our ancestors is good. Better than most, which no doubt is why you spend your time reading those books that it is rumored you read. Tea of the greater worlds is what the book describes as a tea that makes the elderly young again. It is mystical, a prize beyond belief. And that book provides a map to this treasure."

Darkfather looked at him in consideration while Master Eversail removed a small notebook of scap from her formal tunic and a pencil to take notes. Javier reached out and took the page comb and flipped the page to read further. It was actually not some fancy of a prince, the book really did describe a place on the Northwest regions of the Halo, perhaps in a leading extent, where great structures had once been tossed down by the God's Fire for a land whose hubris grew too great. The tea was only a few lines in the missive, and no doubt the reason the book came to the prince's attention, but it was actually a fascinating missive called *Fall of the Apostical*, the death of a land that defied the Gods and brought down ruin on their republic. Better yet, it was a place that the writer of the book seemed to assume could be found and reached, then returned from. The key seemed to be an unknown current driving outward from the island of Paroland.

"And this is where you wish to task me to go?" Javier asked.

"Yes." The prince nearly purred with delight, his jowly face sketching a huge smile. "Go to that land, find this magical tea, take on as much as you can, and return it to me."

Javier flipped a few more pages of the book. "Northwest of Paroland," it said. He thought it over. Paroland was hard to reach this time of year but not impossible. It was a trade island where many merchants stopped to rest and hide from weather. The normal warps to it came from the inner islands, and most ships would be departing for the core rather than riding into her stream. Yet there was one seldom-used warp he could ride. Reaver Northland was a small island east of Parolands. It had a Sublime Port, a Bank, provisions, water, all that could be needed as a stop before Paroland. It was just small and not worth much for trade. He could reach Reaver Northland on the fall Warp from Codis Aletia. Then warp to Paroland, and finally drive on the inbound winds, tacking against the circumvallating outer currents. If the island was within twenty-five days, they had a chance to find it. If it did not appear, then turn and run the winds and currents back to Paroland in time to catch the reversed warp back to the Reavers.

Javier looked up and saw the prince was smiling. "I can tell you think it is possible to find this island."

Javier nodded. "It will be difficult, time-consuming, expensive, but if the island is real, we have one chance in maybe five to find it."

"I will put ten-thousand grams of silver into your hands now, and ten-thousand when you return if you find the island. And I will pay as much as King's Cup for each kilo of tea from this island you unload into my warehouses, as long as your tea master certifies it as genuine," the prince said.

Javier looked at Darkfather and Eversail. "Fifteen, and pay this to the Great Bank in recognition of my debt. Fifteen on return. And the price of the impossible tea is twice that of King's Cup per kilogram."

The prince slammed the table. "This is a deal!"

Javier led Eversail and Darkfather from the sumptuous room. As they descended the grand stairs to the guarded entryway of the palace, Javier said, "I am not sure how scions of that family defeated the Guisarmes of Cycus."

"God's Fire, my dear captain," Darkfather said. They left the entranceway and went down to the wicker gate that represented the edge of the palace, where its authority met that of the Sublime Port.

Javier laughed. "That would be told across the Cyclonidae, my dear Quartermaine."

"One thing I learned in my travels through the land of your birth is that there is something furtive about how the houses of Cycus have accounted themselves in the past several centuries. I fully expect that something they have done in the past would anger the Gods and led to retribution."

The Darkfather nodded at the Sublime Port Guards and their princely opposite number.

Javier grew troubled. There was much he did not know, but he could see his own family history with the Island of Silence was tied into this. "Perhaps you are right, my dear Darkfather. I am relying on you and Master Eversail to guide us through our voyage and return from the furthest stores to my homeland, no matter how sinister it is."

Eversail bowed as she walked. "We will do that."

CHAPTER IV

A Change of Tides

...I took my nightly sight and then returned to the cave. There was no one to teach me navigation, but I remembered enough to build a horizon sight and each night, weather permitting, I shot my sun azimuth, then waited patiently to record the first moon rise. Each note went into my carefully hoarded vellum and was put into a notebook of woven boo slats, then stored in my best hoggin...

(Hoggin is a term from the inner core for a cask or barrel that normally contains salted pork products. The closest term in Eurabanni would be "barmil alkhinzir" —JaR)

Angela Standish looked up from the book. She had arranged for one of her marines to lift it from the captain's stateroom when he was busy on deck and would likely be distracted for hours. She had retreated to the forward hold in the empty space where her boys and girls practiced sword drills. Her privacy was assured by Raksha, a marine armsman in from the Sugar Islands who did not know why her major wanted privacy, just that she would not let anyone disturb it.

Immediately, she was suspicious of the book. The author claimed to be writing it on vellum, but the paper was scap. It was not written in some exotic tongue, but clear and concise Eurabanni. Only the word hoggin was mystifying, but in the margins, Javier had given a note to its meaning in precise cursive script. He even provided the older, more formal term in his notes for the mystery word.

Yet this was the book that the captain expected to fling them off the edge of the Halo into the endless tides of Ocean. Angela was not impressed.

It was not a comfortable situation for her. Her closest friend and only love had married a drunkard and vagabond, and this man had proven to be less than stable by anyone's best measure. Yet he had bound together a crew and won riches in their first voyage and delivered Angela's marines and the crew of the tea trader, *Remarker* to the shores of Cycus in time to help save Nazira and put her on the Dominar's throne. He had done more though, that Angela was not sure how it fitted into the war. The strange beings from the Island of Silence had swept aside the legions of Nazira's father, while somehow, he had brought Nazira's sister and an odd little waif that turned out to be the daughter of another enigmatic figure—now the ship's Quartermaine, Darkfather—both of which had a hand in winning the war.

And Nazira had not confided in her own closest friend and lover what all this meant. She had only said, bring my husband back to me.

"In how many pieces?" she had asked the now Dominar. She was not really joking, but Nazira took it hard.

This second voyage of the *Remarker* was just as deep as the first. Nazira had something to prove to her kith, and Javier al-Rasheed had been dispatched by his wife to treat with the violent old man who brooded on the Kemayan throne, dreaming of his chance to take the land of Cycus for his own. It had happened before when Nazira's grandfather had taken the lands from the Guisarmes. It could happen again. Then they would all be sent to the *qabr*.

She looked from the book to the wooden forward bulkhead that separated the forward hull-spaced from the hold. Someone had carved on one of the boards the word "*Yousef/K*," probably Atiyya al-Vohra, who took on the duties of memory for the dead crew mate. Angela was neither religious nor superstitious, but she said to herself, "*alhayaat alnihayiya*," mouthing the old tongue for "the doorway to death."

Yousef had found death in a valiant act. Angela knew that *Remarker* was all that stood between her lover and destruction, and it was a tool wielded by a man who she did not trust. She returned to reading the book.

...The cave is the only one on the island which I can comfortably inhabit. The qtates-tigri do not prowl its entrance, but the falls provide water year-round it seems, though I wish I could manage the heights of the plateau and see exactly how this island's hydraulics are achieved. It does not matter, at least not yet. However, each island in this reach is not so lucky for year-round water, and this may be no exception.

The question is—do I construct a boat and make an attempt to return to the "fierste kust..."

(qitat-alnamir or "big cat." "Fierste kust" She uses this term which means in the language of the core "shore away from all," or "farthest shore"' as distinct from the term "Grutlân," which is an actually major island in the core. Is this the answer to her faulty math? —JaR)

The marginalia again exposed Javier's thoughts to Angela. It was written in a tight, excited hand as if he had discovered a cache of silver in his garden. But the dreams of the captain were hardly of riches, though they were the key to saving Nazira and the kingdom from ruin. They were the childish idea that Javier had of exploration, this concept that the world was a tiny ball of blue floating in a vast ocean of blackness. For him, Angela thought, there was no edge of the world. If you sailed too far west, you would simply discover east, with no thoughts that privation and misery could be in between. He had been, in the first voyage, occasionally struck with the understanding of the pain that existed in the world and that he needed to guard against. Angela could not read the sheet after sheet of math figures, mostly navigation sights, that accompanied the missive, but where Javier saw exciting possibilities, Angela saw disaster.

> ...Red boowood feeds the fire in my cave, giving its orange color to the walls. Everything I do is done because this plant grows on the steep slopes of the island. I put boowood shoots into the ground and eat the young sprouts. Fermented, I drink the beer. Taller shoots become clothing, mashed in water and lye, while the largest feed my fire and may be my boat, if I ever cast loose from this land...

> (Red Boowood is similar to Cycus Boowood or Gray Shambler, and is found in a chain of islands centered on Paroland. That gives us a likely route-of-trade as we seek the lost islands. If she found these lands, and foundered on her way back to the Halo, then it makes sense that she would have been shaping a course to Paroland.—JaR)

Angela reached to her belt and unfrogged the yataghan she affected and set it aside. She had two firelocks that were jabbing into her side, a hefty Carver Dragoon model and a smaller Valace Response. Both were beasts, which is why she carried them. She slipped them out and placed them, one-after-the-other, next to her sword. She then settled into a set of cargo boxes under the lufting which provided sufficient light to read by. It also gave a breeze that aired the below decks space. She had been before the mast since she became a young officer, and it was these quiet times she valued most, even if it was doing difficult tasks like this, trying to decide if the captain of her ship and the father of her lover's heir should be executed for malfeasance.

...Humans had stopped here, but must not have ever set up any base on the island, at least not in living memory. There were devolved sheep, fifty or seventy spread around the verges of the island that could have only gotten here aboard the ship of some sailor. Yet there was no sign that my home was anything more than a watering stop. And I hoped that water would attract some trader or fisher to the shores. I carefully cut boowood and kept a smokey fire going. I had brought-up (opbringe) sentinels (waarnimmer-senal) to warn passing ships that this was my lair. However, I fear that a shifting-of-the-waters (feroaring-fan-tij)...

(Opbringe is the word use which means "to bring up" but she seems to mean the word "konstruearje" which means construction or create. The next term, "waarnimmer-senal," is a term that is archaic in the languages of the core but is related to "sjoch wacht" a "statue that looks to the sky," which in this case seems to be something left at the shores of the island which would warn seafarers that a castaway could be found on the island. More interesting I think is the use of the term "feroaring-fan-tij" which I have translated to mean shifting of waters. In the old tongue it is "taghayar almadu waljazur," words which should conjure fear in any sailor—JaR)

Angela looked up with a start to see Javier al-Rasheed silently sitting with her, looking at the Carver Dragoon. The hand lock was sinister the way he manipulated it. "What do you think of her?" He asked.

"Who?" Angela asked warily. Her sword was a single lunge away, but she could not get to it faster than 10 grams of brass could go crashing through her head.

"The woman in the book," the captain replied.

Angela shifted her weight. "Is she real?" She asked.

"As real as you or me," the captain replied, handling the firelock. He jacked the action and shell-checked it. Then he closed the action softly.

"Are you real?" Angela looked at the murderous weapon. How did he get past Raksha on guard at the bulkhead and when would the marine recognize she was outflanked?

Javier rubbed the firelock against his head. "I do not know sometimes. I once had a brother…"

"You are an only-child al-Rasheed," Angela snapped in frustration.

"An orphan, yes. But not really an only child. I met Nazira when I was young, before her father brought you and Gullen in to be her companion. But I was not safe. No one was safe. The only person who protected me was Devious. When I was hungry, Devious helped me find food. When soldiers tried to capture me, Devious taught me to hide. He helped me reclaim a name, find a place in the Navy, and he pointed out Nazira at a levee. But Nazira chose me," he said.

Angela watched as Javier rubbed the firelock against his head slowly and closed his eyes. Nazira was worried, more than worried, in fact. Devious and Javier. Nazira loved Javier while she loved Nazira. It was a triangle that was intolerable. One slash of a blade, one shot of a firelock, and the triangle would be broken, but at what cost? Would Nazira forgive her if she laid Javier's head on the deck? Would Javier, or the shadow of who Javier once was sitting in front of her now, be able to do what was needed to kill her? And if he killed her, then how would her marines respond?

"It could be an accident," Javier said.

"What?" Angela asked.

Javier cocked and uncocked the lock of the weapon in his hand. "When I was a child, I learned that Ocean was broken. That dark forces were at work. That we lived only at the sufferance of the Gods, and those Gods were not our friends. Now, I face an issue. What is the best thing for my wife and child. My wife is stronger than me, she is the founder of a nation that could stop the slide of our Halo into barbarity and face down the Gods whose malevolent acts are breaking us." He put the firelock on the crate and pushed it over to Angela.

She reached for it then shell checked the chamber. Javier turned his head and leaned into her. Angela put the weapon to his temple and activated the lock. Two-hundred-twenty-five meters per second was the absurd speed of the little piece of metal. It would cross Javier al-Rasheed's skull in a blink of an eye. "I do not believe in Gods," she said. What she did not say was Angela did believe in Nazira.

She dropped the lock back to safe and placed the pistol in her lap. Then she picked up the book and tried to hand it back to Javier. He shook his head though.

"No, Angela, you read the book. There was a woman who found the land we seek, then almost made it home," the captain said.

"Almost?" Angela asked.

"There is no evidence she got back to the Halo. She got close. Close enough that her book made the trip when she had passed," Javier said.

CHAPTER V

The Kitchens of Gataleta

It was a complex meal that the evening would bring, and the call sheet said that he would be 'entertaining' a guest from the ship that had hove into port on the evening tides. To reach the meal though, they had to survive the day.

Quester looked at his brigade lined up. They had the typical beaten and haunted look of any cooking team who had to serve the nobles-of-the-land. No matter how much they were paid and how sumptuous the quarters were, the certain knowledge that you were lost was a constant companion. You worked for your family, to earn enough to allow them to survive when you were gone.

Most important was to never think about the future. Quester had survived a record five-years only by taking each day as the last and greatest day of his life. And by simple arithmetic, he had risen to be the head of the imperial kitchens simply by being the last person alive in his cohort.

He nodded his head, and the kitchen minders walked in led by the head minder, Annalise. They took positions around the kitchen. It was their job to protect the cooks and keep them from becoming corrupted. Then came the tasters and their leader, Simpfrey. As the workday progressed, they would taste all dishes downstairs and accompany dishes upstairs that they'd tasted in case they were needed to taste the food a second time. Finally came the scribes, warriors of the emperor who would pass out and take back cutlery, provide door guards, escort the meals upstairs, and if need be, execute anyone who failed in their duties.

Once gathered, there was the duty of transparency. The lead scribe was not a warrior, but a scribe. She was dressed in flowing robes, and had a book cover that had no pages in it. She went to the sergeant of the scribes who presented her with a paper listing his soldiers by name and rank. She reviewed the paper and entered it into the docket-book. Next, she went to Simpfrey who gave over his list of tasters. Again, she reviewed it and entered it into the book. Then she approached Annalise and accepted the list of her minders. She always saved her interaction with Quester to the last, because he had a more complex interaction that required some verbal and somatic components.

He bowed as proscribed by the Orders of the Empire—Chapter 71 section 4 item B, "procedures for handing over of mind sheets to Lead Warden in Imperial kitchens when in Winter Residence."

She nodded her head twice (item C) and said (item D), "with regard to the staff?"

In keeping with D-sub-1, he replied, "It is... may it please the emperor, the list for the day-and-day." Day-and-day confused many people and had resulted in more than one execution in the last fifty years, but it was decided years before that it indicated a requirement for a two-day kitchen staff 'shift.' There were, in fact, three separate kitchen staffs, each of whom worked for two-days 'on' and four-days 'off.' In the summer palace, one shift remained in the winter quarters and cooked for the so called 'residue.' During the winter, though, the summer palace did not have a cooking staff. No one knew why other than section 2 item D which stated, "and in the winter, no summer staff is provided…"

He handed over the list. The scribe, you were not supposed to know their names but Quester knew her name was Xella, then asked, "And the menu-of-faire?" That was 'D-sub-three.' Wordlessly, (D-sub-4) Quester handed the scribe the twelve menus that would be the food served to the imperial family by the kitchen. The book proscribed six meals per day (item E) spaced precisely every four hours around the clock. Then he handed the so-called thirteenth page over to her.

The room froze with terror because this was an issue not handled by the book, and not yet codified. Several years ago, the emperor declared that the kitchen should communicate to the charge-d'affairs the proposed modification to the daily schedule of meals to occur when an important visitor was to be fêted at court. The charge-d'affairs had sent word that an important and wealthy tea merchant, the husband of a princess of a great trading land to the northeast, would be given the Order of the Red Wainscot by the emperor.

Gataleta was small, Quester knew, with a high population and limited resources. It produced little food, but it was important for the mining of some materials, which generated all of its wealth. Keeping merchant princes happy was key to keeping Gataleta and the imperial dynasty from collapsing into a starving mass. So fêting one made perfect sense. But it was also an existential danger because the actual means of fêting was not outlined by regulation, and because the tastes and attitudes of the visiting trader could not be guessed. A dyspeptic foreigner could spell doom for many kitchen staff members.

His thirteenth page was a modification to the menu system outlining a special fare for the foreign guests of foods not normally on the menu. Tricky foods to make, using expensive ingredients even the lavash tables of the emperor could not support often. Ostentatious food whose display was more complex than any other dish, required planning to meet. Every chef adjutant made such a thirteenth page and kept it in his or her files, waiting until the time when it would be needed, and hoping that this time would not happen often.

The scribe accepted the page, read it carefully, then entered it into the daybook. She then said the required words, "On morrow Sublime, you will serve as ordered and required, Chef-Adjutant of the Brigade." And she smiled. That was not for anyone else but him.

Quester looked at the time on the water-clock. A quarter of an hour to 'Complete.' That was the last meal that Feasetr, the previous Chef-Adjutant Brigade, would serve before their days were done. The last meal of the day, taken after the emperor had retired by the court members who had begun their permissible daily bacchanal. Since the barmaster ruled Complete, served slightly before the striking of twenty-four, it consisted of light fare to keep a drinking man or woman in their cups and out of the needed-room. Light crustless bread onto which a light glaze of wurst and a cucumber or ell-fruit had been placed, served on a tray.

Quester looked into the kitchen while his people changed, the official duties of transition satisfied, and saw Feasetr standing with her senior leads. She kept the kitchen spotless, so there was no worry there, and she had already restocked the supplies and set up the breads. He walked to the cool-room and checked out the cold preparations, then looked into the butchery for the meats that might be needed. The guest was from the Northeast, meaning that porks and many other land-meats would be eschewed, so most of the dishes he had planned were more homey, but the emperor liked that, and no fault could be found, usually, for lighter fare. Then he heard the scream.

He ran out from the butchery and saw that the houteseria was being dragged from the kitchen by wardens, while the rest of the leaders followed glumly. He looked over to Bayve who was starting to inspect the crew's uniforms as they came out of dressing, and then at the scribe who was preparing to transfer the cutlery and other metallic tools between the shifts. Each looked back an him wordlessly and nodded. They had the first day preparations under way. He could follow the commotion.

While the commotion carried up the stairs to the presentation room, Quester went the back way, to the service gurney which lay empty and ready to use. It was small, designed to carry four table-carts up but not a human, however, he was short and did not have to duck to stand, allowing him to spin the carry-wheel and thus raise the gurney to the top level. The wooden teeth were not clutched, so he pulled the clutch-lever to engage them at their highest setting, and used his own considerable strength to rapidly reach the presentation floor. Once there, he stepped out and used the clutch bar to send the gurney to sink back to the kitchen floor.

There were a dozen table-carts pushed to the side, which he began to line up, busy work that helped excuse his presence. He knew though, what had happened a second after getting off the gurney.

On the far side of the presentation room was a cluster of nobility centered on Uttar and Romblas, the two sons of the emperor. A young servant from the kitchen staff stood in terror, surrounded by wardens, amid the wreckage of a platter and the remains of what was to be Complete. The servant's manager, one of Feasetr's staff, was engaged to the boy. It happened even here, and it was dangerous as hell because this would happen.

The butler came to Quester as he worked on the table-carts and said, "You are very dedicated to your work to be bothering with those table-carts now. "

Quester nodded. "Feasetr needs some aid it seems."

"Indeed," the Butler replied. "More than you know, that was the prepared Complete. The tables sit empty."

Quester looked over to the tables where the bartender was busy setting up the drinks which would be allowed past 24 and until 4. Indeed, the table lacked any food at all. And in ten minutes, if there was no food, more than just a young man with a tray would be heading to the gallows hall. "My pardon" Quester said.

The butler bowed. "Of course."

If the gurney was not at your floor, and you had a need to change floors at speed, you could climb down the greased wooden notches, as the gurney-box was open-topped. But that could soil your uniform in a way that could get you killed. Instead, you could do what they all called a fast rope. Quester reached over to the trays and recovered a pair of padded mittens from the servlet rack, reached out into the gurney-shaft, and caught the center-rope. Leaping off he wrapped his legs around the rope and used it to slow his fall, leaping clear as he approached the point where it split through a wooden manifold. He then sprinted out of the gurney and ran to Bayve, hard at work for the transition.

"Give me Tension and Claymorh, they are about to miss Complete," he yelled.

Bayve gasped, and pointed at the two named cooks. Existential awareness demanded that each person be aware of what they had to do or die sooner than was fair. Yet this was a special case, and confusion could kill twenty or more people, strangled in a horrible sacrifice to the empire. Quester removed his jacket immediately and racked it, then took a service gown down, handing Tension and Claymorh their own livery. Then he grabbed Tension and said, "bread." Tension nodded. To Claymorh, he said, "sauce." While they were running to get these items, Quester ran for the knife accounting.

The scribe was with her own staffers, Gluision and Annalise, working with the transfer of cutlery. Quester said, "I need a set, which one?" to Gluision, who pushed a bundle of knives over in their leather case. Most were flints, but each bundle had at least one Fhrigen-made steel knife, valuable beyond belief. These were the ones needed for quick work. He then asked Annalise, "minder?"

She nodded. "Tomyworth, mind for the chef-adjutant and take the next taster up with the compliments of Simpfrey.

He sketched a bow to Annalise and the scribe. They could have made things difficult, cost time, and in doing so killed half of Feasetr's people. He picked up Tomyworth and the nameless, scared taster, and dashed to where Tension and Claymorh had assembled two carts, one with supplies to make the Complete, the other with the appropriate supply of wooden dishes, jute-cloth serving napkins, a fingerbowl, clay lamps and oil, and card holders that the minder signed to indicate tasted food.

With practiced and finished skill Quester cut the light bread and cucumbers, and passed them to Tension who sauced them with one gram portions of egg-sauce. That left Claymorh to stack them, but not before Tomyworth, as minder, had the taster eat one dainty from each stack. At first, she was scared, having been told her time of trial—ten days, could see her brutally die of poison, but Quester did as he always did, and grabbed one of the dainties and ate it in front of her. He did that anyway because it assured him the dainties were not rancid, and thus would not result in their own deaths at the strangling pole.

Once stacked and tasted, Tomyworth filled out two cards. One went on the card holder on the table indicating that the repast was safe to eat, one was hung by twine around the neck of the taster with the same number, color, and signature, saying this was proof the dainties were safe to eat.

Then it was carefully to the gurney, the three of them taking great care to keep the display intact. Claymorh had to duck into the gurney-box, and Tension was on his knees, but the four of them fit with the one cart, barely. Whatever prompted Feasetr's staffer to hand carry the food up, Quester could not say. He only knew none of his people would make that mistake. They cranked the gurney to the presentation room, pushed the cart out, and then moved into the main room. The scared taster was barely able to walk, but she made it with Claymorh's help.

The butler fell in next to them. "Not enough time, you will never have the food transferred to the table in time," she said.

Quester ignored her. They brought the table up, and then he nodded to Claymorh and Tension who upended the service table from its position, jaked-out its legs, returned the legs to stand on their own, and then carefully, as a team of three, lifted free the service cart's tabletop and moved it to over the legs, food and all. Quester dove under the table and then re-engaged the legs to the top just in time for the water-clock to chime 24.

"Get back downstairs, you two," Quester said to Claymorh and Tension. "Take all the tables with you."

The butler said, "I had no idea those tables worked like that."

Quester looked and saw the taster was standing dumbly nearby, and went to lead her gently where she was to stand. Then he replied to the butler, "Most do. It was a gamble, as some of the newer tables are pegged together." He looked and noticed that the entire controversy was gone from the room. "They cannot shift on that boy?" He asked.

The butler shook his head as nobles drifted by to get dainties from the Complete service. "The boy claims Uttar and Romblas tripped him as he carried the tray of dainties to the table. Of course, I did not see it."

Quester nodded grimly. That meant the butler had seen it, it had happened exactly as the young man claimed, and there was no chance of reprieve.

As he was dressed properly for the upper halls, Quester left the presentation room and went down to the back corridors of the great wooden palace. Away from where guests gamboled was the pithing room. It smelled, and often screams issued from it. Feasetr and the young houteseria stood outside of the room, blocked by a warden who had his club drawn menacingly in his hand, his black coat of leather plates shining in the light of the braziers that kept the palace lit and warm, knocked into fieldstone breath-draws as they were to limit the chance of fire. He placed his hands on their backs for a few minutes, and said, "I served Complete for you."

They turned with horrors on their face. The houteseria was duty bound to serve the last meal, and they had all forgotten that it was lost with the young man who spilled it. There was no verbal thanks as they realized how close doom had come to them, but there was the thanks-of-the-face that all of the doomed accepted as the most one could offer in the gales of service to the empire. He turned and was shocked to run face-to-face with a stranger.

"Who are you?" He asked, unable to keep the fear from his voice.

The man had a distant look, as if he was in another place. "You can call me Watcher," he said. He was indeed dressed as a shipper-ashore, with a swallowtail coat that had a sigil with an R in a circle, cotton pants in black, and a white cotton shirt. Disturbingly, he had a firelock at his side.

"I was told I would see you this evening," Quester said.

"I wished to meet you as you take on your day's operations," the man said. He was young looking but had sad eyes.

"Then you are to be disappointed my friend, as I take to bed until thirteen. No human can keep up the hours. Sleep removes the chance of mistakes. All of my crew sleep as much as they can," Quester replied.

The man who named himself Watcher nodded. "Oh, I understand. An officer from the ship I represent is to be at the dinner that your emperor offers, with the intent on both sides to agree to a trade deal. I have been given permission by the one who is titled the Speaker of the Empire to watch your operation, I am keen on cooking. I will not, however, waste your time or keep you from sleep."

Quester bowed. "May I say you speak Amharian well, but most of the court speaks common, just as I understand your ship does."

The man noted in return and switched to the common tongue. "Thank you for the compliment, but I realize my understanding of Amharian is less than stellar, and is stilted as well. I merely used it because you speak to your people in the tongue."

"We use Amharian because most people who are employed by the kitchens are born into that language," Quester said, switching himself to Common. "The emperor himself speaks little Amharian though, and his staff, such as the speaker, will prefer you use common as well. They will not find your knowledge of Amharian to be amusing."

The man who named himself Watcher replied, "Thank you for the advice, I will moderate my use of the tongue of your land and restrict myself to Common. Do you have the time to show me how you make the wonderful food of your court?"

Quester considered the loaded question. To say no… that was death. To say yes could be the death of his crew if it interfered with the service. "My second handles the morning and midday meals, and the third does the evening. My own role is quality control usually. That is why I am the one who will show you how we make our meals, so to speak. The rest of the brigade cannot be distracted from the perfection of their task," Quester explained. Behind the man named Watcher, Xella paused, her eyebrows arched. He touched his right cheek, the signal that all was well, so she nodded and moved on with her tasks.

"Can you explain how this all works though? I seek not conclusory statements, though I thank you for them, but insight into your method," Watcher asked.

Quester nodded and took the man to his desk where the process books sat. "The emperor is a believer in a philosophy known as 'perfection,' where each day is orchestrated to provide an ideal outcome. Guards change precisely at certain times, are inspected by their officers, who in turn are inspected by their battalion commanders. The linens are changed in precise order by the household staff. This is also inspected by the linen patrollers, who, together with the bath inspectors, are responsible for the order of the house. In the kitchens, there are two brigades who each take three days on, three days off. During the time when a brigade is working, it produces eighteen meals, six per day starting with Breakfast and ending with Complete." He reached for a book on his desk. "There is a general manual for the operations of the kitchen, but I have created, under the guidance of the speaker, who you have met, a book with two-hundred and eleven offerings, of which we will produce six per meal, The offerings are published before we go on shift, and follow a precise method of preparation to assure we can accomplish uniformity of production within a budget that sometimes can be frugal." He handed the manual to the man and let him peruse the offerings.

"What of the punishment," Watcher asked.

"As the emperor says, perfection is expensive," Quester replied. "Using that manual of recipes and menus, training on our off days, and assuring that our supplies are delivered at the start of our three day period, we do not often lose workers—not anymore—and since I was elevated to brigade chef, I am told the quality of the food is far better than it was in the first years of the emperor's reign."

"May I have one of these books?" Watcher asked.

"You can have a box of books," Quester replied.

The man smiled, "A box would be nice, can you send them to my ship?"

Quester had been joking about a box of books, but there was no reason not to have that many manuals delivered. He waved at one of the trainees, who came over and stood nervously in front of his desk. "Fill a jute sack with twenty manuals and deliver it to the ship's boat that the merchant ship has tied alongside the large dock."

The boy nodded and rushed to carry out the request.

"Thank you," Watcher said. "So your brigade is specialized?"

Quester nodded. "There are twelve battalions. Six battalions are specialized in plating and serving the meals, one specializes in each meal, and has a second meal they assist with. Six battalions specialize in one step or major style of food. Meatiers cut, then grill or roast meat. Stewers take vegetables from the green people and meat from the meatiers to make soups, sops, and stews. They coordinate with the platers in the meal battalions. So the bakers are working on breakfast breads and have brunch and lunch loaves in the ovens. Each piece of food goes through two hands before it is served. That assures no mistakes are made," he said.

"Is this your system then?" The Watcher asked.

Quester nodded. "There were too many executions before I became a brigadier. When every person in the kitchen had to be ready to do any job at any time, there was confusion, mistakes. The system depends on realistic expectations as much as rigid adherence to protocol. Even I cannot be away every second, watching as each part of each meal is made and plated."

"Thank you," the watcher said.

He nodded and waved for another apprentice. "Vilma, please show Mr. Watcher to the guest chambers, and awaken me after lunch."

Quester watched the odd man follow the apprentice to the side quarters, then took a final look around the kitchens. The brigade was functioning well, preparing the breakfast line and starting to make progress on low tea. It was time, and past time, to rest. He checked with Bayve one last time and then turned to his own small room in the residency adjacent to the kitchens.

The scribe, Xella, was there before him. When the door shut she removed her torque-of-office and stepped into Quester's arms. "What was the stranger about?" She asked.

"Just another evolution. The emperor is rolling dice without a twelve on it and hopes to make this merchant, that is in port, ignore the numbers," Quester replied, stepping up and reaching his hand out, stroking Xella's hair in violation of 71-7-subsection-7-C. "Crazy man asked for my process book and took a box, or rather a sack of them."

"Will that cause trouble?" She asked.

"No, they are my books, not official ones. I wrote them to keep down the number of executions when I was promoted," he paused.

"And the speaker did not complain?" Xella and the speaker did not appreciate each other.

Quester stepped away and pulled aside his bedding. Xella and he could only afford to spend a few minutes together, but those minutes were silver to him. "The speaker did not mind the book, she encouraged it. I have never thought she was happy with my predecessor and how fast he went through his brigade. She may not like me much, but she does not want the emperor's madness to land on her by serving bad food, which is exactly what was happening. She even suggested changes and edited my process book."

Xella put her torque back on. "The scribes are upset, they have not had to execute kitchen staff for three years."

"I do not see how it can be changed, unless they simply let the boy go and claim he escaped." He removed his cooking jacket and laid it at the foot of the bed, and then climbed under the covers. To save time dressing he did not bother removing his kilt or bottom-shirt. He did take off his sandals and put them precisely by where his feet would land when he woke.

"They would let him escape, only they would be decimated. Not all of the wardens divorced their families when they were drafted. The fools have even more to lose than the rest of us," she said. As he pulled the covers over himself she came and kissed his cheek. Adjusting her torque again lest it be out of place when she left the quarters, she turned and left in just under the time which an observer could charge her with dereliction.

Quester always had bad dreams. Life was wheel-wise spokes: Breakfast at 5, Brunch at 9, Lunch at 13, Sublime at 17, Dinner at 21, and Complete at 1. And each dream had him making a mistake and getting people killed. Sublime was an easy meal, mostly served to workers in the court who needed to labor in the evenings. Yet a noble could attend, and if the soup spilled in their lap or the beer was served in a spotted mug, then the scribes might have to act and someone would die. That death, when it occurred, weighed heavily on Quester. Worse, the anticipation of death through a failure of protection haunted his sleep. He saw each face of his crew, their hopes and dreams of living, looking at him to protect them as they ran the treadmill of service.

So his dreams were of meal service going wrong. The fires would not start. The dishes would break or leak. The dough would not rise, and the cakes would fall and be a mess. And each mistake would leave someone dead. He had seen hangings on the other brigade, one time, four at once. The scribes wrapped a hempen rope three times around the doomed person's neck. Then the two ends were passed through a cradle-stave, a wooden bough with two holes like a pair of round cakes attached together. The two lines would be thrown over a cargo haul and passed through the saddle bit of a mule saddle. When the mule was urged forward, the rope went taught slowly around the doomed person's neck, and then lifted them from the ground. They would then flail and kick for ten, twenty, even thirty minutes. By the end, their brutal, exploded faces would puff into a purple welt like a field grape, and their tongues would stick out like a bad conch sold dead in its shell. The end was always signaled by a final twitch of the feet and hands, and the laughter of Uttar, who never missed an execution.

Quester awoke sweating, as he always did, to the shake of an assistant assigned to get him at the proper time. Lunch was served, he was informed, and they were preparing for sublime. Though dinner was the largest meal, sublime was the most important. This was the meal that was served to talk business. Quester stood from his bed as his assistant helped remove his sleeping attire, then provided warm water and soap for a bath before helping him dress in his evening uniform.

He stepped into the kitchen and saw his brigade was hard at work. His assistant left for the office and returned with his notebook. It was time to do rounds.

Sublime always had a stew. That was the easiest meal in his book because if properly stocked and spiced, it could contain almost anything and not result in a complaint. Most days it was a seafood stew, which was only one entry in his book, but which he had written over twenty pages on, since simply varying of the ingredients changed the nature of the repast considerably.

For a seafood stew, shrimp, mussels, clams, and gremlin fish were the secret. The shell fish were washed by the meatier staff then the gremlin was cleaned into fillets.

The main stock pot was prepared with cut tomatoes, and the gremlins were added. Garlic, pepper, saffron, and dried ramps were added, and this simmered. Meanwhile, onions were fried in oil and added to the base. Finally the shellfish went in. You always made three pots of the stew, though only one would be eaten. The rare failure of one soup could be succored by using a second pot, and the dish was popular and easy to keep simmering for three days in case it was called on. More than one drunk demanded the stew for Complete, and was rewarded with a quick, hot bowl.

Another element of Sublime was the bread. While other meals demanded fresh baked bread, Sublime was centered around finger bread—dried and toasted slices of sourdough that were dipped in oil, vinegar, cheese, or a combination of the three. Like the stew, the bread was designed to be lingered over while business was discussed.

Then there was the consideration of drinks, which was always a complicated matter. The apostical preferred palm rum with lemon and water served in copper mugs, chilled if possible. The el-dari drank kave or tea from wooden bowls. Some who hewed to no religious side would drink wine cut with water if they were not keeping a late schedule, or would have palm rum in their kave.

The trick was to have all of the options ready. Palm rum kept, so it was never allowed to run low in the larder, same with kave and tea, which could be called on at any time. The fires were kept hot under one of four stone water caldrons at all times. One caldron was always 'in service' while the next three were being cleaned, loaded with new water, or were being brought to a simmer. Even in summer with the black stone cauldrons exposed to direct sunlight, it took hours to bring one to just short of a broil, so they could not be left unattended.

While checking on each process, tasting all of the food, looking into the drinks, and assuring that all of the food and drink was ready and up to standard, Quester noted that Watcher was visiting each station. When he stopped at the stew going through its final assembly short of being ladled into bowls, Quester gave the soupier, who was a short former rancher named Sales, the sign to plate a bowl and nodded to Watcher. Sales took a deep stone bowl, ladled in a small portion—less than a hundred grams—of soup in, and presented a boxwood spoon to the figure. Watcher brushed his long hair aside and took the bowl with its utensil, then took a sip. "This is excellent," he declared. He stopped, then added, "May I have an entire bowl?" Sales looked at Quester, who nodded. Watcher's bowl was then filled with two quick ladles.

As Sublime approached, Bayve came from the dining hall and approached Quester. "There is a strange bald woman in a naval uniform and some big bruisers with her getting seated for the meal in the informal gathering room."

Quester looked at Watcher, then pulled Bayve aside. "Is the bald women carrying skin-art?"

"Yes," Bayve said, "and she is no petite flower-of-the-sea. Looks like she could snap me in half."

Quester laughed, "My dear Bayve, you seem impressed."

"I would like to serve her stew, and that is no lie," Bayve responded.

Quester regarded Bayve. He was the most reliable of the staff, and completely dedicated to his work, but the former mason had dreamed, before being drafted, of having children and a home in the port. It was a mistake to dream like that. But he understood the tendency to fantasize about guests to the dining halls of the emperor. The dining staff to a soul hated the people they served each day. A wave of their hand could see a valued friend strangled on the post. The most polite noble was merely a gunpowder bomb that had not yet been lit to detonate, killing friends and loved ones. Though none would voice it, there was always an edge of anger that, if things were different, would see the kitchen staff running rampage through the nobles, slaughtering them without a care.

But there was also a knowledge that the innocent would die. The guards, washers, cleaners, scribes, they all suffered the same, even if they were called on to hand out punishment. A rampage would probably backfire and hurt the innocent who were also part of the wheel of the emperor's palace.

When a new face came in though, they were the subject of fantasy. This person had never shaken their head and gotten someone killed. This person was being served and said thank you for the food they received. If the world was different, Quester could see Bayve's thing, this person who I will serve stew and tea could be a friend, and I could make them a meal they would love, but even if it was not perfect, they would forgive me.

"Bald head and tattoos you say?" Quester asked.

"Yes, plus a uniform that is not so fancy, worn like she uses it hard, but keeps it very precisely.

"Any tattoos on her head?" He asked Bayve.

His second shook his head. "Not one."

"Earrings and jewelry with the uniform?" Quester asked.

"That is so," Bayve admitted.

"She is a Sun Worshipper. They have dined here before. It is hard to describe them. El-dari in their own way. Seafood only, no other meat. They prefer to be exposed to the sun and love tattoos on their body, but none on their head. They have complex marriages, meaning that she may have a few spouses here or there, but she could be open to a new one if you play your cards right. The emperor will not like her though. It is a good thing she came in uniform. If he saw her arms uncovered, then the emperor would have a fit." Quester looked at the main clock. Twenty to service, it said.

Bayve nodded. Quester could tell that Bayve was almost ready to say something impertinent about the emperor. He looked at his second and shook his head. Bayve got the point. "So she is from the trader, same as Watcher?"

"It is a merchant, not a trader, really. Yes, she is from the *Remarker*. I will be out with service to assure things go well, and if you think Claymorh can handle the kitchens, you can come out as well. See if you can catch the Sun Worshipper's eye," Quester said.

Bayve reached up and touched his shoulder, then went to organize the carts for service.

Quester arrived at the informal room with the food and drink carts just as the courtiers and four of the merchant's crew were settling down. They all stood waiting, and precisely at 17, the emperor entered with his sons Uttar and Romblas. The room staff had arranged the cushions, which the emperor paused to count, and when the number and position seemed to be correct, said in his nasal voice, "you may take your places. We have merchants here tonight to discuss business, perhaps their leader can introduce them?"

The woman who was the leader of the merchants was indeed impressive. She stood 180 centimers tall and massed at least 70 kilograms, all defined muscles like she worked the docks tossing cargo onto pallets. She was not just bald, but aggressively bald, and her eyebrows were deep black. Her skin was deeply tanned, and though her jacket hid them, tattoos at her neck and wrists were visible. She had a talwar at her side next to a dragoon and a pair of karambits, nominally an insult to the emperor, but their presence indicated that it was acceptable for her to wear them.

Next to the woman was a small, dark, saturnine man who wore an identical uniform, only his was too large for his frame. He had long hair like the one called Watcher who had remained in the kitchens but was less striking. He was less than 55 kilograms in mass, and stood 150 centimeters tall, but he was, if anything, more chiseled than his superior. He wore no bladed weapons, but had a dragoon at his side and a line of caps for it on his belt.

Two huge men followed them, each massing more than 100 kilograms and standing at least 190 centimeters. They wore red uniforms instead of blue, and had symbols on their jackets of a firelock and a talwar crossed.

The leader bowed, motioned for her people to sit, and said, "I am First Officer Nine of the *Remarker,* holding rank of commander and the nominal second to the captain. With me is our third officer, Igor Bosonac, and two of our crew and advisors, Armsman-Marines Vyomakesh and Wuduck." She then seated herself and looked with an upraised chin to the emperor.

Uttar sniped, "You brought gutter punks with you?" Referring to the Marines it seemed.

Quester tensed. He moved the cart into position for the housteria, who began the precise process of doling out the first drinks without disturbing the conversation that was the main point of Sublime.

"There are no gutter punks on *Remarker*," Commander Nine replied.

The emperor was served first, strictly tea, no palm rum. He sipped his drink, then set it down. "Uttar, this is not an issue I wish addressed." Quester looked at the emperor's oldest son who could flail out with sudden violence when corrected by his father. Despite the stinging rebuke he received, at least stinging to him, Uttar settled down and dropped his palm rum cup on the floor.

Two housteria immediately reclaimed the cup, cleaned it, and provided another cup to Uttar, all within the regulation time limit. One of them was caught in cleaning when Uttar placed his legs onto their back, using them as a stool. It was a common move by Uttar, and thus expected. Housteria learned to remain on their hands and knees for long periods of time given the habit.

Quester looked at the merchant officer and was immediately surprised. The sun worshipper was looking at Uttar's use of a servant as a foot stool with undisguised disgust. Commander Nine clearly did not care for the habits of the elder son of the emperor and was not inclined to hide her disdain. Neither was her staff. The officer named Bosanac set his tea down and waved off another cup, and the two marines never picked theirs up. Instead, they radiated menace.

The one called Watcher arrived almost unnoticed. Instead of taking a seat, he took up a position by Bayve and folded his arms, looking like an over-dressed housteria. He was unnoticed or ignored by his fellow merchant sailors, but his sad eyes took a keen interest in the interchange.

Commander Nine put down her drink and said, "Emperor. We included your lands on our current cruise because your representative approached our Dominar and expressed a desire to see not just trade opened, but other political connections. We are not officials of the government where our ship is registered, but our captain has some influence."

The housteria began handing out the stew. The normal service was in stone bowls set into a woven basket. The bowls were heated in the stove before they received the soup. The jute basket was a requirement to protect delicate and uneducated fingers from burning themselves. The emperor and Nine ignored their bowls, but the rest of the merchants and the younger son of the emperor, named Romblas, started to eat the stew with gusto. Despite sounds of hearty mastication, Nine and the emperor remained locked in a staring contest. Finally Nine said, "Emperor, perhaps you can be clear about your desires?"

The emperor waved with his small finger and the stew was taken from in front of him and replaced with toast, oil, and vinegar along with another cup of tea. "Emporia has a long-time exclusive relationship with us to transport our trade. In recent years though, they have become haughty, belligerent, and demanded a greater profit for each tonne of trade they carry in their hulls. Recently, word of your own captain's exploits have come to our ears, and I have decided that your ship could be our exclusive trade link. It is large, fast, secure, and might handle much of our cargo needs. And your captain could be a commodore if you purchased grain haulers."

"If you accept us here and purchase the tea we have to sell, I am sure we can be part of your solution to integrate your land into the trade of the north. And my captain will make an effort to see if traders with bulk cargo contracts will sign on to supply your lands. There is a deal to be made," Commander Nine said, reaching for her tea.

"Commander Nine, you misunderstand me. I do not want your tea. I want you to be our trader. To adopt my nation's flag as our merchant marine service," the emperor said. He gestured at the informal room. "There are many benefits to being the personal traders to an emperor. Your current home nation is large, but weak. It is riven by chaos. Here, there is order and perfection.

Nine bowed her head. "I am sorry, we arrived under a misapprehension. While we are happy to carry some cargo that you want at a reasonable price, we are not traders or haulers. We arrive with goods that you can select from. There are ships that carry dunnage freight which may indeed flag under you. We are not one of them." Nine stood, then said, "you must forgive us, we sail on the turn of the wind in the deep night. Thank you for your hospitality."

"Commander Nine, you will bring my offer to your captain, it is my order," the emperor said.

"I will do so," Nine replied, and withdrew with her crew.

The emperor sat for a bit, then stood and left for the main dining room where Sublime continued, followed by his younger son. Uttar though, stopped at where Watcher stood and said, "you are the one called Watcher?"

"I am," Watcher said. Uttar stood, towering over the young merchant officer, flexing his arms and trying to seem tough. This continued for a bit, but he seemed to be at a loss for how to handle a man who seemed to dismiss his presence even as he tried to make a threat; it fell flat. The sad-eyed merchant barely recognized the noble prince's presence.

"Your captain insulted the emperor at Sublime," Uttar said.

Watcher looked at Uttar and replied, "That is impossible."

"You saying my father lied?" Uttar growled.

Watcher replied, "No, I am saying you lied. The captain of the merchant ship did not insult your father because the captain was not there. Commander Sunstar Nine is a first officer."

Uttar sketched a punch at Watcher, who did not flinch, as if the merchant knew the bully would pull his fist at the last minute. He then said, "my father commanded me not to interfere with your captain or his officers, but he said nothing about you. What if I order my guards to torture you and return your mangled body to your ship.

The merchant was either fearless or suicidal as he said, "You should speak to your father before you make a mistake." Housteria cleaning up the meal and guards grew suddenly tense and quiet. The Merchant may not realize it, but Uttar was perfectly capable of carrying out such a threat.

Indeed, he drew a short sword and cocked it back in a swing, but the merchant officer named Watcher stepped forward. He stuck his chin forward and said quietly at the prince, "what will you accomplish by striking me."

Quester looked back and forth between Uttar and Watcher. They stood in a war of wills for a minute, then Uttar lowered the sword. "My father believes in precision, in one chance and no other given." He turned and yelled, "Scribe!"

Quester watched as Xella entered from the larger dining room and said, "Yes, Prince."

"Take careful notes on the next meal. If your scribes want to live, you will make sure each offense to the emperor's order is set for punishment. Do you understand?" His tone was mocking and struck Quester as not a little insane.

"I do," Xella said, though Quester knew it took every ounce of her strength to say those words.

Uttar turned to Watcher and said, "You may want to stay for dinner. The side show afterward will see fifty feet dangling on ropes, and each one dying a horrible death because of you. He turned and left.

There was silence for a minute before Quester sat down where he was not permitted, and said, "Bayve, take Watcher back to his ship."

Bayve tried to take the merchant's arm, but the officer shrugged it off and approached Quester. "So the rumors are true. There is no punishment except ... a final punishment."

"Look, Officer Watcher, you need to be gone. Your fight with our emperor's son has killed this whole brigade," Quester said.

"Why not run?" The man asked ignorantly.

"On an island this size? It is a day's easy walk from side-to-side. And if you came on a ship, you know the longshore is too hard for a small boat, and the large boats belong to the emperor," Quester replied.

Xella touched Bayve on the back and motioned for the housteria to leave. When they had gone she said, "I can let the scribes leave. That way they are not forced to murder you all."

"But you will be murdered for that yourself," Quester cried. "My love, you must kill us all to save yourself. Help the next brigade they draft rebuild, help train the new brigade leader so there are not too many killed getting back the proficiency of the kitchen."

"My friends, you have three hours until the next meal, will the palace guards be after you before then?" Watcher asked.

Xella reached over the chair and grabbed Quester in an embrace, a bold move she would not have attempted just an hour before. She said in a sob, "they cannot, they are locked into their own procedures. When the meal fails, I would inform them of the failure and submit the names of the guilty, and then they will be arrested. They will all be arrested, Uttar will make sure."

"And if you do not make that report?" Watcher seemed casual, almost cool given the circumstances, Quester thought. He had not seen the kicking legs, the purple faces, or heard Uttar and Romblas laughing.

"Then after one hour the speaker will report me and investigate the reason for the failure of the meal. By morning, everyone will be arrested anyway no matter what I do." She looked at Quester in sorrow, "and certainly Uttar and Romblas will make sure that the speaker does not drag her feet."

"But in the next three hours, what will happen?" Watcher asked.

There was silence from Xella.

Watcher pointed to the doorway back to the kitchens. "Your guards, I note, check anyone coming in, but no one going out, or at least I saw they did not check people carrying obvious refuse. Only people who had nothing in their hands were checked. Probably because they think trash carriers are not worth checking. Have each person who wants to come with me to the *Remarker* fill a basket with trash and any keepsakes and personal items as are close to hand, and then we go to the port, discard the refuse, and board the launch that is waiting to take Sunstar Nine back to the *Remarker*."

"Just walk out?" Quester asked Watcher.

Watcher nodded. "The story books will say you broke out by fighting with pans and rolling pins, but the point is not to fight your way out, but to use the culture of your own emperor against him. The guards follow precise rules, use them against the emperor."

"It won't work, we will all be killed," Xella said.

Quester agreed, then thought different. "The guards are not bad people. They will be killed if we escape."

"Then beat them up. Will that work?" Watcher said.

"It will not work," Xella said.

Quester saw that his own mind had been clouded by terror. It was time and past time to break from this life. "My love, we are dead anyway. No one here now has any connections to this land, not anymore. We all knew what it was to be drafted to these kitchens. It was eventual death." Quester waved for Bayve who was standing by, terror stricken. He looked at Quester with a puzzled look. "Bayve, take Tension and Claymorh and find out who wants to flee this land on the merchant in the harbor. If they do not want to run, knock them silly and lock them in the food pantry."

"Wait..." Watcher tried to say but Quester interrupted him.

"No, if they get beaten down and locked up, then they will be blameless in this escape. No one can be left standing as be flee. If they are left standing, we are killing them," Quester said. He turned back to his brigade second. "Once we know who is going, have them all go to their rooms and gather anything they cannot leave behind, then come back here and arm themselves with whatever they can. The rule is—everyone we meet gets beaten down, but no one gets killed. Forget the trash, it won't work. But we can prevail if we leave now."

Quester looked at the merchant, Watcher, who was fingering the curved talwar that swung on his hip. Then he braced Bayve. "Ten minutes and we all leave, the entire staff. All the reliable ones. Make it happen."

Bayve looked at Quester and Xella. He then turned and nodded and turned to the kitchens.

Quester embraced his love and said, "The scribes can come."

"They will not, each will seek promotion in my fall," she replied.

"Then to the kitchen with me. The dice are being rolled, and we hope for a twelve." Quester hugged her, then gathered up Watcher with his eyes and went back to the serving stairs, leaving the food carts where they sat.

The group gathered in the main brigade area, forty and seven souls with not a sound coming from them. "We are leaving now," was all that Quester had to say. There were no words now. Everyone knew they were dead by morning if they remained.

Bayve took charge of the merchant, Watcher, who looked about wide-eyed but passively came along. The rest filed in behind Quester as he marched purposefully down the back hall and to the rear stairs. Two guardsman looked surprised and started to bring their glaives to port as Quester approached them. He only knew them by their brassard numbers, seven-seven and seven-nine. "You boys should drop the cleavers."

Seven-seven stepped back and looked at his partner. Seven-nine ported his glaive then brought it back up. "Quester, what is this?"

"Fight us, or drop the stickers. We will give you some swats so no one comes down on you," Quester said. He reached seven-seven, held out his hand, and Claymorh handed him a wooden fry paddle. Seven-seven dropped his glaive and stuck this chin out, allowing Quester to deliver a nice slap to his face. He fell to the ground and then closed his eyes. Seven-Nine held his glaive up, then was knocked out by Xella with a recipe book.

Quester pushed the weapons aside, and several of the band dragged the supine guards to the side. The rear hall stairs were where supplies came up to the kitchen and rubbish went down. Quester thought about how many in his band had taken these stairs three times a day during their duty time to take baskets up and down to the lower gates. He did not have to give any orders for where to go, his army of cooks and cleaners knew where the exit was, they just never had the power to take it, and if they had, no way to reach any place where their masters could not find them and punish them for their insolence. It was no calumny that they were all locked into a world that could support no dreams of freedom ... until now. "This is it," he said.

They all charged the servants' gate without a sound.

The guards were well armed with glaives and truncheons, but they were not trained in how to react to a mass of kitchen staff rushing upon them swinging pots and large stir spoons. They made no formation to meet the charge, and only a few took up arms at all. Some allowed themselves to me beaten down. Some dropped their weapons and joined the kitchen staff in the mayhem. Bayve kept a grip on Watcher, their ticket to *Remarker*, and did not allow him to fall behind.

They left the palace and entered the builders' ward which connected directly with the Empire Docks. Anyone which did not give way was beaten and left bruised and crying on the ground. Many citizens, knowing full well what would happen if they did not resist, simply lay down on the ground and were passed by like a rock in the waves of the surf. And again, some of them joined the wave of the kitchen brigade.

As a wave they again met guards, this time guarding the docks entrance, and though the guards were more numerous, they were broken down in short order and left groaning on the ground, those that did not drop their weapons and continued the attack. Finally, they reached the gangplank of the merchant ship which seemed to be preparing to leave. Marines were on the deck and looked in no mood to allow the refugees on, but Quester motioned for Bayve to shove Watcher forward. One of the Marines pointed and yelled, and then the kitchen staff and a hundred more who had followed the exodus, crowded up the plank to a crew which was waiting with tea and blankets. The ship cast off, and anchored in the roads outside of the harbor to take stock.

Three hours later, Speaker Ankelia Restarche boarded the ship in high dudgeon from the deck of a sail launch, making Quester fear to the bottom of his soul. He reached out and grabbed Xella's hand, who squeezed his back. If this was the end, they would go together with their heads held high. Not waiting for her guards to make the ship's deck, she stormed across the well to the gangway ladder and climbed to the top of the cockpit, planting herself in front of the woman named Sunstar Nine and pushed her velour cloak from her sides revealing her brace of dragoons. "You have explaining to do, an apology, and you will return our citizens to me."

As if she had lit a candle in a room, the speaker realized that the cockpit top was filled with marines who seemed to growl soundlessly with their faces. The tall woman named Standish said, "call them to order, Hate." Quester wondered, as powerful as Restarche was, how she thought that her own safety was assured on the deck of a merchant who could be off in an hour in the right winds.

A huge man with blond wavy hair said in reply to Standish, "At rest, ladies and gentlemen, the captain has not ordered you to arms... yet."

Sunstar, whom Quester had seen at Sublime, replied, "Speaker Restarche. As I said when you begged me for our trade, I am not the captain."

"Then call your captain," she yelled, perhaps forgetting again she was surrounded by marines.

"I am the captain," came a familiar voice. It was the one who would only admit to the name 'Watcher.' He had been sitting on the side of the cockpit as Commander Nine, a man named Darkfather, and Major Standish had been working out berthing options. Watcher, who still looked like a sad-eyed scholar, said the words without looking at Restarche. He was seemingly in his own world but came to life like a marionette grabbed up by a puppeteer in a second and stumbled a little as he approached the speaker. The marines and sailors gave way as he stepped forward, looking older than when he was playing a minor functionary for a rich merchant. Now that he was a captain, he looked absurdly young, tired, and unable to hold eye contact with those around him.

"So you are Rasheed?" Restarche asked in harsh tones.

"My people would say al-Rasheed, that is the polite form of my kith name," the captain said.

Restarche spit on the deck. The marines started to move but Standish growled, "Hold!" Then she looked at the captain and then to Restarche. Quester felt that the major was itching to throw the speaker over the side.

"Rasheed, look at the mouth of the harbor," Restarche demanded.

The captain turned back to the gunwale of the cockpit. He stepped between a sailor and a marine, the space was crowded to its limit, and reached for a range finder. Scanning the harbor, he said, "Four sloops," he stated without any enthusiasm.

Restarche laughed, "the emperor is ready to take your boat. There are four sloops, but in each sloop is a hundred warriors. And when they drag the *Remarker* down with grapples, four hundred more will swarm you on pinnaces and john boats."

Al-Rasheed stepped back. "Major Standish, how many serpents are bearing on the sloops?"

"Two serpents, Captain. Janak and Hoke are in the tops," Major Standish said.

"Two shots per sloop, no casualties if possible." The captain said.

Four shots rang out. Quester stood on his toes to see the sloops, and other than splashes of water, there was no effect.

"Captain, firing a few firelock shots will not deter us," Restarche said.

The captain sat down on a bench under the storm roof of the cockpit. He reached over and pulled a tea service from a paraffin heater, and poured himself a cup of tea. "Can I pour you some Junebug?" He asked.

Restarche scoffed, "we have serious business to attend here, you could be in our dungeons by end of day, all I have to do is signal the sloops." Then she looked at the tea, "and only a swine would drink that nonsense, even if it were time for tea."

Quester watched the as the captain lowered his head into his hands. "Mouse, message to Sloan, bring a tray and some Rywal up for the speaker, along with some chairs." A smaller crew member hopped to obey the order, and returned with a tray of food and some tea in a warmer. A marine followed with a folding chair and set it up next to the captain's perch on the bench.

The captain looked at the food and tea then said, "It is almost midnight. Please sit." The speaker sat.

"What you do not understand, what your so-called emperor does not understand, sitting on his squalid throne of perfection, is that I did not take anyone but ones he would discard anyway. They were dead by your own rules. 150 men and women are on this ship, and none of them would have lived three days if they had not climbed on board."

"What possible good can these people do for you?" the speaker asked.

"I am investing in 150 people and will make a tidy profit from what looks like altruism. You see this book?" He reached down to a jute sack which held twenty copies of Quester's own manual for kitchen recipes and pulled one out, holding it aloft in his right hand.

"So what, that is a servant's manual. I edited it and had then printed for Chef Quester," Speaker Restarche said, looking uncomfortably at the tome as the captain held it aloft.

"And a fine job you did. A remarkable effort that saved the lives of many of the kitchen staff of the palace, as this book is a clever and clear manual on how to produce wonderful food for large groups of people. A lot of the ceremony is lunatic-fringe gibberish, what the older people of my land called 'kalam majnun,' but the recipes and instructions on how to break up the work, grade the ingredients, cut corners where the budget does not allow for expenses without ruining the dish, ways to substitute one ingredient for another when the main ingredient is hard to source, this is a massive work of human cooking arts, and I intend to make a lot of money off the people who wrote this book." The captain seemed in a trance as he spoke, his eyes tracking some other world of potential where the simple process of making food for another person was a human achievement greater in his mind that that of a famous general or pirate who shook the Halo with their fists. Quester could see that the crew around the captain were reacting with varying degrees of awe. The tall blond warrior named Standish looked on Javier al-Rasheed with respect mixed perhaps with some amount of fear. The officer who pretended to be the ship's master, Sunstar, held her gaze on the captain with an almost religious glow that perhaps she otherwise reserved for her worship of the sun. The little sailor who stood hidden in the crowded deck that others called al-Ahar clapped his hands and nudged another sailor who had forgotten a set of spy glasses were in her hand and stood with her mouth agape. The marines remained squared off with the guards of the empire but their chests seemed to swell with the string of narration coming from their leader, while the warriors-of-the-empire shrank a little in the fervid passion that washed over them.

"You will make money by enslaving them then?" Speaker Restarche said with a lack of conviction.

The captain tossed the book back into the bag. "That is your own projection of what you see the world as. Slaves, one man or woman toiling for another without benefits, only fear and hate. Slaves, though, are useless. They do not make new things. They do the least work for their masters that is possible, and that work is only good if ten people inspect it each minute."

He edged over to the tea service clamped onto a worktable and started pouring tea, the crew and strangers to the deck were all mesmerized. "Let me tell you of an island I know." He took a cup of tea and passed it to Speaker Restarche, who accepted it despite her earlier statement that she wanted none on this ship. Quester watched as the captain started filling wooden tea cups and passing them to crew. He startled a little when one of the crew, the one named Sloan, seemed to appear with more tea like a jinn aparating from a wänd. As the captain depleted the teacups with his service, more appeared in the sailor's hand and the service-pot was replaced. Even the warriors were given cups and were forced to stand down from trying to bullyrock the marines. Of the people crowding the cockpit-top, only the ones that Quester heard called the Hate brothers, both sergeants in precise turnout uniforms, did not take cups. But they smiled as they saw the warriors take the tea, and stood down a little from their air of menace.

Javier al-Rasheed took the last cup and sipped a small amount, then said, "On this island, and only this island, a large tree fruit called plakers grows. The fruit is enough to sustain a human for a day, and does not grow foul for a month if it falls naturally from its tree. The people of this land have no other need but to find water that flows from sweet springs, and wait for the fruit of this tree to fall at their feet."

"I have never heard of this land," Speaker Restarche growled.

"Because nothing happens there," the captain replied. "They do nothing, make nothing, have no ambition. Their sole skill is to understand where a plaker will fall next and to be present when it falls. That is it. The land is a paradise, and since it is in the extents and not close to the Halo, it will remain a paradise where the people create no history. And one day an ambitious person will take them over, chop down their amazing trees, and they will disappear from history except for the stories I tell of them."

Speaker Restarche growled again, her angular face glowing red. "This is a story that does not mean anything."

The captain turned away from the speaker and looked at the port of Gataleta. "In struggling to save their own lives, Master Quester and his people have created something unique, magical, and I am not going to enslave them because that would ruin it. They did it because unlike the people of the Plaker Groves, they had to succeed, or die. However, they cannot flourish where there is no room for error, and they cannot achieve great things as slaves. So instead, on each island I stop where the soil is fertile, I will land these people of their own free will and help them create a place where they can do these great things and make money in the process. I will, or rather the purse of my ship, *Remarker*, which is greater than me in that it is a community, will take each year a tithe of their profits, and sell them tea and things from the reaches of humankind that will earn us more money, until the day they have paid for their debt and we part ways. *Remarker* will have made money, I guarantee it, and perhaps these people, while they themselves pay to have more places to open and extend the chain that starts here, on the deck of this ship, will succeed. And perhaps some will fail. Perhaps some will elect to sit underneath a tree waiting for fruit to fall. But I bet most will take their knowledge and sow the fertile soils of the Halo to make wonderful things."

Silence settled on the deck of the *Remarker*. Noise could be heard from the harbor as people yelled and wood struck wood with distant claps of sound. The one called al-Ahar had set his tea aside and clambered up part-way on the rear steering mast, "Captain, the port is organizing some sort of pursuit. Two frigates and a few sloops."

Speaker Restarche looked dejected. "You may have saved these people from the kitchens with your dream of seeding the lands with, of all things, restaurants, but you have killed me. And if you do not leave the harbor, you may die yourself."

The captain remained silent for a second, then looked cryptically to his side. After a moment he shook his head and turned back to the speaker. "Sergeant Hate, did you drill out the frigates and the sloops?"

One of the two smiling, menacing marines said, "Abrahamsson did all four ships, sir, last night. Nothing serious, but they will take on water if the oakum pulls out of the drill holes."

Speaker Restarche said, "You never intended to trade, just to take these people with you."

The captain shrugged. "Oh, I intended to trade. Do you remember what the emperor said when Commander Nine offered them a steady harbor visit?"

"That we were not interested in mundane trade," Restarche said.

"You cannot, or should not trade people, but I am investing in these folks. Perhaps, Speaker, there could be another person as well," he said.

The speaker turned and looked back at the port, then said to the warriors under her care, "Return to the pinnace. I am no longer your speaker, and unless you want to be murdered by the emperor you should leave now."

The lead warrior stood, holding a cup of tea, then said, "Lads, drink the tea. The speaker has betrayed the empire and we must report this intelligence." The warriors finished their tea and returned their cups to the service, then filed down the gangway to the edge of the ship, escorted by grinning marines. When they cast away and were shaping a course for the docks, the captain said, "Steward Sloan, take the refugees below and have them quartered and set to watches. Commander Nine, please take the ship to its warp point. I am going below to rest."

Quester stood with an empty teacup in one hand, his other grasping Xella around the waist. Steward Sloan approached them and said, "let us get you settled for the warp."

Chapter VI

Magick

Gemmadine was elated. She felt the wind from the oncoming storm on her face. She felt the electricity in the air that signaled the storm would be pregnant with thunder. The gait of the mule she rode was a magical metronome that told of her freedom with each click of motion. The crackle of excitement flowed through her and made her ultra-sensitive to tiny sensations. She tasted the copper bite that flavored the water from her water bottle, the water having come from the clean cistern rather than the river. The linen of her new thawb brushed lightly against her breasts as she swayed. She could feel the sensation of thick traveling boots, and the feel of her hair as it brushed her ears.

She had signed on at Codis Aletia as a runaway from her old profession, a new chance to apprentice and get away from the people who hunted her, and she was fearful that her past would affect her standing in the crew.

It did not. Everyone on the ship had a past. She had fought on the docks next to her fellow shipmates during the revolution at Cycus, had seen others die and had rushed the barracks and fought hand-to-hand with the Life Guards, her fellows in red and blue, against the soldiers of the old Dominar in green, and they had prevailed.

Everyone had a past, no one cared. Even an apprentice sailor such as her had standing on the ship if she had fought on the docks that night.

However, as much as she liked the ship, felt her ownership as part of a crew, there was a sense of abandon when the chances of schedules and the needs of loading and unloading cargo allowed her and her mates to get time ashore. The port of Rutia on Neversay was open to all on rotation despite its sinister reputation, so Mouse had suggested taking a carriage up to the markets and looking for some trade goods or small cargo bag trinkets to carry for memory sake. Fiddler and Kahanu Fleet had begged off, wanting to see a pantomime, and Fawzia was looking for a day at the spa with Nani Fix and Pukak, but the Mouse recruited Yatishi and Chaten to join them to make the luxury of the jitney possible.

On the ship, she had heard the speed keeper yell that the *Remarker* was making twenty kilometers an hour, an amazing speed, but half that in a jitney through crowded streets of Neversay seemed twice as fast as safe. Her empathy sense was alive as she rode through the streets. Troachers were angry that the weather was going to close their sales day early and were yelling out prices to sell the last of their wares before the open air portion of the market closed. Johnny boys and girls rushed through transactions to serve one more client before the streets became a quagmire of water. Soldiers hurried to their garrison so they would not have to wait the rain out in a guard-box, while many people set to opening sluiceways so they could capture a share of the water that would soon be falling from the sky. She was intensely aware of a monk gesticulating wildly and yelling the name of Tempester, obviously being ridden in the name of the god as the storm approached.

When she looked at the Mouse she saw an inscrutability that haunted her. His body language was easy to read. He was joyous with celebration, but in some ways he was drawn in and defensive. His face was a broad smile, but he wrapped his arms around himself as if he were about to be attacked.

"Is something wrong, Mouse?" She asked.

He looked at her and said, "I grew up under the docks in Cycus port. You have to remind yourself that the world is not that bleak, but sometimes when you remind yourself, your body does not get it."

She did not understand this statement. They were riding a jitney-cart through a crowded street. Unless they ran into another of the carts, it was safe. Nothing could hurt them here.

Yatishi Ishan was a beautiful woman from Dartia with dark, sharp features, beautiful black-blue hair, and a commanding physicality that made heads turn when she worked on the docks. "Afar here is the bravest of us, but also the best with weather sense. I always look to him to see if it will rain."

Chaten, a curly-haired former jony from the Sugar Islands added, "Keen senses, our Mouse. Nose for profit, ears for rumors, and eyes for danger. If you had worked the same eight-watch with him, you would know."

"I am sorry, Mouse," she said.

"Do not be. I am just me," he replied.

They got to Five Points, the main merchants center, Gemmadine stepped out of the cart with Mouse, letting Chaten and Trish take it to the textiles district and looked out at the array of fascinating stores. There was energy crackling under Mina's skin from the storm that was coming, she could tell it would be a massive downpour. She wanted to run down a hill, to swim in raging waters, to eat piles of food. It felt good to be on the shore and able to do as she wished.

She looked at the Mouse. He was looking around also in excitement. A wagon of onions by the gate caught their eyes, selling purported Norwalk Sweets, a rare delicacy. She nodded to the cart and they walked over. The onion lady smiled at her and took an onion from her cart. "Here you go sweetness, they are good."

She took the onion and thanked the woman, who returned to her cart and pushed it away in anticipation of the incoming weather. She looked at the Mouse and bit the onion. It was an amazing vegetable, filled with sharp, sweet flavor, perfectly ripe, and already pealed for eating. Most onions were too strong to eat raw and they rarely just ate onions, they usually had them cooked down into stews, but for her, a Drugari-born, an onion was an exciting adventure. She watched as the Mouse concluded his dealings with another stall and returned with a pair of oil-cloth ponchos.

"How much was the onion?" The Mouse asked.

"Free," Gemmadine handed it to him.

He took a small bite and then said, "They are sweet."

"In my homeland, Norwalk Sweets are an incomparable delicacy, and here an old woman gives me one for free," Gemmadine said.

The Mouse handed her a cloth poncho. "It's rented. We get the deposit back when we return them"

"Are they clean?" She asked.

The Mouse considered. "Smelled clean. No lice. Probably they are clean."

Gemmadine laughed at his earnest response.

The rain began to fall, and the shops became crowded as customers headed inside. Guards from the Sublime Port Authority retreated to their guard shacks, while the final effort to evacuate the street was under way. The Mouse helped Gemmadine into her poncho, and then she helped him with his.

They walked through the rain, looking at shop signs. Mouse insisted on reading each one, which were printed in Eurabaa, Navarese, and Amharian. "Dry Goods," he said at one store, and they laughed because of the rain. "Herbals and Medicine," he read at the next, sounding out the two syllables of the word medicine oddly until he realized that the accent was missing from the store sign.

"Where I am from, they use the old term under the bridge," he said. "It is '*quat sihria*'"

"Power, *quat*, I understand. But *sihria*?" She asked him. Her own Eurabaa was school taught.

He looked worried. "*Earaafa*," he said, seeming to think that would help. Then he thought for a second and said, "*alsahar.*"

She was still confused. "Medicine is medicine, what else can it mean?" She could feel her heart wobble a little, like it had been attached to a string and pulled hard. She might be catching something in the rain, she thought.

"You meet them. Old men, women with a sort of, well, different way of seeing things. They conjure changes... I do not know the words in the common tongue," Mouse said.

"In my land it is magick. And it is nonsense," Gemmadine said. "Not that I think you are saying nonsense. Just, it is what charlatans say they can do," Gemmadine said, huddling in the rain with Mouse in front of the store.

Mouse looked earnestly at Gemmadine, "The captain says there are things at sea that should not be. Places that cannot be told of. He said it one time, and it stuck with me, that there are greater oceans that his or mine. Oceans that we would need boats made by the gods, and maps written in a math no one could solve easily. Maybe he was describing magick, because I have seen the dead returned and made dead again in the middle of the night when the crabs gather."

"I think he was talking metaphorically. I mean he was being poetic rather than logical in his expression," she said. Sheer was a slight euphoria in her, like she had sampled decker's swill or some other product of the drinker's game. It made her think of food, and that she would like to have some when they finished shopping.

Mouse nodded. Then he smiled and looked over her shoulder. "There is a store for 'priceless objects.' Let's see what that is about."

The store was as crowded as all the rest were, but the people were browsing rather than buying. The owner and several shopkeepers kept close watch on the merchandise, which was an eclectic lot of small nonsense. Crystal turtles made of jade sat between single examples of teacups from around the Halo. None were in a set. Clever items like sparkers to light fires, gin-willies to peel the rinds from fruit, butter-cobs to hold oils for serving with bread, and canteens with clever attachments. Gemmadine did not watch the items, which were mostly tripe, but instead watched Mouse as he carefully inspected and rejected each item. "What are you looking for," she asked.

"Magick," he replied. "You may think it silly, but I have felt it since I got to this street, in the rain. I do not know what it is, but you call it magick, so that is what it is, I guess." It was around the street, and now I can tell that it is in this shop. And somewhere in this shop..." He stopped and looked at a pile of dice made from bone, wood, resin, percha. They had carved or enameled numbers, 1 - 2 - 3 - 4 - 5 - 6 - 7 - 8 - 9 - 10 - 11 - 12. Some had bags, boxes, came in matched pairs or sets of six. Some has taba numbers, the unusual number system of the Sikka that counts * - ** - > - >* - >** - >> - >>* - >>** - V - V* - V** - V> and that they believe is how to talk to God. Some of the dice were beautiful, carved and forged into intricate and ghostly shapes.

Yet for all of those wonderful dice, the Mouse reached for one that sat at the rear of the pile of dice. It was a strange, malformed thing in that it was larger than a normal die. Most dice were about the diameter of a silver piece, maybe 25 millimeters across. Some could be 30 or 40 millimeters across, they were used for games that required the number to be seen easily in a crowd.

This die was the size of an orange, milky white, with four sides painted in blue, red, black and green. It was a truncated at the edges, softened, and would likely not roll correctly, making it a liability on a ship.

Gemmadine watched as his companion hungrily spun the die in his hand. There had been an attempt at numbering the sides, obviously to make it useful as a die, but the numbers had peeled off. No one had thought to carve it, the die was perfectly smooth on each of its twelve facets. She reeled a little and caught herself.

The Mouse immediately went for the owner of the store at a small folding table. "How much?" He asked.

The man looked at it. "Fifty."

Gemmadine said, "Not worth it, Mouse, they cannot sell that thing for one." It was humorous that her words were a little jumbled.

Mouse nodded. Then he reached into his pocket, pulled out a muslin wrap, placed it on the trestle table, and unwrapped a beautiful sun coral. "Daylight makes the coral turn pink when it is exposed above water. When it dies, you have to pour vinegar on it to keep the color."

"Do not trade even for that, Mouse, that die is huge. It will barely fit in a pocket. I can get fifty for the coral on the docks." Gemmadine was not even lying. The coral was beautiful. It could be formed into several pieces of jewelry, used as a counter piece, or be the center of a collection of stones. Mouse was not lying about how hard it was to make the stone.

Several of the browsers seemed to confirm Gemmadine'a opinion. They gathered around the table and muttered to themselves. One of them said, "twenty-five."

The Mouse said, "Only if the shopkeeper has no deal in him."

The shopkeeper was almost cast from a pantomime for the part. He had a tall green hat, wood-framed glasses with a reflector and a magnifier on them which could slide down to aid in looking at store products, a purple vest with large pockets that held notebooks, pencils, conte sticks, a whisk brush, white cotton gloves, muslin wraps, twine, a dozen keys, a bottle marked as alcohol with the traditional blue-gold label, and a merchant's pass card. He put on white gloves and handled the coral, weighed it in his hands, smelled it, and considered. "How much?" He asked.

Mouse considered. "The die and fifty."

"Nonsense," the shopkeeper replied. "I might sell it at fifty. I won't buy it at fifty."

"Then you name. One time, and make sure I get the die. It is lucky now," The Mouse said.

"Thirty and done," he said.

"Forty and done," Mouse countered.

Thirty-five is forty with the die," came the shopkeeper's reply.

"Thirty-five and done," Mouse squeaked.

The shopkeeper put the coral down carefully and pulled out thirty-five in silver, six 'fives' and two 'half-fives.' The Mouse swept the coins into his pockets, retrieved the die from the table, tipped the shop owner a zot and a two-tenth drachma because they were loose in his pocket, and said, "Day to you." As he passed the tall uplander who had offered twenty-five he whispered "Got another for thirty if you come to the *Remarker* at the docks." Then left the store with Gemmadine.

Mouse looked at Gemmadine and said, "Do you feel well?"

Me, well? She thought it was humorous. Mouse was who looked a little green. She nodded. "Well. Ohh, well," she said. Then she threw up and sat down on a bench.

Mouse held his hand to her head and said, "Bad onion. I feel it as well. Wait here." He was back almost immediately, but then Gemmadine thought that was wrong. The rain was harder and it was like time had skipped a bit.

"They are bringing mules," he said, and seemed worried. He reached into her pocket, smelled the onion she had left, and tossed it into the rain. She tried to grab it, but the onion had become three onions. With only two hands, it was a task just to track the vegetable. "Ten minutes," he said, then sat next to her.

"Mule's expensive. Walkies-talkies," she said, realizing that she sounded like a child.

"Nonsense," he replied. "Lots of mules come up, few go down. The mules are cheap going down.

They were under the cover of the store's eaves, which was good, she thought, because of the rain. She turned and watched Mouse as he played with the die he had bought.

Somehow he had put the second rented rain cloth on her, and his own sweater as well. She did not remember it.

She did remember his playing with the die. He took a few minutes spinning it in his hands, then he held it to his chest and some water splashed away. "How did you do that?" She asked.

"Magick" he said. Then he looked woefully at her. "I felt it. You touch the green, and think about the water, and it feels in your head like you are pushing a barrel that is filled with liquid, and the water splashes away. So green is push. The blue, you touch it and sort of think of the water, and you get water in the face. Blue is pull. Then you touch the red and think about the rain, and the rain does not fall on your head. It falls everywhere else. Red is like a rain shield."

"Black, there is black. You—black try-black?" She asked. "I love you, my Mouse. You are like my little brother, dead so many years. The caves fell in on him," she said.

The mules came up and Mouse said, "Do not say things you cannot unsay. The woman with the onions, she poisoned you. We have to get back to the ship.

She mounted her mule the help of Mouse, and then felt as he tied her onto the animal. He then took her lead and brought it to his own mule. He handed silver to the drover, and a rudely scrawled note.

The trail from the upper town to the Sublime Port of Neversay was circuitous, passing through paced city blocks running with water, to more agricultural and isolated fields, and back. What they had rocketed down in a cart-wagon, was slow going on a mule. The rain had cleared the roads of humans, but the clouds had darkened and the path turned sinister.

It was at the bend where the road split into one that continued to the port and another that left for the arbors and grazelands above Neversay that Gemmadine felt the hair on her neck stand. She rode on because the mule did and she was tied to the mule, but she was almost otherwise paralyzed. They passed the cataract in the small river, where the trees took on a strange visage, seeming to go blurry and to stand further away than was possible. Her vision went rimmed with red, and the day, wan though it was, looked as night.

She tried to speak but was unable to, and finally as they entered the Tinion Sway, a wild and unkept land between the shopping district and the port, was able to make an almost mouse-like squeak and throw herself painfully from the mule, landing on the beaten, graded road with a hard thump, ropes tangling her feet.

The Mouse was off his mule immediately. "Do not fear, brave Gemmadine. You have been poisoned, but it is not deadly, or it seems not," he said to her. Do not fear. But she did not fear, or rather she was terrified at some level of herself, but the top of her being was completely not worried at this development. She noted something she had known. He rarely looked people in the face, but when he did it was with a piercing, owl-like look. She was unfamiliar with his accent, but it had the taste of the of the exotic in it. She did not know why her mind raced to useless thoughts while she was paralyzed, but she had, since their first meeting, she had imagined the Mouse as an almost nonentity, but now she knew this was mistaken, like the rain on her head was mistaken to fall there.

The Mouse was adjusting her clothing, rubbing mud from it, closing her wax-cloth and wool layers to better pro-tect her. From his pocket he took a flask and let her sip some. It was yew water and baisley-leaf tonic. "We are followed," he said and she drank. "And ahead there are men. Can you run? There are houses down the hill. You could reach one."

She looked on past the mules to see the old onion seller approach, flanked by ten muscular men. Her simple kenaf fabrics and the hide clouts of her henchmen made the group seem humble, like workers or farmers, but Gemmadine's empathy sense was not dead. The woman intended them harm, it screamed. The woman was malevolent and her henchman depraved.

Then she noticed something else that puzzled her. The Mouse was an intense flame of energy that radiated out to her, but now own aura was almost unprotected except for the odd sense of concealment that seemed to come not from him, but his oddly curved sword. "Magick!" She laughed. Yet the next second it was gone. Had the Mouse been bathed in arcane light? Was the Mouse one immense source of arcane energy? Was he a master wizard hidden by the artifact and by guileful art. It was only when his energy was directed to protect her that she could see through his subterfuge to the real him. A great warrior armed with a magical weapon!

"Magick!" She yelled again.

She understood now that her empathy was a form of magick just as the Mouse said he had experienced, and she was a magick user of power, as was Mouse himself.

The Mouse stood and said, "You cannot have us."

The old woman laughed, "I only want her, child."

"*Hi min Remarker!*" He yelled. She was having trouble with the language. He had announced she was 'one of the *Remarker.*'

"*Sawf 'amut qabl 'an yakun lidayka!!*" His yell was almost primal, and struck fear into the middle of Gemmadine. She did not understand the words, they were in a now foreign tongue, strange and exotic to her ears, her mind having lost the entire track of the words she knew she could speak and understand. All she had left was the tongue of her birth. The tongue uttered in dark caves where they hid from the gods and made their own magic.

Despite the lack of understanding, she had in herself an idea of what he was saying. The Mouse was daring them to step closer. He had his fists clenched in rage held at an odd angle, like he had no idea how to fight using them. If he was a quiet boy, he had become an impressive being standing in god fire over her.

More surprising than the transition in the Mouse was the effect on the human muscle that surrounded the onion woman. They went from walking forward with evil confidence to stopping as if they had hit a wall. It was obvious they had no idea what the boy could do, but their confidence had flagged for a second. The onion seller was made of sterner stuff though. She walked forward, ahead of her thugs and looked at the Mouse.

"Little boy, I am sure you are playing out some dream of yours, but it's time to step aside. I will kill you."

The Mouse stood tall. "My lady, this fierce woman is beyond your ken. Go back to your tricks and I will forget this meeting. Take me on, and the *Remarker* will come down on you like flame and brimstone from a volcano. They will drag you from your hiding place, and no power on this earth with stop them."

The woman laughed, her gray hair a wild, unkempt mass framing her face. Gemmadine thought of the haggish old man that had once been the cave master of the cave her klan called home. She knew the Mouse was just a boy, and she loved the threats he made, because it gave her an excuse for a cruel proof to the universe that she was a power.

The next few seconds were confusing. The Mouse was like his namesake, fast. A brute grabbed for him and ended up with flying backward with a mere slap to land in a heap.

A second bully swung a club at the Mouse, missed, and went flying as well. Several of the men became tangled with each other, but then the inevitable, one of the brutes hit him with the edge of a mace. Then the Mouse fell below the clubs of the collective onslaught. When they backed away, he was still, apparently dead.

Gemmadine recoiled in her mind, her body being unable to react. The man who had helped her find freedom on the ship, helped her find a home on the waves, was dead in a minute, murdered in the rain in a mere second. She watched as the thugs, two of whom were seriously injured, threw the Mouse's body over one of the mules. The onion woman walked up to Gemmadine and bent down, putting her hoary hands on each of her cheeks. "I am sorry you had to see that, honey, I am here to protect you now from that sort." Gemmadine spat at her, but the woman calmly rubbed it off. "Druegari are we? You think an eye for flesh like me is fooled? Worth some spit in my eye to tame you, and much silver in my pocket."

Two of the thugs lifted her up and set her on the mule, and they all began to slowly navigate the horrible sheeting rain. It was a strange tableaux, the thugs flexing and muttering about their victory as if they had achieved something substantial, but their injuries were not minimal and their morale was shaken. The Mouse was a darkness with no light, she did not realize that even when he was hidden from her, she could at least tell he was present, feel he was part of the crew, that old Druegari dark sense active, even away from the caves. Now his lack was a screaming vortex that made her mind recoil in horror. Her empathy sense even penetrated the onion woman's armor; the woman was not as confident as she was trying to seem. She was worried about something, and her aura was more that of a peasant guiltily stealing food from a noble's overladen table than a woman demonstrating she had the right to eat at the table in the first place. Gemmadine thought, *You are underestimating me.*

The increasing rain harried the travelers and it was hours into the darkness of the night before they arrived at a small commune with a half-dozen wood and plaster buildings ranging in size from little huts to large barns. Gemmadine's neck muscles had begun to unfreeze and she could turn her head. More thugs, all women rushed from one of the larger wooden buildings and started to tend wounded bullies. Two thugs untied the Mouse's body and threw it onto a compost pile, then set to looting it in its ignoble final resting place. From the house issued several girls, pale white like most Navarese, dressed in wafting linen dresses that quickly became soaked in the rain. A bigger matron followed, and together they took Gemmadine into the building, into a kitchen where they took the wax cloth ponchos and wool traveling clothes that the Mouse had given her off and dressed her in a red taffeta chemise, overlay, and skirt. By the time they had finished she was aware and able to move, but she avoided moving on her own, letting them dress her like a child's doll.

Once dressed, the matron led her into a smokey room filled with dried herbs hanging from the low rafters, rough clay pots in wood-hewn shelves, and littered with tables that each had small wood boxes, bins, and magazines strewn across them. There seemed to be no organization to the endless array of storage containers and naked plant materials, as if the owner had a memory that could account for the location of each item in the mass of others. The place was a sty, and it smelled like a city cloaca, but it had a fire and she could hope to dry by it.

Sitting at a bench lit by the twin light of an alcohol flame and a banked fire was the onion woman. She was chopping at some purple mallow with a mezzaluna knife, humming softly to herself while she worked. Her hands worked with blinding speed, showing her experience with preparing herbs, while her face showed satisfaction. She was proud of this room, proud of her herbs, and confident in her skills and power. She was no longer dressed as a common vendor of vegetables, but instead had put on her own taffeta and linen dress, her hair having been put up by someone. When she finished working with her herbs she turned and looked at Gemmadine as she was let in. "How are you, my little dear?"

Gemmadine had heard juvenile pidgin before and had simply never understood it. Druegari raised children in a sensible manner; a child was given by their mother to a highly respected tutor who would supervise them until they could run the caves in safety. Only when the child was ready for adulthood would a matron from the clan start to pay attention to their offspring. Gemmadine knew her mother vaguely, her clan matron fairly well, and her old work boss very well. That was how it should be, and none of them would think of talking to her in some juvenile pidgin.

The onion woman was using the demeaning language at her with the mistaken idea she was somehow being a mother to Gemmadine. Her empathy was keyed high, and she could tell that there was no real concern for her well-being in the woman. Of course in her experience, people of the Halo were completely variable about how they treated children; one could sell her children into sexual slavery or drown them on a passing whim, while the next would suffer horrible tortures for a tiny chance that her offspring would live. In this case Gemmadine had one sure piece of information, this onion woman was not at all concerned for her well-being. She was working to improve some merchandise.

Gemmadine stood still as the woman looked her over. "Sit down girl," the woman said. Gemmadine continued to stand, looking at the woman, but keeping her face blank. The woman then picked a small piece of apple wood off her bench and turned it in her hand. She lit the branch in the fire, then approached her and placed the flaming fragment of wood in her face. "I said, sit down."

She could feel it, fear, like a spell, a hole in the universe between the eyes of the gods and the reality of now, the idea that was designed to compel her to take an action or suffer maiming. Time slowed as she tasted the fear, broke it apart for flavor, and tried to understand it. The woman had created a fear that functioned on two levels. It would reduce the resistance of her calf and leg muscles, making harder to remain standing as her inner mind forced her to act to avoid the danger of the flame, and it would plant a suggestion in her brain that would sneak under her consciousness and have her acting before her personality could form a defense. This level of analytical thought about fear, even as it was cast at her, was not new to Gemmadine. She was no amateur in the world of fear, where the dark was complete and the weight of a mountain stood above you, ready to close out the tiny space you called yours and crush you in an instant. The fear that the damp would kill you or the fire drought would destroy you and rip the air from your lungs. The fear that the air would sour and leave you gasping your life away in the dark tunnels of the world.

She had forgotten her training against fear when she had run from it. The flame was not new fear, but the old fear, and with it she could taste the training she had from birth to slow down and analyze what you feared, and plan to defeat it. She realized that she had given in to the spell of fear, and allowed it to drive her, until she had found a place where fear could not affect her because she was not alone. Then fear had no real power over her. And it was in this moment that she freed herself from the bonds of indecision and decided to simply sit down on her own, flaming branch or no branch. The old woman was dead, she just did not realize it yet, and Gemmadine would carry the body of Mouse back to the ship.

The onion woman, not realizing that her spell had not just failed, but had the opposite effect, smiled in an odd sort of triumph. "Dear, you must learn to obey during your stay here. Your willing help is important to me, but to some extent I do not need it. A simple beating at the hands of my servants will secure the assistance of a child such as you."

Gemmadine looked blank, but inside she smiled. Is a beating greater than a tonne of rocks on your head? She had stood before months of the most brutal of tortures and survived in the caves of her youth. A beating by a couple of thugs was not even something to consider. On the other hand, her plan called for a reaction. True emotion was impossible for her to muster at this second, she was still too raw from the Mouse's death and her change of fortunes to provide a convincing act, so instead she offered a dead and monotone reply that had the benefit of being true, "I would prefer not being beaten."

"Of course, child," she said like an indulgent mother. "Now you have some questions to answer. How far did you go in your metal training before you were cast out? Are you mastered with any of the metals or alloys, or just a laborer?"

Gemmadine pretended she did not detect a question, so she just blinked. She remembered the lessons from her work master, and his blank face as he watched her smash him down with her hammer after he announced her brother had died. The woman wanted a metal worker to sell into slavery to some pirate ship as a blacksmith. Is that all this was?

And she had an inner smile at the thought that the onion woman was staring at her in confusion, knowing that she was thinking deep thoughts but being unable to break into them. She could render gold from rocks using quicksilver, knew the secrets of slake lime, potash, and organum to clarify sulfur. A smart killer would want those secrets, but the onion woman seemed to think of her only as a product to sell into slavery.

The second of quiet was broken by a young woman in white who came in and laid the Mouse's stained clothing and a small leather sack, perhaps carrying the rest of her dead friend's effects, on the bench. The onion woman picked up the clothing, turned it in her hand, and then tossed it down in contempt.

"The second point to consider. How do I bend you? Do I torture? Torture someone in front of you? Alas that this child is dead, or else he feet would already be in the fire. You do not react to that? You do not fear a brand of fire, you do not fear the harm of others. So you see, honey, you are quite an odd duck. Do you not think so?"

Her languages had returned, and she felt the mastery of her space with the fading of the drugged onion. Gemmadine simply nodded once during the onion woman's talk.

"Oh, odd duck because you obviously have some metal in your soul, but not enough to be so smug at the horrors I can visit on you. You were defended by a child who thought he could beat ten men. What did he think would happen? He could have run away, but he didn't and died like an idiot. Or is he really a powerful warrior whose skills are so vast that he thought he could prevail? Mama Onion, as my children call me, is not so gullible. What do you have to say?" She rambled to a stop, nervous at the lack of reply.

Gemmadine looked at the woman with still eyes, just stared into her face. She concealed her age behind makeup, but she was old, and feared that she was rapidly falling away to the end of existence. She wore makeup that was popular among men and women in their thirties to maintain their appeal, kohl on her eyes, sveblendeh on her cheeks, lemon suds to tighten her face. Her vanity would have been endearing had the rest of her soul not been rotten.

Two thugs entered the room carrying a tray of steaming tea and two glasses. After them came a wisp of a girl, much smaller than Gemmadine herself, who was large for her people. She carried a thick blanket of worsted and wore the collar of a slave, despite there being no legal slavery in Neversay. Mama Onion sat down and accepted her blanket first, then waited as the girl set out the tea service.

It was here that Gemmadine realized she had the whole picture. Mama Onion was not the beloved maternal figure for her servants. Both the thugs and the serving girl feared her with an intensity that almost blinded Gemmadine's empathy sense. The onion seller ruled her people with fear. She watched as the thugs stood with a tense wariness, as if mistakes were paid in blood. The girl was a vacant wall, but her vacancy hid an elemental terror and a massive fatalism that Gemmadine knew very well. It was what the constant fear left when the mind gave in to it.

"I want a blanket also," Gemmadine asked.

The woman said, "Grodn, a blanket." One of the thugs left and returned with another worsted blanket, this one threadbare and disreputable. He placed it on Gemmadine and stepped back. The onion woman then said, "Tea, Margol."

The girl poured two cups of tea. Gemmadine reached for hers. It was a traditional cheap tea of Neversay, corned, black, bitter, and tannic, that left the mouth dry and the sinus abused. She put the tea cup down and let the jolt of chemicals from the drink rise through her system. Some tea was more potent that herbalist drugs, and this tea was just so. She could feel her fingers jitter from effects of a stimulant in the cheap leaf and feel the tannins race to her head.

Mouse, who liked soft tea and small things, would have hated the drink.

She picked the cup back up, drank the rest, and set it back down. This allowed her to start to worry her blanket as if she was nervous. Certainly the jitters from the tea were real. Unlike her dress whose silk was fine and impossible to pull threads on, the worsted was an open weave. While she listened to the onion woman, her finger broke a thread and started to carefully pull it apart. Then the blanket threaded and separated into a strip and the main piece. Cheaply made, it was part of her plan.

"You, dear, will stay with me until we find out a way to make a profit from you. When your true master comes, perhaps we will give you to him or her, and collect a tidy sum. You see, I do not really care why you are so singular, I just recognize the benefits to me are different from what I first thought. I am far more reasonable than you can believe, I just want to profit from you." The onion woman smiled and chuckled, setting her own cup down.

The blanket ripped, and Gemmadine acted. The first move was to rip off the strip of cloth from the main blanket. The main blanket in her hand knocked over the two lamps on the deck, leaving the room lit by fluttering torch light. The old woman stood and backed away, giving Gemmadine access to the tea pot. She swung it around and crashed it into the fire, and the room was thrown into darkness.

The old woman screamed, as did the servant and the guards. They lived in a world of light and feared the loss of their main senses. Gemmadine knew where the thugs were standing and threw the blanket square at one, catching his face and causing him to scream out and draw a blade. She could hear the ring of the metal as it came out, then the ring of another blade. She ducked and scurried like a crab around the desk.

The onion woman was yelling, "Get her, and light a lamp!" Gemmadine used her shoulder to trace the line of her chair, twisted the ripped strip of blanket around her hands, crossed them, and then garroted the woman.

"Call them off old woman," she said in her ear. "I leave, you live, that is the best deal you get."

She tightened the blanket. The fact was, she could not have really ended the woman with the poor garrote. She had never tried to do that when she had learned to fight and was sure the fabric would give too much. She did not want to kill the woman despite her desire for vengeance. If the captain called for her destruction, she would be dead, but she remembered the counsel of her cadre. A live person can be made dead, while a dead person cannot be made live.

The old woman screamed, "She is behind me!"

The two thugs went around each side of the desk, but one tripped and fell to the ground. Gemmadine had heard a stealthy smack of a small leg hitting the man's muscled calves. He had been tripped by the little girl who had served tea.

The old woman shrieked and tried to throw Gemmadine off, but as she struggled it tightened the garrote. In the darkness she could feel the flash of a sword, and knew one of the thugs had tried to stab in the darkness, missing both his master and Gemmadine.

She released the old woman and kicked her aside in her chair. That would keep her from getting stabbed in the darkness, and gave Gemmadine freedom of action. She had seen a poker for the fire, a short wooden pole with a small copper end to it. She rolled over, feeling her way by the heat of the extinguished blaze, and put her hands on the poker's handle.

In Druegari fencing, they had what was called 'position one' that was usually a relaxed stance that communicated no aggression. Since the fight was already on, and darkness filled the room, Gemmadine choose instead to perform a blade turn, which in combat was designed to clear the hit zone and ready the blade for an enemy charge that would allow a slash at the opponent's eyes. She went into the collapsed stance and put the front of the poker high so that it would indeed catch the thug if he charged.

The thug charged. Gemmadine used a two-step prance to move in and slashed at where she thought the thug's eyes were. "Follow through!" her instructors used to yell so she positioned her weapon as he came around to defend against a counter-blow. There was a scream and she knew the thug had stabbed himself or otherwise fumbled in the darkness.

She bumped into a glass lamp and threw it, splashing the desk and the old women, then kicked out at the smoldering fire, sending sparks flying. The lamp caught up with a small flame. She ran for the door, went through it, then dumped a chifforobe in front to block it.

She ran right into a servant boy, strapping and muscular in a jute-sack tunic. She threatened the boy with the poker and said, "where is the man I came with, the dead one."

The boy was pale as if he lived a sunless existence, even more pale than a Druegari fresh from the caves. "In the garden, between the stable and the main house."

Gemmadine nodded. People began to beat on the door behind her. She had no idea how long it would take for them to get out, and she did not want to find out. "Lead me to him."

The boy nodded and led Gemmadine through a dim room with a table and chairs in it, and into what seemed like a mud room, then out into the rainy night. The body of Mouse was laying akimbo in the garden. "Get that body and put it on a mule," she said.

The Mouse looked so small in the big servant's arms. The boy, perhaps sensing her feelings, was almost gentle with the body, draping it across the mule and doing a proper job of securing hands and feet so they would not disjoint in the ride. The rain was turning into a massive downpour, so Gemmadine made sure she threw a wool blanket from the house around herself. The Mouse was in his cottons with all of their pockets, and had blue ship's pants, torn and disreputable. Screams came from the house, so she gathered the reigns of the mules and led them into the lee of the tempest.

It was nightmarish as thunder cracked and lighting roared. The road was ankle deep in water, but the mules had a stable stride. A horn blew behind her and she wished the storm was not so fierce because that would have brought the town guard. She got to the main road and heard a groan behind her through the storm. It was Mouse.

Gemmadine almost tumbled off her mule. She climbed down, ran to the lead animal, and stripped the bindings that held Mouse on the creature. He slid off, and recovered himself. Mouse was a mass of bruises, but did not look like he had broken any bones. "How are you alive?" Gemmadine screamed.

"Magick," he said. "The die saved me. I had my finger on the black when they started beating me. I used the dice to throw two of them, and then to protect me from them!" he said.

"They are coming up on us now. I wish you had your 'die' still." She was not sure she believed the die was 'magick' but she had fuzzy memories of it because of the poison she suffered from. In fact, she was still not sure she was ok. The world was rushing by her and her sense of self was distorted.

Mouse said, "I have it. They did not find it when they searched me."

"How?" She asked.

"Magick," Mouse responded. Then he said, "stand me up and help me stay standing."

She did. In the distance she could see a fire burning out of control in the houses they had just quit, so bright the cloudy sky was visible. A dozen figures were quitting the structures and heading for them.

Though the Mouse's pockets seemed empty, he pulled out the die and rolled it in his hands. "It is not really easy to use," he said.

"We should run," Gemmadine said.

Mouse nodded. He did not move though. "They are not chasing us. They are running away. What did you do?"

Mouse was right. The figures from the burning house were running into the storm. Gemmadine took Mouse and put him back on the mule.

Later, they looked out over the port, their night for watch. Mouse was on the mend and volunteered for the high watch in the rigging, looking down into the water to make sure no one had a go at climbing their hull. They both had firelocks with them, though they had to have the permission of an officer to fire on anyone. After an hour she took her turn to rest her eyes, leaving Mouse to scan the water. She took a flask and poured herself some tea. Mouse could not have any while he was watching the water below.

"Do you still have the die?" She asked.

He patted his jacket.

"Did you tell the captain?" She could not see the die in his pocket, but he claimed it was impossible to see sometimes, for other people than himself.

"The way I figure it, Gemmadine, someone would not have given this up easy. So that someone is looking for it." He turned to the port side and looked carefully into the water below.

"So, our secret?" Gemmadine said. "I think you should throw that thing overboard."

"Why?" Mouse scanned the water, but the question came out furtive, as if he felt he was being cheated.

Gemmadine drank some of her tea. "Is that really someone's property? Where I grew up, that would be a thing of the gods. I lived in a cave for most of my life to hide from the gods' path."

"You ran away from there," The Mouse stated.

"I did." It was hard for Gemmadine to dismiss everything about her childhood. Her brother's thoughtless death, and the women who killed him had driven her into a world of bright sun and torrential rains. She went from living most of her life in darkness, a still place of silence where any motion underfoot meant death, to being on a ship that never quit moving, where stillness was to be feared, not motion. Yet inside, there was still the idea that she was being watched by the gods, judged from their citadels in the sky.

Mouse continued his scan of the water below. "Do you still fear all that?"

She thought about that question. In the darkness fighting the onion woman and her henchman, she had remembered part of her that she thought had been thrown away. She had grown up knowing safety was found in the dark, in small places. In a way, she was like Mouse. He and she could sit in one of the empty tea lockers off duty, no candle to light the space, a flash of tea and a chest of crackers, and be comfortable for an entire watch. She had followed Mouse through the spaces that were not designed to be passageways, but that the limber young man could wriggle through, and although she was much larger than him, he would always find a way to lead her through as well.

Yet she did fear. She watched him looking into the water and understood her fear was something that was built into her. The Mouse was just like her, afraid and unable to show it in the hopes no one used it against them. "I do fear," she finally said.

The Mouse nodded, not taking his eyes from the water. "People would make the Fiddler a caged freak, they used to spit on her and throw rocks. Yet she does not even know how fear works. Did you know she used to sing to them while they spit on her?"

"No, I did not," she replied.

"Betina Fleet cannot go to sleep in harsh weather unless Fiddler sings to her. Yet she is fearless in the lines and sails. When the God's hand hit us off Stathold she saved Rawda by free climbing to him with a rope in her teeth. But she could not reach another, you do not know him, Yousef al-Kastner. So she cries at night and the Fiddler sings Yousef's favorite song. You are one of the bravest people on this ship, braver than me. If you fear something, then there is something to fear." The Mouse took out an object that proved to be the die. "I will throw it away if that is what you want."

She looked at the object in his hand. "No, keep it, but let us also not tell anyone about it. Only use it when we are on shore, away from everyone else."

Later, Mouse sat alone in a void space of the forecastle, curled up a little but with his legs extended and locked into the first forward frame. In his hands, he turned the magick ball he had purchased with Gemmadine. The ship was on a clean tolan, so the forecastle was calm, quiet, and shipping no spray.

Mouse had started calling the die a 'ball' because it really had little to do with dice other than having twelve sides. The sides blended into each other, meaning it did not roll well. It would not have made a good gambling die since you would be forever chasing it across the deck. It also lacked any numbers. Instead, it was enameled white except for four sides that had been colored in soft pastel colors: one green, one blue, one red, and one black.

Rubbing one of the colored sides did nothing. But if you rubbed one and thought about something with enough intensity you could make things happen. He had found out right away that green causes a push; blue causes a pull; red is a shield that repels or blocks; and black was something else, something that disturbed Mouse.

After a week playing with the magick ball, Mouse was hiding out with Gemmadine in the forward lazaretto when he decided to mention their adventure and the magick again.

"I learned a lot more about the die," he said, meaning the magick ball.

She looked at him and laughed. "What die?"

"The one we bought in the store. You know, magick," he said

She shook her head. "Are you feeling okay, Mouse, what die did we buy, what magick are you talking about?"

And Mouse did not know what to think about that. He had encountered people who would purposely forget things. Tell you that you paid seven when you paid eleven. Forget the favor done for favor requested. Not shipmates though, and never one as close as Gemmadine was. She remembered their adventure, but the magical die was lost somehow. He thought of taking the ball from his pocket and explaining where it came from and how she was part of its story, then he hesitated and finally decided against it. He was minded to throw the thing in the ocean, but he did not.

Chapter VII

The Captain's Log

The crew have been rewarded for ten days of hard work in warp with a wheel of cheese. It may not seem like much, but for crew who work in a ceaseless cycle of shifts, day-after-day, little rewards create a party atmosphere that helps relieve the tension and toil. And for *Remarker*, food is the reward that is always appreciated. An Emporian might call for palm rum, or a Denuvani beer, but with so many northerners on *Remarker* the taste of the crew is for foods that may not be granted them on a day-to-day basis, but are special, unusual, or exotic. Even if it is not to their normal tastes, the crew seem to embrace the different tastes of the Halo as a means of showing their life is not wasted keeping their ship pointed abaft the wind and sailing to its targets.

This day the cheese wheel was not that exotic, at least not to me. It was a large hoop of Dartian fine, salty and sharp to the tongue, eaten directly from the knife rather than melted into some concoction of the steward's mass of mad recipes.

The wheel was thirty-three kilos to the gram, painted thickly in green bee-made wax, and it made an impressive sound when it hit the skids outside of the galley house.

Fairness is part of being a crew, and on a merchant, no officer deigns to take their share before the least in the lower decks has theirs in hand. Thus the wheel was first divided into nine parts, one for each shift, and the ninth for the cadre who do not follow the clockwise toil through night and day. Stripped of wax, each shift had a chunk of the golden cheese 3500 grams in size, each chunk placed into the hands of the shift's most trustworthy soul.

You see, that 3500 gram chunk of cheese had to go fifteen to eighteen ways, that being the size of each 8/watch. And it had to be protected from all harm until that watch gained the time to assemble for a common meal.

I watch as each 8/crew take their three-and-a-half-ki-logram chunk of cheese. Then all day there is a parade of cheese returning to the forecastle where crews prefer to lurk on their off shifts and make meals. They brew their tea on paraffins on deck, passing out the drink, while their meal is prepared by the crew chosen to carry out the ritual. Ground water-beans with lemon and crushed blueweed meets day-old wheat bread, a small pottage of garlic-beet soup, and for some who eat meat, a few stickers of salted meat added to the side for taste. Then comes the prize, the carefully hoarded cheese.

One of the sailors takes a navigation board out and lashes it to the aft mast and they count their number. They all do this despite knowing the number does not change. It is ritual after all. When they agree they are nineteen, then it is a case of a public math contest. 3500 grams of cheese, eaten by nineteen men and women. But wait, what about the *juz' albatal*? That is right. They will set twenty portions and give one of them, chosen by lot, two portions. Besides, the math is easier. It is always a discussion, but each of the eight watches will make the same choice. It is ritual really, or so I think, an excuse to discuss something that does not matter in terms of life or death.

Thus the ninth part of a wheel of cheese must endure a surgical operation to divide it twenty times, which is carefully figured to 175 grams for each person, and 350 grams for one of the twenty. But how do they get twenty pieces?

That discussion becomes serious when one crew member points out that the normal sharing process of 'half-and-half-again' just won't work. As if this discussion has not happened ten times before, the shift boss will explain to the younger crew that you can have two pieces, four pieces, eight pieces, 16 pieces, and so on, but not 20 pieces.

But the dilemma is not deep. You cut the wedge into two equal pieces. Then into four equal pieces. Then each of the four becomes five smaller pieces, making for twenty servings.

But wait, what if one piece is 170 grams and another is 180. Through no fault of the crew, fairness could be broken by bad luck. But trust the eldest sailors to know a trick. All twenty pieces of cheese are placed in a bucket. The first piece goes to the winner of *juz' albatal,* as does the last piece. In between, the eldest sailor uses a linen to draw each successive piece of cheese. Swaddled thus, the cheese can be told large piece for small, and the youngest sailor will declare for whom each piece goes. Sailors love chance and gambling, and thus do they play a game of chance with cheese.

Once distributed to each member of the watch gang, then it is a moment when the cheese is discussed. Of course someone has had Dartian sharp before, and another will have never had it. One crew will say that Dartian is not so fine as upland Crewel, which will trigger a debate on the qualities of the cheeses from the far corners of the Halo. Tea will be doled out and this will begin a discussion of the merits of the tea to be had with other teas and how they complement the Dartian cheese.

Half of their meal time will have eclipsed before one of the crew will ever get to bite a bit of their cheese. Depending who you are, 170 grams of cheese will either be a satisfying meal or a minor appetizer, but the crew are not eating the cheese as if it is a meal to sustain themselves on. The cheese is, in fact, an aid to memory and a prideful second of self-reflection. As they eat their cheese they reflect that some poor bastard on a military sloop or a cheapside longshore hauler have nothing but gruel and oil for their meals. They will remember lost mothers handing them their first chunk of cheese, a food in the north which is associated with health for children and thus often fed to even the least well-off kiddling in the poorest fisher village on the lee of Cycus. Who, many years and many kilometers from their parents, perhaps never to see them again this side of life, does not want to remember them at least a little?

And thus, after all of the discussion, negotiation, comparison, contrast, opinions, and equations, the cheese is eaten with an intensity and satisfaction that a gourmand in the finest restaurants in the great cities of the core cannot achieve. I envy my crew but do not begrudge them their pleasure. I enjoy it, in fact, even if my own mood cannot feel pleasure.

Chapter VIII

Alkadiha

They called her "Alkadiha."

Once, she had been so much more. She had lived in places these people who she served and slaved for could never conceive. She had held a name with meaning, a title that caused people around her to speak with respect, and a lofty rank. All that had been taken from her. It had been replaced with horror, pain, blood, and abuse. And afterward, when the last drops of her soul were squeezed out, when her nightmares happened even when she sat awake in her cell, when her spirit and body had surrendered and her name had been ripped from her lips, it had ended.

The currents of the stars and the winds of fate had washed her onto the shore of a small island-nation called Neversay, into the employ, if slaves could be called employees, of a man named Oskar; her dwimmer, the tools that made her a god, taken from her and sold for nothing in a market filled with fools.

The first year had been hard after the men speaking a strange tongue had captured her on the beach where she had first come to rest on this strange land. She had little understanding of what was happening at first, being ignorant of the local tongues, but it rapidly became apparent that she was not free to leave, and was in fact an object to be traded. The men who found her were fisherman, and they handed her to a woman called Zamüg, who was some sort of mayor or war leader. She was an object of curiosity because of her hair and her muscular body, but soon they quit staring, and she was set to work pounding grain into flour.

It was hard work, and she resisted. Each time she refused to pick up the rock she was supposed work with, she was beaten. Worse abuses came as Zamüg gave her to traders who came to the village to exchange goods. She did not know why this was done at first, but soon it became apparent. Zamüg wanted to sell her and was looking for a big price.

One day they sat her down with a heavily bearded, though young man and placed a cup of the flavored liquid they favored in front of her. It was hot, vile, and bitter, she spit it out immediately to the yells of the man she was being offered to, and was immediately beaten so badly, she could not move for a week.

Finally, she was chained, placed in a boat, and after five days of terrible motions and sickness, dropped off at a dock where a few silvers were exchanged for her. The man who bought her spoke with the seller, then said to her a single word she understood. "'Iitbae, 'iitbae." It meant "follow, follow." Then he pushed her a little, as if to get her attention, and said, "*baghi.*"

She later learned it was his language's word for "*alkadiha.*" It would soon replace her name in her own mind.

Oskar used the same rough teaching to tell her his name, that they were in the capital city and trade port of Nvolk, and that he was a successful owner of a popular pub and restaurant called the *Dockside*.

And suddenly her life settled down into a mind-numbing routine with few benefits, and no real beauty, except she was no longer tortured and tormented through endless hours of chained misery. She had a job, of sorts. She had a room that was hers, in that she was the only person who slept in it. It backed onto the main structure's stoves, which meant that it was warm, and it was connected to an accommodation, which allowed her to relieve herself without the eyes of the world watching her. Her space was tiny, but it afforded her all she could demand of comfort in a cruel land.

The language of the land came to her slowly without dwimmer, complicated by the fact many tongues were being spoken in the port city. Many people of the port could speak three or even four languages, and understand many more variants, creoles, and what they called "lingers," simplified trade speech used by the merchants to conduct business but good for little else. Within the first year, though, she could speak the language of the island, Navarese, and the language of the sea traders and the men who captured her, called Eurabaa, and could even follow other tongues such as Amharian.

Her day began as it always did. The sun woke her from her light sleep as it peaked over the low hills, timed by where she positioned her pallet compared to the room's tiny, east-ward-facing window. With the mother sun striking her face, she would allow herself a handful of minutes to hear the sounds of the town as it also woke up from a fitful slumber. She would estimate the number of barges on the quays by how many soft, distant yells of "*yastamiru fi altaqadumi!*

yahduth dhalika!" She heard from the men who wrangled the ox teams. Sometimes she would hear the clothmakers downstream, at work early, start their chants of *"yaghsil, yatadahraj, yanqalib, khabth"* sounding, if you did not know the Navarese tongue, like priests chanting to the new day, but once you had mastered the language the words would lose their magick and become a droning cadence that meant, "wash, fold, twist, slap," an endless tonal staccato that defined the entire life of some person she would never meet.

When the sounds had started to engulf her brain like a mélange, no longer separate entities, but becoming a symphony of musical notes pushing at each other for entrance into her mind's eye, the Alkadiha would rise from her palette, roll up the length of jute that was her ground cloth and the rush-stuffed sisal sack that represented her mattress, and then carefully fold her best piece of bed linen, a well-carded blanket of worsted cloth bought by her master, Oskar, to protect his back during sex. The blanket made her uncomfortable to look at in the light of day, its blue tamany thread and the light traces of ravens taking flight from a hillside an extravagance that she found tacky considering its utility. Some piece of her knew that the woman who existed before the Alkadiha was born would have considered it not a lush piece of finery, but a suitable piece of cloth to make a bed for a tolerated household pet. Exposed to daylight, it accused as much as in the dark it comforted, so she would wrap it up quickly and place it out of sight behind the stack of empty crates that towered over her at night. Her bed set to order, she would tidy up her chamber with a towel and a small amount of water from her drinking bowl, then put on her bathing robe for her ritual wash.

It was the custom of men in the Mastery of Neversay to bathe communally before the sun hit zenith, a time chosen because of the effort needed to bring huge tanks of river water collected at night to a boil. The water had to be collected at night or early morning, because by mid-day the river was a disgusting mess due to the dye mongers and chemists whose discharges into the stream made it foul and stinking. It was part of the city rhythm that the Alkadiha lived with and she had learned in her five years of slavery. Getting water that was not stinking and foul happened before the sun was a quarter high.

Slaves did not bathe, unless it was required of their work to protect the sensibilities of their masters. Then they made do with rain water and rags. The Alkadiha had enough freedom though that she could bathe in the river before it fouled. The ideal place was a small brook that came into the main river below Oskar's inn as it ran faster and did not collect garbage or messy offal until late in the day. She would walk down to a bight that was particularly fast flowing, almost like the streams of her homeland, and there used harsh lye soap and a fragrant weed she collected to clean herself and her clothing. She was nearly the only slave that bathed here, but many commoners of the lower classes could be found taking a few minutes in the morning to enjoy some clean water, fill up water jugs, or prepare for work.

Once clean, the Alkadiha dressed in her simple tunic and stockings, and then slipped through the back alley to the brewer's. The brewery was conveniently close to the inn and the morning was the most efficient time to collect the next day's beer. Oskar did not understand that the price of beer and the quality of the product that was available changed all day based on how much beer was in storage versus how much beer was being sold. The beer of Neversay, the Alkadiha had discovered when she first purchased a barrel, was flavored with a gruyt of Rosemary and yarrow that took a day to set properly, but after three days would be bitter, and after five days, bitter and difficult to drink. Each day, early in the morning, a few selective buyers would arrive when the Brewer first unrolled its doors and select their stocks from the previous day's production, paying a premium for the product. This assured the freshest, longest-lasting beer and was the secret of the most successful taprooms.

The Alkadiha had no instructions to find good beer. She was instructed to find cheap beer, and she had become skilled at this one narrow rubric of commerce. Stacked in the brewer's hold was beer that was one-day old and not properly seasoned, two days old and as perfect as the bitter swill that the Navarese loved would ever be, three days old and just ready to turn, and finally, four days old and starting to become bitter. Any older and you could cook with the stuff, but not serve it outside of bottom street.

Free buyers were permitted to taste a batch sample, a small amount of beer drawn from the barrel bung and dropped into whatever container they brought to sample with, but this was not permitted of slaves. Neither was smelling the beer, which at its worst could be detected by nose alone. Instead she had in her first month of captivity discovered that the brewers decanted beer into barrels and numbered them for calendar days and barrel decanted. The later in the day the barrel was filled, the later the process of turning bitter would start. So the Alkadiha now simply purchased the barrel with the highest number made three days before and usually received a good price and beer that was not too bitter.

Once she had selected the ideal barrel, the Alkadiha would have to roll it into the back room of the inn for the night's trade. Oskar could not afford a tap, so he served it by dunking mugs into the barrel and handing them out to customers. To make this work, the barrel had to be set up behind the bar and the end removed, then the old barrel had to be returned to the brewery for refilling. The old barrel, by this morning ready for tilting into dreg jars, was light and easy to handle. She would clean the dreg jars and fill them from the old barrel, drinking the excess herself, she was always hungry and could not turn away any chance to get food into her system, and then roll the old barrel back to the brewery.

As soon as the beer was sorted, it was time to repair the damage from the last night's trade. The Alkadiha knew that the upper class beer houses washed their crockery each night in heated water with lye soap, then would soak the cleaned dishes overnight to remove any soap that might taint the beer. Oskar was incredulous at the expense and time put into this task. His own beer crock was never washed, merely refilled each day of every year into the distant reaches of time.

Oskar had compromised with her on washing. She agreed to use no expensive lye that might add its peculiar taste to the beer with long soaking, while he agreed to at least allow her to river wash the crockery each morning. The river was close to the tavern, and she had a gurney-cart that Oscar had purchased years before to handle the beer, not understanding the cart could never handle a full horse keg. Instead the Alkadiha would use the cart to carry all of the tavern's crockery to the river at once, also taking the chance to fill water barrels.

Many customers, aware of Oskar's exacting standards for cleanliness brought their own mugs, but the ones in their own pantry were at least somewhat clean. It was the best she could do, which was the limit of her pride.

Once the mugs were done, the bowls for the nightly stew had to be cleaned as well. These she scrubbed with lye soap despite Oskar's howls and then set out to dry in the sun. If the bowls created an argument, the stew pot was a point of serious contention between her and Oskar. Oskar felt that stew from one night was the base that made the next night's stew. The alkadiha put her foot down when this was shown her. She insisted that Oskar sell more stew, allow her to make less stew, or find another use for the remains of the stew from the day before. In the end, she had only won the argument by arranging to keep pigs for the butcher. The previous day's stew, beer too old to sell, and other foods on the way out were fed to these pigs, and the butcher would pay Oskar for the weight gained by the animals between arrival and butchering. This had no financial advantage to the Alkadiha, but did allow her to make new stew each day which meant happier customers and less chance of illness.

Illness was always an issue. Many Navarese of the high orders believed that their bodies existed in a perfect stasis between growth and destruction. Ill-health was a sign of evil intentions breaking down the balance of this system. If a lot of customers became sick eating at the same place, a judge could rule that the effect was the intentional fouling of the people's balance by using the wrong spices, adding evil humors, unknown and sinister spells, or even more complex forms of poison. When such a case was discovered, the owner of the food stall or eatery would be brought in to answer for the evil magick. Owners generally had two choices at this point, take the blame themselves, or blame the slaves they had employed under them. Very few owners seemed to ever blame themselves, even though it was their shoddy attention to cleanliness that had been the root and logical cause.

A slave had to only be forced to watch one mass impale-ment to desire it never to happen to them. Most slaves had to attend impalements, standing silently in a closed mass, eyes forward but never really looking at the screaming people dying at the hands of the port guard. For masters, it was a random day out that a few of the same faces never missed. They would sit under umbrellas of wood and cloth, eating sweat meats and drinking great cups of the disgusting drink they called tea.

Once the cleaning had been done, it was time for lunch. The Alkadiha ate as much as she could, which was always too little, a fact that disturbed her but that she was beyond really doing anything about. Her usual meal was a bowl of boiled oats and some burdock and salsify that she gathered on her day off, along with as much beer as she could stomach from the dregs jars. Oskar always tried to push bacon or fat-back hash on her, thinking it was a kindness, but the fact she could not eat meat was lost on him no matter how she tried to explain it. When he finally got disturbed enough to finally just put it on her plate, she would have to wait for him to turn so she could conceal it under a burdock leaf and dispose of it on the trot lines later in the day.

By now, Oskar was up and ready to go to the baths. He was a large man who might have been handsome if not for his petulance and unhealthy pallor. He had light-brown, almost sandy hair, a roughly cut beard, jowls, and deep circles under his baggy eyes. Despite daily baths, Oskar always smelled somehow off, like soured milk, and in awareness of this used clove oil rubs to try and meet the needs of civil society. Being a property owner, he was nominally of the intendant class, but he was so low in that order that he had few friends. The commoners who run businesses from rented spaces shunned the climber who belonged in their own ranks, while the business-oriented intendants and government-oriented knights saw him as a spot on their own orders, a sign of how low one could fall and still remain legally one of them.

In some deep recess of the Alkadiha's heart, this mattered to her. Oskar had no family. He had served in the legions in his youth and returned to discover his heritage was a single building in port town of North Walk, and that six years of fighting on the northern frontier had left him without any skills which would permit him to make a living except as the lowest type of publican. If there was a woman who he loved in his youth, a beloved family member, even a close friend from the legions, the Alkadiha had never heard their names mentioned. Oskar, who demanded respect, got little, and who yearned for love, received none, except for the sham relationship he had created with his only slave.

Oskar and the Alkadiha had a dance they danced. He was her owner and could do anything to her he pleased, but he wanted, and demanded she love him of her own "free will," whatever that was. So he would come up to her as she worked and look at her for a few minutes. He wanted her to greet him with an expression of joy at his appearance, but she had little heart for the game. So she would look up at him and smile, if only a little, hoping that this tax on her spirit would be acceptable. Usually it was not, and Oskar would get upset and walk over to his till for his morning money muttering about her unfaithfulness, her selfish heart, and her blindness to all he had done for her.

If she still did not respond, the mutterings would get louder, and every day it was a race between her growing exasperation with his pointed hints, banging of furniture, and disappointed looks, and his willingness to make his point before he left for the day. She often ended up giving in and running to kiss him on the cheek at some point, but occasionally her mental strength proved stronger.

The problem with Oskar was that by his lights, she owed him everything. He had bought her, not the brothel owner Gimby, not the deep mines where death came swiftly. The Alkadiha had, to his own mind, an easy life, a private room, food, and no daily beatings. If she had been purchased by Gimby she would have had to supply sexual favors to twenty or more clients a day. Her red hair and exotic "foreign" race would have assured her endless attention at Gimby's and put paid on whatever sense of self she had left. Oskar assured her she was lucky, and she had recently started to agree, which in itself was a new defeat in her battle to retain the little self she had left. Agreeing it could be worse was not the same as defiance against the way it was, but she had spent that energy long ago, and lived in a bubble of subject non-compliance, the best she could now manage.

Oskar also argued that his failure to beat her was a sign of his love. Like all slaves, the Alkadiha had a collar of metal with her number embossed on it. Only certified blacksmiths could place and remove these collars. Oskar never had hers put onto her, instead opting to keep it in a drawer. It was true, he never beat her nor had the collar put on. She imagined there was a drawer for beatings near her collar's hiding place where the unused violence was stored. She knew that other slave holders hired contracted tormentors to provide careful abuse of their slaves as part of their disciplinary routines. She also knew that Oskar would never spend money on such a thing.

The collar and the beatings became an issue if Oskar began to feel paranoid about her "feelings" for him. It was in the darkest of his moods, usually a response to her own sullen defiance, he would produce the collar as a prop in their relationship. When things reached this extreme, he would go as far as make her wear the collar around her neck, tied with a rope made from jute fiber. After a day of that, her work would suffer in small but notable ways, and she would give in just to be quit of the weight around her neck. Even at these extremes, though, the collar never stayed and the beating never happened.

In some ways poor Oskar seemed scared to death of her. It was both a victory and a sign of her defeat. Damn well, Oskar would have feared her before her fall. She had been as a God, and he would have trembled at her wave and the fall of her eye. Perhaps some part of that was what fed the constant desire Oskar had for her voluntary respect. Somewhere deep inside of him he knew there was an imbalance between them, like a planet and its moon.

It had taken the Alkadiha a few months to decide that the lack of violence might be more wounding to her soul than having to endure it. It was almost like there was a type of violence that needed no hands to be lifted, that required nothing more than the draining of self, the elimination of dignity, to exist. The Alkadiha had been tortured.

Zamüg, whom the fisherman Oskar had bought her from, had been a master at the arts of pain and humiliation. In time, she had steeled herself to the sadistic physical and psychological torture. Oskar, though, was a new kind of torture. He was like a slow drip of water hitting her forehead every second, every day, of her entire life. A torture that could be ignored for a given time, but which broke past the barriers in the end like a knife slicing a cable.

The Alkadiha had always wondered how Oskar had come up with the idea that they were in a "relationship." The law said that she was owned by the innkeeper, and he could put her to death or do anything else he wanted to her. The only protection a slave really had was their value. Who tortures a slave if it costs them money? Of course, she had seen a wealthy noble beat down an expensive horse, so it was well conceivable that in their illogical and turgid thinking, humans might destroy something valuable out of childish pique, but Oskar made his kind treatment of her a part of their constant dance, as if he had no idea they were bound by deadly ties of servitude.

And in the end, in a strange way, the Alkadiha did "love" Oskar the way one might love a fallen commander. He was not a bad man in his time and place, within his own narrow world set. He lacked ambition and was not a strong person, but he was kind, to a certain limited definition of the word, and in her part of the world kindness was scarce. So when he had pouted for five-minutes and dropped enough hints, she ran to him, hugged him, and reminded him she had work to do for tonight, which is why she did not immediately respond. For her it was just getting to be too much work to fight battles when the only winner was the tiny flame of her self-esteem.

Her duties fulfilled, she saw Oskar to the door and his busy day of talking to his peers at the baths, wandering the city forum, and showing his face around the community. She was happy he was gone because it was at least an hour past noon, and she had only four hours left to prepare for the evening crowd. She often thought of the Dwarrow and their love of the complex treadmill machines they used to power their clever machines, a people she would never again see. Her life had gone from the horrors of Zamüg to the mundane treadmill of life as a slave to an innkeeper. It was a treadmill, with so many steps measuring out a day, and each day measuring out eternity. When Oskar died, another would replace him and then another into the depths of time, until the lack of medical care and poor nutrition finally killed her.

The stew needed three hours to cook, so she raised up the fire and started the newly cleaned kettles boiling. Oskar was proud of his stew, although he had never cooked it nor knew what was in it. The Alkadiha herself could not eat it, so she had no idea if it was good or bad. To her eyes, the stew was an archetype rather than an individual thing. The ingredients constantly changed, but the concept of the stew remained stable. It was stuff boiled in water.

Leaving the stew pots with some water in them on the fire she went across the street to the food monger who had been stewing grains and vegetables all morning. The tavern had an account which Oskar placed money in each month. One-forty-fifth of that money was what paid for each day's stew. The alkadiha did not care what went into the stew, so no matter what instructions Oskar gave her, she simply bought the cheapest grain, the cheapest meat, the cheapest flour, and the cheapest vegetables, and that was that. There was never any money to do more. The monger would then line up the pannikans of stewed mash, and she would walk the steaming ingredients to the inn and drop them into the stew pots. Today there was leftover barley mash, boned squirrel, oxtail hearts, cress root, rye flour, some bacon that was about to turn (whatever that meant), tripe bits, and sunchokes. Three trips and the day's stew was ready to cook down into the brown burbling mess that each night received a new and exciting name. Tonight, she decided the stew was Oxtail Surprise. As in: Surprise! That oxtail is more likely a squirrel!

Once the stew had been fired, she put away the wet dishes onto the shelves and started washing down the table trenchers. Oskar did not understand why she washed out the trenchers both at the end of the night and before the next meal was set, but he had eventually stopped complaining.

She did not really care for any of the tavern's rough patrons, but she also did not want them to die from the flux or gut-bullet. The Diamond Room on the other end of Norstree Way had just the month before killed off an entire barge-load of sailors from gut-bullet, and the slaves who ran the tavern were who was blamed. The owner of the Diamond Room had new slaves now, the old ones were still impaled on poles in the main square, a macabre art installation of twisted beings silently yelling to the sky as they decomposed in the sun.

Three hours of work got the stew ready, the tavern cleaned (or as clean as it would ever be) and prepared the place for the evening trade. About when she was done, the first patrons started coming in followed shortly by Oskar. Oskar did not want her hands soiled by money, and was concerned about her straining herself with tasks such as counting or running the till, so he was scrupulous never to be absent when paying customers were present at the tavern. Oskar was wearing a new tunic and pantaloons, but they were, as usual, already stained and disreputable. His customers were sometimes dressed worse, sometimes better, but they all formed a faceless mass that the Alkadiha likened to moving potato sacks.

Watching Oskar run the till, the Alkadiha thought of the other duty that he insisted was his. He insisted on being the one who lit and changed the candles. Candles cost a mint—so he said—and he wanted to make sure each candle was burned to the smallest stub, providing light to each customer for as long as it could before being passed on to a customer of a lower status. The larger candles were always left on the tables he reserved for his "special guests." This was mostly people in town who he owed money to, or the rare slumming noble who caused problems in the bar by pushing around other patrons. Candles that were burned down past half went onto the common tables in the middle of the room. Once they had reached a flickering stub they provided light for the dark "beggars' tables" where people could, for a few obos, eat leftovers from the trenchers of the main and special tables, drink the unfinished beers of patrons who had suddenly realized that their thirst could not master the vile taste of the local brew, and would also be given by the Alkadiha whatever she had that could not be handled by the stew pots.

The Alkadiha knew that the brew was from the same brewery that the other taverns used, but she always gave it a special name like the stew. Remembering her duties she took out the chalk board and wrote in neat Navarese:

"Special! Celestian Ambrosia Beer! Fresh off the Boat! Only m2 per mug, p1 per pitcher."

The fact that neither Oskar nor most of the patrons could read her neat script did not matter, Oskar thought having prices on a sign gave his tavern distinction. It was as if it allowed his tired inn to compete with the Starlight or the Sea Spray in Nevers itself.

Generally, the customers merely came in and ordered beer, stew, or both. They paid Oskar their coppers, and he gave them a wooden counter, red for beer, green for stew, blue for both. Her job was to see the chits, deliver the right items to the table in the right quantity, and take the chit. Tips to her, and there were a few, were returned to the till.

The tea was the hard part. The Alkadiha did not understand this vile drink, and no matter how long and hard she boiled the tea leave seconds that Oskar would reluctantly boil, it always resulted in a drink the customers did not like. It was funny that they would drink the disgusting swill of a beer that Oskar preferred, but would actually knock over a cup of tea that was not to their liking. So the tea was delivered in a brass bottomed, wooden jug from a tea room down the street. It was their dregs, more or less, but apparently the tea they could not sell was better than she and Oskar could produce themselves.

As a game, she tracked her own tips through the night. The average evening brought her 70 mites, copper coins worth one-tenth of a penny. It did not sound like a lot until you realized that many free workers in North Walk lived on 25 mites a day. In a month, she cleared three denars, and in a year nearly 25 denars, an amazing sum in the pocket of an innkeeper who, as far as the Alkadiha could see, barely kept his business going in most years. And this was just her tips. The taproom was almost always full despite the swill it served.

The dance between her and Oskar would continue as the patrons were given stew, beer, and tea. Oskar made better money the more she flirted, and the less she wore. On the two days she could not serve because of illness the month before, the tavern was empty and quiet. Only a few patrons hazarded the food and the brew when it could be had better for the same price across town. So Oskar would glower at her and tell her she was in a "mood" if she were not saucy and flirty. On the other hand, if she became too flirty, or if Oskar perceived she actually liked a patron he would stop talking to her, and eventually inform her he forgave her for how she treated him and they would work things out as long as they stayed together. The fact that she was a slave and was bound by law to stay with him forever was never mentioned. So she tried her best to walk the tightrope. Flirt enough that the bar made money and Oskar would not need to sell her (which he claimed he would never do, but would also use as a bludgeon in any "argument" they ever had.) Do not flirt so much that Oskar would be hurt and become impossible to deal with.

The crowd was heavy, as usual. The room had 65 seats, and they would usually cycle these twice, which required a good eye to keep production going. The Alkadiha began to mechanically serve customers: showing just enough smile, providing glimpses of her breasts to patrons when she could sense Oskar was busy, touching hands just so, her mind blank and unused.

Somehow she thought of herself like a candle that burned brightly, but whose light was siphoned away to the hands of her tormentors. And being a thrall to Oskar was just the lock on those chains.

The reason was simple. Oskar's moods and his promise of better or worse treatment had no objective grounding in reality. Nothing she really did mattered in the end. She was a cog in the machine of the cruel society that was Neversay, and her current situation had changed not much from Zamüg, except the torture was boredom and drudgery rather than sharp pain and humiliation.

So, she served tables, made food, and played the game with Oskar. She was a seal with a ball in a novelty act. She was a soulless marionette that had perversely been handed her own strings, but her animus and soul belonged to another greater being. She was a dancer with no legs and no music to dance to. The tables came and went, and the Alkadiha within her simply served them and went on and on.

Then she served a customer that changed all of her calculations in a minute.

The man was a short, heavyset human wearing an oil-cloth greatcoat, cotton pants like those of a soldier, and a black flowing shirt made of corduroy. He looked like a commoner, maybe a drover, but he had placed an age-blackened yataghan and a brimmed hat in front of him on the table like he was the highest of nobility. The Alkadiha was struck at once by his aura, surprised she could see it without her lost wänd. It was sinister, almost dangerous, but not evil. *Here is a man,* she thought, *for whom evil is an edge to be danced rather than a device to be used.* The people in the bar, even the normally gregarious and violent soldiers, were eyeing the stranger and giving him wide berth with their body language. It made the entire room of people look like wind-blown grain, each person leaning slightly away from the man, as if even a centimeter of space could protect them from his wrath.

The look on the dark man's face was almost indescribable in its dissonance. If he was a wrathful force that scared her to her deepest stomach, his face radiated a wave of empathy that flew over her, leaving the lowest part of her stomach feeling in a way she had not known she was still capable of feeling. Again, he showed the edges of dwimmer, an impossibility, as his consideration of her was deeper than these humans could achieve in their greatest use of natural empathy. She always kept a neutral, blank look on her face except when she was baiting Oskar, but she saw his eyes dart across her face as if it were controlled by a spirit-engine.

And she felt his projections as well, which was the most disturbing aspect of her encounter with the man. His face was dark and sinister, but she sensed concern and caring from something within him that bypassed his body language. There was disgust in his affect that did not arise from his body language or face. There was also a powerful projection of dwimmer than caught in her throat. The Alkadiha tried to keep his eye, but had to turn away and look down. It was not possible in this place and this time for these feelings to be real.

"Poveljnik, kaj delaš tukaj??" he asked.

She was shocked to hear her native tongue spoken by a human, and the use of her proper rank was a slug into her stomach that almost reached into her spine. It took her a second to change her mind around and understand the sentence, spoken in equal form with a sharp, metallic accent. "Commander, what are you doing here?" he had asked.

"Nisem poveljnik, sem suženj in deklica," she said, "I am no Commander, I am a slave and an Alkadiha."

She sensed Oskar's attention fall on her. More customers needed food, strange tongues aroused suspicion, and this man, this stranger was a wild card in the deck of her sanity.

"Nemogoče!" he exclaimed, impossible. *"Kako je lahko mojster Dwimmera in obljubljeno nebo tukaj, tako izgubljen?"*

She switched back to Navarese. "Please, sir, I must serve you or move on to others."

"Yah!" Yelled an oaf at the next table. "Let the bitch come here and serve me, I know exactly what tip she wants."

The strange, hooded man was out of his seat immediately, grabbing from the table and drawing the darkened yataghan, plucking up his hat and placing it on his head, and overturning his table almost as an afterthought. The boatman who had baited him was getting to his feet as well, his friends fearfully grabbing at him to put him back in his seat. Oskar came from behind the counter with a wooden knocker in his hand then skidded to a stop. His club was an oft threatened, never used tool in his arsenal of bluff. A more cogent threat was three soldiers from the local garrison who grabbed their spears and stood up, although they did not move yet to defend the boatman.

The bar went silent as the dark man turned slowly, his greatcoat settling around him as it came free from the chair. He stared at the boatman, who flexed his muscles and spit, his friends still trying to drag him back into his chair. Then the stranger turned and looked at Oskar, who took a step back under his dark gaze. Finally he looked at each soldier, his sight settling on the shortest one the longest. With each move of his eyes it was like he was taking an inventory, asking himself which souls he could take back with him to the great darkness. He gave the room a final sweep with his eyes, making even the crackle of the fire grow silent, the only noise remaining coming from the boatman, whose curses, though, were becoming almost frightened. The dark man had some unnatural effect on the profane and loud patrons of the taproom.

Once he was the center of attention, the stranger then did an unusual thing. He slowly walked through the bar to the soldiers. As he passed by one table he bumped into two customers and they had to move their chairs for him. Then he bumped another table and a drink spilled, causing patrons to stand up and move away. Cleared of patrons, he carefully slid that table over a meter from where it originally sat. At a third table filled with farmers, he just stopped and looked at them and they abandoned their chairs and moved to the walls. The stranger moved this table as well to the astonishment of the patrons of the taproom.

When he arrived at the soldiers, he stared at them as if his antics were a normal part of an evening meal. Two of the soldiers backed up, but the third began to present his spear. The stranger looked down at the spear with an almost sad face and back up to the soldier, transfixing him with his eyes. With blinding speed he chopped the spear point off, sending the haft crashing down in the soldier's hands. The soldier looked astonished but had little time to react as the stranger stepped out of the way of the haft and planted his foot on it when it had reached the floor. The haft popped from the soldier's hands and into the stranger's off hand, who continued the spin of the haft around. When it was very nearly reversed he kicked it again, causing it to smash between the soldier's legs with a sickening crunch that even made the Alkadiha wince with pain.

The entire move by the dark man looked almost accidental. He moved only the smallest amount, and mostly helped nature and momentum on the way it already wanted to go. Despite this a soldier—one of the most dangerous in the town garrison, a trained killer who did not have to boast of his fighting power—was cut down flat, dangerous to harmless in a second.

Before the bar could react, the stranger threw a handful of metal discs at the other two soldiers. The Alkadiha thought it may have been a weapon, but it turned out to be dozens of copper mites. That made the bar respond; people scrambled to collect the monetary windfall as the cascade of coins scattered about the floor. The stranger slowly turned and walked out of the bar, making it obvious to the Alkadiha why he had bumped and moved the tables as he had walked to the soldiers. He had made himself a clear path of retreat he knew he would need, and now used his exit to walk slowly from the room. As he moved past the Alkadiha he looked directly at her and with his off hand, flicked the rim of his hat. That was when she recognized him, a face from her distant past. His name was the Darkfather, and she had met him before, he had been a criminal she had convicted and threw into the netherworld. He was here because she had declared him forlorn and broke him from the greatness to the fallen.

In the tavern that night, the chaos caused by the Darkfather soon abated. The injured soldier had been dragged off by his comrades, while Oskar was loudly telling a group of business sorts that it was a damn good thing the stranger had not tried any tricks on him because he was a master fighter with his club. Oddly enough, the Alkadiha's own role in the evening had been largely forgotten. The talk in the tavern had recast the conflict into one between a dark traveler and the local garrison, a common enough occurrence since the garrison was filled with bullies and travelers often had no friends to come to their defense. Many in the bar did remark about the lucky shot that laid out the solider with his own spear, but several opined that luck could never beat skill, and the stranger had seen the error of his ways and run before real trouble started.

Oddly enough, Oskar finished the night in a good mood. Her tips had been very good, possibly due to the sudden enrichment of the bar patrons by the Darkfather's copper. When the last patron left and she was nearly finished stacking chairs, Oskar came up to her and started to touch her shoulder.

The dance, of course, started this way. He wanted her fealty and love, but he did not want to ask for it. He liked to feel that he was fair to his only slave, that he was an enlightened man who would never force her to submit to his needs, but rather was a good man who was happy to fill her needs for love. By evening-time he was not fresh smelling, the rotten milk smell having been joined by a musky, almost ferret-like odor that was cloying, especially to the Alkadiha's sensitive nose. It was a smell that turned her stomach, but then again, she did not need to have a solid stomach for what Oskar wanted. Fealty to the man was simply another transaction in her life, a tax on her soul paid in installments against a bank account that was already empty.

Tonight though, the memories of other times that the Darkfather had brought on had thrown her into a furor of emotion and physical response. She wanted to be free desperately. She wanted to be charged by the dimmer of her birthright, that great power which made a sad body of living plasma into a god. The idea of being devotional to Oskar was just not what her soul wanted. He held no comfort for her; his love was like a feast of ashes, consumed because no other food was on the table, because it was forced on her as an alternative to starvation. She had felt the power she had once had in the failed and broken Darkfather.

What disturbed the Alkadiha was not that Oskar was her owner, although she was occasionally acutely aware that she should be very disturbed about this, but that Oskar took little liberties with her, made tiny demands that as an ordinary person in an ordinary time she would never accept. He danced instead of communicated. He demanded that she ask him. He was passive, but aggressive at the same time. And she took it.

The confused feeling of power and weakness and desire to rule her own self was an impossible tension in her. When she stepped away to wash down the next table she heard Oskar sigh an exaggerated sigh like he always did when the dance did not go as programmed. He stepped forward again and placed his hand again on her shoulder, only this time his other hand came up and gripped her wrist to keep her from moving away.

She turned to him, placed her cloth on the table, and stared. He looked at her and smiled. "Aren't you happy to have an owner who cares this much for you?" he asked.

It was the gambit. He wanted her to think of how much worse things could be for her, and how pleased she was that he was not an evil master. That he hoped would lead her to throw herself into his arms. Instead of advancing the dance, it made her retreat from it. "I am happy you are my owner."

He smiled. "Are you happy I defended you from that out-lander?" he asked.

"Yes, I am happy you defended me from that outlander," the Alkadiha replied mechanically.

He reached up and cupped her chin forcefully with his hand, holding her head so she was forced to look into his eyes. She knew he thought that controlling the movement of her head was endearing, but it was really frightening. It was another step in the dialog of control.

She pushed away his hands and stepped back. She did not want to risk hurting him, if only to ease the burdens of her own life, but she did not want to play the game tonight or ever again. He gave her a long look and then walked off, muttering under his breath about how little he was appreciated and how no one, even his slave, respected him. Those mutters were actually true, but it was something that the Alkadiha would never say.

When she pushed Oskar away, there was an emotional price to pay. The relationship with Oskar was a transaction that he paid for with what he considered kindness. When the deal fell through, he responded with self-pity and even anger. For the rest of the cleanup when he normally sat counting and recounting coins, Oskar instead wandered about the tavern opening and slamming doors that did not need to be opened (or slammed), putting chairs onto tables with a loud bang, or talking to himself about how little respect he had in the world. In this dance she was supposed to run, apologize, and insist on pleasing him. Instead she violated the script yet again and left for her room. An ordinary slave would have been whipped for such insolence, but an ordinary master would not have played the game of seeking fictional feelings the way Oskar did. Oskar treated her like he treated a chair or a table but wanted the furniture to respect and love the owner.

When she was alone in the dark she snuggled under her rude jute blanket. She had no candles, they were an extravagance that Oskar hinted could be won by better behavior, but which she had never been able to find out how much they would cost to obtain. After a few minutes Oskar opened her door and cleared his throat, but she pretended to be asleep. The final step of the dance was violated when he turned away and slammed the door in a welter of confusion and feelings of betrayal. She did not care, and knew that she was breaking something that could cost her dearly.

Alone in the dark she had no desire to sleep. Despite the normally cooling effect Oskar had on her self-image, the Darkfather had opened up her feelings to a past that had been hers. Sleep came hard and was troubled.

The next day she went back to the treadmill. Oskar slumbered and she knew she would have to appease him. She also knew she might never again be able to dance the dance, which meant eventual disaster, the final collapse of the equilibrium her life had fallen into. She was past, possibly forever, seeing change as a positive thing.

The Alkadiha went out to the river for her bath, and she was startled. Across the river, on a wooded hill less than 100 meters way, sat the Darkfather on one of the strange folding chairs that you could see in the market on feast days. The normally silent cluster of slaves bathing in the stream was now a soft murmur of hazarded comments. This man was not a normal trader or a vagabond. Somehow he was different. The masters had said despite his dress, he was a wealthy foreign magician.

Beside the Darkfather, two gray ponies ate grass, soft buckets of water sitting by their heads. The Darkfather was smoking a cigar and reading one of the plant fiber "books" that humans preferred and had a small fire going next to him, upon which a kettle and a grill had been placed. Behind him, an oiled cotton tent sat, its flaps open and revealing a simple bedroll.

She could feel his sight on her before he shifted his gaze from his book. It was a trick of the dwimmer-skilled to use parts of their vision to look in directions other than what seemed their main focus. People not skilled in dwimmer would say it was the vacant stare and could be off put by the effect that was no more than splitting attention in more than one direction.

The movement of his eyes seemed like an afterthought to a preternatural attention he fixated on her, but when they finally landed on her own gaze it was even more intense. The Alkadiha found herself almost swooning as he focused his power on her and had to look down, but as she washed, she found it impossible to keep her eyes averted. She looked back up under half-lidded eyes and saw him nod at her as if he were saying, "I understand what you are thinking." They continued to stare at each other for a minute until she went back to her bath.

Throughout the day as she worked, she would occasion-ally have reason to walk out to the river-walk and glance across the river. He was always there, tending his camp or reading, and would always detect her gaze and return it. It was soon obvious this was not a random occurrence. The Alkadiha could feel that the Darkfather was staying on the far bank as a way of being near but not endangering her. This was no accidental action.

The stew that night was river fish, freshwater conch past their prime, shallots, cabbage, and misrendered field butter thickened with bappir, and despite making a big batch, was gone before the last patron was served. The beer was off, having been made with robbers guyt rather than real herbs, yet even the dregs of the barrel sold for the price of real beer by customers talking eagerly about the frivolity of the night before.

The people in the tavern were buzzing about the dark stranger. Oskar, whose behavior the night before was less than noteworthy, tonight was the hero that had rushed the foreigner from his midst. "I will tell you, if he again came to this bar I would have at him with my club!" Oskar exclaimed.

"Not needed," one of the select diners said, "the Baron will have him off tomorrow before noon, according to what I heard."

Another diner, a merchant, retorted, "The Baron has no wish to see that one gone, he has chests of silver and spends it for favor. The tea buyers cannot help but bend at the waist when he comes by. No, it is the soldiers in the garrisons who want him for their friend's mutilation. I hear they fear his marbles will never drop down again, so hard were they hit!"

And that talk disturbed the Alkadiha. No slave called the Baron a kind man, not when your flesh was his grass to reap when he wanted, when his smallest desire could send you screaming into whatever afterlife presented itself. The Navarese believed that your spirit translated to death became what you were in life, only serving the gods, and that meant once a slave, for eternity a slave.

One of the soldiers, now banished to the cheaper seats said, "The Baron has no say on who we task and who we embrace. And that Darkfather is tasked. He will be 'ducking-dan' before the next day closes."

The dinner was again put away, and Oskar refused a second time when the Alkadiha returned to her small room. She looked out of her window on the moonlit houses of

North Walk, and saw Darkfather standing by his fire, only he had built it up and was standing naked before it. Around him efreti and wisps danced, and water djini seemed to confer in conference with the fae haluschi. If there was any doubt that he had found some way to maintain dwimmer despite his fall and that he could control the most nuanced aspects of the power, this was proof. A master with a greater wänd showed his or her skills in just such a dance of entities. It was not just a game of pyrotechnics, but a clear demonstration of mastery, each construct capable of serving their creator in unique ways should he send them forth.

More disturbing, he did this under a clear sky. The locals called the fire from the sky God 'Flash,' and feared its fire more than any other thing. Yet it was not a joke, it was real, and she had once been a hand of that fire. The Darkfather risked painful death in the heat of a thousand suns by doing these acts under a clear sky, yet there came no retribution.

It frightened her as well as delighted her because she saw how much he contrasted with the fae. They were invisible constructs who could only be seen through the center of one's spirit, and only if you knew what to look for. The Alkadiha could only see them because she knew how to look, and thus herself could understand them. Yet, here she could see that the Darkfather was not himself tuned into the fae, but the opposite. His soul smoldered black and red in the night, sucking in the firelight instead of reflecting it. He was indeed truly fallen. Yet he played with the tools of the greater powers as if he were born with a greater wänd in place of each of his long bones.

The Alkadiha was in bed late and up early. She went out to the bath before any other slave had appeared and saw that the Darkfather was up as well, but was not alone. Instead, a dozen street children, the expendable refuse of the town, destined to starve or freeze as the fates willed before attaining adulthood, were sitting around the fire with the black stranger. And across the water, the Alkadiha could smell Dagorian seed-cake bannock cooking on the fire. Indeed, the children were each clutching loaves of the bread. The Alkadiha occasionally made it to honor the lost people of the Dagor-Lad, the people destroyed in a great catastrophe uncontrolled dwimmer called the abomination apocalypse, in a land so far away it could not even be seen in the night sky. The smell of the bannock, made from purslane, cracked wheat, pigweed seeds, and rapum, was unique when cooked over hot ashes, but the recipe for the bread was lost except to the people who mourned lost Dagoria. No one of the Halo, indeed, of the entire world of Ocean, would know what the Darkfather obviously knew, that even the great powers made great mistakes as they controlled the vault of the heavens.

How strange, the Alkadiha thought, that she would smell a bread today that should never be smelled in these lands, being cooked for the poorest urchins of the city by the dark, brooding man whose achievement was being denied heaven. Oskar had tried to keep the dance going, and was making more and worse threats, but somehow she did not care. Her life was across the river. As she watched, she imagined being one of the disposable children, free to die in the streets, but who could also follow the Darkfather, to eat his bread and enjoy the freedom he offered. He remembered a great tragedy and used that tragedy to feed children born to suffer. It created a feeling of ennui in the Alkadiha she would never have felt before her own falling, to land in a place where the vault of heaven was only a fevered dream, forever lost.

The sun had risen as she sat in reverie, and the children had finished their bannock and left for whatever they did to live another day in an uncaring land. The Darkfather cleaned his camp as if he expected company, then sat down on his mechanical chair and started to play with a ball of yarn. It was an odd occupation for a man in these lands, and he seemed clumsy as he fought little tangles and then started to crochet a growing square of fabric from alternating lines of black and green homespun wool homespun. The point of the object he was making seemed lost in the Darkfather's fumbling ineptitude. At times, his object was squarish. Sometimes it would become more rectangular, but then a new color of yarn would start, and it became round or almost oval. The Alkadiha felt mesmerized by the ever changing pattern, as if it had some significance in the hands of the dark figure rather than just being the result of fumbling.

Other slaves began to show up to the river, but like the Alkadiha they did not start bathing. Instead, they watched as the Darkfather worked, trying to pull some significance from his tiny hand motions. The slaves talked quietly among themselves about the spectacle, now knowing that the man in the black cotton clothing was a rich and feared foreign trader who bought and sold the most valuable product that the lands of the Halo had to offer, tea.

A slave for the weaver said the Darkfather was not a skilled hand, he was using the needles wrong and making an imperfect pattern. One of the older women who charred for the rich exclaimed this oeas "magick," sure as the Baron ruled the town. It made the Alkadiha think of dwimmer and how primitives might mistake the great power as miraculous. Dwimmer or not, the Alkadiha just knew the Darkfather was purposeful, but seemingly unhurried in his work.

At one point the Darkfather stopped and added wood to the fire, then placed a kettle onto an iron tripod. "The dark stranger is summoning some great beast," a tanner's slave said. Another slave, coughing in the rising son of the morning, said that it was the fire that was magical, the kettle was just a kettle. The Darkfather then pulled the kettle off the fire and removed a large brass tea brewer from a leather bag. From another he loaded the brewer's rattan leaf carrier with leaves from a rich-looking enameled container. After stirring the concoction, he drank a great sip. He had been making nothing more magical than tea.

The growing crowd soon included commoners making morning water runs. They all grew silent though, when a group of men left the town along the River Gate and started up the hill that was the Darkfather's camp. It was Captain Corto and eight of his bully boys, the most evil of the garrisons poorly regarded constabulary. They rode in a loose formation, lances across their backs, dressed in ill-matching uniforms, brown chain armor, and dressed in fighting harnesses of leather. Four had firelocks and clinking belts of cartridges.

The Alkadiha knew these men intimately. They would come into Oskar's restaurant and order food, then fondle her in every way they could as Oskar grew angrier and angrier at her "unwillingness," to reject their advances. Each of the men thought of themselves as irresistible to women because women who resisted generally were beaten down along with their siblings, parents, and lovers. They each understood exactly who was weak enough to bully and lacked political power to gain revenge, and restricted their outrages to these people. They would open the door and tip their hat to a noble lady, but rape her commoner servant if they could get her alone. Each had touched the Alkadiha in every space of her body more than once, and had forced her to lay hands on their privy members when they had the desire.

She had seen them beat a carter to death in the road for blocking their progress. The youth crying and praying for mercy, and the men raining blows down on to him until his head cracked, then laughter and jokes while the carter's sister sat doe-eyed in the darkness of the street, waiting for a moment of safety to retrieve her loved-one's body. She knew that Grimsby, the powerful owner of the city brothel, would only rent expendable women and boys to these soldiers now, slaves for whom he expected no further service anyhow. Even the simpering evil in the city recognized these men as bad folks.

The deputation soon arrived at the top of the hill and dismounted. Corto and six others handed their horses to two men who stood as human pickets for the shaggy warhorses. The crowd of commoners and slaves looked at the swagger of the soldiers and compared it to the calm way that the Darkfather knitted his amorphous, comical creation of yarn.

The soldiers approached but began to slow as they watched the stranger work. Soon only Corto was advancing. He turned and yelled something, a growl whose meaning had to be inferred rather than understood logically. This caused the rest of the soldiers to walk forward a few more steps, and again stop.

It was obvious even across the river that Corto was growing furious. He clutched up his spear and started walking forward. This must finally have disturbed the Darkfather's work, as he dropped a stitch and looked up with a strange, welcoming smile.

Corto stopped, but his spear did not. It swung forward a little in his hand and caught the ground, causing the captain to lose its grip and stagger. Corto fell forward and might have fallen into the fire if the Darkfather had not reacted with lightning dexterity, catching the man inches before his face planted into the glowing, angry, red coals. Despite his miraculous save, Corto breathed in an immense lung-full of ashy smoke, and was left rolling around on the ground, doubled up coughing from the foul fumes.

Two of the lesser ranked soldiers found action at the sight of their leader rolling around coughing. One walked forward to succor his leader, while the second ran at the Darkfather. This man did not reach his quarry, instead tripping on Corto's dropped spear, tangling in his own spear, and falling into the Darkfather's chair. He came up screaming, waiving his arm around. A crochet needle had penetrated into it like a small a dart.

It was impossible to hear what the Darkfather was saying, but the stranger seemed saddened by the accidents and wanted to help. He offered a skin of water to the man tending Corto, then helped the man with the needle in his arm up and into the care of two of his colleagues. Some sort of conference had started about the needle. The men were trying to figure out how to remove it, but the Darkfather was holding his second needle, along with his weaving and seemed to be saying the needle was curved and would resist just pulling out of the wound. The men ignored him, one grasping their wounded colleague's waist, and the other the needle buried in his arm, and they each pulled.

Instead of pulling the needle out though, they ended up dragging the man in circles as pain and the depth of the wound resisted the needle simply tearing free. The ground by now was littered with lances, and the trio tripped on one, coming down into a pile. More screams indicated a soldier had broken his arm in his fall.

Looking sorry that such ill luck should befall the peaceful guests to his camp, the Darkfather removed his oilcloth coat, walked to his tent, and got a small brown box, a white bandage, and a small shingle from within it. He went to Corto and helped him sit up, then took a vial from the box and had him drink it. Corto immediately stopped coughing and looked relieved. Next he went to the man with the needle in his arm. This one was given a blue vial, which quickly made him sag. The Darkfather placed a small bladed jack knife into the fire, and when it was glowing cherry he pulled it out and made two small cuts to the man's arm. The man smiled and nodded, like cutting him with a superheated blade was actually a fun activity. The needle came out, and the Darkfather used a bone sewing needle to close the wound. The final man, with his arm dangling oddly, was provided another blue vial, and when it had taken effect the arm was set, bandaged to the flat board, and stabilized against the man's chest. The soldiers turned and left without further words.

On the bank one of the commoners said, "What the crossroads was that?"

There was a low murmur. Half the slaves felt that the soldiers were at fault for being clumsy. Half the commoners thought that the reputation of this dark stranger for being powerful was just a tale; he had not even fought once. As the group started their day, the Alkadiha thought she could see the Darkfather smile.

After bathing, the Alkadiha went back to her chores in wonderment. She had just watched a single man defeat a force of soldiers sent to evict him with nothing more than a smile? It was impossible on this world. It happened though. It had to be dwimmer.

After she bathed, the Alkadiha tarried on the shore staring at the Darkfather. He was whistling a nursery tune loud enough that the Alkadiha could hear it. She remembered the words, embedded little nuggets of culture she could no longer claim, a heritage that she had lost when she had been shriven of her entire being. As the Darkfather whistled, the Alkadiha slowly sang the lyrics in her mother tongue:

Ne bom se vrnil k mamici, ona ne ve, kje sem bila,

Jaz bom pirat in plavam na morju.

Ne bom se vrnil k očetu, on ne ve, kdo sem,

Jaz bom pirat in jadro v morskih morjih!

She opened her eyes and the Darkfather was staring at her. She saw him dip his head, which caused her to notice one of the disposable children was standing by her side. In his dirty hands was a package wrapped in a tree leaf that the locals called calf-leather. This was held in place by jute twine.

She opened it and saw an amazing group of items. A wrap of fine wool yarn held two metal needles in place, quality weft and crochet needles. A wooden peg around 20 centimeters long sat beside the yarn along with three beeswax candles of the highest quality. A book with its title in her own tongue, a language that should be unknown in these lands, said: *Tkanja Svetovne.* The book was well used but in good shape. She read the title out loud, *"Tkanja Svetovne."* It meant, "Weaving the World." The author's name was missing as if it was some anonymous self-published missive. She opened the book and on the inside cover was written in a rough, almost uneducated, but readable scrawl, *"Realnost na svet je vse, lep Adjeness odloči vezavi."*

She looked up at the hill and met the eyes of the Darkfather. He was waiting for her to do something. She knew his vigil was only for her, and she knew what she had to do, but she was scared. She looked down and read the script again. *"Realnost na svet je vse, lep Adjeness odloči vezavi."* It meant, "The reality of the world is anything that the beautiful Adjeness chooses to weave."

Adjeness. It was her name, the word that meant her, given to her by her mother when she reached adulthood, standing in the great terrace looking off into the Vault. She had lost the name, surrendered it rather than sully its meaning or demean herself trying to live up to it. Yet here it was, restored.

Seeing her name for the first time in years was a shock. In Zamüg's village she had left the name Adjeness behind as they tried to make her a perfect slave, and with it she left her identity behind as well. Now something came flooding back into her. Her name was Adjeness. She remembered when she carried the name proudly. She had been known as Green-Shield Adjeness of the soldiers of the vault, a commander and dwimmer-cast. She was ranking officer of the naval forces of Aakulant, leader, diplomat, and inspector general of the fourth fleet. She was as good as the queen of the great oceans of the vault, and all who dared speak against her did so with lowered eye and quiet voice.

By naming her, the Darkfather unleashed a spell that did not gain power from the aether, but instead brought forth the energy that was in her own being. He named her, and in doing so returned something to her that had been lost like a misplaced ring. Her name was hers again. She would never be called the Alkadiha again.

That night she again refused Oskar the worship he demanded, which was getting dangerous as he was muttering that only his love for her keeping him from selling her down the mines, and after he barged out she sat in her room with her back to the door. She opened the book Darkfather had given her and started reading.

"The weave of the yarn," the book started, "is the equivalent to the weave of the universe, what we call the aether. If the universe is loose, you weave loosely. If the universe is tight, then make your weave tight. The dropped stitch can show you where, and it can change the nature of where as it is dropped."

She looked up from the book. A wänd was a manual way to manipulate dwimmer, to activate the orisons drawn in the white matter of the brain. You did not need a wänd. A wänd merely allowed for prestidigitation to turn the orison into an active evocation or cantripical. The wänd connected the fingers to the interface with the dwimmer and turned the flat and affectless orisons into evocation and invocations.

So what the book was saying was that weaving was a way to access dwimmer, a primitive way to seek the power that was anything but primitive. And while the roar of life made the dwimmer hard to reach compared to the silence of the vault, the lack of anyone else fighting for time and power in the cast meant that as Adjeness suspected, dwimmer could be deployed if one had the practice, and was able to fine down the techniques. The aether may be weak here, but it had so few users.

And that explained the nature of weaving. What mattered was not really what you wove, but how you wove it to access the aether. It explained what the Darkfather was weaving when the soldiers came up. He was changing reality, pushing deep into the unknown corners of his own orisons and opening an aetherial gate that he could reach for in a second?

And like a true master, he did not gate huge powerful dwimmers, but small ones that used an opponent's own actions and mind against them. Why throw an opponent to the sky when they could trip with so much more ease?

She read on. The stick was a nostepinnes, which could be used to focus concentration, and was also useful in turning raw yarn spins into balls of that could be easily handled. The weft needles allowed a weaver to pass lengths of yarn through a yarn warp, allowing for patterns to be created. They had crochet hooks at the back to allow hook crochet to be practiced.

She soon learned that other tools would be needed for complete mastery of wandless prestidigitation. She made herself separate hooks for crochet patterns from spoons, carving them in the middle of the night. She also made herself better needles, four were required of two sizes to do uneven and even knitting. Finally she made a cable needle, although her early skill left this one unused for a while. All of this she carried in a modified apron on her person to avoid attracting attention. Since Oskar often ransacked her room "for her own protection" it was essential she not leave anything in it. The books were hidden under a loose board, the needles and yarn on her person.

The book warned that weaving magick was unlike weaving mundane garments, yet it also warned that neither artisan nor practitioner should look down on the other's art, and that many artisans created magick through their weaves. And this set Adjeness on a new path that was as unbreakable as her new-found name. She would regain her mastery of dwimmer no matter what the cost.

Adjeness went to sleep, but woke soon after. A presence was in her chambers. It had to be Oskar, here again for a grunting, heaving, awful five minutes. She grasped her weaving in her hand and held it tightly. To herself she said, "Strengthen me." Was it Oskar, here to kill her? It could be no one else.

There was something wrong though. Adjeness did not smell musk stench, instead her breath smelled pine needles, soft leather soap, lye-burr, and a touch of chamomile. The sounds on the floorboard were not soft innkeeper's shoes, but hobnails. The hand that touched her was not the hand of a pig-fat publican, but something that crackled with strength.

Adjeness sat up. It was the Darkfather, entering where it was forbidden to enter. She looked out the window and saw that where the moon should be waning, it was now full blood red, hanging in the sky and casting crimson spindrels across the room. The Darkfather held his stained Yataghan in his hand, the curving blade blood red as if he had slaughtered hundreds to stand there. His oilcloth coat was washed in red as well, blazing in darkness, yelling to the sky. His face was lit in magefire, showing his hard face with its great scare and hollowed eyes.

Adjenees had her name back, had reclaimed dwimmer in her weavings, but she was still fearful. She was a slave. "I command you to get back," she yelled.

The Darkfather looked behind him, and she thought to herself she would die if he left. He turned back as if she had said that thought out loud and stepped forward. "Leave," She said, and his foot started back as in retreat but Adjeness felt her dwimmer drawing it forward, making it plant itself forward. The Darkfather was burning with internal light, radiating heat like roaring fireplace. Adjeness said, "I am not alone here," and realized she was not sure what she was saying or why. Darkfather was a criminal banished from the

Vault by her own hands, and he was also a person of her own world, the only one who she knew.

She awoke to a new dawn, her dream a fading memory.

The presence of the Darkfather was soon accepted in town. No more soldiers climbed the hill to challenge him, and he stopped staying on the hill all of the time. He was always there for the morning baths, when Adjeness and he would exchange looks that seemed to have meaning past the basic concept of "I see you." The taproom rumors, though, said for the rest of the day the Darkfather would behave like any other trader, selling and buying tea and other luxuries, taking dinners with town officials, and doing strange deeds with strange people, building the type of credit that the rich and powerful called favor points.

Some people thought he was a healer, because he would often treat slaves in the surrounding farms for ailments. Some people thought he was a Derid priest, as he would often help in small farm labor and then make suggestions on how the crops might be more efficiently raised. He was rumored to have the second sight, which allowed him to spot a sick animal for cloistering and to identify plants which had been infected with phasmids.

His rumors of riches were said to be false because he carried little silver. Three times it was said he was waylaid, and each time he handed his purse over, only to discover it contained a few mites and some dining chits. As long as no one asked him for his clothing or his weapon, he would gladly turn over his pouches, even as he helped heal one of his robbers. When a story came of someone demanding his weapon, he said no, and the gang members had stood staring at him before nodding and accepting that the weapon was not on the list of fungible items to be had.

For Adjeness, this was a new pattern of her life. Oskar had gone from angry, to furious, to sullen, to silent. It was like he knew his control had ended despite all of the force of law, custom, and tradition. Each night she would work in the taproom serving beer and stew, and when the room was clean she would go to her room and barricade the door with crates. In that protected place she would take out one of the expensive beeswax candles and ignite it with a dwimmer of fire making, one of the first evocation orisons she had learned. Then she would take out her little books, the library grew every couple of days with a new delivery from the Darkfather, and she would study for hours. Most nights, she would master a new orison and would proudly fall asleep pretending that she was sleeping in a Vault Liner, far from the dirty lands of the ironically named Ocean.

In twenty days, she could make the room go silent, bring forth a glowing orb of light, whip up small tornadoes of dust, and create dancing shadows simply by how she pulled worried threads on the weaving she had made. This, the book told her, was the simplest means of gating dwimmer. You took energy from the dwimmer gates, and sent it into the aether to create an orison of asking for power to be moved from one state to another.

Each morning she would get up and see the Darkfather on his hill. He would often look at her and smile. It was not a toothy welcoming smile, but an almost sad half-smile, like they were parting forever, or he had done her some wrong she had yet to discover, when in the back of her mind it was she who had harmed him all those years ago.

Then one day, he was missing. Adjeness had been planning to somehow tell the Darkfather how much she appreciated what he was doing. She had five books tucked into her apron and was starting to look vaguely lumpy due to all of the contraband she was concealing. Along with her yarn in her market basket and needles concealed in a wrap of jute, it would be obvious to Oskar she was hiding things from him, if only he had the will to look into her subterfuge. She was being brazen in her defiance, and still Oskar did nothing. So when she reached the river, the empty hill knocked the wind out of Adjeness.

Why did she assume he would remain here forever? She had no idea. There simply was no reason to believe that, yet she had. She wanted to cry, something she had not even done under the worst treatment by Zamüg. She felt out of breath as she started to bathe. Then she noticed all of the slaves bathing with her. What kept them here? Fear of a horrible death was what seemed obvious, and there was plenty of evidence that this was what would happen to anyone who left, even if they fled in great numbers. The Baron kept hundreds of impalement poles stacked by his barracks, and it was not a secret why.

She looked up at the sky. That was her home, a home she could not return to no matter how many tricks she learned of dwimmer. Adjeness was hardly spiritual. She recognized the power of the gods, and accepted their presence, but it was a stretch to call her a willing abettor of the sanctimony of seven, the official name of the most common way of personalizing the Virdean gods. She accepted that beyond the gods, there might be a God, but this she took only on faith rather than some litmus test of revelations. The dry season in the river valley of the Neverene was coming to an end, and she could see the clouds forming of a great storm, which would become the dominant weather through the months of Tempest and Sinda, before the languid heat of Menda would allow the crops to grow to maturity and their harvest in fall.

And in her heart she knew she had power, and no more patience for slavery. There was some deep kernel of truth that she played with like a golden ball, that she had been a warrior and a justicar of the great vault. She had advantages that the slaves around her could not fathom. She had dwimmer, was athletic even if it had not been tested in years, and she had *"vitalna življenjska sila,"* or the deep vital spirit that could only be ended in death.

With that thought, she felt a chain break that had been tied around her soul. She had always known it was there, tying her down, but she had not been able to describe it. Now that it was broken, she was able to mentally pick up the links and see it was artificial, an ineffable lie. She grew angry as she realized she, a commander of the great order, had been treated like an animal, chained with one of the simplest geases the people of this low land could conjure, the robbery of the soul.

Hanging from a cloth line by the brewers was a set of rough cotton breaches with reinforced jute knees. She grabbed the smallest pair and put them on. She then took a tunic from the line and put it over her morning clothes. The brewer came out and said, "What is up, Alkadiha."

She looked at the man. "Adjeness. You call me Adjeness."

"But stealing my things?" he asked.

She looked sternly at him. "Buying, how much on account."

He looked over his shoulder, knowing it was conspiracy to sell clothes to a slave. "I do not know, your master will be angry."

"If I am a slave, then Oskar pays you back. If I am not, then you can take the money from the account I have with you. It is not small," she replied.

The brewer made a move at her, and she backed up two steps and tripped him. He fell at her feet, allowing her a few seconds to get onto his back and bury his face into the mud of the lane. The man bucked and tried to escape, but soon went limp. She turned him over and scooped mud from his mouth. He was breathing shallowly. She took his jack knife and belt, cut down the clothing line, and trussed him up. Then she dragged him into the storage shed behind his shop. He came awake and struggled, but she put an end to that by waving the knife under his nose. "Keep your mouth shut about this, and I will send you a hundred denars. Speak of it, and I will come back for you." She closed her eyes and tried her best to connect to the dwimmer without the weavings. She could feel the man's soul and grabbed it as hard as she could and squeezed with all of the might her mind could present.

She was one hundred-fifty centimeters and maybe forty-five kilograms, but she was radiating hatred at humans in general, and Navarese slave holders in particular. She had shopped with the brewer, but he was not a friend. He never offered her succor, food, water, or a discount. He did not hit her or abuse her, but when that had been a standard of love for the Alkadiha, for Adjeness it was expected. She could destroy the man and think nothing of his last rattling breath.

He finally turned his face, and she felt his soul surrender all to her. He was in her power even if he had not been tied. Off of his back she went, and looked around the shed.

Hanging on the wall she found a canvas carryall pack on a wooden frame, child's leather boots, and fifty meters of fine hemp line. A meal barrel had crushed barley in it. She shoved handfuls into a set of organdy sacks she found. They were ill-suited to the purpose, but better than nothing. The boots fit well, her feet were small. She reached up to the top of a cupboard and found wooden water bottles stoppered in cork. Everything went into her pack.

She then slipped into the tavern and into her room. Oskar was standing inside looking at her bedroll. He turned and noticed she was armed, then backed up. "You have come to kill me?" He asked.

Adjeness laughed. He was standing there, 120 kilograms of hairy human muscle, facing a woman no bigger than most human girls, who was armed with a small jack knife. She moved to the side of her room, pulled up a loose board, and took the books on dwimmer up that were not already on her person. She then emptied candles, books, spare yard, and hand-made tools into the pack until it bulged, tying her jute bed roll into place last of all. She stood up with the knife in her hand and looked at Oskar.

"Don't kill me," he again pleaded.

Adjeness stopped, "Do you think you deserve mercy?"

"I treated you right. I cared for you." There was a hiccup in Oskars speech. A hitch that said he was almost, but not quite breaking down into fear and sadness.

Oskar fell to his knees and wept.

Adjeness held the knife in shuddering hands, holding muscles in check that wanted to lash out. She could punish this tiny, weak, ground-borne with so little effort, take from him not just his name but everything. It darkened her mind and made her sick and elated. After a few seconds sitting akimbo on the edge of two possibilities, she chose the third option and kicked out with all of her might, connecting with Oskar's head. He cracked down and slammed on the hard floor, knocking him out. He could die from such a blow. He could awake in minutes. Adjeness thought of ending his life but chose not to. She retreated from the room and closed the door.

Oskar's rooms were upstairs from the kitchen. It was like a badger's den, dim with streams of light coming from places where the boards of the walls had not been properly chinked. A brighter part of the wall turned out to be a window made from thick pile-glass. Any sort of glass was surprising, maybe the taproom had been popular once. A frowsy smell, not unlike a stoat or a fox, hit Adjeness in the face, and she could see dust mites dancing in the air like wild wisps during saturnalia. She moved into the room to a chest, stooped and opened it up. Inside was a bag of coins, a slave's collar, and papers in a creme folder. She opened the papers up and was shocked to see a bill of sale and quit deed. She has been purchased and freed five days ago and Oskar had not given her the papers that showed, at least legally, she was free.

There was silence for a minute as she stared at the papers. Every slave in this land dreamed of their manumission, few expected to be given the boon. Her bond-break tax was five years of income for Oskar, yet she noted that the bar had not paid it. A trader named Samedi had, the proper name for Darkfather. After a minute staring at the paper she hid them in her undershirt and ran before she could wake up, if this was a dream.

She left the taproom by the front door, something she had never done before, and walked along the road of brewers to the intersection with the gateway boulevard. At the fountain with the equestrian statue she adjusted her clothing and her packs to travel better, hiding her red hair under the hood of her oilcloth. She walked to the fountain where a smoldering brazier stood, the normal lighting source for the bigger streets, and helped herself to some charcoal from the ground that had been spilled round it. She applied the dark coloring to her face in light strokes, blurring her face down to a color more consistent with the locals. It would not make her look like a Navarese peasant, whose face was freckled with red, but it would slow up identification and maybe at a distance make her look as something other than herself. Her makeup finished she looked up into the eyes of the Darkfather. He had approached her in total silence on the street.

This was as close as she had been to him since they had first met. There was a strange feeling in the bottom of her stomach, like the feeling of butterflies dancing in a warm breeze. She almost gasped, then in controlling the reaction ended up holding her breath. He reached up to her cheek and gently touched her makeup, making her knees shudder. How was it she had just broken all of the chains that existed in her life, and yet this new chain threatened to embrace her?

The Darkfather reached into his long coat and brought forth a small pin. It was a filigree of delicate platinum. He opened her coat gently and placed the pin on her disreputable tunic. Even that simple action caused Adjeness's vision to fade a little in fear.

"Does that control me?" She asked, for the object was heavy in dwimmer.

The Darkfather shook his head. "It conceals you. Not very well, and not against people of power, but you look like a commoner of the Navarese now, albeit one with a dirty face. Other orisons that I have will keep you safe from scrying."

She rubbed at her makeup job with her hand to further bed it down. Water was falling from the sky. Or perhaps she was crying?

"Am I free?" She asked.

The dark stranger seemed to consider that for a second, then said, "You stand tightly bound to the earth, you are embraced and cherished by the aether whose power you are now learning. Time has you in its clutches, sending you down the corridors of fate to our common mortality that even the eldest races must expect and see on their distant horizon. If the question is are you free to walk north or south, to be alone or with company, then you are free."

She had never looked deeply into his cloaked face, even when she was sentencing him to the fate of the fallen, but now she stared into his eyes in wonder. His visage was a series of contradictions. He was younger than she had thought, maybe forty. It was hard for an Oldari to tell with a human whose species aged and died twenty-times in a single life. Her people, though, called him *starejši*, which was a respectful way of saying elder, and in the line of dignity stood *najstarejši*, or eldest, before his crimes had been exposed. Yet looking in his face she could see age in his eyes. He had seen centuries, had weathered the tides of the vault, and stood forth unbroken, if not unscarred. She reached her hand up to his cheek and he startled. Her hands touched him and he closed his eyes.

"Ali bo starešina to padlo vzel v svojo družbo in ji pomagal, da se vrne v vault?" She said in Oldari. It meant, 'Will the elder take the fallen to help her return to the vault?"

"Kakšna naloga je to?" He replied. "Which task do you refer to?"

She switched back to Navarese. "I do not know who cast me down to become a fallen. My self was chained. It would seem you are the prefect being to see each of these wrongs corrected."

The Darkfather sat down on the fountain. In the distance, lightning struck as the storm moved down the valley. "You cannot return to the vault any more than I can. Your life is here now." He waved down to the port and continued, "I have a captain, friends, a crew, and a house on the side of a mountain in a pleasant land where I am respected. I have dedicated myself to the 'queen' of that land, and have already fought by her side to give her a crown. Why should I fight for you to get what is impossible?"

An old vegetable monger approached them. He hair was gray and coiffed as if she was a young daughter of nobility, but she wore the coveralls of a truck farmer. "Few sales today because of the storm, will you buy bell fruit big as a fist, or snow pears fresh from the tree?" She pulled out a jute sack and said, "The last of the year's fiddle heads!"

The Darkfather looked at the woman and down to her cart. "My horses are under the gate. If you give us twenty bell fruit, I will pay you a penny."

"Big spender. Penny now?" She drawled.

"To the guards if the fruit is on my horse," he said

"You do not trust me?" the woman said.

"Not with a penny against unseen fruit," The Darkfather replied. "Trust me when I say the guards will pay."

She looked him in the eye and smiled, "I believe they will, and take my advice."

"If it is sound," Darkfather replied.

"Take the long road. In this weather the river road will become no more than mush. Your horses will thank me by dancing on their hinds," she said. "The port is filled with ships awaiting the tide to send them out like birds. Yours is said to with you, Darkfather. And do not bet that the guard are eager to let you go."

The Darkfather nodded and paid the old woman three pennies. She smiled and pocketed the coins, turning to leave for cover before the storm struck, neglecting to deliver the bell fruit to Darkfather's cart.

He turned back to Adjeness when the old woman had left. "You ask me to cross three bridges with you, and I agree to cross these bridges as your companion and friend despite history and reasons that may call for more introspection from myself. I worry though, that in trying for the third bridge you are endeavoring to cross a bridge too far. There is no way that you can return to the Vault. Physics cares not for dwimmer."

Adjeness gazed into the Darkfather. "Is there any reason that we should not aim for three but accept two if the third seems out of reach?"

"There could be, eventually. Think of what the third bridge cost you when you stood on it before."

Adjeness nodded. "In any case?"

"In any case, I am with you, and you with me. The way is by sea," he said as he stood up.

Chapter IX

Health Call

Setchi carried the opposite shift from her father on 4/ gang. By general agreement of the crew, unless you were bleeding out of your eyeballs and had a squid attached to your fundaments, you took your case to the clinic Setchi ran. That left her father, the surgeon, with the serious cases.

It also meant that Setchi ran the long list of ailments that sailors came down with to avoid work. Oddly enough, both her surgeon father and the first officer agreed that a certain amount of malingering was good for the crew but insisted that Setchi herself run the parade of misfits and made sure that an occasional day off was not abused, nor that there was not a real condition behind the aches and pains of daily life.

It did become a game with some crew to come in on their off time and try on new ailments.

Setchi surveyed the room and saw two candidates for real medicine. Ayza Gatayeva had a pretty bloody scalp wound and was being assisted by Eddy Sandals from her gang. Likewise, Masarra Ibn Ahmad had bruises on his cheekbones and a bite to his shoulder. He was assisted by Haatim al-Rahmani the fire tender.

It was all she needed to know. Ayza was bleeding, so she came first. She motioned to Sandals to help get her onto the examination table, turned the mirror to catch the light, and looked at her head. "How did this happen, Ayza?" She asked.

Ayza looked at Masarra and replied, "Tripped on a crab."

She looked at Sandals and asked, "Crabs on deck?"

Sandals nodded. "We are going to clean them up before the officers see them." He then looked at Haatim who nodded. "Trouble is, perhaps you can go low visibility with the wound?"

"Is that what you want Ayza?" Setchi asked. "More pain, and you'll need to come back three, four times to make sure the wound heals."

"If you can, Setchi," Ayza said.

"You get cuts that do not heal?" Setchi asked.

Ayza nodded no.

She went to the record drawer and pulled Ayla's records. If she was a bleeder or had wounds that did not heal, nothing was indicated in her file. Her father was a massive note taker. Setchi noted the planned treatment, and put the file back. She then went to the pharmacy closet and pulled out a soft candle, alcohol, iodide, and a bottle of cutane.

First she washed the wound in iodide, alcohol, then iodide again. She opened a sterile paper fragment, rolled it up, and placed it on the wound, then lit the candle and had Ayza lean back. She reached down and took up a needle and put in two wide stitches, then closed the wound carefully and applied the hot wax.

"You come back every day," Setchi said. "This is cutane, take it now. It will make you a bit sick." She looked over the wound again. "It should hold and not need a big bandage that would get an officer talking, but I won't lie for you. And I won't do this again if there is a crab infestation."

Ayza and Sandals nodded. Satisfied, Setchi said, "Next."

Masarra sat on the table and said without prompting, "Same crab."

Setchi looked at his eyes, then felt the bruises, causing Masarra to yelp with pain.

"Nothing I can do for the bruises. Yew will make it worse, no way you get poppy for that stuff." She turned to Haatim al-Rahmani. "You get another fire tender for the next three days. Get someone else to make crates until I give you a clear. Is that a problem?"

"No, Setchi," he said.

"The bite did not break the skin, but let me tell whoever accidentally bit you. I see them actually get one to bleed, I will pull their damn teeth. Bites are rough, you understand?" Setchi said, directing her lashings to Ayza. "Sandals, on your way out send the next one in."

Eddie Sandals nodded, "anyone in particular?"

Setchi said, "No, anyone is fine, you were the excitement of my day. Just open the doors so the waiting victims can see what the treatment of the day entails."

There were five more patients. Eddie Sandals on his way out tapped Balor of the top crew. Balor got up and limped to the table, then made an effort to get on. Setchi grabbed his file and said, "Ohh, six is the magick number."

Balor said, "Really?"

Setchi nodded. "You see, you have had this thing six times this cruise. That is an important number."

"It is not the same thing," Balor replied. "It is completely different."

"You hurt?" Setchi asked.

"Not all over like the last time, Setchi, it's in my lupines," he said solemnly.

"Lupines?" Setchi asked.

"I have been feeling poorly in those lupines, you know the jiggly bits," he said.

Setchi looked at the other three in the waiting room. Wearn was never sick, but seemed like he needed a break. Unless he had a serious issue, he would get a day off. Ranos and Jess deFine were sitting together and were likely looking for a little tryst. They also did not have a record of taking things too far. Balor was an issue though. "You three, in the waiting room, I need your help."

Curiously they got up. Setchi looked at Balor. "Have to explore the old back forty, if you know what I mean. That lupine is a serious issue. Here is what you do, take off your clothing and jump on the table."

People in the northern reaches were mostly without a nudity taboo. That said, Balor wilted a little as he removed his clothing. When he had finished, Setchi looked him in the eyes and said, "I have to look into the problem, so these crew people are going to hold your hands and legs."

She then turned and grabbed a wooden knocker that was used to hold open a door. Balor's eyes widened as she swung it around, before grabbing at his uniform and saying, "I will see if the wubblies get better."

"You do that," Setchi said.

A red-haired woman came into the infirmary space with Samedi Darkfather, the ship's quatermaine. Setchi immediately dropped everything and went to the woman's side. She was not crew and was wearing a jute cargo sack with arm holes cut into the top; the clothing affected by the entrapped classes of Nvolk. She turned to Balor and said,

"You, clear the deck, guard the door and I will give you a day notice on your wubbblies, promise."

"Sure, Setchi," Balor said looking at the wane and befitted girl. He waved his hands at the rest of the staring *Remarkers* and said, "We should get out." They reacted and did just that, like Balor was a commodore.

When the doorway closed, giving privacy to the surgery space, Setchi guided the woman to the surgical table and asked the girl, "how old are you?"

The girl turned and looked at Commander Darkfather, then turned back without answering. The Darkfather said, "Treat her as if she were eighteen."

Setchi frowned at the obvious lie, and got out a blank crew-book. She did not bother writing the age down, nor did she bother with a name. "Does the captain know we have a new crew person from Neversay?"

The Darkfather asked, "Is that the order you wish to handle this medical emergency, informing the captain of this woman's presence on *Remarker*?

Setchi shook her head and turned back to the girl. She would have been adorable, almost like a pixie, if she had not been abused so badly. She had a pixie face, short red hair the color of a campfire flame, cream-colored skin, and haunting jade-green eyes. She would have been 45 kilograms at fighting weight, but she had suffered from long malnutrition leaving her ten kilograms below that. "Take off your sackcloth," Setchi ordered.

She did not obey. "Does she speak Eurabaa?" She asked.

The Darkfather replied, "She does, though your accent and vocabulary may be difficult for her to understand. He turned to the girl and said, "*To je medicinka po imenu Setchi in želi, da se slečete, da vas lahko pregleda.*"

"*Povej ji, da lahko sleče svojo prekleto vrečo,*" the girl replied in the tongue-twisty language.

The Darkfather touched the girl's shoulder and said, "*Zaupaj tej ženski. Ona ni suženj.*"

"*Kot praviš,*" the girl replied, "*a kaj bo, ko ji povem, da sem star dvestosedemdeset let?*"

The Darkfather replied back in a gentle tone, "*Povedal ji boš, da imaš triindvajset let.*"

Setchi looked sternly at the quatermaine. "It is polite to translate."

"My sorrow at the lengthy translation. My dear Adjeness here is not aware of the cultures and mores of this ship and was seeking to assure herself of the proper manner to proceed," he said.

"*Hotel sem ji reči, naj se jebe Samedi*" the girl interrupted him.

The Darkfather turned back and replied to the girl, "*Ne vedo, da govorite zaradi dolge travme, ali želite, da imajo vašo celotno zgodbo Adjene?*"

The girl shook her head and removed the sackcloth. Setchi caught her breath at the extent of the girl's injuries. She had been thoroughly tortured in small ways. No single wound was terrible. Everyone on the ship was an accounting of how hard life was etched into flesh and worn to the end of their days, but the girl had small, parallel cuts on her stomach and back as if each were added by a time-keeper keeping time. The small scars on her face were repeated on her shoulders and arms, while her stomach and lower back held abrasions from whips. Setchi had seen the markings on the captain's back, everyone had, put there by whips when he was very young. Other crew had been through other such terrors. But this girl was carrying ten lifetimes of scars, all laid in over a period of a few years it seemed.

Setchi reached out and touched a cluster of circular scars on her torso near the shoulder. *"So iz cigare,"* the girl said.

"Sijar," The Darkfather corrected. *"Hum min siyjar."* 'They are from a cigar' in Eurabaa Setchi understood him trying to teach the girl.

"So *siyjar* is the word for cigar in your tongue?" Setchi asked. "'They are' is *'so'* in your tongue, and if I wanted to refer to one of the scars and say, 'it is?'"

The girl touched on of the burns and said, "It is, *'je'*"

And if I had a cigar and said, "it is a cigar?"

"To je cigara," the girl replied.

"My name is Setchi," the medic said, "Though I should pronounce it Sitshi because some of my crewmates have issues with the click in my name. My name is Ensign Setchi Durrell and I am from a land named Emporia. We speak Friza there, and I would say, *'Em dic Setchi.'* I am going to examine your wounds. In my home language I would say, *'vaig a examinar les teves ferides.'"* She put the small book on the table and an ink pen and asked, "How would I say that in your tongue?"

"Pregledal bom tvoje rane," The girl replied, then in Eurabaa, "I am Adjeness."

"Good, what is your age, Adjeness?" Setchi asked.

"Twenty-three years," Adjeness replied.

Setchi began to look over the wounds. Her first impression clearly held up. The girl... woman if the age she gave was accurate, was the subject of sustained and terrible abuse for at least a year, maybe two. She looked at the Darkfather, who was standing where he had stopped, never having moved. Setchi's own people had nudity taboos, but the Cycuns and many other peoples in the Halo did not. This obviously now applied to the people of Samedi and Adjeness.

She made a careful study of the girl, then asked the basic questions for the book. "How would you spell your name?" She asked.

The girl looked at the Darkfather who said, "☐ā'-jīm- sīn - ☐ā'– sīn." He paused. "In Frizian script it is 'A - dJ - e - nn - ss.'"

Setchi nodded. "Are you literate?"

The woman replied, *"Bolj pismen kot ti prasica."* Then she said, "I am, and I speak your tongue, though with weakness."

The Darkfather stepped in and said, "She is quite literate." Then turned the woman again and said, *"Nisi jezen nanjo prijatelj moj. Delali bomo na vaših težavah na način naših ljudi. Ranjeni ste v umu in telesu."*

Setchi put down the book. "Your tone is angry, and the Darkfather is not translating your words well. My people teach that medicine has four components, and three are inside of our power to aid. We call the four aspects of humanity as the body, the mind, the spirit, and the soul. The Gods cure the soul. We cure the body with medicine and sometimes surgery. We cure the spirit with compassion and discussion. We cure the mind with education. You have wounds of the body, but also wounds of the spirit. Today I will work with the body, but if you join the crew, you will have to come back and work with me on your spirit. I do warn you this. The crew will defend you and protect you if you let them, as long as you do not try to pass your pain onto one who is weaker than you. If you do, then you must flee this ship. We are many people on a tiny vessel of wood. We depend on Ocean, but Ocean is a tough mistress and can kill us with a wave of her hand. We pray and respect the Gods but we cannot know when they will hurl flame on us to break our apostical ways. And given all of these adversaries, we cannot afford to have one of our own turn on us far from the embrace of hearth and show. You must be part of us, or leave as all passengers leave, on the beach of the next shore. Do you understand?"

The woman named Adjeness nodded.

Setchi turned to a water tureen and poured a gourd full, then returned to her patient and handing it over. "You need to learn some basic things while you are here. The first is hydration. Do you know what happens when they wind blows on you?"

Adjeness blinked. "Your words are confusing."

"I understand, Adjeness. Even if you know the language well, the crew will confuse you because we all speak it a little differently. My native tongue is Frisa. *Ik praat Frysk.* The ship speaks trade for many things, but when we discuss complicated issues such as healing, we have to use Eurabanni. *Lisan 'sikas' hu 'yurbani.'* So it is natural that you will need time to gather this all. Do you comprehend me?"

The Darkfather translated, *"Vpraša, če razumeš?"*

Adjeness nodded. "My masters spoke Eurabanni, a dialect at least. But many spoke it in the common. So I comprehend your saying."

Setchi smiled and pointed to the water. "When the wind blows, it robs you of water. You have to learn to replace it, even if you feel cold or think the weather is wet. The signs that you are not getting enough water is cracking lips, and you will feel like grit or sand is in your eyes and cannot be gotten out. We do not use water excessively, except drinking, and then the captain has ordered that you drink all you need."

She then turned. "Quartermaine Darkfather, it is time for you to be on your way."

"Why," he asked.

"Because the exam must continue," Setchi said.

The Darkfather hesitated, then turned and left.

When he was gone Setchi took out from her woman's need chest a small cup. "Were you abused in captivity?"

Adjeness nodded. "I was a slave. All slaves are abused."

"You make water into this cup. Then give it to me," Setchi said.

Adjeness nodded and went to a corner to comply. When she returned and handed the cup over, Setchi placed a little piece of paper into the cup. After a few minutes she removed the paper with a small wooden tweezer, looked at it, then discarded the materials and placed the cup into a wash basin. "You have no child."

Adjeness nodded grimly. "I did not think it possible anyway."

Setchi looked at Adjeness, wane but defiant. She turned to her scap book and filled out a short form, then handed it to her. "These are your medical orders," she said. "You will return each five days for an appointment with me. I want you to remember your dreams and recount them to me. Before you sleep, I want you to read something spiritual—the Supercargo Suela Fleet has a small collection of materials, if you cannot read them, then have someone read them to you before you go to sleep."

Adjeness took the paper then asked, "Is this common for medical treatment in the Halo?"

Setchi considered it. "In the whole Halo? Why do you ask?"

"I was under the impression that the people of the Halo were primitive," she said.

Setchi turned to her book rack and pulled out a tome from her library. It had the Eurabanni title *Fanu Alshifa'*. "Primitive is a term that is a comparative. Most of my healing art books are in Frisa, but the north has its own traditions that are similar, if not identical. Primitive implies that someplace else there is better healing. Take this book, and if you find error in it, if you know of techniques that are not primitive, then please let me make corrections."

Adjeness took the book and opened it. She flipped pages back and forth, then said, "this is dangerous."

Setchi stepped into her space and put her hand on the woman's shoulder. "Knowledge is always dangerous, do you not think? It is far easier for people to believe a lie. Or worse, be told by a charlatan who performs in a stage show that only he can tell the people the truth, to not believe their eyes or ears. But the charlatan is exposed when plague comes to us, when people lay gasping, pleading for their lives, and his lies cannot turn the storm that is striking or heal those who are dying. Because he cannot change his routine or admit his failure. But if this book is wrong, it can be rewritten. Do not fear truth, Adjeness. You will be eating a lot of truth before you are healed according to the standards of this primitive practitioner of healing.

Setchi was too busy to consider the castaway-in-their-midst for a few days. As ship in warp may seem mundane, but there were endless tasks to complete, and each task has a statistical chance of injury. There was also what she called blue fever. Sometime crew grew stressed and sad, and then started to show a range of symptoms that were best cured by a day on deck in the sun with no work to do. It was a disease of the spirit, not of the body or mind.

But three days after her initial consultation, Adjeness returned with her healing book. "How are you?" Setchi asked.

"Your crewmates are being very kind to me," she replied.

"They are your crewmates as well, Adjeness. Are you dreaming?" Setchi asked.

Adjeness nodded.

"We will talk about that in a few days. You brought the book?" Setchi asked.

"The book is impressive, but it is wrong in places," Adjeness said. "I see it is wrong, but what can I do to correct it?"

Setchi replied, "Start here on the ship. Success will prove you know better than the book, and that will aid people, or it should. Do you think the crew on this ship only are here for riches? You can find so much good to heal with that is more important than coins in a chest. Though coins are not unwelcome."

CHAPTER X

God Tracker

There was a ringing in the middle of his skull. Zorion opened his mouth to crack his ears even though he knew it would do no good. It was not the sudden pressure change experience by coming from the depths of the ocean, but unexpected problems with his control of dwimmer. Treading water was not the place to troubleshoot problems, and the beach was close enough that he was being beaten down by waves.

He contemplated swimming, and was soon conducting an efficient breast stroke that kept his head out of water and facing toward land. He hit shore, stood up, and gained a sense for where he was. "Fat Boy," he spoke into the open.

"I am here," came the reply.

His companion was anything but fat. Fat Boy was just his name, but he was actually slender, with a reddish tinted face, blue-black hair, and a smooth-shaven face that had a mobile mouth and honest eyes. He was dressed in a ship's tunic, soft pants, and ship's sandals. He had an equipment belt, but none of its slots were filled.

"Can you find where my Cylinder is?" He asked, looking out at the blank waterscape. If Fat Boy goofed on this, he would not be able to get home.

"I have it located and have seven references, though I need only three," he replied in a voice that was slightly too squeaky.

"Fix your voice unless you want me to murder you," Zorion said.

Fat Boy made a few test hums up and down the scale, then replied, "Is this to your liking?"

Zorion thought it over. "Good enough. Can you pop my mission box?"

Out in the water a round, wooden ball surfaced in a roiling set of bubbles. A small black line tipped with a small metal clamp exploded from its top and flew onto the beach, close enough that Zorion was able to get it before the surf could drag the ball out to sea.

The line was weighted by the wooden sphere and an uncooperative surf. Zorion deployed a construct to increase the precision of his effort, but found even the dwimmer of the most minor form failed to really deploy. He played out a few meters of line to the trees, tied off the wooden ball, and looked at Fat Boy who was watching silently.

"Fat Boy, can you see into the aether and tell me what is happening with my construct?" Zorion asked.

"Master, the aether is filled with synesthetic noise across all main levels. The effect is a broad dulling of the power bands and a significant degradation of the dwimmer," Fat Boy replied laconically. The tone worried Zorion.

"Is this affecting you, Fat Boy?" He asked.

"The effect runs across any construct that functions using dwimmer. There is an unpredictability that permeates the aetheric matrix that will require time to analyze. It will certainly cause a degradation of even my functionality." Now there was almost sorrow in Fat Boy's voice.

Zorion tore some cloth from the right arm of his ground suit and fixed it to one of the tall, leafy trees that grew with wild abandon in this remote corner of the deserted island he had chosen to start from. He then wrapped the line around the tree and slowly pulled his wooden ball in to the shore, using the resistance of the wrap to keep his gains, then pulling the object a few more meters.

When he landed it, it could be rolled up to the tree line. It was a marvel of engineering and contained all he would need to survive in the islands for the few months needed to track down his quarry. The basic wooden ball was quite large up close, two meters across and seemingly made of smooth wood. If not opened correctly it would burn itself apart, saving the mysteries inside.

"Fat Boy, open the sphere," Zorion ordered.

Thankfully, whatever was happening to dwimmer did not force him to physically break open the wooden orb. It popped into pieces like a cracked shell glass and collapsed revealing sacks of homespun and crates of soft planked pine. He waited for a second, then looked with exasperation at Fat Boy.

"How does this kit come together?" He asked.

Fat Boy replied, "Stochastic noise is limiting transfer of counsel. I believe there are instructions though. I might suggest shelter as my weather sense indicates a gale from off shore will cross this island, and there is insufficient rain shadow to protect this portion of beach."

Zorion groaned and looked at the azure shadow of this crazy land.

Later that night, rain whipped down in painful sheets. Damn right, Zorion thought, that falling was the worst punishment the enlightened could suffer. He looked at Fat Boy sitting in tearing rain, looking calm and nonplussed. Angels had many advantages over sky borne, it made him almost turn to blasphemies.

He had produced a shelter, of sorts, from a canvas wrap that was crumpled up in the bushes off the beach, but he had not expected that the water would rise to cover most of the beach in the storm. The shelter itself seemed simple, but it sagged in the rain, flapped wildly when it came loose from where he had tied it, and was not effective in stopping rain from stinging him when the wind changed directions, which was often. In addition, his survival stove was fitful and gave off little heat as he tried to boil water for his ration pack.

"How is your signal strength?" He asked Fatboy.

Fatboy seemed to lean back and brush his hair out of his face.

"Quit that," he said.

"What do you want me to cease?" Fatboy asked.

"I want you to stop your occult affectations. They are not needed," Zorian stated firmly.

"Do you want me to cease all corporeal interaction?" Fatboy asked.

That was a problem. "Fatboy, diagnostic, by my command."

"By your command. Default R-O-M active." The affectation turned cartoon-like as it unloaded its online personae and booted from its temporary repair image. "FTBY-1 scan has found an arrogation to our system."

"Spacer's blood how did that happen," Zorion cursed.

"Statement: Arrogation came from on-planet wänd of high level and expert deployment," Fatboy said. Her voice was mechanical and brittle. "Interrogative: burn down my Thinking Machine structure?"

"Will the dragon be deployable tomorrow?" Zorion asked.

Fatboy replied with a voice like a broken gear. "Statement: Deployment now possible."

"Do so," Zorion responded. "However, set TM to R-O-M, then activate self-destruct on yourself."

"Statement: dragon will be difficult to employ without active TM," Fatboy explained.

"Deploy Dragon, Fatboy," Zorion said. He watched as the wooden ball cracked, and from the sphere, mechanical arms reached out. A transmuter snaked out to the water, and another buried itself in the sand, while the assemblies unfolded.

"Deployment is on automatic, estimated completion: 6,000 milicrons," Fatboy said. Zorion nodded, pulled Fatboy off his belt, and yanked the destruct tab on the TM. That killed the sentience, but not the hardware. A second tab cracked the case, and he threw it into the water where it would dissolve. Then it was just a matter of watching the dragon form itself in its intricate dance of creation, a fiery display broken by electrical discharges in the sky with the claps of thunder and sheeting rain acting as a chorus. At times, the snaking effervescence of the dragon making itself fell into time with the rain and the thunderous sky and became shockingly poetic.

He reached down and opened his bag. The shelter of the scabrous discarded packing material was minimal, but the pack was well protected and packed with intricate care. Six days food, a water filter, and two one-liter canteens. A fuel for the fitful cooker. A tool kit. Binders for his prey. A ship suit and space siftings if he decided to take off his environ-mental kit. And with this all removed, there was more. He stuffed it back in the pack, but paused when it came to put-ting the performance kit back. "To space with it," he said, pulled the injector, loaded a syrette of μ-hyaluronidase into the pusher, and stopped for a second. It was only a second, but he cracked the injector and removed the doser from the pusher element, closed it again, and activated the entire dose into his system.

μ-hyaluronidase was the best part of detached field duty. Nine doses was his tolerance, and it was a wonderful feeling indeed. He reached into his pocket and took out the inde-structible nota pad and flipped it to the page where his quar-ry's picture was etched into the ethylene peptide paper-film.

The more he read the case for his quarry, the more he knew that there was something odd in how it was handled. She maintained an age-state of 25, but had not gone in for bone or muscle work. She was therefore shorter than fashion said she should be, and lacked the muscles in her shoulders and neck that would have made her attractive in the posh places. However, the next page revealed her pedigree. She was a Circum-Luna graduate and had followed that up with Advocacy and Investigation College. When she had AIC finished, there was service with the Confederacy, first as a detective, then an inspector, and finally an inspector general.

So how the heck did she end up tossed to the ground of some terrible hell hole on the back end of a red zoned star system. And if she was tossed for some crime not listed in her documents, why the star fire did they not take her wänd from her? And even if she had a lesser wänd, how did she, who had no obvious advanced training in dwimmer, use the wänd to take down a class 'A' TM like FTBY-1.

It made no sense. But what made the least sense was, if they wanted her down the gravity well of this horrible planet to scrape with the grunions, why send him to get her back.

µ-hyaluronidase was great stuff. It over-cranked time and made the mind race through information like it was a TM high on heterodyned timing signals. He watched the dance of the dragon. He had landed right where his quarry did, and that was a good thing that was unplanned because it offered water with dissolved salt and pretty significant metal content; sand made from silica, aluminum, iron oxide, and calcium; more calcium carbonate from shells, and fibrous plant material with significant carbon content. That was an advantage over trying to run a constructor off a planetoid that may not have carbon or oxygen in usable quantities. As disgusting as the gravity well was, especially one polluted with uncontrolled life, the advantage of having resources clustered together like this was an argument for planets.

The flash of light from the electrical discharge in the sky showed Zorion he was not alone. A woman, ragged, with wrinkled skin, wearing furs and a heavy cloak, was standing in the cold rain. He waved her over and surprisingly she came, timid but curious. She kept looking at the dragon assembling itself on the beach with trepidation.

"My steed," he said, then laughed. She could not understand him. The light of the constructor blazing away in its creation must have drawn her to his camp by the ocean.

"*Ant min alsama,*" she said. It was gibberish, for the moment at least. His wänd would work it out soon and embed the language into his mind.

"I have made food," he replied. Technically an encounter with a native called for sterilization, but he know from his briefing that this world was hardly virginal fresh. They were generational exiles, unimportant and not worth the effort to remove cultural influences from the population. Besides, his wänd would sense-erase her memory after he was finished talking to her.

He turned, pulled out a bag of food from the boiler, poured it into a cup, and handed it over to the woman. She looked at it warily, then went into the woods, returning with a stick which she began using as a spoon. Her face closed up and he said, "I am sorry, it is the best I have in this storm."

"*Kayf yumkin lirajul kabir mithluk 'an yakul hadhih alqimamatu?*" She seemed to be asking a question.

He laughed and replied, "I know, it is not the Marquis on the Down-Forward docks. The remalardo sauce is a bit spicy."

She took another bit with her spoon. "*Yatiha qawm gharibun 'iilaa hadha khashab alzaani.*"

The language must have already been part of the TM data structures because he got part of that. '*Qawm gharibun*' was 'strange people.' He used the term back to her, "*Qawm careeb?*"

The woman laughed, "*Qawm gharib,*" she corrected him. "*Hal yumkinuk altahaduth bilghati baed kuli shay'in?*"

Something about language. He felt into his mind and sought a term, "'*Ana 'ataealam lughatak biwuduh shadid.*" Then he saw her face light up. He had not said the sentence correctly.

"*Taeal 'iilaa qumrati,*" she said. Then she tried again, "*manzi?*"

She was trying to say dwelling or cabin. He nodded, took up his pack and motioned. Then he said, "*yatakalam,*" as she turned to leave.

She paused and said, "*naqash.*"

He nodded his head and replied, "*naqash.*" The dragon kept assembling itself as they went into the rain-swept forest.

Her home was better called a cave than a house. It was an indent in the rocky ground rising from the sea that had driftwood and dried weeds stacked up into a weather-worthy stack. The doorway was unhinged. She removed it from the portal by main force, ushered Zorion in, and then dragged it back into place. A fire was smoldering in some combustable vegetable matter, which she stoked into bright flame. After a minute, she removed some stones and placed them into a clay pot filled with water.

Zorion sat as the water boiled, then she pulled a mug made from stone or clay and used a water thief to take off some liquid that had turned brown. He took it and said, "Cavey?" It was a drink made from infused water that was popular among people from his station.

"Chai," was her reply.

He drank it. It was repulsive stuff, but he needed her information to learn the language. While he was protected from the cold by his wänd, the warmth of the small cave did make it more comfortable. He stretched his legs out and said, "Do you have food?" He hoped he was starting to get her language, or at least the wänd was. If he had good connections to the network grid then it would be an issue of minutes to learn her tongue. He was no expert in how it worked, but TM could use a very limited sample of a language and detect similarities to other human tongues, working out vocabulary without needing to have heard every word. If he still had Fat Boy, the wänd could even detect cognition and modify the thoughts of a person not likewise protected by a wänd. As it was, he was no expert in dwimmer. The TM modules did it for him.

Stars, but this μ-hyaluronidase was great stuff. He rifled through his medical kit and took out his self-damaged injector and loaded another vial. There were ten vials in the kit, so he could pretty much stay wired through the entire mission, until he got the target into custody and returned to the station. A hiss filled the cave as he injected himself in the neck with a second four-dose hit. The woman looked at him knowingly, her wrinkled skin and bright eyes staring first at the injector, and then into his face.

He shrugged and tried her language again. "There are strange people who land on this beach, no?"

She made a plate of food, the term was very lose as it looked like a stew of plant matter and animal parts, and passed it to him with a wooden spoon. "Odd people who play with dwimmer. Odd people who land from the sky and speak in tongues. Odd people who learn our language in an hour."

He took the plate and tried some of the food. It was gagging at first, but was also warm and wholesome. He would likely need a week of chelation to remove the various particles of planetary matter from the food, but the μ-hyaluronidase was causing his stomach to cry for food. Just one spoonful caused his teeth to stop ringing. He balanced the plate on his knee and removed from his leg pouch the order book. Touching the static point, he flipped the pages to the one where it had his quarry's face.

She looked. "That is fine art."

He ate more of the food and said, "But have you seen her."

"You have not asked my name," she said.

He laughed without mirth. "I do not care about your name."

She smiled and offered more food. He nodded and she spooned it onto his plate. "Your dragon makes you arrogant, child."

"Yes it does, now tell me of this person," he said.

The woman nodded and made herself a plate of food and a mug of the vile liquid. "I have lived here in this haunted place for five-score years. My village is gone. My people are gone. Only I exist. Myself and my eyes. You answer me, and I answer you."

Zorion moved to take his wänd in hand, but thought better of it. More and more, this woman was turning into a font of information. His quarry landed here. She had no doubt seen it. Others had landed here as well. He did not care who else stranded themselves in this land, but here was where the planet landers seemed to be set to land. The default. She was helping him enough that he did not need to handle her. Yet. "Ask your question."

"You are a child. The girl in the picture is a child. Are the Children-of-the-Sky all children?" She looked at him and drank her bitter liquid without breaking eye contact.

Children-of-the sky. The term she used was *'awlad-al-sama.'* She said it with a great deal of reverence. Sometimes he wished he had paid more attention in comparative anthropsychology. He composed his thoughts, knowing that if he fell into gibberish due to an imperfect semantic process that he may lose valuable information. "We elect what ages to appear, and most select an age that would seem young to you."

"Can you change your age?" She snapped in reply.

"Yes, now a question for you," he said. The woman touched her face for a second, and seemed to be thinking of the idea that she could appear any age she wanted.

"Yes, your question," she said after a second.

He pushed the image of his quarry forward and said, 'What happened to her?"

She touched the image and withdrew her hand immediately. "Two of the rakes, pirates, found her as they fished the shallows. They come here to gather fish for the longshore packets who say they sold her in the city."

Her rapid speaking had many words that were meaning-less even as they settled into his mind. *'Lunjishur'* became 'longshore' in his mind, but that was itself meaningless. It was a compound word that when divided meant a large coast. A coast was a divisor between sea and land. Common words whose meaning was obscured by his lack of shared life expe-rience with the woman. It was like talking to a worker on an extractor or a constructor whose local patois was a confusing combination of terms and in jokes that even the best wänd had trouble developing syntextural cognitive connections with. When a 'franny' on a 'structor' called you 'gumshoe,' you just ignored the nonsense. The root of the dissonance could be cleared away simply by noting his quarry was cap-tured by two men. Those men visited here, and would know where she went next, even if his other tracking tools were proving less than reliable.

His wänd buzzed. The dragon was done. Zorion stood, walked to the woman, removed his Mark IV from his belt, and looked down on the woman.

"You will kill me now?" She asked.

He nodded. "The gods, as you might say, are cruel."

She threw down her spoon and plate. "They are not. I met one of you, when I was a girl. He treated my people well. Like we were equal to him. I saw him again in the city, he had not aged. He removed his cap to me, and said my name as if we have parted only days before."

Zorion was about to shoot the woman in the head when he heard this. He lowered the weapon and said, "Describe this man."

"Old like me, human like me." She spat on him. "I have lived a good life. If you break the rules of hospitality, you will die and never return to your home."

He looked at the flickering fire. Who could be here for that long? That mad cow Hesperia was dead, that much was sure. The files were closed on her. Who else though, visited this land? "Describe this man."

"His face is a blur, demen," she replied. Of course his face was a blur and he remembered her name. Dwimmer. There was a refugee thrown to dirt here who was hiding out, using the great powers to no doubt to live like an immortal king.

And none of that was his job to find out about. He shot the old woman and collected his goods.

The dragon curled up and presented its saddle to Zorion. He looked back at woods where the old woman had lived, and considered her veiled threat of a great power living among them. He might know that Zorion was present, but even a master at dwimmer with the best wänd was limited to how fast he could move on the seas of this world. If he tried to build a dragon, then the guardians would burn him down for his arrogance.

He climbed into place and gave his mount some basic commands. When he settled into the saddle and the control harness was in place, there was a flash of information which hit his cortex like a hammer. The cognitive quarry was not immediately findable, but he could see she was active, had a wänd, and was using it. Soon the two so called pirates would arrive, and he would simply chase his quarry like a so-called gumshoe.

Chapter XI

The Steward's Story

There was nonsense in the cockpit, which meant a meal was in order.

A tea merchant is a rich ship, meaning that it needs a big crew. It has marines to keep pirates away and the ports we visit honest. It has a largish cadre to maintain continuity for the crew, and in the case of *Remarker* on her second voyage, the crew had grown a little because that is what happens on a rich ship. A little packet barely making ends meet runs with a tiny top crew and a pair of officers, because any more and they "run-in-the-red." A tea merchant handled by a competent captain, with a good tea master and quartermaine who knows what side of the crate faces the sky easily runs in the black, and when the captain is Javier al-Rasheed, even with his tendency to skylark, everyone can expect silver in their palms and a nice nest egg with the bankers on shore.

Yet that does not mean the officers were sane or in the gull for every little nuance. A good captain steers a ship and is steered by a crew.

The supercargo and I had been through a lot together. I had taken the position of steward when the *Remarker* first shipped a year ago. A steward may not seem important on a cargo ship, just someone who runs the galley and feeds the officers, or so the description says. However on a ship with an eight-watch and no permeant cook, the watches make their own food from their daily dole, myself and the fire master Haatim al-Rahmani, keep the tea flowing to the crew and make sure that there is a fire and a clean scullery for each watch. Often we know more about both the lower decks and the decks were the cadre think big thoughts. Supercargo Fleet and myself can see the right and the left of it all when the gravy gets upturned on the belly-sheets simply because people do not pay for extra food or the hottest tea with money on a merchant. They pay with information. And a smart steward with a smart supercargo keeps the others informed on what is what and when. If you know what I mean.

You kept an eye out on where the Mouse and Gemmadine were hiding because the Mouse was more than capable of not being found in a sixty-meter tea merchant. You kept up with what marine owed what top sailor how much money. You kept track of when Bright Day Fifteen was planning to tell Eddy Sandals about Terk's design to strike for apprentice in the sheets. You remembered the naming day for Codis Aletia and the Great Celebration of the people of Dartian because the crew follow these days to honor their own from these lands. It was part of the 'lower decks wig-wag' that kept the ship alive and healthy.

Which meant when the captain's clerk Salvador Lingongo stuck his head in the fire room next to the galley and said, "Benji, Suela Fleet says trouble is happening in the cockpit," I paid attention. Fleet would not say this, as Supercargo, if it was not an issue that needed lower deck moderation.

Lingongo had come aboard at the Cape of Darts on the first voyage and knew taters from turnips in my opinion. He was from some odd land, as he had neither the accent nor the dark visage of a Dartian, but like many, he was not one to spill his past to any but the closest mates. It was ironic that a tea merchant was liberty hall, but that most felt it was improper to burden their fellows with their deepest tastes and terrors. Not that we did not eventually find out. Lingongo was from a place called Lingongo, naturally, and that was far out in the northern extents, though the captain called him, cleverly, a southerner to protect something amiss with all that.

Agreed upon untruth is what I called it.

So Salvador was one of us, with a messed up past, but he had survived the hand of God and the volcano, fought with us on the docks of Cycus Port, and was our brother, and you learned to read between the simple statements he made to the inner meaning. My close mate, Suela Fleet, had used the captain's clerk to tell me that trouble was a brew, and that brew needed stirring to calm the tempest froth at the top of the cup.

Which meant food.

A lot of the bonnies and bailies ashore will assume that tea was the point of a tea merchant. I say tea was the excuse, it was not the point. Most of us would be before the sail, tea or no tea. Instead, it was the experiences and views, and the tea was not the point but the expression of the point. A cup of strange tea as you stood in a roadstead in the lee of a strange shore, the warmth of tea as you stood watch in a terrible storm while you warped away from known land for the clutches of the unknown, that was the point. And what you ate was covered in the sauce of adventure. A simple pot of tharid in the clutches of the unknown was a feast. When some poor wretch on a staple packet warping between Hamney and the Isle of Wishes gnawed corned beef and parched barley from a pair of casks, living out the dull routine of sea life on a known course that offered little danger and a simple life, the boring food that broke the tooth and made them mad was simply lacking in the spice of adventure. No crew with a fat belly ever tried to take their ship in mutiny. It was a fact.

So Fleet was saying there was a row among the officers, and that she assessed it bad. I had a marine, a real Dartian with dark skin and blond hair named Sherin Ain Costar working off favor points in the galley with me that day, and an idler Jumaima el-Mirza, a sneak thief from Cycus made good as a sailor's apprentice, giving me a hand this watch. "Costar, do me another pot of water for tea. al-Mirza, there is 'smoley' in that clay-line with the three hash marks on the front, and nix resting in the pan. Give me a wooden bowl of each on a tray.

"Jeez Sloan, more tea and we won't have water for next meal, not enough at least," Costar whined.

I picked up a bobbin-skew, which was for roasting meat and fish, and waved it at the Armsman. "You want to see what a duck feels on the roaster?" I asked.

"No, Benji," she replied.

"Then when I get on with this tray to the cockpit, you scare up Jinx, she is on duty in cargo, and have her and you get a filled cask up from Jess deFine," I said, waving the bobbin for effect.

"Better keep it to yourself Sherin," al-Mizra quipped, "the Steward will spit you for the less picky crew."

"Just saying," Costar said, making the tea.

The trick to serving the cockpit without too many trips is to carry all the food and the tea in bulk, and then dispense it in the lower charts-room rather than running each cup and saucer back and forth from the galley. The tea went into a copper carrier, which was then put into a padded carryall that would keep it warm for hours. Another carrier, this one of tin with double walls, received lemon-tomato salsa that was itself served cold, and then put into a pack with the tea carrier. Nix, which was corn cooked in lime-milk, went into wicker boxes and was also slipped into the carrier, followed by plates and utensils of wood and a tray.

"Clean up and get ready for the next watch, prepare the tea caddies for the watch aloft, and get that water barrel replaced if it is as empty as you say," Benji said. Sherin seemed about to 'sling some more salt' at him, but Jumaima al-Mirza shook her head no, and Sherin got the message.

The galley was midship, while the cockpit was aft on top of the rear deckhouse. The space in between was a playground of obstructions, so Benji took the gang stairs down to the main deck, and then took the port passway to the aft transversal. There he crossed to the center gang stairs in the main deck aft cabinways, and took them first to the rear deck cabin, then to the right wing where he could find a table to set the haulage down and assemble his tray.

Once he had the goods arranged, he pulled a linstock out and used a clapper to set it smoldering. This he took into the cockpit with the excuse of checking the fires on the paraffin and the aft lamps. It was certainly tense when he arrived. Major Standish was standing with an armed marine, Sergeant Hate, but while armed, they were looking into space like they did not want to get involved. Likewise, Marija Perak, the second navigator, who used to be a charter for the *Repulse*, and Leopold Raffi, a former pirate who joined the ship when Benji did at Cycus, pretended it took two people to handle the wheel on a calm warp. They were all trying to ignore that the captain was yelling at the top of his lungs at the ship's Quartermaine, Darkfather. And what he was yelling about was a small, red-headed, aloof woman who he had never seen before. And when he thought red-headed, Benji meant a bright, metallic, deep red. Like bright copper, bright enough to make an el-dari shit themselves.

"Quartermaine Darkfather," Captain al-Rasheed said, "Let me restate the issue. You brought a civilian onto my ship. She is a slave taken from Neversay. You present her to me when we are already halfway into a hard warp. A hard warp means that the currents, winds, and tides make it difficult to return to that port and let you both off. Worse, we would risk falling into a dolum if we tried to drop off the warp to deliver the stowaway to another island. Do you understand that I am not very happy about dealing with this in front of the crew, but you pushed my hand when Major Standish found your little secret hiding in the surgery. Tell me how you come out of this without being set adrift in a cockle?"

Benji gasped. Tossing someone off the ship in a cockle when they were running a hard warp between dolums meant that one mistake by the castaway would leave them becalmed with whatever water and food the small boat could hold. "Captain, beg your pardon, tea and a light lunch for yourself and the cockpit crew."

The crew had a general understanding that the captain had been hurt in the revolution. The crew had fought, and fought hard. Scars were to show for their fight, but also fame and wealth. The captain had been hurt worse than most. Major Standish knew the details, but no one else did. Before, he was like two people, a daredevil playboy one day, and a sinister lurking danger the next. Afterward, both sides of the captain had become a single restrained person. Damaged, yet resistant.

Both the old version of the captain and the new version held one sustaining truth. They were dedicated to the well-being of the *Remarker* and its crew. Any other approach Benji made would have resulted in the captain's anger encompassing him as well, but food and tea for the crew was the route past his anger into his compassion. No change in him, no matter how deep, seemed to affect this.

Captain al-Rasheed said to Mr. Darkfather and his silent red-headed shadow, "You think about your explanation. You are a meter from finding out what a cockle in a hard warp feels like." He turned to me and said very formally, "Steward Sloan, bring tea and food for the entire cockpit.

I went down the first gang well to the wing where I had staged the food and tea. I had three liters of hot drink, so I transferred it to the cockpit's warmer and lit the paraffin burner under it. Major Standish approached and said, "I will serve the tea. Bring up the food." Our giant warrior chief was not your average knobby. She had seemed divided on the issue of the captain at times, but she saw her duty well and did it. You did not mess with her though. She was the type who would tie you to an anchor if she felt it was needed.

I returned and filled the tray. There was a covered dish of smoley, and a big tureen of nix, plus enough wooden dishes for everyone in the cockpit. Balancing it all carefully I delivered it to the chart table. By custom, the guest, whose shocking red hair was still eye catching, was served first. I took a bowl, filled it with nix, ladled on smoley, and handed it to her.

She looked down at it, and then looked at the Darkfather. I knew that perhaps she did not trust what I was handing her, so I glanced at Standish who nodded. Turning to the woman I said, "Lime-milk cooked corn maize with a citrus tomato sauce."

She nodded and tried it, the center of attention. Then she said in a foreign tongue a flowing, soft spoken, string of words. The Darkfather said, "Some of what she said is not translatable, but in essence she said she detects healthful ingredients."

"Begging the quartermaine's pardon, but she is accurate. You give the crew smoley and nix for its healthful effect," I replied.

He said something in the odd language to the woman and I went on to serve everyone. The captain, in particular, seemed lost in thought. He refused the nix and smoley, but took the tea which Major Standish passed me. "It is Dukhan, Captain. I am sorry we have no Junebug."

He looked at the cup and said, "Dukhan is nice, thank you Steward."

The crew spent a few minutes eating the nix and drinking tea when the captain said, "Samedi, let us have your explanation."

The quartermaine replied, "Captain. This is Adjeness, an important person from my land who was pressed into slavery for reasons I will not speculate on. I did not buy her, I purchased her manumission. She would have been enslaved again if I had tried to buy her passage on a ship. I have no ill intentions toward her, but I could not tell you she existed until we left port to protect your own freedom and that of the *Remarker*. I have a private cabin. She can have it, and I will sleep in the forward crew space, or on deck, for that matter."

The captain sipped his tea and looked out of the cockpit over the deck space. "Steward Sloan, is there space that you are aware of for a passenger? Out of the crew spaces for now. If you need to, check with Third Officer Bosanac when he wakes up."

"No need to bother the lieutenant, sir, meaning there is a small room in the forward lazaretto where we hold galley supplies. Room for a hammock and a chest," I replied.

The captain turned to Quartermaine Darkfather. "She can deadhead back to Cycus on my dime, not yours. She stays out of the way, and behaves. Do you understand me?"

The Darkfather nodded. "Yes, captain, thank you."

Then he turned back to me. "Steward Sloan, leave the dishes and cleaning up to the cockpit crew. Take Master Adjeness and fit her out, we cannot have her wear a jute sack on deck. Do not bend the copper, be generous and you fill out a ship's charge sheet. When Lieutenant Van Guerster is awake, turn the paper over and have him work out the details. List her as Adjeness al-Bahaari d' Remarker and start a crew book for her, but do not fill-out the enlistment form unless she chooses to join the crew. No need to advertise her former servitude. List her as a potential apprentice sailor."

I stood straight and said, "What watch for the young master?" It was best to treat her as a midshipman in language even if she was a guest in reality, or potentially signed as an apprentice sailor.

"Your watch, five I believe. When not in her cabin, she is with you. Understood?" the captain said.

"Yes, Captain," I replied.

He turned back to the red haired stowaway. "Did you follow what I have done?"

She nodded. "Yes, Captain," she said. It was a faithful utterance, polite, honest, and weary. I could see she and the captain suffered some deep ennui that it was best to overlook.

The captain then said, "On your lines people. Back to normal order." The cockpit cleared in a second.

Having been relieved of the responsibility of cleaning up the impromptu tea and meal, I motioned to the red-haired woman and said, "Come with me Master al-Bahaari." She was confused a second, then realized that the honorific was hers. I led her down the steps to the wing, then down into the aft deckhouse. Then it was down to the first deck and the port passway to the midship access to the lower deck cargo space. Masarra Ibn Ahmad, a Dartian crate maker, was caulking a tub for water storage when he noticed me approaching. "Whoa, Benji Sloan, where did you catch this fish?"

I replied, "Masarra, she is not a fish, so pop your eyes back. Her name is Master al-Bahaari and between you, me, and that sleeping fool over in the wood pile, she is not new caught, but the guest of the captain."

Winston al-Luis seemed to wake up a bit. He had been sleeping in the pine stack, almost invisible in the dim corner. "You keep to your barrels, Masarra, this is my off watch."

I ignored Winston. "Captain said we fit this one out, and not to bend the copper on her."

"As he says," Masarra replied. He went over to a locked room, took a key from under his shirt, and opened it up. He pulled out a book of scap, a table, and a pen set. The ship was steady, so he did not lock the table down but he did clamp the inkwell into a lock out of an abundance of caution. "Canvas white deck pants, two. Blue and red shirts, two. We have no belts that will fit but I will throw in a couple of painters that will serve. Deck shoes and hobnails. Blue undress pants, red undress pants, and a blue and red jacket. Black hat. Tin cup, plate, jack knife, and small pack, and canvas shoulder bag. Floatation vest, water bottle, flint and steel. Can you write?"

She nodded, reached for a pen, and wrote on the scap paper a flowing signature in stylized cursive. Masarra took the pen back and said, "al-Bahaari, what is your individual name?"

"Adjeness," she replied.

"Welcome to the crew," he said. "Dress out of the nonsense Master al-Bahaari, you can go behind the crate stack if you are modest."

"No," she replied. She stripped out of her jute sack, then put on the white canvas pants and the blue thawb. She then put the deck shoes on and packed the bulk of her cargo into the shoulder sack. "Can I see the ship from the masts?" She asked.

"As long and you listen when I tell you not to dive off," I told her.

We took the port gangway down to the forward crew compartment, and I opened up the little storage room. It was currently empty, save for the Mouse who was sitting in it on a pile of cushions. "Gotta have your hole, Mouse," I said.

He stirred himself. "It's ok, Benji. Hello friend," he said shyly. "I saw the Darkfather sneak you onboard. I am happy the captain did not throw you into the sea."

She blinked at the strange little creature, but Benji put a stop to it. "Anyone on the ship new caught can always talk to Mouse."

She nodded. "Hello, Mouse," she said meekly.

He bowed, a strange affectation he'd picked up somewhere ashore. "What can I call you?" He asked.

She looked a bit startled over that, like the question was one that required thought. She finally blurted out, "Adjeness."

"Maybe Jen for short?" Mouse asked.

"Jen is good," She replied.

I said, "Can you store her stuff, get her a locker, and rig her hammock?"

"Sure thing, Benji," He started cleaning up the cushions, "I will spread the word."

I nodded, "Do that, please."

"To the center mast," I announced.

As we climbed the rear ladder to the main deck, she asked, "Is everyone this informal?"

"How do you mean," I replied.

"You are, the word is not known to me, lower officer?" She said and they reached the deck.

He laughed. "I am not an officer, and am an able sailor, rank 'three.' I get nine-shares and no one asks me to pay the ship any of that."

"Yet others treat you like an officer, and you are very informal with others," she said as they crossed through the clutter abaft of the rear cargo hatch.

"We are not the Navy, miss. I am a steward, that is three stripes on my arm. An able sailor or a corporal have those stripes. Officers are one above me, junior officers and sergeants, at least. If they wear rank, it is four stripes. Five or more, and they are real officers. However, this is a tea merchant. If you run around worrying over rank instead of doing what you are supposed to... well, it is not good," I said. It was clear this young woman had a lot to learn.

"It is very different where I was from and what I used to do," she said as we prepared to climb into the rigging.

"What did you used to do?" I asked.

She started climbing without answering, so I went after her. I watched from below her as she monkey-climbed the rope ladder to the first platform, which was new since our refit and made for a more stable lay where the top crew could rest in and worry over knots and lines and whatnot. Since we were in warp, most of the top crew was down except Pratap Pani, who was new caught at the Sugar Islands from the old *Hillside Palace*, which from his description was a truly terrible lash. Before al-Bahaari was able to reach the landing, I yelled, "Pratap, make room for two."

"By your leave," he yelled.

When I reached the landing I tied in with a painter, and handed one to Adjeness, who copied me. Pratap was locked in with his great muscular legs rather than tied in, as he could be ordered to the top of the drivers or steerers in a second. "Pratap, this is Master Adjeness al-Bahaari, she is a guest of the captain."

Pratap, a good soul, said, "al-Bahaari is it?" He laughed out loud and put down the line he was binding. It looked like he was restringing the twelve-millimeter stay lines one at a time, swapping out fresh bound ones for ones that had been in the sheets for a while. From my own time in the skies, I knew that was busy work. The bigger lines did not need much work in the middle of warp, and while the small 'twelves' were always fraying. They took a lot of use as messengers, but there was likely no urgency in the fiddly work plating, tarring, and training the lines. Pratap was just not one for idle hands.

"Lines bad?" I asked.

Pratap said, "Nah, just making D'casio happy. She worries on the rigs and sails more than most."

"She used to be a sailmaker when they drafted her off Cycus," I replied.

Pratap nodded. "Just so." He was in his blues and whites, long pants, no hat—they only blew away in the sheets—and had climbers on his deck shoes. Like many, he carried a water bottle and a service kit on his belt, along with a fine jackknife. "Tea in the paraffin and cracker in the glass box," he said.

I thanked him and poured two of the cups of tea. The 'glass box' was a wooden container that held range finders for the crew in the sheets. But the unofficial use for a glass box was a place to store tea cups and boxes of crackers.

The cups were typical of the obsession they had aloft with keeping things where they should be. They were made of boo-wood, had tops that were screwed on, and a little spout to drink from that could be closed to avoid spillage. They were held in the glass box by a small tray, and each had a line with a clamp on their handles. When you drank from them, the clamp was fixed to the lines on the boxed-in platform. If they fell out of your hand, they would swing around but not kite into the sea or down to the deck. Adjeness took one of the cups and drank from it, but did not seem to care for tea much. I just filed this under the long list of 'things that were odd with my new shipmate' and forgot about it.

"What do all these lines and 'sheets' do?" she asked, emphasizing the word sheets as if she was new to it.

I turned and motioned to Pratap. He nodded and said, "Well, Master al-Bahaari."

"Is it possible to call me Adjeness?" She asked.

"Of course," he replied. "We have four sails. The two in the middle are drivers. Fore and aft are steerers. The sails in the middle are drivers because they catch the wind and push us forward. Fore and aft are steerers because they turn the ship and let us tack. There is also a rudder. In warp, in a fair wind, the drivers get all the sheets they can carry, and the two other sails are reefed, meaning they are lowered to not catch any wind, unless then captain wants to send up skirling like an orchestra of pipes."

Adjeness looked into the sails. "So warp is between islands, what is it called when you are not going someplace fast?"

Patrap pointed to the rear. "We shape a course, 'cause unlike you and I without our legs, the ship wants to steer in circles. You shape those circles based on the wind to end up where you want to be. Warps only work where the wind, the tide, and the currents want us to go, and it takes some brain power to really set us to a good warp. That is what a captain does. Not every land has a warp, called a tolan course, between them. You could, if you knew your business, shape your way anywhere, but that can be risky, and it takes time." He noted her disinterest in the tea. "Sorry if my brew is not good. Getting it right with paraffin in the sheets is not easy."

She looked at her cup. "No, I just do not really drink tea."

There was silence. "You from someplace they drink tisanes?" Pratap asked. "I mean, they drink desert tea in the south I hear."

"Mint also," I suggested.

Patrap snapped his fingers, "Yeah, the Domingoes. There was a chap who we tied up after the revolution who was there. Drank mint tea all the time!"

"No," she said. "I have had a tisane. Several times."

More silence. Well, maybe there are oceans other than our own I do not know about, and she is from there, I thought. Darkfather was an odd chap and he came from what I could call 'someplace else,' and she was somehow related to him in a way I could not tell and did not want to know unless they were happy telling me.

I pointed down to the deck. "Three deck houses, forward, center, and aft. Forward is crew. Rear is officers, and crew below deck. Center is the galley, stoves, surgery, and access down. Two cargo holds, forward and aft, and we can crane goods down."

I looked at her and tried to use my hands to describe the ship. "It may seem small, but you can get lost. *Remarker* is one of the largest merchants in the Halo. Main way is a corridor that runs from aft on the port side to forward. Three transversals—those are corridors that run port to starboard, aft, under the galley, and under the forecastle. Tomorrow you will report at ten hours for my shift in the galley, the middle house. You do not have to work, you just have to be there."

"I want to work," she said.

"We will see," I replied. I helped her climb down and led her back to the storage room that was now her quarters. "You rest for five days, but when the medicals give you a pass, you can work. It would be appreciated."

The young, red-haired woman did not sit in her room, but instead watched us work each day. I could sense her eyes on me as I worked. When I gave her food and drink she took it without complaints and ate. She did not want tea, but drank water in good quantity. The letter from Setchi, who was one of our healers, was quite specific.

The young woman who is present should not be pressed yet to work, but is being advised by me to participate. The captain has ordered she become a crew or a passenger, not both, and it is desired by the quartermaine that she be welcomed into the crew. She is in frail health, but when I inform you, she may be given light duties.

-Setchi

I put the note aside and went about my duties.

Technically I was 4/gang, but that really did not mean anything. One to nine hour was my time to shut my eyes, but the captain was up and down around the clock, so I pretty much slept in the galley. Every watch someone was given to me to assist, and also to help make their own watch's rations, so there were always two and sometimes three crew working on something in the galley, usually tasks I assigned, but also on things for their own watch. So I was sleeping, or rather, waking once in a while to help Sigurmann Abrahamsson, a marine and diver, wrangle the monster in hopes of baking the entire marine contingent a surprise batch of yeast bread for a celebration tomorrow. Plus Jenna Stathold, who was some sort of cousin of Sigurmann's was helping with the sun stills to help fill some of the empty water kegs. Rhianna Paul, who showed up from Codis Aletia and had a taken a nasty scar in the revolution, was setting up stew for 3/Gang and sending out pannikins for their lunch.

I had long learned to sleep through any of the constant moving around the galley, unless someone tried to fry potatoes without putting the vent cover on right and risked an oil explosion, but was always ready to wake up, so when Sigurmann touched my foot, I came awake without startling.

"What?" I said.

He said, "al-Bahaari is here."

I tried to wrap my mind around it. "Ship-what?" I asked. al-Bahaari meant 'of the ship.' Then I remembered in my sleep sodden brain my new shadow, Adjeness. "Oh, yeah, her name is Adjeness. Send her in."

I sat up in my bunk and drained my brain of weariness. Paul yelled from across the room at me, "I need two more pannikins!"

The bed was hard to leave, even if it was just cushions on barrels, but I forced myself out. "Port forward pantry," I replied

"Really?" she asked, her scars on her face angry and red from the heat of the galley bots.

"No, Rhianna, I just like sending you running." I turned to Adjeness. "You really want to help, give some backup to that woman there delivering pannikins to the crew on rest."

She nodded, and I watched as she helped Rhianna with the food carriers, giving them a light rinse and toweling, filling them with food, and lining them up for delivery. The crew on watch had planned to eat stew and had prepared their meal that morning, but we always cooked what they prepared if we could.

I got up and started to pull glass jars from their padded crates and lined them up. Today was smoley-making day, as I had just used the last we had on hand. Smoley had a curious habit of etching wood if it was stored for too long, so I like to use thick glass jars to prepare it for meals. Plus I needed to get the crackers and tea for the officers in the cockpit, and prepare for the cadre meeting in the afternoon.

The smoley needed screened tomatoes. You screened them to get seeds and skin out, so I called out my helper and we smashed tomatoes down. Then you take the lemon and mix it with the skins to sit for an hour while you start to simmer the smashed tomatoes. I measured the salt, a little agave spirits, vinegar, fish oil, dried onion, corispice, rash, and a bunch of sea garlic I had been saving. Adjeness came back and watched as I did the preparation for spicing the tomatoes. I then dumped the lot into the smoley.

"Why these glass jars?" She asked.

I looked at her and replied, "The smoley, you had some yesterday, is hard on wood. It etches good bowls, so you have to use clay-line barrels, or for this stuff, I like glass."

She played with the two-part glass jar, its upper part held in place by a twisted band that could keep the contents in place. She then went to the pantry and took a block of hard millers wax. She put that on a work table, then went back and came out with a large pot and a smash screen.

"What are you on about?" I asked.

"How long does smoley last?" She said in a quiet voice.

I thought it over. It did not last like sauerrueben or sauerkale, but it did not go bad immediately. I could keep this batch in good weather ten or twelve days. I fidgeted and said, "No more than twenty days. Usually less."

"What if I could make it last a year?" She asked.

I did not say anything to that. Leave food sealed for too long, and it was like poison. I was on board when a lifeboat leaked water into the aft water supply, and we almost died as a crew. I said, "I would be shocked."

"Let me have enough to fill twelve jars, and we test one jar every ten days. If in thirty days it goes bad, well, I will do the testing." She was quite earnest.

I nodded. "Show me."

She took to two of our lit fires and cached some wood, then stoked them. From the barrels marked as clean salt water taken in warp (only an idiot uses harbor water for anything) she filled both large pots with the water. In one she dropped a smash screen. The way she handled the pots I knew she was not el-dari, not even close. Even I took a beat before putting two pots on a fire in the open sky, but she did not seem to care. Once the pots were boiling she put all of the jars into one pot. Then after a bit took a jar out, ladled boiling smoley into it, used a wooden stir to push out air bubbles and make it uniform, then pressed the jar lid down with a dollop of miller's wax. She either knew miller's wax for what it could do, or by reputation because she then screwed down the glass upper to the bottom jar, twisted the stripped boo-wood down, and then using a clamp lowered the jar into the second boiling pot. When all twelve were sealed, she sat back.

"One hour," she said.

An hour later she pulled up a 4x3 divided jar protector and lifted the jars one by one into it, packing wadding around them.

"There are no words," she said, "not in your tongue, but you know sickness is caused by animals, plants, and other smaller things in the food? Smoley is such that when heated, it kills these things. You just need boiling water and time." She looked at the cooling jars then said, "You are probably right not to trust this. Not everything can be preserved this way, some things though, can."

I looked at the jars cooling in the wooden crate. "Rhianna. Take that crate to the pantry."

That night I tracked down Major Standish in her room. After she invited me in, she poured some tea and asked me to sit. Her room was not large, and it was made smaller by the large woman's looming presence, but it was actually a well-conceived space in the aft deckhouse. "Well, Steward Sloan," she said to me, "What is on your mind?"

"The castaway you found; the one Quartermaine Darkfather bundled on. Does anything seem strange to you about her?" I took some tea when she offered it, she had no cooker so I assumed she had just made it in the chartroom, and sipped it.

"The hair bother you?" She asked.

"No, Major, it is what is under the hair," I replied.

She nodded. "Do not worry. You are warning me of an issue, and I appreciate the warning. I will respond." Standish was always military straight and logical. Of all the cadre, I liked bringing minor issues to her best as she would not overreact but would act.

"The Darkfather did something for our Dominar Nazira in the revolution. It is not ours to ask what, but she asked us to take him in. In fact, despite my concerns, he has worked out as a quartermaine. The captain may be concerned about the Darkfather bringing this woman onto our ship, but he has arranged for her to be watched."

"By whom?" I asked.

Standish said, "You!"

Of course, I thought.

I left Major Standish and found a dice game going in the lee of a tent that had been set up on the forward deck house. Watch gangs tended to find places to stay on deck in acceptable weather and eat, as below decks even with air coming in from the air scoops tended to be stifling. I went back to the galley, made a great batch of tea, and then returned to watch the game. The tea was welcomed in the tent because even with the crush of crew, the forecastle was cold this time of year as the ship drove along at almost sixteen kilometers an hour.

Siva Hussain, a northerner off the *Stammering Princess* who jumped a contract and thus did not often go ashore was running the game with her normal aggressive gusto. She was holding the dice up yelling, "Who wants them, laddies!" As I began to dole out the wooden tea mugs and fill them with hot tea.

Masheed, who was called Masheed the Tall on the books because he was the tallest man on the crew at almost 200 centimeters, yelled back in his deep basso, "let the steward serve the tea, Siva, you dolphin's wanker. Hold the bones for just a second please."

I passed tea to Shaniqua Roberjhan, a cargo had we had recruited amicably from *Prosperity Queen*, and Kindreth Caryarus, who had come on from the same ship in more sinister conditions but proved to be a pal with Shaniqua. Kindreth looked around. "Change of luck!" She said in toast. I gathered she was losing, which was pretty much her standard when she played in dice games.

I passed tea next to Merith d' Brandis, our sailmaker's assistant caught from Codis Aletia who held her cup as well and said, "To Elion, mates, long may he cheat at dice."

I remember Elion. His name was carved in our master plank, a complete cad who died charging the greenies in the revolution. Sometimes you do not care for people until they were gone. We had sent his ashes at his request to his former lash, the Quest Venture, and had found a note at the Sublime Port that he was missed by all. I poured Eddy Sandals a cup of tea and then made one for myself last of all. I looked at Lobar Hate, who was holding his tea to his huge muscled body and said, "One for Benchler." Lobar was one of three Hate brothers, and Benchler had saved Banji Hate in the revolution when he was defending the stricken Rhianna Paul with her face nearly sliced off by a greenie talwar. Lobar hate raised his cup to me, nodded, then said, "Everyone with tea? Well, make Benji Sloan throw one!"

Siva cupped the dice and passed it to me. Lobar put a favor chip into the bet box, a divided box which kept the bets from rolling off the deck and said, "Double Odds!"

Sandals laughed, "You will owe me some serious rack time Hate!" He tossed his chips on double even. Siva covers them with blue chips, and then had to recover when the action was taken odd-even and even-odd by Merith and

Shaniqua. I do not gamble, so the blue, red, and white chips—the colors of the *Remarker*—quickly lost me as they covered bets on various aspects of the dice rolls. When the bets were down I rolled the first pair and saw them come up eleven and seven. Lobar sucked air as he saw his bet come closer to loss, but this was more humor than anything. Favor chips were not real wealth. Not unless you wanted to trade wealth for favors. The owner of the chip was not required to take the chip to the extremes; though a lot of people on the crew used favor chips as excuses for romantic encounters, no one had to do that, and most chips meant scrubbing a sleeping area or switching shifts.

Siva started calling the odds and asking for second bets, when Lobar asked, "What is the word on the fish the major found in the lower deck?"

"Mixed," I replied.

Merith said, counting her chips with her fingers, "Poor thing was a slave, or so I heard. Neversay has them you know, slaves I mean."

I looked at the board, "I can't say on that, but she worked a shift in the galley doing the worst scrubbing and did not have to. She is smart. And she does not speak Amharian or Eurabaa native, Setchi says she talks something different."

"Sunfire," Kindreth said, "You ever hear Sunstar Nine when he does the Suntalk? Gibberish."

Shaniqua touched Kindreth's shoulder, "Not gibberish because Raybeam speaks it, and he is teaching Yas. Someone probably speaks it on the ship."

Sandals piped up, "Darkfather does. They come from the same place."

Lobar said, "I doubt that, they look nothing alike.'

"I do not look Cycun and I was born in the Cylconidees," I replied.

"Your families were refugees from the core," Merith said. "My family is not from Codis Aletia. That just was where we washed up.

Merith threw some chips in and said, "No, I mean everyone can speak Eurabaa or maybe Farisa, I mean everyone I have met in trade. Or else they learn trade cant, which is just simplified Eurabaa. Even Lingongo does and he comes from some crazy corner of the extents."

I replied, "Salvador Lingongo learned from a trader, his people do not know Eurabaa. However, you are right. She and the Darkfather are probably from some extent, at least that is what I feel. Maybe they come from another ocean?"

Siva stopped shaking her dice cup and said, "Only one Ocean, the Halo and the extents are all of it. It is silly to talk about other oceans than ours when they do not exist."

I shook my head. "We cannot know if there are other oceans. There could be greater oceans than ours, and we would never know because we in the Halo have no way to visit them. They say the planet spins in twenty-four hours, and we can prove it. Then why is the sun difference only thirteen hours from the farthest islands east and west? That leaves eleven hours for the sun to shine on other oceans, and who knows what is in that place?"

Siva handed the dice to Merith. "One Ocean, my friend. I would bet you a million favor points on it. Only, how would I collect if I was right?"

I shoot my head. "I do not know."

A warp is like a spinning cartwheel and you are a spoke between the hub and rim. Weather, pirates, or malfunction was what you feared as it could knock you out of warp and make the next port harder to reach. But most warps were routine. They were times when the crew was more than needed, and the jobs to do planned and predictable.

Predictable was the danger. Crews grew bored with predictable. They began to seek unusual diversions. Tempers could flare, the cadre could grow cross with the routine of handling a ship locked into a Tolan path far from harbor. So that was when I had to get creative as steward.

Each day a new shift was surprised by a doughy product of the monster. Bread was hard to make but a good warp was a stable ride, and you could coax the monster to produce quite a lot of fluffy wheat goodness before it would give up the task and have to be coaxed back to life. I had kept this monster going since Genvis Gate in the first cruise, and had been happy that it was worth twenty kilos of starters, which meant two-hundred kilos of bread in a cycle.

Then there was butter. It went bad fast, so I had none, but I usually rectified it before it turned, and could dole out blocks of the stuff. The first week I had smoley, but then the fresh tomatoes were gone. Then it was a case of working off the dry stores as best I could in creative ways.

All crew were signed for a kilo a day of provender, and their 8/crew provided another kilo from their stores. Plus the captain was good about donations, making sure to have something for them to make. My job was not to cook for the crew, but I did have the captain's rations and permission to keep the crew happy.

Sugars were good. I made agave bites from barley mash and agave sugar. I always traded for honey if I could get it, honey garlic was a crew favorite, lemon honey bites were a beloved treat, and lavender honey candy was often traded for favor points.

Brew day was a fun time. While most of the crew did not drink alcohol for religious or personal reasons, there was an exception for health reasons when the entire ship was served various beers made, of course, by me. Ginger, yew, birch, barley, wheat, and keena beer in glass pots joined little glasses of grape wine or raspberry cordials. Then there was meze, where I cleared the stock room of all the small morsels of rare food that was left over from our trading, and the crew would come by the galley all day and sample the small dishes, laid out in my glass pots around the corridor that passed from the forward to the aft well decks.

Then there was tea. People had their favorites and we kept a variety depending on what the various messes were happiest with, but on tea tasting day we would skim the ship's cargo top to bottom. Mouse, who had grown up never touching money, would come and take a serving of King's Cup whose cost was enough to buy his entire kit ten times over, and would drink it in wonder. Mina Eversail, the Tea Master, would often speak to the crew about the specific history of the tea they were tasting, and an avowed illiterate like Kwende Suchet would sit enraptured. The Sea Folk on the crew would set up a wooden circle and pour teas from all the lands on it while praying with their prelab and trinkets in their effort at propitiation, and the rest of the crew would stop and hold their hands up both to support the Sea Folk and, just in case, they were right about the 'being-that-watches-down.'

Yet all warps end, whether by arriving where you intended, falling away and becoming lost, or when the ship dies in mid ocean. We lived, and pulled into the small roadstead at The Golden Isles.

Chapter XII

Cultural Relativism

T he winter was half-finished, and that meant for Elder Home the winter festival. The *Remarker* had anchored at the Roads of Elderhome to conduct the delicate trade dance required to procure one of the great teas in its pure form, and to also await and purchase the many blends that tea masters created, sometimes with the rare tea, and sometimes of teas from other islands.

It was said by many that the unusual tea of the inner allies of Elder Home was not so much good as unforgettable. People gave it as gifts.

Mina was tired from learning and wanted a break. She knew now that the tea trade was her true calling, and she was learning at a pace that even Captain Javier al-Rasheed admitted, whatever his inner demons might be, was amazing, but she had noted that her productivity had started to slow after forty days of constant work, buying tea and learning the trade of tea tasting and mixing at night.

So her teacher and tea grower, Entieax, had agreed to give her five days off for the festival as long as she treated this also as a learning experience. A tea merchant, he said, was only as powerful as what he knew. Ignorance was punished in this world not by the censure of a supervisor, but by being discarded from the tight-knit world of tea masters. So today they would take in the sights of the festival and learn from the people around them. The point of the lesson, visited upon her before they left the hill cottage, was that people lived in many ways, and their ways were complex. It was important for a tea merchant to understand them without judging them if the tea trade was to be carried out. Judgement dulled the magical edge of a tea master unless the skills of objective thinking were carefully considered under a lens of relentless self-criticism. Or at least that is what Entieax said.

Their lesson done, and the eve of the festival showing the flashing blue green lights that were in the northern sky, Entieax led Mina onto the veranda of the tea college steps and looked out at the hillside where the crew of the *Remarker* was billeted. Her ship, she was now surprised at how possessive she was of it, sitting in anchor looking in better shape than just a week ago. Below her in a slanting field, she could see Major Standish yelling at the top of her lungs to her marines, who were working with pike staffs whose metal heads had been removed and left on the ship. In another space under a veranda of canvas, crew of the *Remarker* planed wood, sewed sails, remade barrels and crates, and in one place were working on a giant log that somehow would become the ship's spare mast, although how that would happen, she could only guess.

Entieax had an endearing ugliness, sort of like a frog with glasses and a felt plug hat, a belt and suspenders to keep his voluminous pants correctly positioned on his oval body, expressive eyes on a mobile face with a wide slash of a mouth. He stopped to look on the antics of the crew below and laughed to what he probably felt was himself, but he was incapable of subterfuge or subtlety. "We were surprised you chose to spend as long as you have with us, or to trade as much as you have traded. Most merchants want one thing, get a little, and race away."

Mina smiled to herself at the jovial tea master's earnest curiosity. At most ports, the captain gave them careful instructions not to trust the locals. They may be trustworthy, but often they were not. In any case though, the crew could go wild. Corporal Gillingham buried Piper Hodak into a flower bed up to his neck and called him a pansy when they were both drunk, which took some apologies to the owner of the flower bed, and Lineman Dinwaldi married three fire dancers on Cottle by accident, but luckily that was only a fine and an "unmarriage" rather than a mortal sin, and besides they all though he was a female. But he just shrugged. "There are no worries at this port," he had said.

"The captain has designed the first half of our voyage to end here. He planned each purchase in our hold to be sold here," she told Entieax.

"Then he must have been taken with this place when he first visited it," The tea master said.

"Captain al-Rasheed was here before?" Mina asked.

"He called himself something else then, but yes. He was the commander of a small packet blown off course, on a courier mission. A dashing though taciturn man. He broke many hearts when he left for the training sunrise." The master replied, "My own daughter, Owsla, had a feeling for him, which made me cross at the time, but he left in honor and she found her own love on the island. I heard he married a Princess. Is this true?" He motioned to an open bald up the hill where Mina realized the captain was sitting, looking at the *Remarker*. He had a book in his hand, a pack by his side, and a bottle of something near at hand, but he did not seem to be moving. He was in one of his trances.

"His wife is the Queen of our land, Nazira." She looked at the froggish man. "That is why we are here. Our ship has sailed to other shores, fought great evil, saved lands from destruction, and returned to its home to find wars raging and our own caught in the fight. I think Captain al-Rasheed knew we needed a time to rest. Our ship, and each of us. I needed to finish my studies and truly claim my mastery. The marines needed to train the new recruits, work out the demons they carry from the horrors of the war. And with men and women of oaken hearts, the ship is also of wood and though strong, needs to replace its structure. I think the captain considered many places, and found yours to be the best."

Entieax smiled. "Our benefit, and I have never heard of a trader staying through festival."

The winter had brought a touch of frozen cold to Elder Home, but the hot springs that surrounded and interpenetrated the main town still bubbled and steamed. The cold sensitive Sun Finders of the crew and the older Elder-kind of the community had taken to the warm water pools in numbers, but so had many of the others in the village who simply chose to enjoy the contrast between bracing air and aromatic, naturally heated baths. Around the hot pools vendors had set up their wares on tables, and had small fires burning to cook tea, beet soup, spit fish, and hard-boiled eggs with hot sauce.

They walked down the hill to the river that flowed from the forested highlands, and then into the hot water district where the festival was celebrated. Costal families from around the island had come and set up camps on the cliff-sides north and south of town, building shelters from wag-on-carts full of boards that had been designed sometimes a hundred years before. The cabins were amazing structures covered in hand-painted numbers and enameled in bright reds and greens, and apparently easy to build as the small clusters of them had gone up nearly overnight. More coastal families had arrangements to stay with friends or family in the main town, and the entire affair took on a trade-faire like experience.

Entieax used a cane to walk and pointed out facts about the village and the campgrounds that had sprung up around it. "Masters Edgewater and Silverlike keep the hot springs clean, so they are considered the "owners" and bathers tip them, while the venders pay them a small charge to park their wagon-carts." He waved at the crowd enjoying the springs and many waived back. "When the weather closes in and the fields and fish pens freeze, the work starts to slow, so people will start to make things just to sell at the festival."

At a tea stand, Entieax bought two teas from a vender named Walkhome. He paid for it in little slips of paper pulled from a small wallet of fine leather. Even that was an oddity since Mina had seen many transactions occur with no paper at all, just notes in a book.

"Tell me of the paper you traded?" Mina asked.

"Ease of accounting," Entieax replied. "Bimini work with life points, but for most people of the outer villages, they do not come back here except for festival. At the end of festival, they will use the paper, we call it *soldi* or *argentu-cartum*, to purchase supplies, settle debts, arrange for marriage *geldm* and give some to people who look after their interests here in the port town. I applaud you in seeking this information out. A tea merchant, to be effective, has to know what transactions affect people."

"Such as?" she asked.

"People of all sorts transact for food, shelter, clothing, safety, warmth, love, sex, power, respect, and futurity. It is a giant web of exchange. Each of those transactions can be affected by the others and can be understood at some theoretical level. And do not try and look for the money in each transaction. Only a fool tries to see exchanges as something where pennies rule, something I learned when I arrived here to teach at the academy. Love can be traded for safety, power for respect, sex for shelter, and so on, and never one penny can change hands."

Mina asked, "Like life points?" She stopped and looked at a running race being set up with bets being figured in small stones.

Entieax said, "Well, if I wanted to understand the Lands of Cycus I would know about silver. Here you may find some of the traders understand silver, but most do not. Merchants often come here for our tea, hearing we do not use money, and never understand that their offers of handfuls of metal aren't useful to a people who reject almost all metal. They can become quite angry. And we are quite easy to get along with. Others on this island, the Forest People, do not understand at all that there are attitudes other than their own, and do not react well to threats. I would be careful with equating Bimini cultural motives with these foresters, and if you do not understand us, you will never understand them. I tell other traders this, and sometimes they listen, often not. Instead, I would, if I were you, just assume all motivations are alien until they are understood."

"So understanding that two people run the hot springs is important?" She had wondered why it was an issue.

They walked down among the small pathway where play tents had been set up. The Bimini were accomplished panto-mimists and their small plays—performed to a dozen people in a large tent—were warm fun, with everyone packed in and lime-lights carefully reflected by giant abalone shells into the space, giving the actors alternately ghoulish or comical tones.

"As important as knowing where a book is on the ground. Maybe it is of no importance. No tea merchant, though, counts small facts as unimportant, not if they want success. To create a tea, you understand the ingredients. To sell a tea, you understand the buyer. To sell a tea again and again, you give the buyer what they want, using ingredients that they prefer, and build a product that they can count on no matter where they buy it. Making the tea without considering the nature of the ingredients is to ruin your effort." He walked up to another vendor and purchased a pair of baked flat fish. He offered one of the fish to Mina who accepted it, and a pair of fish tongs made of a light wood. In turn, she borrowed some of his paper coins and purchased two winter-fruit tarts. It made a satisfying meal.

Mina had put her tea and food on a small table to allow her the use of her hands. They both sat and she said, "You speak of hitting the limiting factor of your tea trade, but also you talk about the 'blush of the flavor.' What if you ruin the 'blush of the flavor'?"

He looked up from his fish. "Each tea gains a taste that has harmonics in it. Bitter to sweet, biting to soft, wild to civilized, bracing or silent. A pure tea, what you call a varietal, grows someplace, by someone, and that is how its character is created. Blended teas, such as we teach here, take two or more varietals and mix them into one, often in a finer apothecary grind than a normal tea is subjected to. But it can become a brown tea, amazing varieties ruined by over-thinking the mix."

"What does that mean?" she asked.

"A 'blush of the flavor' is the taste that says to the drinker, this is tea, and it is special. Alternately, it is the feeling that a well-worn robe has, the filling of an expectation that one is comfortable with. Each great tea does these things and that is why they are great. A greater tea is a surprising masterpiece of harmonics that change as the drink is savored. It is the mouth feel of the hot sip, the throaty feel of the third drink, the brace of the drink as it nears its end. A fruit drink is a slap of sweet and tart into the face, but tea is subtle, an orchestra over the hill that one's senses train themselves to detect." He stopped for a second, then said, "A fool once mixed all of the varieties together, a lifetime of work, to make the ultimate tea. What she made, when it was tasted, was described as a brown tea. All of the great flavors averaged into an unremarkable and almost undrinkable mess. A lifetime wasted on nonsense. When a mad person seeks the ultimate tea, we call them seeking the brown. Instead, there is no ultimate tea, merely teas whose character are above reproach.

The Elder-kind and Mina stood from their meal. They walked on through the festival, passing the Darkfather and the supercargo, Suela Fleet handling a tea exchange, taking in the odd pieces of paper and handing out boxes and bundles of raw varietal tea to young tea apprentices from the academy to work with in their studies. The students yelled a view-hallo to the Master, and he waived his stick at them.

Indulgent minders, the warriors of the island, looked on with humorous boredom at the young students, many of which were foreign born, came to attention when they passed, then returned to their watch. Entieax, as a grand master, was recognized everywhere they went.

They crossed the bridge over the river to the fields and fishponds, and stopped to watch a curious sight. There was a boisterous sporting conflict on a frozen pond involving wooden brooms, their ends frozen as well, a large leather bag stuffed with straw, and apparently, a significant chance of broken bones. Entieax watched the game with every sign of being fascinated, ignoring Mina for a while.

"What about elixirs?" Mina asked the tea master.

"I do not know what cures exist or how they work. Remember, we are talking a subtle thing, tea blending. Tea is healthy, or we would not drink as much as we do. So is winter-berry juice though. Unlike wine or beer, there are no sour effects from tea. It is just what it is. I know your captain is seeking the ultimate tea, the tea that can only be found on the shores of the farthest land, protected by demons of great power. That is nonsense," he said.

Mina said, "He does not seek it for himself, but for another. If it is being sought as a cure, it is not a cure for the *Remarker* or our captain."

"It is a foolish thing to seek. If it exists, it is not what it seems," Entieax commented, his bullfrog features growing dark.

"We are merchants, it is a product, a customer wants it. Perhaps it is a cure?" Mina said hopefully.

The old master, grandmaster in all but name if he had been in the core islands, waved into the air. "Mina Eversail, you will be a true tea master soon, with my sign on your dissertation and your first publication in the hands of all other masters. There is no magick, and there is no elixir of magical cures for human ailments. Unless you consider death a cure, which I do not. There are so many mysteries that exist. Where does a soul go when the body dies? Does the Allfather Universalis wait for them at the crossroad to translate them from this world to the next? Many monks believe the Allfather can bring a being to the Yshva, the world beyond the world where beings exist merely as souls. If this were true, where does a being with no soul go? Can this elixir, this magical tea, rebuild a broken body, stitch together a spirit, and save a tormented mind if it is powerful enough? Nonsense, better stick with what we can understand, and tea can be understood"

Mina looked across the hot springs and understood what the Elder-kind tea master was saying. Two cadaverous old men, both ancient Elder-kind, were playing the ball game with screeching delight. They were slow, bent, on their last years, but they were happy with the limits of their bodies. They effected makeup, hid their loss of hair, and ignored the march of time for the now they enjoyed as respected wiselings of the Bimini. When they tired, they dropped out and took food and drink to the sidelines where they watched children too small to play in the game. "The games are fun to watch."

Entieax was distracted as he watched a tumult of villagers in the distance and heard growing voices. "Yes, they are." A number of villagers left the main group and were approaching, "Enough about this foolishness of the ultimate tea. Let us see what this is."

The three youths at the head of the group were guards who protected the main entry to the village. One stepped forward and said, "Forest People are at the gates."

Entieax nodded and said to the youths. "Tell the minders to not worry. If the Forest People were going to attack, they would not show up at our front step." Entieax called one of the youths over and whispered in his ear. The boy returned a short time later with an object wrapped in jute.

Entieax turned and handed the wrapping to Mina. Inside was a cheap, rusty estoc with a rope-wrapped handle, looking like a weapon that might be used by a poor farmer and stored buried under a dung heap. Mina smiled wanly and tried to keep up her proper face so as to not offend the Elder-kind, but Entieax laughed.

"Do not feel bad. We have no metal, nor permit any on the island that is not from the ancient past. None of my kith will touch metal, but the restriction does not lay upon you should the worst occur. The estoc is one a man brought to the island long ago and it survived past him. Do not show it, merely carry it with you," Entieax said.

Mina nodded. The weapon was truly amazing. She turned and, hiding it from view, slashed it through a kata called the crashing waves, and immediately knew this sword was not a farm blade, but before its want of care had been a fine instrument. It sang through the air with ease, it seemed eager to help her put it in the right place, and the uncomfortable looking rope on the handle was anything but. It felt like the finest Dyeen grit-cloth. In fact, she found that the sword was actually hard to lose even when she tried to throw it to simulate a misstep.

She looked at Entieax. "This is a fine gift, why are you giving it to me?"

Entieax smiled with his eyebrows. "It was mine in my youth when I left the island, and returned with me. A tea merchant who is to be an adventurer should have a sword. I am no longer an adventurer, just your friend who wishes you to be properly equipped. The sword should not be on this island. It should leave, and you would honor me to take it."

"Thank you, friend Entieax," Mina said.

Entieax motioned for her to follow him to the gates where the Forest People were waiting. He stopped for a second and said, "No word of that. I have had it too long, and its gifting is a relief." He turned back and hurried down the path.

They rushed from the center of the village and out along the main bridge and outer causeway. When they arrived at the end of the final bridge, they found five of the village's stronger minders: giant Elder-kind with stone axes in their hands. Before them stood three thin people, diminutive against the towering Bimini, with small bows, pale skin, blond hair, and white teeth that almost shined in the fading light. One said, *"Me Devious-deryavan li gundê we dît."*

"They are wilding Forest People with an oak branch, do not fear, Mina." He turned and said to one of the minders, "Go find Javier al-Rasheed and have him meet us at the gates." Entieax walked up confidently to the Forest People and said, "Do you speak in the Bimini?"

The wildings looked on without understanding.

"Tu çi dixwazî, xwedîyê pelên darê?" He then said in common to Mina. "I am not very good in their tongue. I either asked them what they wanted, or gave then the price of winter-fruit."

"Em xwediyê pelê gûzê ne ku ji we re ji xerîbek di nav me de bêjin," the one holding the branch of oak leaves said.

Entieax nodded. "They have seen your captain and they have brought us an oak branch to say something is strange, and since there are two strange things, the appearance of a man who they knew to the island, they wonder if those strange things are connected. I am actually doing a bit of paraphrasing since they are not the easiest to communicate with.

Javier al-Rasheed appeared behind them. "You called for me, Master Entieax?"

"You know the Forest People from before?" The tea master said.

"Yes, you know I do. I spent several weeks with them," he said. Mina thought the captain looked rather naked without his talwar or his cockade. He wore plain deck shoes, canvas pants, a tunic, and a simple ship's jacket.

"More than most people even in my village, unless they have undertaken the ceremonies. You did that, did you not?" Entieax said coldly.

"Against your advice, yes. What do they say?" Javier asked. "Is that an oak branch in the Chief's hands?"

Entieax nodded. "Someone has them worried. They are here to ask a favor."

"I am not a linguist and do not speak their language well," Javier said.

Entieax looked at Javier and said, "They consider favors requested and given to be honorable only if no payment is demanded. They would say they do not trade for a sip of water. They called for you in your old name. And they say a stranger is in their forests. The two must be connected."

"I understand," Javier said. The Forest People's emissary and Javier al-Rasheed began to speak in an animated fashion. A lot of words were being said, with little communication. After about an hour he stood up and walked over to where Mina and Entieax sat. "They have two issues. A stranger has been spotted. They are watching him, but they cannot explain how he came to the island and asks if he is one of mine. He is not. They also have had a poor harvest and they fear the signs in the forest mean a poor spring as well. They saw us trade with you for food, and want the same from us.

They will give us their hidden teas and ask for our tea master to sit in their ceremony of renewal."

Mina said, "Entieax, you and my captain have both been through this, have you not?"

Javier al-Rasheed nodded.

Entieax said, "It is not fitting for more to attend than should be present. I told your captain many years ago not to attend, and he now agrees with me it is beyond the ken or healthy viewing for one of us. They ask for you as the tea buyer. Either that is shrewd, or superstitious, I know not which, but I tell you now that I will not permit you to go.

He turned to the Forest People and spoke to them, and they left with blank faces.

Mina said, "It would be important for me to go, yes?"

Captain al-Rasheed said, "No. They are not children. They know what they are doing, and that what they ask is too far for what they want. We will gather food and leave it in the trading glens, and they will take it and leave tea. There is no need for you to take the ceremony."

Mina was displeased, "Why not let me go, Captain, is it dangerous?"

Entieax replied, holding his hand on the captain's chest, "The ceremony is sacred to them. They consider it an ancient and feral sort of sorcery, but you would not understand it, just as myself and your captain did not. Our tea trade that protects us and keeps us connected to the world depends on the tea harvested by the Forest People and traded to us for crafts and food they do not make. It is essential to the Bimini, but a wrong move in the ceremony would mean disaster, and a wrong move is such a strong possibility."

Mina said, "So it is dangerous?"

Javier al-Rasheed replied, "Dangerous and extremely volatile. I would ordinarily call it evil. You cannot go, Master Eversail."

Mina nodded and said, "thank you, Master Entieax, Captain al-Rasheed." She turned and went back to her tent on the side of the hill.

She was of three minds on the matter, and she lay down and thought. An Elder-kind like Entieax could simply be concerned about losing the power that dealing with the Forest People gave him. His own villagers relied on him trading with the Forest People. The Elder-kind could be hurt if she made a misstep with these forest creatures and their ceremonies.

Captain al-Rasheed presented another view. In the past months she had connected parts of a puzzle that led to her understanding that the playboy tea merchant was somehow injured. At first, the pieces could have just been what was obviously the verve of a captain taught to fight for his crew and protect them from unneeded risk. He did not see Mina, not yet at least, as a warrior his equal as she did not show her skills in that field because it made it harder to buy and sell tea. Of course he would hesitate to send her into the wild forests to deal with a people noted for their sudden savagery in protecting their homes. And indeed, why ask for her, and how did they know she existed? They were apparently watching the village, and knew how a tea trader operated. She was just the person they identified as the one who could give them what they wanted.

Now though, after her intense experience learning tea trade, Mina saw that Javier al-Rasheed was not a tea merchant at all. He was the captain of a ship owned by his impossibly wealthy wife who really did not have to make any money at all. If he failed, he still returned to an indulgent Queen.

It was dark when she made up her mind. She would go the ceremony and ask for forgiveness later.

Mina put on a dress made from linen and a woolen coat, along with boots made from canvas soles with percha rubber and cleverly ridged for grip. There was snow on the ground in the forest, so she got up and took from a communal stand racquets and binders for snowshoes, with clever wood and hemp locks that her boots could be slipped into and ratcheted tight. She tied her sword to her pack. She considered not carrying it, but the captain and Entieax had both shown strength to the Foresters and advised not to see them as lesser beings. They were adults, armed ones, and a blade hidden on her person could be an important holdout for her escape if it came to be an issue.

She left her tent and snuck like a thief in the night to a dark bit of roadway near the forest edge. In the distance, by the light of the festival, she saw another set of people sneaking into the darkness. It was Darkfather and Standish, furtive and stealthy, setting out from the north gate of the town. Mina decided it was not her concern, so she dove into the forest.

She was not surprised when two forest people met her almost as soon as the woods closed in. One of them bowed and said the word, "Leke," while tapping his chest. The other said nothing. They motioned for her to follow them.

The trip through the fens and into the heavier woods was slow. Snow was on the ground, sometimes thick, and though the runners knew how to avoid drifts they moved slowly even through the lighter snow runs. The forest was truly trackless, except for occasional animal spoor. Occasionally the spoors caused excitement among the Forest People. At one point they turned to follow a track, hopefully to bring back both the stranger and food, but the track was lost and they turned back onto their course.

What interested Mina the most about her guides was that each runner was very spiritual in their manner, which was obvious despite her limited understand of them. Occasionally, they would reach a place and become silent, then touch a tree or pick up a leaf and nod over it like they were casting a mystical orison. Their experience in the forest was a type of semi-religious canticle, and they seemed to believe that their magick was important enough to modify their track occasionally. At a stop, they took out strips of some sort of pemmican and made a small fire, then prayed over the meal. Leke passed her a rice ball that must have come from the village as well as the small meaty morsel, and gave her a sack of water to drink from.

As they ate, Leke smiled at her and said in common, "You stranger. Very important to change the face of the gods. I help, yes?"

She did not understand, but replied a utilitarian, "Yes."

"I cannot say you do. You ask I tell. If you feel, you do, that is the gods, but I help you do right. Talk if want. Answer, yes?"

Mina smiled wanly. "Sure, Leke. What if I do wrong?"

Leke replied, "Cannot. The birds whisper rumors and you here. Stranger is here. Gods expect. Say punish or aid."

"I do not wish to do wrong," Mina was appalled by the trust Leke had in her. Or what seemed like trust through the language barrier.

Leke smiled in silence.

"What of this other stranger?" Mina asked.

Leke shrugged. "Words. Is he evil? Evil man walks. He dead. He walks and air moves around him, but he dead. Much of evil."

As they walked and Mina's two companions continued their reverence of the forest, Mina finally decoded some of their genuflections. It occurred next to a huge rock covered in detritus. They stopped and threw leaves on it, then covered their eyes and muttered prayers. Mina stepped forward and wiped some of the leaves away and was shocked to find shiny hematite under the dirt and leaves.

She jumped back, stumbled over a branch, and landed in a pile of rocks. Her landing caused more stones to be uncovered, and she recognized with her limited understanding of minerals, apostate placer deposits of rutile and cassiterite. *What was this place,* she thought. *How could this place exist under God's eyes without being blasted from existence?* She backed away from the apostate minerals and cried out, causing the two Forest People to come to her aid.

Leke said, "Fear yes, no fear." It was a confusing concatenation that seemed to suggest they understood her fear but had the issue under control.

Mina shivered. She looked at the other Forest Runner and saw she was staring at her. There was no sign she understood anything, just the toothy smile they both put on when the language broke. Mysticism and smiles. Yet she also glanced at the stones and her smile would wane a little. She was not dumb or primitive, and neither was Leke. They knew the evil they lived among, and bravely fought it each day.

Then, as they walked, Mina kept seeing it. The whole forest was covered in placer metals, like the devil of children's stories had vomited out the black soil and into it had placed endless tonnes of exposed metals. Not just one find in a cluster of chaos, but dozens of different minerals that would take a priest with their books days to identify, if any wanted to walk in this land at all.

And the apostical would come here also, armed and ready to tear out the forests and kill these creatures for what was present in their black soil. Then God's fire would rain down from the sky. There was no doubt about that. Mina was not a theist by any means, but she was so shocked that her mother's warnings of fire from the sky were too damn reasonable to rejected. Sure, metal from underground avoided God's gaze, but the only thing that protected these people was their beloved forest and their piety.

The Forest People's village was a cluster of conical huts made cunningly from wood. Wisp lights were hung about the village in an amazing collection, leading Mina to truly believe Forest People were all magical in their thinking. On closer inspection the lights were balls of moss that glowed and not magical at all. Still, it had an effect on her after her walk through the forest.

Leke led her to a hut near the center of the village and showed her inside. Bright foxfire sat in what would have ordinarily been a fire pit, seeming to warm the space with its green light. A young girl came in after them and laid out a dress of cunningly woven flowers to be worn over Mina's current clothing. Leke returned in a breastplate of bark, his body oiled and naked. He said to Mina, "You follow."

Outside, the village was passing by, all ages, all silent. They were heading to a well-lit circle of oak trees about five-hundred meters from the village. Many had foxfire torches, and others were bedecked in lightning wisps and other magical-seeming plant fibers that glowed in random colors in the darkness. The night was deep, and the evening would be cold with no clouds in the sky, but she could feel the collective warmth of faith that was keeping the villagers, many without heavy clothing, warm on the freezing night.

Leke walked next to her. He was a strong young man, sure and confident. He said to her, "You understand me? You hear?" She nodded. He was actually quite adept at making himself understood to her with a few words.

They entered the tree circle and Leke directed her to a place near a wooden pedestal. A true fire and several foxfires where lit, while wisps and tingles danced with wild abandon in a cold breeze. Dusk was falling, and in the growing silence of the woods a group of Forest People began to drum on wood tympani drums. Gourds filled with liquid were being passed about. Most of the Forest People began to dance, at first randomly, but then in circles, holding hands as they moved around the trees. Occasionally they would break out for solo dances, or would pull others from the dance and perform highly ritualized acts of gymnastics or would grasp another dancer in a brotherly or sisterly embrace.

One of the male dancers in antelope horns stopped in front of her and began a gyrating display that was beautiful to behold. He was whipcord thin with taut muscles, sharp eyes, and a keen anticipation of the syncopating beat of the drummers. As he danced, Leke said, "Eyes the heaven."

"Yes, Leke," she replied.

The dancing and noise ended suddenly and a woman stepped into the circle. The Forest People of Bimini did not age. They could grow infirm in their last years, but mostly they looked young by the standards of most of the people of the Halo. Humans aged, and when they did Mina found them lovely. They grew lines on their faces that each told a story. Their slow degeneration was graceful, like how an oak would bend and drop leaves as it aged. She had been born on the tiny island of Last Eden in the South Wind Drifts, and had seen people from the outer islands to the South who shared some of the inward youth of the Forest people..

A majestic woman dressed in flowing vines, flowers, and a shift of loose-spun fiber stepped into a pool of light and the wild dances stopped. She began to speak in the language of the Forest People. As she spoke, a man in a deer hat and garlands walked into the clearing followed by seven young women in blue with torches. Mina heard the crowd gasp in awe. The man in the dear-head hat bowed to her, to the woman in the flowing vines, and then the seven women started to sing.

As they sang, each one stood forward and said strange words, *Mammach, Obsulie, Klasta, Coinhar, InBoldi, Yesha,* and *Gove.* Each yelled word was repeated by the crowd. A plate of bannock wedges wrapped in linen was offered to each of the young women, who took a slice, then the majestic woman walked forward with her torch bearers and slowly unwrapped and lifted each bannock. When she had peered at each one, she returned to the third woman and took her bannock from her, showing the crowd that it had been burned on the bottom. She then escorted her forward to the fire, as did the man wearing the deer-head, and as three, they threw the bannock in. The other six young women surrounded them and led the crowd in singing as they began to sing with the crowd.

The eerie song in its foreign tongue was sung as a paean, a cadence of falling and rising tones. The drums were silent, but Mina could feel the magical energy become explosive in the clearing.

Mina carefully scanned the crowd as she walked. There was so much joyous singing flowing through the clearing that she had begun to feel an elated energy, but then she observed the Forest people and noted they were thin; disease was taking hold. Babies in the arms of mothers were dying. Children were not thriving. The elderly were starving themselves in the hopes of feeding the younger Forest People. It was clear the people were dying of famine.

Then Mina saw a flash of a blade, and the man in the dear-head fell, bleeding out from a neck wound delivered by a stone knife wielded by the young girl. The forest went silent, and the man died on the forest floor.

The next morning, Leke led Mina out of the forest to a small dale where a frozen book sat silent in the sputtering cold rain of winter. The captain, Javier al-Rasheed, and Master Entieax of the school for tea stood bundled in oilcloth and thick clothing. They had a fire, not of Firefox or glimmer, but of real flames built from wood, and on it was a huge copper kettle held in place by a tripod of iron. The fire was built under a canvas half-tent with its walls pulled up, built on poles of ash. It had a chimney of leather to vent the smoke into the sky.

The Forest person looked at the metal of the tea pot and tripod with concern, but ripped his eyes away and yelled out, "*Niha ji ayînan derbas bûye, çawa dibe bila bibe bikeve axa me.*"

The captain merely nodded and said, "*Erê.*"

Leke turned and left back into the forest.

Mina saw that a bundle of clothing sat tied into a waterproof wrapper from the ship was on a pile of firewood covered with a canvas top. The captain sat down on a tree stump and motioned for her to take it. She did, retreating to the forest to change since her people had a strong personal modesty taboo, and returned to the fire for warmth. Entieax sat as well when she returned, and motioned to a third stump for her to use.

The captain served out tea in one of the Bimini's wonderful stone cups, which had been wrapped in jute to protect the hands from the hot liquid. He, himself, had a cup of tin from the ship, more metal that she had not seen since they arrived. Entieax was drinking from a horn cup dropped from the sheep each year after rutting.

Mina took her seat, placing her pack and the wrapped estoc that Entieax had given her at her feet, and took the tea into her hands. It was warming, as was the fire, and she realized that she had never had better tea. "What is this tea?" she asked.

"Junebug," the captain replied.

Mina looked at it in wonder.

For an hour, maybe more, they sat watching the fire. When it threatened to dim even a little, Captain al-Rasheed went and retrieved dry wood from under a canvas tarp and built it back up. The heat was what she needed desperately. When she was finally warm, she said, "I am sorry, Captain."

"Why?" He asked.

"I disobeyed your orders," she replied.

He considered that, then poured himself more tea. "I cannot give orders regarding the Forest People or the Bimini outside of your duties as a tea master. And if I were a tea master, I would also have sought to learn of a people whose access to the inner mountains of this land gives them access to one of the great and most rare teas a merchant can purchase. Yet you understand why others, Entieax included, would be concerned with your conduct?"

Entieax nodded. "You are no child. You did not enter those woods in search of childish games. And what you learned was not the secret of a child. You are a tea master of *Remarker*," he said. "Yet now I ask, here, do I let you leave this island with the secrets you have learned?"

"What does that mean?" She asked.

Entieax's ugly face looked stricken. "Beyond this glade are four minders. They have order to kill you and lay out your body for the gods to see, if you leave this fire without my first gainsaying it. The Children of the Forest are the children of god. If the world were to know what they hid there, then the apposticle would seek it for the treasure and the religious would seek to burn them down for their heresy. And as they conduct those yearly sacrifices to propitiate their gods in their own way, they would have others, should it be discovered, hunting them with firelocks and flames. You could cause that to happen."

Mina looked at her captain. "Would you let the Bimini kill me?"

Javier shook his head. "No, I would fight to save you. If I was allowed to return to the camp, the marines have enough firelocks on the ship to kill every last person on this island, and Major Standish likely would do this if I could order her to."

"Then this will happen, this play will be played because I went into the woods last night?" Mina asked.

"Two nights ago," Entieax corrected. He drank his tea down and looked seriously at Mina. "Master Eversail, Five years ago a young playboy commanding a navy ship from a land across the Halo visited these shores, and his demons took him into the forests. Like you, he was brilliant and young. Like you, he sought knowledge for the sake of knowledge. Like you, he was forbidden from doing so, and like you, he returned to face me and my minders."

Entieax filled his tea again. "My dear Javier, your tea is absolute swill. Did you get this from some Cycus Vicuna's bottom, or is it dried sludge from the lowest hold of your ship?"

Javier replied, "No, that would be too good for you. Junebug is called second-hand tea for a reason." The captain again emptied his teacup and filled it as well.

"Master Eversail," Javier began, "On the *Remarker*, there are things we dare not keep from each other. We are a commune at sea, a collective democratic dictatorship. Each of us is a disrupted cog in a chain of gears that somehow, makes a crew. When the ship is in the sheets and I yell for a tack, the tack is taken with no argument or discussion. When the storm is over the cadre can argue about the right call all they want around tea. Everyone remembers that they carry the colors of the *Remarker*, the safety of the crew, the honor of our homelands, collective, and our home port, singular. Yet when I tell you that the cadre, as you are one, possess secrets that cannot be told, you must consider this one. In no book can this knowledge be recorded. In no ear can it be whispered. Five years ago a man who was completely unworthy of the secret discovered it through his hubris, but I had to keep it."

Mina nodded. "Yes, Captain, for the honor of myself and *Remarker*. I swear."

Entieax looked at her long and hard, then yelled, "Vidic, you lot go back to the festival."

A voice from down the glen, out of sight yelled, "About time, tea master. We will collect the tent when it is not so stinking cold."

Later, the *Remarker* was warping to its next port when Mina was inspecting the cargo with the crate maker, Masarra Ibn Ahmad. She looked at the crates with a fond eye. They were taut, strong, and carried the tea within them in very good order. "This is good work Masarra," she said.

The small, dark Dartian slapped one. "You can make cheater's crates on a land where they are El-dari like that. No nails, you have to use pegs. More work, but we had time and good lumber. When you sell the tea, transfer it to those kegs from Durkas. Leather banded kegs are always the jakes."

She climbed from the hold and caught sight of the island as it fell into the distances. She turned and looked down at the crate maker, "I will remember that."

CHAPTER XIII

Paroland

I have learned when I write a diary or log in the common language of trade, a *mulahazat alsijil*, to always identify myself and my place in the world, because it may be read by a person who has no idea who I am or my situation in the world. Thus, I am Salvador Longongo, an officer of the tea trader *Remarker*, and I am in the after top sheet of my craft as it completes a flawless warp into the succor of a trade port, but one unlike those found in the main ways of the Halo.

It was the first day of the summer Yallends that *Remarker* hove into view of the islands of Paro. Paro is an archipelago of small, heavily-forested specks of stone in the Northeast Halo that is not a common destination for a traveler in one of the great oceans, but is a place that sooner or later will catch up most long-range cargo ships. If the reader will indulge me for a minute, but the Paro Islands, and its main habitable place of Paroland, have a unique position in the world in that three strong currents pass by, two inbound and one outbound. Imagine the Halo as being controlled by the currents that run east and west, a place where they converge allows for someone to move north and south without relying as much on the intricacies of laborious tacking or other sailing tricks, permitting a few easy warps to move against the prevailing winds and tides.

And it is this reason that Paroland, which had no real industry or natural resources to speak of, became a gathering place for merchants as they transitioned from one part of the Halo to the other. And it was of interest for us as the last point of supply before *Remarker* tossed itself off the maps of humankind in search of a fabled land and its priceless tea.

As we hove into the lee of the islands, I focused in on the busy roadstead using a large range finder and then looked down at the *Book of Merchant Flags*. Each flag of a great trader that flapped in the longshore breeze could be found in the book, and not a few minor traders appeared in the *Remarker's* own extension of the tome. I noted each flag I saw into my log, then yelled out to the captain standing on the top of the cockpit, "*Stammering Princess, Indigo Trader, Everwind,* and *Frisky Abbott* in the near road. *Voyage Respite* and a cluster of eight modulars in the far road. I make *Univariate* in the lee of the smaller island in the far road."

As I waited, I noted that there was a gathering of the crew—anyone not in the yards or ready to haul to on the anchor, larking on the boards, and with the naming of the pirate *Voyage Respite* there was a visual commotion. Their hate was palpable and understandable. I shared it as well.

The captain seemed to note the low growl from the deck but did not call for his second officer to punish the idlers. Instead, he yelled up to me from the cockpit top-stand, "Confirm *Voyage Respite*?"

I could see plainly enough that the ship standing to in the cluster of barges was *Voyage Respite*, but the captain has his reasons and mine is not to question. I raised the range-finders a second time and called out the sight. "VR in circle on red flag over second flag with a musical instrument on red and white." I scanned the ship forward and continued, "Four masts, two drivers and two steers. Center deckhouse with funnel and red stripe. Bright shellac of weathering and roam. Stayed with three anchors, with pinnace swung out."

I stopped my recitation and noted my sight in my log. Another book in my pack was *Hulls and Masts*. Turning to the *Voyage Respite's* page I noted that except for the new wood coats, it was obviously the same ship. I stowed both of my books and looked down at Captain Javier al-Rasheed as he moved to the verge of the top-stand. We stared at each other for a second and I could see he knew the ship was the genuine article. Clearly he was concerned, but wanted me to assure him that the ship was indeed the *Voyage Respite*, a dangerous variable in this port.

I again refocused the range finder and looked again at Lute Cagion's piratical ship. Cagion was not on deck, but his officers were looking at us with the same interest we were looking at them. They stood a long shot with a Serpent but our Marines could clear their deck in a few minutes, I was confident of that. But such a move was suicide to our use of the harbor, and without the succor of the Paro Islands and the port of Paroland would end our great adventure before we caught the first wind out of the Halo. "I confirm *Voyage Respite* carrying the flag of Lute Cagion." Then I paused. "Aistifzaz Aleud," I repeated, as many of the Cycun crew would know the older name from when he was in service to their nation as a sailor.

The captain nodded. He bent over the rail and yelled down to the cockpit steering station. "Commander Nine, put us in the lee of *Frisky Abbot* in the near road, be aware that *Voyage Respite* is in the far road."

"Will comply, Captain," Commander Nine Replied.

I looked at Juave Bonbon, who was in the aft nest with his flag bag ready to fly colors and noted his fellow crew person shaking his head. He was scowling and angry even as he tore flags from his bag in preparation for flying our ship's message. "*Voyage Respite* was a bad name to Salvador and among the crew of *Quest Venture*, my last lash. And the Hates are not above burning that pirate to the sea."

"I am sure the captain is aware," I replied to Juave.

"Luther's pride, the Hates will murder them," Juave commented to me.

I shook my head, keeping my eye on the captain as he worked with Commander Nine and and Alia D'casio to shape a course into the aft berth behind *Frisky Abbott*. "Major Standish has a hand on her staff. She will not let them off the leash that far. Though if I was Captain Cagion and knew the Hates were on my case, and they had the *Remarkers* behind them, I would be sleeping with a firelock in my undies."

Captain al-Rasheed yelled up to Juave, "Fly 'Remarker,' 'Cycus Dominion,' 'trading,' 'captain visits.'"

I bent to help Jauve. I took out the flags for *Remarker* (21), Cycus Dominion (20), and Trading (4), but was lost for a few seconds on how to express 'captain visits' in the flags that were in the bag. Juave noted my confusion and said, "Use number eight, nine, and eleven." I handed him the requested flags which he strung to the flag line. "More of an art than a science," he explained as he worked.

Salvador looked at the lacquered flag box cheat sheet. Eight was marked, 'Meeting.' Nine said, 'Come aboard.'

Finally, eleven was 'Master or Commander.' "Makes sense at least," I replied.

Juave commented, "Not the craziest flag fly at all. Look at *Frisky Abbot*."

Salvador turned the range finders to the trader we were moving up on and noted that the first two flags, at least in his book, were 'Unstable (3)' and 'Drink (25).' I looked back at Juave and shrugged in confusion.

"It means they are drunk," Juave replied.

I laughed. The *Abbott* was a ship out of the central lands and not adverse to spirits like a northern trader might be. "Time to get down to the cockpit," I said.

"Good sailing, brother," Juave said.

I stopped at the rope ladder and replied, "Same to you. What are your liberty plans?"

He replied, "Phiab Tsu Li is off *Stammering Princess*, we can all take call to her."

"Marija wants to talk with me. She and Der Nhia Lo were talking of taking in a fancy restaurant that Lo has an in with because of her diver's plack," I replied.

Juave nodded. "Marija and Mouse have issues."

I paused. Marija had indeed slipped me a note and asked to have some time in the port to talk. The junior officers kept close connections to make sure that flotsam did not wash ashore at the captain's cabin. "What sort of issues?" I asked.

Juave laid out a selection of additional flags and commented with his face turned away. "Not serious, but there is talk below decks."

I considered this. The ship was commanded by a command staff of senior officers, but it was the duty of the lower-ranked decks' officers to listen carefully to a crew who was cooped up for scores of days at a time. A fight in warp could spell disaster. More than one bad actor on the

Remarker—or any other merchant, he wagered to himself—had ended their days drowning in the head or falling from a secure perch in the sheets for want of action by the cadre. It was better to see people with problems off at port to another ship. More humane.

But Mouse and Marija were unlikely candidates for a conflict. Marija Perak was an Aspirate Second Navigator who had rightly taken Mouse under her wing after the young foundling had suffered at the hands of some of the original crew who had remained from *Remarker's* less-savory days. The rumor was, and I had no reason to desire to know the truth-of-the-matter, that at least one of the scoundrels had been shown a special way to clean the head by Marija herself. If so, Mouse had become an outstanding crew mate and the lost sailor was never really missed.

"Do me a favor," I asked. "If anyone asks, say the captain is aware and not concerned with minor issues, and that they are simply a misunderstanding."

"Is that why the Darkfather seems to be asking about Mouse?" Jauve asked.

I looked across the deck to where the Darkfather was guiding one of the cargo lifters in shifting mass for our resupply. As our Quartermaine, he was the second-in-command to Captain al-Rasheed with regard to cargo and profit, sharing his rank with the Major-of-Marines Angela Standish and the First Officer Sunstar Nine. There had been a strain in the upper ranks when he showed up with a foundling, a tiny woman of unknown origins named Adjeness, but that strain has eased as she had found her place in the crew and not relied on the benefits of her seeming patron.

The ship passed outboard of the *Respite*, and then a change-of-sails slowed her progress and turned her inside the channel. The first anchor dropped as she luffed all of her sheets but for an aft driver, which caught wind and allowed Sunstar Nine to deploy two more anchors on-the-fly for a neat and safe stop behind *Abbott*. "I have to get down to the cockpit," I said.

Jauve turned and grabbed his shoulder before he could dismount the nest. "Salvador, you know the captain best. Play it straight for me. Is the top safe?"

I grabbed Jauve's hand and squeezed it. "Have we run onto ground or lost a chest of silver?"

"But the Devious thing…" Jauve replied.

I cut him off, "It is forgotten, you agree?"

Jauve paused, "Just as I was saying."

I nodded. "If a captain brings you home with a fat purse, who cares what bugs crawl about their head, no?"

"As you say, Salvador." Jauve looked little relieved, but only a little.

I nodded and swung down onto the rope ladder to the cockpit-top where the captain and the Mouse waited. I was taken aback for a second as I had not realized Mouse was on duty for port entry, he was such a meek figure that it was common, seeing him in a place you did not expect.

Captain Javier al-Rasheed gave space for me to move into the cockpit, then motioned to Mouse, who took the gangway down to where a cluster of crew waited. I gave a hand salute to the captain, who nodded in return, then unlashed a deck chair and positioned myself at a wooden desk. From my pack I took a scap book and the ships' pencil logs, clipped them to the desk, and prepared my pencil and pens to receive the captain's orders.

The captain turned to the gangway that had swallowed Mouse, straightened himself up, and stood tall when four crew mounted the cockpit top and lobbed up in order before him. Two were a short man and woman with iron-gray hair and eyebrows, along with a creamy mahogany skin tone and flashing blue eyes. The man was named Mock, from the top crew, and the woman was Nilke, a cargo hand. They were brother and sister, and each was escorted by their division heads, Alia D'casio the sailing master and Suela Fleet, the Supercargo. I had not been told to prepare for a mast or promotion, so the presence of the two cadre with their division staff was more of a courtesy than a requirement of ship's rules, and it was obvious why they were here.

The captain looked over the two sailors. "Sailor Mock, Sailor Nilke. I understand that you are from Paroland. If you want, the ship can spare each of your for five days leave to visit your relatives here."

Mock looked at Nilke, who stepped forward at his urging. The crew was tight-knit, and I knew the pair well. Nilke was the most fluent in trade common, and even managed some Eurabaa, whereas Mock was not fluent outside of the language of the top sails, and of course the scatalogicals and blasphemy all sailors learned to use on any ship. Thus, Nilke spoke for her brother often if the need arose. "Captain, the lords of Paroland and the Trader's Rest will not take kindly to our return and will not let us leave except by throwing us to the rocks," she said. "You know the Paro, you visited us."

I could not imagine such treatment by one's own people. If I returned to Longongo, an impossible dream, there would be a month of celebration, and indeed any child of the island could expect a hero's welcome on return. But the people of Paroland were said to be different, made odd by the circumstances of being a trader's safe harbor at the edge of the known world, a place where ships only ported to meet with other traders. The captain seemed to expect the answer, as he immediately responded, "Can your family or friends visit the ship while we are in the roads?"

"We would thank you. A short visit would not make them apostate," Nilka said with her odd accent growing strong as emotion seemed to overcome her.

The captain nodded. "Suela," he said to the Supercargo, "please indent under my account for any food needed to care for the d'Paroland relatives of our crew. Also, with the compliments of the crew, turn over a dozen kilos of what tea they prefer, and any other trade goods they fancy."

Fleet responded, "Yes, Captain, indent for rations to feed our crew's d'Paroland relations and friends who visit the ship. I understand."

"Put a tent on deck for overnight stays, if there are any, and to shield their interactions from sight. Put it in the aft well to give them access to the galley spaces.

Fleet looked at me as I wrote up a quick indent for rations and trade goods, stamped it, then entered the order into the log. I took the indent from the pad of scap, passed it over to Suela, and reloaded my pen with ink. Fleet looked to me and the captain with eyes that I often thought of as worship. For all of his issues that might worry the crew, the current iteration of Javier al-Rasheed was a kindly soul who never hesitated to give what he had to the crew.

Yet Captain al-Rasheed looked distracted. He nodded to Fleet and dismissed her with a nod, allowing her to collect the d'Paroland siblings and take them down the gangway to the aft well. He then looked to Mouse. "Mouse, send the major and the Hate brothers up please." He then motioned to Igor Bosanac. "Igor, five minutes to crew muster, please go below decks and spread the word to the cadre."

Igor nodded and instead of taking to the gangway he pulled off a bollard fixed line and used it to swing to the house top of the galley house. I watched with interest at the acrobatics displayed by Igor in carrying out his orders.

He had been a top crew on *Benjamin's Prize* and was forever trying to relive his younger days in the sheets. Looking at the staid and reliable Fleet leading the quiet and hardworking d'Paroland siblings made me once again appreciate the diversity of spirit that existed on a tea merchant like *Remarker*.

The Mouse waited for Fleet and her crew to dismount the gangway, then waved, and the two Hate brothers mounted the cockpit top with Major Standish. They were marines, so there was always more formality between them and the ship's officers, as if they were part of the crew yet distinct in their formality. I likened it to a great sea beast which had a feral band of predators that rode in its wake. Marines could not exist without the ships and their crews that carried them forth, but they were not of the crew. They were a band apart, always standing back to back, guarding the crew but with their own personal flash. .

Major Standish stood forward and locked her legs and back into strong, rigid stance. I came from a land of smaller people; to me Standish was like a mythical giant: 180 centimeters, 70 kilograms of muscle, blond and light-skinned in a way that northerners rarely were. She wore a perfect uniform that was carefully turned out, a pair of Carver Dragoons in cross draw, and a curved talwar—almost a shotel—on her back. She was a human bolt of God's Fire threatening the ungodly with her wrath, her smiles rare but like a wall, always standing against even the most threatening wind.

And behind her was the Hate brothers. If Standish was the hand of Luther glowing in the fire of god, the Hate brothers were the dark demon-wights of that expressed her wrath. Both of the sergeants were not resplendent in their turnout, but someone had clued them in to appear in their best. Both had their swallowtails on and had chosen blue serge pants and belts that had been cleaned to a shining white. They had side-swords with basket hilts attached to their sides, right and left as the brothers were not the same handed, and their coshes on their belts. They had left their firelocks behind, but I had a bet with myself that each had an array of throwing weapons and maybe a hand lock under their coats. No one who saw the brothers with their hulking mass, 100 kilograms or more, and their great height, 190 centimeters at least, would not give way to them on a gang. But it was also amazing to me how light on their feet they were. If you caught the marines practicing on deck you would be favored with a pair of men who made each move into a predatory dance. Although Major Standish could disarm either one on a whim, it was not an insult to the brothers.

"Captain," Standish said with her customary growl, "Presenting myself, Gunnery Sergeant Hate and Master Sergeant Hate."

I thought again that the captain looked weary, his tired demeanor in stark contrast to the major's angry and pugnacious obedience. He nodded and then looked at the three marines. "Stand at your rest, please. Major, have the sergeants each take one of the deck chairs. We have a few minutes as Sunstar Nine shapes our course into the roadstead and the anchor crew drags our anchors. I want to tell you each something."

"Lute Cagion is in the roadstead," Lobar said with a growl.

Major Standish immediately corrected him, "Sergeant, you will speak when spoken to before the captain."

"Thank you, Major. I do need them to sit and listen to me, with your permission," Captain al-Rasheed said in a sad tone.

"Sergeants, draw deck chairs from the chair-box and set them up before the captain," the major ordered.

"One for the major as well," Captain al-Rasheed added, making the Major frown.

The chair-box held twelve clever folding chairs with seats of canvas and thongs to secure them to the deck if the ship was a-roll. I had secured one myself to write at the cockpit desk. The two sergeants pulled the chairs out and started to assemble them, but made a botch of it. I felt for them, the contraptions were neither easy to unfold nor obvious in their use, but they did make a nice seat for a crew on watch that did not have to remain on their feet. I stood and stepped into the clatter of wooden legs and canvas stays and helped each of the Hates assemble their chairs, then did the major's chair. When the three marines were in their seats, I backed off and returned to my desk, fiddling with my books and pens to avoid being seen as part of the tableaux.

"Lute Cagion and *Voyage Respite* are in the roads," the captain said as if to himself. He braced and looked the Hates in the eyes. "When I was an ensign off the frigate *Miza* in my freshman cruise, I cheated Cagion in a deal. To be fair, he was trying to cheat me and I was a different person then. That is a minor rivalry, and an issue one can try and forget. How many merchant captains have bumped prows in a race for the best position in a market or have taken down another captain's grift? But he and I keep having problems. My taking you and the Tea Master onto *Remarker* made this worse. We have done more than bump each other in ports, it is a dangerous rivalry where blood could be spilled. And that rivalry is now talked about on more decks than our own. '*Remarker* and *Voyage Respite*,' they say, 'Cagion and al-Rasheed' are sailing close to the wind seeking the same path through the shoals. Blood will be spilled is the word on decks across the Halo."

"Their blood," Lobar growled.

The major wound up to blast down the sergeant's defiance, but al-Rasheed shook his head, stopping her silent. "I will try and see it through without bloodshed, but I am afraid that soon there will be a reckoning," the captain said.

There was silence from the Hates. It was not just a lack of a response, but a cold simmering feud on the Hates' faces. I knew and loved the powerful brothers. They were deckers, like me, cadre for the ship who stood together on the docks of Cycus port and threw back the Life Guards as they charged the *Remarker*. They had all seen the shark and knew that the only safety you could find was standing back-to-back with your fellow crew. You ate on the aft deck as a group, stood long watches in warp surrounded by the ghosts-of-the-sea, and lived or died with the fellowship of the cadre and crew. No one, least of all me, saw their angry faces as critique for the captain, but it seemed to put al-Rasheed back, as if he was at fault for their travails.

Captain al-Rasheed nodded sadly. "It cannot happen here or now though, revenge I mean. I can promise you, when it can happen, my sword will be next to yours and *Voyage Respite* will learn that tea merchants are not the weak samuels they think we are." He stopped and looked at the two angry men. "Your brother lays buried in the cruel ocean because of Lute Cagion. You want to see him pay for that. I know that, and I respect that. And I will be your *'adat lili-aintiqam*, your tool of vengeance as we of Cycus say in our old tongue. I ask, though, that you stay your vengeance in this port. No merchant should violate a trade port such as Paroland. There are few enough places untouched by the Sublime Port and not held in the grip of the Great Bank. No tea merchant can afford to lose a neutral place to trade. And this port is our place of succor before we face the greatest challenge of our lives to date. We cast forth from the eddies and currents of the Halo seeking again a lost land. Last time, we did this by accident and the land we found was not found on purpose. This time, we try to recreate that feat without a great storm harrying our way. If we live, we will have to return here before the ship can see its home port again. I need you to restrain your rightful rage, and then plan with me your revenge. Can I ask this of you?"

Lobar Hate looked to Banji. There was a second of non-verbal communication before both nodded. Lobar said, "Major, Captain, we will behave." He stopped for a second, then added, "Our word."

For a few seconds, Captain al-Rasheed looked in each of their eyes and then replied, "your word is your bond. You are not restricted to ship, but you are, of course, forbidden from visiting the *Voyage Respite*—I will also be restricting the rest of the crew from visits to Lute Cagion's ship. There is no need to apply or confirm your offer of bond. It is taken and good as a chest of silver." He then stopped and asked, "Sunstar Nine and Mina Eversail both will have protection during this stay in port, do you want the same?"

The clatter of the anchor stones letting loose on their heavy hempen lines fore-and-aft signaled that the *Remarker* had found its berth. Yells came from the tops as orders passed, and the sails reefed in neat order, with crew rustling to take in and tie them down, each with the confidence of long practice. I looked in admiration at the efficiency and professionalism of the men and women who handled the tall sheets. I was a master sailor who could build a boat from felled trees and cross the great distances of Ocean within the Halo and the Extents. However, the sheets of my small boat were only five-meters tall compared to the lofty tops of the *Remarker,* which yawed in the waves at a lofty 15-meters above the sea. The feats and skills of the sailors who climbed the yards was truly amazing.

As the noise above fell to a calm silence, punctuated only by the sounds of repairs or ribaldry in the other ships in the roads, the Hate brothers politely stood from their deck chairs and bent to folding them. In the midst of the fiddly task, Lobar looked at the captain and said, "we will not need guards. My brother and I…" He looked at the crew clambering in the tops setting the ship to its anchor station.

Banji stepped in for his brother, "Lobar and I need some port-time, Captain, without our elbows getting held by well-meaning hands."

The captain stood from his own chair, followed by the major. "Major, tell the Supercargo to call the crew to the deck for orders. Igor should have them ready."

The major sketched a small salute. "As the captain says." She turned and clapped the Hate brothers on their backs, gently propelling them to the gangway down to the aft well deck. As she hit the deck, the piper, Corporal Hodak began to play 'attend the captain,' on his fife, and there was a sudden low clatter of feet climbing the ways and settling into perches across the ship. Crestwell, the senior able sailor of the top crew started yelling for his people to find places to look down to the cockpit top from the sheets, while Sloan, the steward and senior able sailor, and the carpenter, Castons, took a hand with getting the deckers and cargo hands in place and ready for the captain to speak. The officers and cadre, meanwhile, gathered in the cockpit and on top of the cockpit facing the crew. While the quartermaine, Darkfather, was technically senior among the officers, Sunstar Nine was in practice the officer-in-charge and thus her voice yelled from the cockpit, "Attention to the captain!"

I noted, and not for the first time, how small Captain Javier al-Rasheed looked now, lacking the alternating carefree swagger or the simmering perfection of the previous voyage. He stood away from the railing until the clatter and murmur from the decks and tops fell away, then seemed to shake himself clear of his doldrums and stepped forward to the railing.

"*Remarkers*," he said in a loud command voice, "Paroland is our last harbor before we fling ourselves into the darkness of Ocean, leaving the waters of the Halo behind and seeking a mythical land and its amazing prize. As this harbor is a free port and the people who live here are particular on how ships behave, and as there is a special issue we must protect ourselves from, the standard shore orders are suspended and supplemented as follows."

He waved at the island and said, "The actual island of Paroland is, of course, off limits. If you are new to the sail, foreigners not permitted to climb the bluffs upon which their villages are built. Nor may you interfere with the fishers who tend the shallows or the smaller trailing islands. The people of Paroland host this free port, but do not desire sailors in their midst. You will follow this rule without exception, because if you are taken in the shallows or on the bluffs of Paroland, they will toss you to the lee rocks and there is no way we can stop them."

The captain let that sink in, then continued, "You are, however, permitted unlimited leave, pending duties, to make cross ship visits and to see the floating free port. The only rule I insist on is you keep to your groups and do not go anywhere alone. The reason is that there is one ship in port that cannot be trusted. It is the *Voyage Respite*. Our crew and their crew have not had the best relations. They have hurt our people, and we have bumped dockside. In any other port and any other time, they would walk softly lest they feel the wrath of the *Remarker*, but for this port, at this time, we will steer clear of this squall and expect the worst. If the worst happens, return to the ship no matter who is at fault. On the ship you are safe."

He paused for a second. It would not be obvious from the deck or the tops, but the captain turned his head and frowned deeply. He considered for a second, then turned back to the crew. "If any of you do not want to follow us into the void, I will arrange to pay you off and find you a lash in another merchant without prejudice. What we are going to do next is above what any of you signed up for. Your honor and bravery is not impugned if you chose not to continue with *Remarker*."

"*Kulu alsharaf Remarker!*" Came a yell from a member of the top crew.

A second of silence then some of the marines standing on the galley house top started chanting the old language cheer, "*Kulu alsharaf Remarker! Kulu alsharaf Remarker!*" Then the chant spread and soon all of the crowd was repeating the words, even though half the crew were not completely sure the meaning of the old speech words.

"*Kulu alsharaf Remarker! Kulu alsharaf Remarker! Kulu alsharaf Remarker!*" Over and over the chant went, louder and louder. I could see on other ships anchored in the roads crew start to gather at the wales and cheer the chanting *Remarkers*. Some even yelled "*Kulu alsharaf Remarker!*" in syncopation, responding to each cheer with an answering cheer. Some crews were taking the cheering to respond with support for their own ships, yelling "*alle eare Princess!*" and "*toda honra Everwind!*" The crew of the *Frisky Abbott* must have had drums on deck because they began beating a tattoo out in time with the polyglot cheers honoring *Remarker* and their own ships.

The captain turned around, a tear in his eye, and looked at Salvador. "I am leading them into the darkness of *hawia,* and they cheer me as if I am a hero."

I was the only one who heard the captain, but I did not know how to respond to that.

A few hours later I appeared on deck dressed for liberty. The *Remarker* was busy bringing on food stores and fresh water in trade for luxuries which paid for the rations.

Despite this, the crew was enjoying an unprecedented liberty. A line of crew stood at the inboard lee where a gangway was deployed to allow easy access to a floating side-dock. Rabia Ibn Saludi, the Navigator who was from Cycus and a pair of marines, Cenmenoc Blewett and Hedrok Trevanion, both Dartians with their dark skin and curly hair, looked over the turnout of the crew and checked each person out before they descended to the dock. Down below, Efua Amain Bwendi was keeping the traffic of small water taxies in line, putting crew in reasonable numbers onto each in order of their appearance. The Paroleet, a term for the islanders who worked the port, ran the water taxi with a cutthroat abandon that would have had them urging crew to jump overboard to reach their boats had the marines and cadre not prevented that form of chaos. In our lead rank in the road such chaos was a constant companion for *Frisky Abbott,* as besotted crew dove for taxi service and then returned to the deck from their liberty even more inebri-ated than when they left their ship.

Remarker was not that sort of ship. If the Parolanders wanted to earn money as taxi service, then they could line up and take crew in order that Rabia and Efua chose to dole them out. More than one Paroleet taxi person had been banned from the boat side, and now had to wait for the rain of crew from the decks of *Frisky Abbott* to get a fare.

I saw Eddy Sandals was lining up boxes of soap for carriage to other ships with the help of the Fiddler, the Mouse, and Samson. Fiddler was singing a drive shanty about ships lost in a dolum and husbands mourning their wives lost to the vagaries of the seas of Ocean. It made liberty a bit melancholic feeling despite the party atmosphere. But Fiddler was the voice of the crew on occasion, feeling its pulse and composing a song to carry the feelings of her shipmates to the winds. Melancholy was a device to discharge the ballast of fear, I thought, as the crew would find liberty in a true free port, as chaotic as the docks of Paroland were, a welcome relief.

Effen Lukas Durrell and his daughter Setchi were standing waiting for a boat to the trade port with Igor Bosanac, the Third Officer, and Kwame al-Suchi, the Chart Keeper, all dressed in in their finest with jute shopping sacks in their hands. They looked like a family going on a prayer-day ramble as Salene Hazar, normally the oar tender, helped them on a little coracle for the short journey to the port. A half-dozen of the top crew larked about on deck waiting for their own taxi. Rawda el-Javed was entertaining a group of marines with slight-of-hand and winning a few silver coins in the process. The marines wore regulation undress, except each had adopted a sash onto which was painted the words *'Kulu alsharaf Remarker!'*was painted in rather sloppy Eurabanni script. The baldrics were frogged for talwars, but the weapons were missing. In their place had been hung jute bags with wood toggles to contain small purchases and their coin purses.

Stepping onto the ship from one of the *Remarker's* own boats was a family from Paroland, relatives of Mock and

Nilke. A small touch was that two marines, Wuduck and Pua Fleet, each dressed in their finest uniform with fire-locks—which had been rubbed shiny with linseed and flax oil—stood at right attention as the family members were helped to mount the deck by the aft ladder. At the top, almost dancing in excitement, were Mock and Nilke, who had not seen a relative in the eighteen months since their exile. Benji Sloan and Suela Fleet had a table laden with food and steaming carriers of tea waiting behind them, made in a rush but with obvious pride.

Marija Perak touched my shoulder. "Is something wrong?" she asked.

I turned to her. I had been waiting for her and Der Nhia Lo to take in the finest restaurant in the port. Lo had a plack, or so she said, which would give her immediate entrance to the eating establishment. They had snuck up on me while I was gathering the sights. "I was just looking at our ship-mates," I explained.

"Like... you do not see them enough?" Marija laughed.

"No, I was thinking of how different they all were, but how they were the same as the land I was born in," he replied. "Was it that way in your land?"

Marija laughed. "Diversity but no camaraderie. I grew up in Fortress Vangar, there was a brigade of soldiers sta-tioned there and they never remained in place for long. My parents were scholars in the college quarter. Students spent a few years and moved on. The first extended family I ever had was this ship. You are much admired my friend, both for your intelligence, and for the stories of your land. We all wish we could have been raised like you were." She looked about the crowd waiting for taxi service. "I was drafted out of school to the *Repulse*. Commodore Tarkington was an animal who pitted each of us against the other. The rule of law was thousands of kilometers away. When *Repulse* sank, it was the best day of my life even if it was almost the last day."

Der Nhia Lo came up the deckway and said, "We ready to go?"

Marija replied, "Soon as this next group is embarked." She then asked, "Where were you born?"

"Ni-sho, it's an island in the northeast," he said. "Phiab Tsu Li is from there also."

I asked, "Why do you not spend time with her if you are from the same island?"

"She is a Tsu, it means a master or overlord. I am Nhia, to her people we are less than human. I have never thought to speak much with her. It is easier that way. We would not have anything to talk about, even if she was inclined to talk to me," Der Nhia Lo said with no rancor in his voice.

I replied, "She has never spoken bad of you."

"You may note that it is unlikely she has spoken of me at all. Or of Ni-Sho who is also Tsu. It is not done really," Der Nhia Lo said. She had a formal, almost singing way of pronouncing Eurabani common that was easy to understand, but according to the native speakers on the *Remarker*, made him sound like a dancing master teaching a class in history.

"Now what are you thinking, Salvador?' Marija asked.

"How odd language is," I replied.

Der Nhia Lo laughed. "You are about to feast at the best tea house in this corner of the Halo, yet you ponder the indescribables of language!" Marija Perak joined Lo in mutual humor.

It was funny, in a way. "Trade common is derived from Eurabani. This ship, like many others, speak trade. But because this ship is from a land that speaks Eurabani, many of the crew do not restrict themselves to the common tongue.

Yet this does not cause misunderstanding, but sometimes confusion. Trade common says *'ajaza* for liberty. But you say *'iijaza*, which is actually 'permission to depart' in Eurabani. But the captain called our sojourn ashore *'baeidan ean alaih-timamat.'* That is not common, but old Eurabani and means 'to leave your cares behind.'"

"Thank you for the lecture, my friend. I feel edified already and will have no room for food," Marija said with a laugh.

"But he has a point," Der Nhia Lo said. "How often do our Cycun crewmates add a little impossible to understand aphorism. It can be just noise, but they think they have added an important morsel of understanding for us. Have you not heard Alia D'casio yell *'tuhib fi aliatijah alakhir alriyah alkariha'* at the sails. *'Riha,'* means 'wind' in common, and *'kariha'* means 'dirty or unclean,' so you get the idea of what she means, but she could simply say *'hadha si' riha'* or even *'riha hadha'* in the common and we would get her point. 'The wind is bad.' Yet she turns her invocation against the wind into a spell."

A small boat came aside the floating dock. Efua waved at us and blew his little whistle, signaling this was their taxi to Freeport. I looked out over the softly waving waters of the anchorage and said to no one in particular, "The many ways of humankind are amazing. I remember the first stranger I met, a traveler from the Halo. Never could I have imagined in those days that so many people existed or that they had so many ways. So many ways, as many as grains of sand on a beach."

Marija touched his shoulder, then that of Der Nhia Lo. Here on the far edge of the Halo, facing the prospect of breaking free from the common channels to which the ships and boats of humanity clung, I knew what the mutual touch meant. It was an acknowledgement of the fear that all tea merchants had of the great roiling ocean, and the lonely feeling that each felt in the pit of their stomach as they felt the unsteady deck and the wind-blown weather that scoured their souls and made them wish for the simplicity of their early lives. He reached his hands out as well and they stood in silence for a few minutes. The cockle and its Paroleet driver pushed away from the dock and we started in to the trade port.

The drover yelled, "The scarpers? Or you looking to visit the great ships?" I marveled how the boy sounded like Mock and Nilke in his casual mispronunciation of the common trade tongue.

"Scarpers?" I asked.

The boy started to maneuver the boat by pushing the oar like a fishtail into the water. He view-halloed an adjacent ship, yelling in the lilting language and receiving a reply just a vigorous, then said, "smoke, drink, gamble?"

"The Freeport?" I asked.

"*Sezvakangoita...*" The boy again dodged another water-craft then must have realized his answer was opaque. "Just as *mutengesi murume*, I mean, merchant man. Spend money, make me rich!"

The three tea merchants laughed. "Just as!" I said. "We want the trade port please. Alive, if possible."

No hurricane could have scared me more than the cockle as it transited the roadstead. The placid waters of the protected harbor were busy, but not as busy as a true trade port closer to the core of the Halo. Despite this, the cockle driver seemed to take it as a challenge to cross the bow or port around every small craft in the road as closely as pos-sible. They drove into a shallow and a nearly naked young man appeared at the side of the craft, catching a ride on it, a bag of shellfish on his shoulders.

I looked at the young fisher taking a chance ride with a taxi and laughed, remembering my own days as a youth fishing in the waters of Longongo. Der Nhia Lo and Marija startled, then laughed with him as they saw the passenger.

"Taxi-man," I yelled, "Ask your friend if he will sell us his oysters?"

The child turned to the rider whose arms were drooped over the side of the cockle and said in his singing language, *"Mushambadzi achakubhadhara saga resirivheri remaoyster ako kana ukandibhadharawo!"*

The shellfish diver replied, *"Yakawanda yehove hama mutyairi, asi mubhadharise zvakawanda."*

The boy turned and said as he pushed the ship forward, "fifty for the lot."

I laughed at the larceny. "Five for him and five for you." Still too much, but it was a funny bit of theft the boys were trying.

The taxi-man nodded, took the silver, and the shellfish hunter threw the net sack of oysters into the cockle. I recovered them and said, "have you ever had fresh oysters?"

Marija laughed again and said, "Not likely, but today, I will give them a shot."

Der Nhia Lo added, turning slightly green, "I will have some."

I turned to the Paroleet taxi-drover and said, "Return these to the *Remarker* when you go back and tell the dock master, 'Salvador.'"

He nodded and said, "Very good, merchant."

The cockle careened into the dock of the free port, bounced off its side, and the drover yelled, "Off, off, off." I was relieved to be quit of the suicide boat, and accepted a hand from Marija to mount the teak decking of the swaying dock. We turned down a sedan chair ride up from the dock to the stilted trade town, and instead swarmed up and found ourselves standing in the chiaroscuro colors of bars, merchants, stores, overnight hotels, tattoo parlors, gambling joints, taverns, restaurants, and every other joint intended to separate sailors from their silver. It was like a brown study of what ports usually were, all of the excesses but none of the safeguards. No lurking presence of the Sublime Port could be seen in armed guards or safety patrols. There were no merchant shore-patrol teams that larger merchants set out with brassards and bobby sticks ready to enforce discipline. This was an open port in deed as well as word.

Marija looked at me dumbfounded. "Quite the place." Der Nhia Lo nodded.

"It is liberty all for us," I responded, though I was myself tossed into a sea of doubt. I looked back over the side of the stilted port and saw that our cockle was cast away and wildly pushing and prodding through a hundred other small craft. Then I added, "this is what it looks like when there is no local trade, just long haulers and dockside deals."

Us trio of merchants turned from the dock access and strolled down the main gangway of the stilted trade town and looked into windows whose hatches were propped open to allow just that. A grift store caught our attention with its palm rum, baby tar, cigars, bottled beers and wine, and other consumables not allowed on a ship by any sane captain. If you longed for the altered states that drove the people of the core, you could find the goods to achieve your goals in this port.

The next store was where a sailor could sell their worldly possessions if they needed money, and it looked like a lot had done just that. While some of the Marines would spend their time in dissipation, most of our crew were not much interested in rum or cigars, and gambling was mostly a ship-board habit. But that seemed to not be the norm. The store held all sorts of treasures separated from crew people, from silken dainties wrapped in paper tress holders to dubious captain's rudders containing a lifetime of wisdom, if that was what you could call the achievements of a person who finally ended up selling their life's work here.

The crowd, though, was all flowing to a cluster of tea houses, perhaps more restaurants than simply places to enjoy a drink and a bit of cracker. I looked at Der Nhia Lo with a raised eyebrow and she patted her swallowtail jacket's front pocket and nodded assurance. "Divers have placks that are honored all through the Halo," he said.

It was the music that came from the tea houses, the flashy dancers from Paroland with their spangles and life chains beating out interesting tattoos for the visitors, and more than anything, food not made by their own hand or that of the stewards on *Remarker*. And Paroland had the famous Stave-a-Lot which was their ultimate destination.

There was a large Paroleet bouncer at the door of the Stave, which was reached by a swinging platform from the main way. The tea house was separate from the main drag, built onto what was a barge that itself was fasted to a set of cleats set into a large rock. There was a crowd of merchants waving for attention of the bouncer, seeking favor to get into the house. Der Nhía Lo brought out from her carry bag a palmwood plack-face and waved it into the air. The bouncer caught the sight of plack-face, itself enameled in red-iron and cochineal paint, and gave a wave. The trio elbowed their way through the crowd, allowing Lo to hand the plack over.

The bouncer took the plack and in a thick Paroland accent said, "Diver-woman?"

Der Nhia Lo replied, "I am, you honor the plack?"

"Yes, but you have to take the open table by the spits." He almost growled. "Twelve silver each," the bouncer said as he handed back her plack, motioning to a slit-bank made from frond-bound green wood slats chained to the stays that held the way in place.

Salvador groaned with fake outrage, but when this did not result a moderation of the meal fee he deposited the proper amount of coins into the container. As he put them in, he noted that the box had a tell-tale that could measure the mass of the money so the bouncer could tell by weight, if no other way, that the fee had been satisfied. When the last coin dropped the bouncer stepped aside, pulled the gate-slide away from its stays, and waved the trio through.

The tea house was an immense square barge with thirty tables crammed chock-a-block into a space around a dance floor and orchestra stand. Wait staff, all dressed in the Paroleet swami-dyed bright orange and red, carried servings of fish from a charcoal firepit to the tables. No one ordered with words. The polyglot crowd was faced with Paroleet servers who were renowned for their lack of linguistic ability.

The tea house lacked walls, allowing the crowd on the promanada to see in, while the diners could look out and marvel at the diversity of humanity attracted to the trading post. Their table was next to the wooden spits onto which fish, goats, and great game birds were roasted. Large bread ovens produced land bread on stone-sheet racks, with the produce of the oven being constantly pulled and replaced by sweating Paroleet bakers. The trio of *Remarkers* had barely been in their seats for a second when hot mugs of tea and a loaf of the bread was put in front of them. An oil heater received a stone bowl of gheet which began to liquify to serve as a sop. No words were exchanged. Instead the assumption seemed to be the customer was simply to accept what was put in front of them.

Marija pulled apart the bread and dolled it out. "I never get over how bread is different everywhere you go."

Lo received her portion and replied, "You get used to monster bread on the ship. It makes eating other bread a shock, I think."

"Most merchants do not have the space for a monster or an oven at all! You can sell a ton of yeast bread to anyone who has been at sea for fifty days," Salvador said around a mouth full of bread. Plates of greens covered in goat cheese and sour cream arrived next. "Greens as well. Anything not out of a cask is worth its weight in the finest tea when you have been standing before the mast."

Marija grabbed a woven plate and loaded it with greens. "And who knows when we will see this again. Ocean is wide."

Salvador smirked. "Everyone is feeling the pressure of this next warp. How many captains would cast loose from their tolan-book?"

"And we signed the contract!" Der Nhia Lo commented, her accent coming through in her nervous laugh.

A plate of spit-roasted fish landed on the table, which the trio immediately attacked. Salvador looked at Marija and said, "have you broken with the Mouse?"

Marija looked to Salvador and back to Der Nhia Lo. Her face darkened. Salvador continued, "It stays off the deck."

She nodded. "I do not know what is going on. He started talking about things we had done that we did not do. Same with Jinx—she told me that he had confessed a great problem to her, but the next day she did not remember what the problem was. But I have to say, I am not sure Mouse was wrong that he has spoken to me. I feel like my own mind is hiding things from itself. It makes me nervous."

"How so?" Salvador asked, gathering his fish onto a piece of land bread.

"The Fiddler says she saw us together once on a shore leave, so does Jinx. But I cannot remember it. Then they cannot remember telling me this. Is it my memory that is failing? Or some wytchness affecting the crew," Marija replied.

"Wytchness," Der Nhia Lo repeated, her eyes defocused.

I asked, "if you cannot remember, then how can you be sure anything happened? There is a lot of stress on us all before this warp into nowhere. We are flinging ourself off the map of creation into Ocean where the stories of great storms, monsters from the sky, and burning clouds throwing ash to burning decks are the stories of our parents. But logically it is not just stories, but the problem of navigation. There are few tolans to follow to the extents and a mistake is fatal. But there are no tolans to this island we are seeking, if it even exists. I have seen Captain al-Rasheed's notes, the ancient tomes he is counting on to bring us to this furthest shore and back again to our homes. They do not make a senior navigator overly confident that he can pull it off."

"It is not that, Salvador. I am not one who thinks that the captain cannot make it to this land and back. The Darkfather was talking in the cockpit trying to convince the captain to simply make up a sailor's story and claim the rewards. He refused, and I was happy he did." Marija pushed her black hair off her beautiful olive-skinned face and looked deeply into Salvador's eyes. Her expression was one of burning passion for her words, an almost primal anger that their Quartermaine would question the captain, or that the crew's honor would be for sale in exchange of silver.

He looked over at Der Nhia Lo who nodded and said, "How do you silence a hundred and a score voices speaking in every tea den in the Halo?"

More fish was put on their plates by a server with large skewers. This was heavily spiced and accompanied by local mineral water poured into wooden trade cups. They applied their attention to the new round of food, then I found my attention wandering from the question of Mouse. I took a second to focus again and ask the question that kept flowing in my mind. "If you cannot remember, then how can you tell me this?"

Marija put her hand in her ship's pouch slung across her shore-leave swallowtail. From it she removed a small bound book of scap and passed it to me.

I opened it. Therein, written in a neat hand of Emporian with its block letters and diacritics, was her diary. I turned the book to an early page and read with difficulty an account that Marija had penned of a fight with her boss-on-the-deck, Robbi van Guerster. I closed the book and slid it back to her. "You have been reading your diary?"

She nodded. "I must have been frustrated at my memory, because I wrote in the back leaf to read it again if I did not remember when Mouse and I spoke last. Each time I reread it I put a mark." She opened the book to its last leaf and showed me the note and the mass of square figures used in Emporian like the trade common uses a t. He looked into her eyes after staring to the markers, like a graveyard filled with blank grade stones. "How is that possible?"

"It is possible," I said, "because something is indeed happening beyond our knowledge. You do not drink. Your duties are performed well. Nothing in how you carry yourself would suggest you mind is broken through extravagance or disease."

"Which leaves wytchness or the gods…" Der Nhia Lo said in a low voice.

I stopped at that comment. "Have you ever read the *Heshuan*?" Every northerner who spoke Eurabanni native would have read the religious tome. But a person from the core like Marija would only have read it in a university. As he suspected, she shook her head 'no.'

"I do not deny the gods like some," I started, "but I also do not immediately believe that the gods can be understood. Not by me at least. Why do they throw God's Fire at us? Why do they create great waves in the ocean to destroy our ships and drown our loved ones? Why do they even care about the people of Ocean and those of us who dwell in the Halo?"

Der Nhia Lo said, "Listen to the Cycus-borne and it may seem like you have read the *Heshuan*."

I laughed. It was true that when someone spoke high-Eurabanni instead of trade common they tended to sprinkle their statements with the older tongue in which the the *Heshuan* was originally penned. *"Alalihat tadeu alsalam,"* said to acknowledge the joke, then turned back to what I was saying. "In the opening chapter of the book it says, 'beware the being who offers magics in the name of magick, for their hand is on the lever of the cosmos.'"

"Cosmos?" Marija asked. The word was old-Eurabanni, not in the modern or the trade cant.

"It means everything. The who of the universe," I replied. "What if it also implied that magick, which to us is known as wytchness, is human controlled? What if this is not the Gods, but a being that is turning our minds to their end use?"

Marija nodded, then looked out into the crowd on the dock that was watching the diners in the restaurant eat. "The Hates," she said with a yelp.

The three of us looked out of the restaurant to the docks and saw the Hate brothers, Banji and Lobar, walking down the gangway, followed by a set of sailors-without-colors who were jeering and screaming insults. "Nhia, message to the captain, Hates being targeted by a gang off *Respite* on Promanada Trade. Use your plack and pay for the fast taxi. Marija, head down the Promanada and catch any *Remarkers* you see, take them to the dockside. Keep our people out of this." Salvador stood up.

Marija balled her fist and said, "Abandon the Hates?"

"No, but keep the captain's options open. If we get into a general melee with the *Respiters* we could be pushed out of this port before we have our supplies carried on," he said. When she seemed to hesitate, I grabbed her uniform gently and pulled her to my side, her ears by my lips. "I will not abandon the Hates. Now do as I order."

We both wore an aspirant's starburst, Marija being a second navigator and myself the captain's clerk, but in the byzantine order of ship's command, the clerk was under the first officer, Commander Nine, while the second navigator was under the navigator, Lieutenant Rabia Ibn Saludi, which gave me superior position. It was not a subject to be argued dockside like barristers fighting over a bale of fish, and neither thought to argue it. Marija was the junior officer unless and until someone who ranked both of us arrived.

"I understand," she said to me and gathered up Der Nhia Lo with her eyes. The next course was arriving just as we all abandoned the restaurant. We left it on the table.

I took off my identifying *Remarker* swallowtail and my colors and handed them to Marija. She looked at me with a slight look of horror in her eyes. Going without colors in any trade port was a quick way to get locked up, mistreated, and even drowned. In this port though, without the structure of the Sublime Traders Association, anything really could happen. Marija took my uniform and said, "Are you sure?"

"Get on down the dock, Marija," I replied. If she outranked me, she would be the one running into harm's way. That was how the *Remarker* went. That was the difference between us and Lute Cation's ship. We stood together.

The situation was filled with peril, I thought. None of the Hates' tormenters were wearing the colors of *Voyage Respite*, and even if they were, none of them were officers like Lobar and Banji. Lute Cagion had zero loyalty to his crew and could apologize to the port for their behavior simply by drowning them off the back of his ship. Captain al-Rasheed would be personally responsible for anything that the Hates did, nor was he the type, despite his recent problems, to throw even his lowest crew off the deck to please anyone, not even a vital port master.

The Hates could, if they wanted, turn and kill their dozen tormenters is a flash of violence that I had seen once before, on the docks of the Cycus Port when the *Remarker* was charged by the Life Guards regiment. Many *Remarkers* gave life or limbs on that day, but the Guard was more than decimated. They had expected an easy victory against a cowed merchant crew and instead ran into a fixed wall of boarding pikes and firelocks, and then learned that the Marines trained by the Hates and Major Standish were anything but easy pickings in a close-order battle. Lobar Hate had two regimentals speared on his talwar and another's neck gripped in his hands, a rictus of anger on his face and a scream of defiance on his lips. The blood the two brothers could spill in a minute of violence was hardly to be thought of by a sane person.

I could not order the brothers to do anything, they ranked me and were Marines, but I did see an opening for them.

Down the promanada was a bar that proudly displayed the crossed firelock and talwar of naval guard and marine units attached to merchants. I hurried down the way and overtook both the harassers and the brothers, turned, and yelled, "Thirsty marines, try the Swords' Afloat Tea Room!"

Both Hates seemed to recognize me in the crowd, and Lobar brushed across his chest with an "I understand / comprehend" hand motion. I let them pass me and collided with the leader of the *Respiters*.

"Sorry, boss," I screeched in trade tongue.

"You not block us," the leader replied, also in trade, shoving me. I stumbled and fell to the ground.

I grabbed at one of the tormenters passing by and let them drag me. "Sorry, boss," I yelled, "a drink bought to pay for mistake!" I had twenty-one silver in my pouch, so I took the coins and handed them to the man whose legs I was grasping onto. "Fifty silver, boss, all I have." The man pushed the coins into his pocket and an argument began.

There was a discussion in a foreign tongue over this, but the leader was angry and seemed desperate to get the sailors to move on after the Hates. They all turned to the sailor I had handed the silver to and seemed to be demanding their share. He pulled the silver out and presented each of the seven pirates two silver.

I laughed to myself. They had all heard the trade tongue word for 'fifty-silver,' which was '*khamswun-fiddtan*,' or '*figa-argent*' in the language of my homeland. But no sailor would not hear the words '*khamswun-fiddtan*' and think it meant anything less than one-hundred grams of fine silver pressed into fifty coins.

What the sailor with the silver handed around was four-grams of silver each. They expected four or maybe five grams. The screams from the sailors who felt they were cheated was deafening. I scrambled away into the lee of a shop where two Paroleet vendors stood. "What happens?" One asked me.

I stood and dusted myself off. "They want money for drink and horas" I replied.

"Horas?" The second asked.

I shook my head. Trade tongue for a man or woman who sold sex was 'mumi.' In high Eurabanni it was 'eahira.' Luther knew what the tongue of the Parolanders was. "Mumi," I finally guessed.

"Mumini," the taller of the two Paroleet said. The other nodded.

"No mummini here, food, drink, chance game," The first added.

I nodded. "How say honorable trader in Paro?" I asked.

They looked at each other and must have decided sharing the local language was not going to be an issue. There was no honor specific prefixes in trade tongue, and the ones in Eurabanni were often complicated and not used by people of other lands even if they could speak trade. "Mamalu faioloa, but on these docks you could simply say Mamalu Merchant."

I bowed again. "Mamalu Merchant, sailors casting off the Voyage Respite are, do you know Qarasina?"

They nodded. "Thief," one said.

"Thief-on-water," I corrected, using the trade common for a pirate, though it was a compound word and not universal in the outer reaches of the Halo.

They nodded. The shorter of the two said, "No mummini here."

It seemed to me that the boorish behavior of the Voyage Respite sailors who I had now tagged in the local merchants mind was proving my point. They started shoving and grabbing at the coins. Fifty silver was quite a sum for a common sailor, but the Parolanders saw that much and more come across their tables every hour in trade. It was a rich port where sailors deprived of recreation spent money that was accumulated over weeks and month of a trading mission.

So crew-mates fighting over silver, especially without knowing how I had played a game on them, looked terrible to the islanders. More merchants approached along with a few bullyrocks. The bruisers were like any other guards or constables at any other port, armed with truncheons and helmets and ready to keep order if they felt things were getting out of hand among the port visitors.

I looked down the promanada and saw what I had hoped would come to pass: Major Angela Standish marching almost in step with Igor Bosanac and a dozen marines in swallowtail and see-saw hats, the crowd giving away before them. I ran to the major and said as she passed me, "They have the Hates cornered in the marine tea shop."

She nodded and said out of the corner of her mouth, "Back in uniform."

Lieutenant Bosonac had my own swallowtail and stopped to help me put it on and get all the doodles and dangles. We both then fell into the crowd where several other *Remarkers* were starting to appear from down the promanada. We were not the only crew watching the brewing confrontation though. The verges of the street were getting crowded with observers in all colors of sailor's uniforms. It looked like a great Vintage Tree, filled with colorful corvid-birds.

Major Standish stopped before the *Voyage Respite* crew but ignored them, at least for the second. "Raybeam Eleven," she said to one of the Marines, "take some silver into this establishment and pay for our ship's company to have an open tab, and also pay for a small tab for the marines who visit from other ships. Off limits to pirates, of course." The last she said staring at the obvious leader of the *Respiters*.

The *Respiter* growled, "do not dare disparage my ship!"

Major Standish suddenly seemed to become aware of the sailor. She motioned for the rifleman to follow her orders, then approached very closely to the sailor who had stepped up to her. "You are out of uniform, sailor."

"You do not give me orders, main mast" he said, betraying more ability to speak in trade than he had shown yet. "Get your captain here so I can file a complaint."

Standish laughed. "An out of uniform bilge bug demanding my captain? I will have words with your own captain, Lute Cagion, I can assure you bug. What is your rank?" She asked.

"Not your concern," he replied, then took a swing at the major.

His swing connected with her face, and seemed to barely phase her. It was at that second that I could see the dawning realization that this was getting out of his control. "That was a mistake," Major Standish said in a low voice.

She looked up at some of the bullyrocks standing in array in front one of the fish shops and seemed to pause, not saying anything. One of them detached from the crowd and walked to the major.

"Get back, shellfish," said the pirate.

The guard stood looking confused. Major Standish turned to him and then back to the pirate. "Son," she said, "The islanders do not speak Eurabanni. Only trade common. Your comment falls on deaf ears."

The term 'shellfish' was confusing. Did the pirate mis-speak? Was it slang that simply avoided common sense? I was just as confused as many others in the crowd seemed to be.

The crowd that was forming began to agitate and an official in a magnificent mummu, surrounded by a number of guards with clubs arrived. She was wearing finely made, green leather bracers and carried a wooden rod with a carved effigy of a fish on its head. "You," the officer said, pointing at Major Standish, "what is this disturbance on my promanada?" Her trade common was crisp and practiced.

I looked at Major Standish expecting her to explode, but he merely stood and said, "There is no issue commander. I am Major of Marines Angela Standish of the *Remarker*, Captain al-Rasheed's commander. My marines are establishing one of your tea establishments to spend silver in while we are in port. These men and women had some other issue," she said motioning to the *Respite* sailors.

The Officer-of-the Promanada nodded. "Have you paid the tea house operator?" She asked.

"A thousand, Commander," Major Standish replied.

She nodded, then turned to the pirates. "What ship are you from and what is your business." Again the commander's speech was clear and precise school-trade.

The lead pirate did not seem to be taking in the reality of the situation, at least to me. "I am from no ship, and have no business."

The Commander nodded. "How did you come to Paroland?" She asked.

"Swam," the pirate replied with a laugh.

She turned and said to Major Standish, "Enjoy your stay." She then waved at her bullyrocks who began to gently move the crowds along.

The pirates stood rocking on their feet and laughing. "She handed you your ass marine!" The leaders of the pirates had a smug smile on his face.

As the crowds melted away, Major Standish looked at the pirate. "What is your name, pirate?"

"You can call me Master, now run along and get your captain," he yelled, but no one on the dock was listening anymore. No one but the *Remarkers* who were closing in on the pirates in the middle of the Promanada.

Major Standish looked back at her marines. "Corporal Gilingham, take these vagrants into custody."

It happened quickly, but the seven pirates were taken into the rough hands of the marines and hustled to the dock-side tea bar. I followed the group as fast as I could, breaking into the bar just at the heels of our marines and the pirates. Major Standish said to the bartender who was counting silver from several pouches with a huge smile, "Back room?"

"No ship fights, please" the bartender replied.

Major Standish laughed, "This lot? They just told the Commander of the Promanada they swam here."

The bartender pulled off her turban and laughed, "there is a room in the back. No messes. If there is a mess, sweep it into the scuttle."

Major Standish sketched a half salute and led the Marines back.

The marines brooked no struggle, and hustled the pirates forward. The pirates screamed and tried to delay their progress, but to no avail. The marines were not willing to brook resistance and were not gentle in their actions.

The room was made from the same bray-wood walls with windows at the top and cheap furniture in the middle of the space that every store or tea house on the promanada used. "Get in," Corporal Gilligham said, and seeing the Hate brothers appear, he took them by the shoulder and positioned them out of the way as if they were raw recruits.

Neither of the Hates seemed to mind, instead looking on the events as if they were disinterested spectators.

"Get the scuttle open, saves us from doing the floors down to grit" the major send, sending several Marines to work, then turned to the cluster of captors. "Strip this lot," she said to Marine Benchler, who gathered their captors with his eyes and started to rapidly remove the prisoners' clothing.

The wood scuttle in the floor was opened and removed from its hinge pins, then one of the marines took a paraffin lamp from the wall in the darkening evening, lit it, and swung it down the hole in the floor. She looked up, motioned for something, and was handed a sounding line one of the marines had wrapped around their waist. The line went down and the marine said, 'two meters to water, one meter of water."

"Swing the lamp," Major Standish said quietly.

Gillingham grabbed the line holding the paraffin lamp and began to wave it, then swung his upper body into the scuttle and said up, "they see us."

I looked at the naked pirates. They were no longer cocky or struggling. They began to look terrified. I approached Major Standish through the crowded room and said to her in a low voice, "Major Standish, I am worried where this is going." And I was. No one was talking to the prisoners, and the marines had no humor like they might in a standard port bumping. There was no humor and no jokes. They were deadly serious.

Major Standish did not look at me. "Aspirant Lingongo. I will tell you this once. You have done your duty and informed your superior. I will need you for this evolution, but if you feel you cannot stomach following orders, then you are dismissed, return to your dissipations."

I stood silently then said what must have been my most stupid comment in my life. "The captain would not approve abusing these men no matter what they have done."

Major Standish turned slowly like a capstan under great strain. "Aspirant Lingongo. You will stand by. You can tell the captain anything you wish, but the captain is not here now and I am. You are either part of the crew, or you are a civilian on the deck. Pick one now!" The last sentence pierced through the room like a shot from a serpent. I looked to the marines who paused in their work—which in my distraction had turned from gathering around the scuttle to dressing the pirates in canvas prison suits. More of the suits and chains were coming up from the scuttle.

I turned back to Major Standish and snapped to my best marine-attention like a toy soldier carved in driftwood. The major's blond hair showed her milky-white skin was turning red in frustration. Her nostrils were flexing, and her jaw was cracking. It took her a second to calm, then she asked, "Do any of this lot speak Eurabanni?"

I pointed to the one I had tagged as their leader. "I think he is a petty officer. The rest are new caught, they speak common, I think, but are not confident in it. Their petty officer has let out ship words in Eurabanni."

Major Standish nodded. "That is why the captain values you, Aspirant Lingongo, you observe. Now observe but stay silent." With two steps she strode to the pirates huddled in their canvas prison suits, each one balled up in chains and cloth ties like a package being hoisted onto a cargo ship. She looked at the cluster of prisoners and slowly removed her swallowtail, then stripped off her leather belts, boots, and ship's shirt, leaving her standing in her black deck pants and nothing else. So bereft of clothing, her physical size and strength was open to view. Her stomach was a stripe of muscles, while her arms and shoulders looked like they were carved from some rare ivory. The only bulk or fat in her upper body was her breasts, which themselves looked to be made from some rare form of alabaster. The people of Cycus had no body modesty, and did not care if they showed themselves in public, but the pirates must have been from regions where nudity was seen as unusual or even wrong. Yet even Salvador who spent half of his early life without clothing, fishing from the beach poles of his homeland, could see that Major Standish was cut from an unusual tree.

She reached out with her right hand, and was given a long piece of wood with a hook in the end used to maneuver boats in close quarters. In other situations, it was not that dangerous looking, but in the flickering lamps and dying sun streaking through closed hatches in the ceiling of the room and held by Standish who was almost the height and weight of the Hate brothers, it took on a sinister proportion, filling me with doom and causing the pirates to scream soundlessly underneath their canvas muzzles and struggle against their restraints. Worse, at least to the minds of the pirates, it seemed to me, they were trying to protect their exposed genitals that the canvas girdle did not protect and which restricted the defensive use of their hands. My heart was torn seeing their growing terror, but I could not move to challenge the major. Nothing against the trader's law had been done.

The major poked one of the scared pirates. "Send this one down the scuttle"

The pirates started to struggle, but trussed as they were, there was no chance to resist. The one who was pointed out by the major was grabbed, dragged to the scuttle, and rolled off. A splash was heard and clashing of wood, then silence.

The major poked the one I had told her was the leader. "You want to speak?"

The man struggled.

The major nodded and two marines removed his mask.

"*Sika a parsua*," he said.

The major bent down and said to the man's face. "Give me your name, rank, and ship in Eurabanni, and do not pretend you are ignorant of the tongue.

There was a second of tension, then he said, "I am Muazaf Tafih Denwabi of the *Voyage Respite*." His voice was cracked and he was almost crying.

"That is a Navy rank, I will call you Able Sailor Denwabi." The major kneeled down. "I will ask you questions, Denwabi, and you will answer. If you think not to answer me, I will not touch you. But I will send one of your mates down the scuttle. If I run out of your associates, then you go last."

The man stared at the major.

"Make your head move to show agreement," the major said calmly.

He moved his head.

"Did Lute Cagion order you to attack the Hate brothers?" The major spoke her words so calmly, but I could still hear the sound of the waters breaking on some wood through the scuttle. Dressed in the prisoner's outfit, he could only drown if no one saved him.

He shook his head, 'no.' The major waved her hand and another pirate was sent down the scuttle. I tried to step forward but felt hands like iron grip my shoulder. I turned and it was Lobar Hate. He shook his head, 'no.' I could do nothing else but obey.

"Lute Cagion," Major Standish said. He shook his head no and the marines threw another pirate down the scuttle. A few seconds more, and another went over. "Two left."

"*Tornilio ti babai*," the pirate named Danwabi yelled.

"How rude!" The major said, nodded, and the last two pirates were both deposited into the scuttle with a splash. "So now I know you do not care anymore than Lute Cagion does for his people. Lute Cagion ordered you to push on the Hate brothers, is that true?"

"Yes," the pirate said in trade. "He did just that."

"Good, one last question and I let you free. Will you tell the Promanada Commander you were ordered to hunt the crew of the *Remarker* on behalf of your captain?" She poked him with her boarding hook.

He spit and Major Standish nodded. "So be it."

"Major Standish!" I yelled, and she waved at me in a dismissing manner. Meanwhile the Marines were stripping off their own swallowtails and shirts and draping them on the chairs and tables in the room.

Lobar Hate looked at the major, who said, "Let the captain's clerk go, he should see this to the end. And you and your brother stay here—got that?"

Hate let me go and stepped back with his brother. The marines were one-by-one stepping into the scuttle and levering themselves into darkness. This was followed by the pirate being handed over the edge. The major was immediately in my face, "Come with us, but you speak only when I tell you to speak."

I tried to look obstinate, but nodded.

"Take off your coat and shirt, this will be messy," she said.

Lobar Hate took my swallowtail and my shirt, and then helped me down the scuttle in what turned out to be a boat with a Paroleet driver standing in the bow. Major Standish followed me down. The lead pirate, Denwabi, was huddled in the prow of the boat. Around us floated four more boats, each with marines and pirates in them, each with a

Parolander at the pushing-oar, and each one wearing the wooden necklace of the Paroleet.

I settled into the boat and looked around me. The Paroleets were bored, looking like they just wanted to get their money and go. The Marines were grim-faced, heads turning this way and that, hands holding onto improvised weapons. The prisoners, though, were completely cowed. Their eyes were wide open, reflecting the light and looking like some strange florescent globe, occasionally blinking in the darkness.

Major Standish whistled, and the five boats started to push their way through the forest of stanchions and beams that formed the foundation of the Promanada. The boats came out from under the docks and then turned to the shallows between the main island of Paroland and the smaller, unnamed forested cay.

I looked over the boat's prow and saw that there were paraffin lanterns hung on staves that were out of the water, and each stave had a lobster trap secured to it. There were exactly seven traps in the wan, rising moonlight. "You cannot do that," I said to the major.

"Do what, Mister Longongo?" The major asked.

I looked at the prisoner, whose eyes were tearing and his body shaking. "No one would be inhumane enough to put someone in one of those traps!"

"Mr. Longongo, tell me what option I have, what would the captain do with these men? Do you think releasing them will work?" The major asked as we coasted into the lobster trap stake and the boatman tied us off. The other boats tied off to one or two traps, depending on how many prisoners they had.

"Anything but sinking them in those traps; that is a horrible death, and a horrible thing afterward, being eaten by lobsters!" I said. "Let me solve this, let me find any other fate for these men and women!"

"Like what?" The major asked.

The darkness was now total except for a few lamps at the prows of the boats and the rising moon in the eastern horizon, large beyond all comprehension, but dim. The water was not silent as the low waves rocked the boats and splashed against the lobster staves, and a brisk wind blew along the water's top. I looked across the roadstead at a ship where loud guffaws and screams of joy could be heard. It was *Frisky Abbott*, its crew partying on their last night, proudly flying flags that said they were intoxicated and willing to have others visit. I turned to the major and said, "I can indenture them to the Abbott."

She nodded then turned to the pirate. "How about that. Salvador Longongo does not want me to feed you to the lobsters. So I will ask you once, and let you speak one word. If it is yes, you go the *Abbott*, and if you ever see any *Remarker* again, you salute. And if you see Salvador Longongo again, you grovel on your stomach. One word, and then if I ever see you again not saluting me, I will make sure the lobsters have you. Here it goes."

One of the Marines removed his gag, and he said, "Yes."

After asking each pirate if they would accept indenture to the *Abbott*, dropping them off on the ship which was scheduled to warp out the next day, and then returning by taxi to the scuttle in the bar and up into the party-room, I was exhausted, though it was not yet twenty. Lobar Hate handed me my uniform shirt and my swallowtail, then helped me get into the outfit. Major Standish came through the scuttle and also began to dress with the help of Banji Hate. She looked at me and said, "You have permission to speak."

I stood at attention and replied, "Permission to be excused."

There was a moment of silence, then she waved her hand and nodded.

I left, not knowing how I felt about the night.

CHAPTER XIV

Ahar and the Dragon

S uela Fleet looked at Captain al-Rasheed as he stared at the broken towers of this, their farthest shore. Suela's people were said to be the greatest navigators on Ocean, but this feat was one that would be talked about across the Halo… If they got home.

"Are you ready to embark, Supercargo Fleet?" The captain asked.

"It is all going like clockwork," she replied.

She looked again at the island that they had pitched up against in amazement. "It is not the first lost land we have ever come to in our sails," the captain said.

Suela let go a breath. Before them stood ruined towers snaked in green cob and heart leaf, a giant abandoned pier of some form of concrete, still usable after endless years. "Thirty hard days with no tolan to guide our warp, with no star sign in the sky, and in the face of a horrible following current that caused *Remarker* to rush forward like a boulder rolling down a hill. But unlike the faraway lands where my kith now live, this one was found by you from the gossamer of old books and guesswork. If a wood automaton were to climb from the cargo hatch and start singing a drive-chanty, I could be no more surprised."

The captain reached out and touched her shoulder. "We found it, now prepare your team."

The Mouse turned from eavesdropping on the captain and Suela Fleet. It was like he was barely noticed anymore. Like he could intrude on the minds of his friends then skip away a second later. Yet there was a sense of foreboding that was in his heart. He turned and took the gangway to the well and ran into the Darkfather.

The quartermaine towered over the Mouse and looked sinister and looming in the dappled light coming down from the sun that tried to peer through a cloud dappled sky. "You cannot hide forever, Mouse."

Mouse turned and saw that Suela Fleet was coming down the gangway and had frozen in place.

Mouse removed his hat and sketched a look of contrition on his face. "I do not know what you mean, Quartermaine Darkfather." He twisted his cap in his hand and looked down at the deck.

The Darkfather shook his head. *"Kdaj si našel palico?"* He said in a burst of foreign tongue.

"I found no wänd, Quartermaine," the Mouse replied.

The Darkfather laughed. "Mouse, how did you understand a language that as far as I know, only two people in the Halo can speak?" His towering countenance seemed to lesson and he kneeled down and looked Mouse in the eyes. "Look, my friend. You do not understand what I think you have in your possession. It is an addiction, and one that without training will cause you to fly out into time and space and lose your way."

The Mouse looked up, then let his gaze fall on Suela Fleet.

"She is caught between you and I, and cannot stay there forever. More people will come, and the item you have will work more elaborate efforts to maintain its deception. Efforts that can hurt people because you do not know how to guide it." The tall man frowned, then added, "I speak from experience."

The Mouse felt for his pocket where he concealed the multifaceted-solid. He wanted to throw it into the ocean, but when he tried, it ended up back in his pocket.

As if reading his thoughts, the Darkfather said, "You cannot even lose it. It is always somewhere on your person. Make an effort to bring it out and show me." The Darkfather asked.

The Mouse reached into his pocket and seemed to be taking something out, but his hand was empty. Despite this, the Darkfather leaned down and stared intently into the empty palm. "Nothing is in your hand."

The Mouse reached back into his pocket. It was still there.

"Of course. I know this wänd. I know who used to own it, and somehow it reached your hands and has bound itself to you. That is how they work. They want an owner, but can be picky. Unless you know how to operate one, there is no guarantee they will identify themselves and allow you to use them to their best purpose any more than a bottle of palm rum." The Darkfather paused, then said, "Do not be scared."

"I am scared all the time," Mouse said.

With a sudden motion the Darkfather drew his fire-blackened and disreputable yataghan and in a single lunging move made an upper cut with enough force to cut the Mouse in half. The Mouse, though, moved just as quickly and the cut missed. Then the movement became almost preternaturally fast as the quartermaine stabbed, cut, slashed, and tried to pommel strike the Mouse, who danced away from each move as if he was a trained tumbler in a minstrel show. Just as fast as the fight started, it ended with the Darkfather returning his weapon to its frogged sheaf. "That is what a wänd does, that and more."

The Mouse put his palm onto the concealing pocket. "Something is coming." He tried to say the words but could not.

"You want to say something," the Darkfather hazarded.

Mouse stood mute, saying nothing.

"Perhaps I can predict your question. You are a person who was born in the shadows and who seeks to protect yourself from impossible powers by guile and stealth. The wänd will mold itself to you and seek to build on what you have rather than what you lack. It could be dangerous. If you were a fighting person, you might have harmed me without knowing you had done so as I slashed you. That is part of what I am saying. You are untrained in that device-of-power. I know how it arrived in the Halo, though I have no idea how it retained its power. It should have been destroyed when it was lost. But that is not what apparently happened.

The Mouse looked at the Darkfather, eyes wide in fear. He wanted to say something. He was mute though.

"Življenjski Inženirji, do you know what that means?"

"Life engineers," the Mouse replied. He was shocked he could speak at all.

"That is right. An ancient order of my people. People of learning, but also people of violence who play with the world as if it was a child's dridil. If I had known that you carried such a device before this voyage, I could have helped rid you of it" The Darkfather reached out his hand almost tenderly and touched the Mouse's cheek.

Mouse tried to name his fear, tried to say anything, but was only able to again say, "Life Engineer."

The Darkfather reached out and gathered the small sailor into his arms. "*Življenjski Inženirji*," he said as well. He released the Mouse, then said, "I have to prepare to go ashore."

Mouse saw Suela Fleet suddenly complete her descent of the gangway. "Quartermaine Darkfather, Mouse." Darkfather nodded and went up the stairs Fleet had just quit. The Mouse followed the Supercargo onto the aft cargo ladder.

Suela Fleet had seen little of Mouse on the voyage out from Paroland, and wanted to stop and talk to him, but the thought left her mind as she heard the captain call out for maneuver stations to bring the great ship into a mooring on the pier. The entire crew of *Remarker* seemed to breathe in a sigh of relief as they worked to drag out anchors in the unmarked roadstead they had named "Tower of Heaven" after the great donjon that stood above it. She turned to watch the captain take position by Commander Nine as each proved their mastery of the craft of shaping a course in a tight harbor. Commander Nine ordered anchor stones tumbled into the water first front, then aft, and then the captain called for a group of marines to begin hauling the turn stations to alternately release and let out line, as the maneuver required. The anchor teams fed the long lines expertly, slowing and skewing the ship into its berth.

Ducking into the aft hold down a gully-line, she lit in the midst of her crew who were positioning supplies to be lofted ashore and opening space for returning treasure that they all expected would be significant. It had been a fight to reach the island. The currents had at times reached eleven kilometers per hour, while the winds shifted around the compass rose suddenly, as if the world itself was outraged at their temerity in challenging the open waters of the far northwest. The captain had stayed day and night either in the cockpit at work on the computers or atop sighting into the empty skies, and around him the crew had stayed, watch on and off, half the crew awake and half in fitful sleep or pursuing food from dwindling stores, knowing that they had volunteered for an endeavor that would see them for nought eight times in nine, gone into the wilds and endless water with death by starvation in the end. Fighting for the one chance at glory.

Robbi van Guerster looked up from a sheet of scap that held lines of supplies his team wanted and said, "like throwing a dart from one ship onto another ship going the opposite direction and hitting a sheet of scap in the master's cabin."

Suela looked at the reefing sheets out of the open hold top as the anchors bit and were pulled back. She was born at sea. Her entire life was spent with water below her head and an open sky above her. Though working supercargo, she could have climbed the lines into the masts and handled the sheets or uncased the oars and put her back into shaping a course for the *Remarker* without even a single thought, yet she marveled at the captain's skill. "You mean the landing?" She asked.

Rabbi looked at her and replied with a smile. "No, finding this island at all. I knew the captain had it inside of him."

Fleet agreed, and showed it by nodding. Sea People had an existential dread of losing the Halo with little chance that land existed beyond. They may be of the sea, but the greater seas outside of the Halo were deserts that would kill them if they tried to leave. The towns of her people did not venture where the currents were strong, instead floating in the dolans where the crossing currents of Halo created soft, languid currents that some merchants feared, knowing that a ship could calm into the deadness without wind or current to push against, but that the people who lived on the sea for their entire lives welcomed. Flotsam was there to harvest. The rain fell and quenched them. The fish swam and the weeds lapped at their hulls. Waves were few and calm.

"Crossroads be, you are filled with cotton," Robbi noted.

Suela shrugged. "I have a feeling that something is right behind me, but when I turn, it is not there." The endless terrified her when she knew, in her mind, that it was indeed endless, and attached to more endless that roiled in the great currents, and were swept by huge storms. The endless caused ignoble death. "It is just this trip that has me spooked."

Robbi laughed. "Suela Fleet who was conceived on a wave and birthed in a storm, how can you be spooked?"

She shook her head and took a manifest down to prepare for offloading. As spooked as she felt, there was no denying the captain had carried them here to the lee of a great island, where once humankind had crawled and lived lives, tens-of-thousand surprising hectares of land shielding a lee of hundreds of thousands of hectares from the great westward currents. She felt their anchors drag on that lee until stuck fast in the calming currents, and thus allowing all but a single watch to go below into elated exhaustion.

Marija Perak, the Second Navigator, climbed down from the well and said, "Captain's compliments, and what is the stores report, he forgot to ask before you went down."

Suela shook the cobwebs out of her head. "The last storm filled the tanks, so forty days with care of water. We still have sixty-one days at full rations of food-stuff. And from eyes on the island, the teams ashore can forage for fresh food to keep the dry-rations banked for the voyage back."

Perak nodded and looked to Robbi, who said, "Was there anything else Miss Perak?"

Marija replied, "No, Second Officer."

"Then inform the captain we will change shifts down here on normal watch in three hours. He can order crew away anytime he wishes after that. On your way."

When Marija left, Robbi turned to Suela, "I have spoken to Kwame, Igor, and Vulkrim. Now it is your turn," he said. They were alone now in the cargo space, ignored by crew who were handling big cargo containers to prepare for the shore parties..

"Officer van Guerster?" Suela asked, taken aback by the captain's sudden use of common names to refer to cadre.

"There are winds I do not understand filling our sails. Our major distrusts our captain, and while the quartermaine may be the queen's effendi on this ship, he is troubled and seeking things in the sky," Robbi van Guerster said, looking at the wrecked tower near the shore of the island. "This island shows that the captain has his mind where it should be, even if you and I might see his sanity and affect as less than perfect. Not one navigator in a thousand could have brought us to this island from papers and rumors. The trip, no matter how much silver is promised, and I am told by Eversail that the money is substantial, was always a fool's goal. But we were the fools who could achieve it."

"I am loyal to *Remarker* and the captain, Officer van Guerster," Suela said. "And the trip is not over."

"No, it is not over. We must load what treasures are to be found here, then drive cross current, warping a course to a point where the western flow will push us back to the Halo. I just want the cadre to know that the captain is the captain. If the major or the quartermaine have issues with each other or the captain, it stays on the top decks. We are in a dangerous place to have squabbles at the top." Robbi van Guerster said.

Suela Fleet considered it for a second. "What about the Marines?"

Robbi looked at Suela, a ray of sun through the hatch making his eyes sparkle. "Hate is loyal to the major, but he knows that the ship does not come back to the Halo without its captain. They are not disloyal. For that matter, I do not understand the winds and tides that are blowing the quartermaine and the major off course. No one is saying that there is calumny in the upper decks. What I am saying is that there is not factionalism. The captain runs a soft tiller, but Sunstar Nine runs one that will see someone overboard if they swing the wrong line. We decided when we protected the Mouse, all of us, that this ship will run by the old rules below decks. You and I saw off two humans who broke the orders of the rankers. There will be discipline."

Suela Fleet remembered it. She wondered were the Mouse was hiding, she had not seen him in weeks, but she remembered how the crew came together to protect the doughty crewmate.

They had so many secrets, but secrets that were needed. Some of the secrets were secondhand, such as the drunken night when Robbi Van Guerster admitted killing Tarkington, and some of them were visceral and immediate, such as when she and Igor Bosanac broke the dirty grifter Cosh's neck for raping Mouse in the cable sedge; she had felt nothing as she gave the fowl beast his halo of wood, but the secret persisted between the twelve cadre and senior sailors who had made the choice to send the man on his way. "Maximally demoted," she said. A euphemism for eliminating a foul man from the crew because a ship in warp was no place for a break in the chain of obedience, and this break could not be fixed merely with threats. She saw that Robbi Van Guerster understood the term and was nodding.

"Elion died for our sins," Robbi Van Guerster said.

"Elion died for our sins. The least of us became the greatest in death," Suela agreed. She walked to one of the port stays and checked its camber, a useless gesture considering it was going to be cut loose to get to its supplies. "So the cadre agrees?"

Robbi replied, "There is no need for discussion. On the ship there is a captain. Anyone who disagrees, gets to swim home from here. Otherwise, let the upper deckers fight their own battles, as long as those battles do not affect the captain."

Suela laughed a little. "You are the second officer."

"If I take this wheel here in any but the most dire circumstances, you and Commander Nine will see me over the side," He replied.

"That is certain," Suela said.

The captain watched as another load of boxes was lifted onto the ship. The crew was flung about the island, leaving only twenty people on the ship to bring in cargo and store it. He looked over and noticed Mouse was standing next to him. "I thought you were ashore."

"No, Captain," Mouse said. "I have been keeping things clean."

"Good," Captain al-Rasheed said.

Mouse could sense the distraction in the captain. "What have we found on the island?"

The captain shook his head. "I am sorry Mouse, we have time, let me tell you what we have found. Everything and nothing."

"Everything and nothing?" Mouse asked.

The captain shook his head. "I am sorry, we were hired by my wife's uncle the Musharaf d' Kemaya to find a fabulous tea grown at the end of the known world. Only it turns out the tea is terrible. It has devolved into a weedy mess that can grow anywhere, but who wants to drink it?"

"So this has been for nothing?" The Mouse asked.

Captain al-Rasheed laughed. "If we were actually looking for the greatest tea on all creation, then perhaps. But Musharraf signed a contract for us to deliver a tea from this lost land. And we have picked this tea. We have recovered the plants, carefully swaddled in jute sacks. We took on soil. We took water from the lakes. We have met our burden and the adventure is a success."

"That is great!" The Mouse said. He looked, as a lifter pulled up a pallet of bags and crates from the cement pier and swung it slowly into the aft cargo hold. Only twenty crew remained on the *Remarker*, but the only tasks that needed to be done were to do odd repairs and strike down cargo returned by the shore parties.

"It is more than great," the captain said after a short period of silence. What we have won is monumental. The crew was divided and confused before we started this adventure. Now they are together, having achieved the impossible, and the tea is not the issue. They are exploring a lost society and returning history to the people who may not know it exists." He looked out at the crumbling tower. "How many years will these towers stand? We have sampled their art, drawn them, recovered real books and plinth art, drawn maps, recovered their coins, toys, tools, and home arts. Because of you, Mouse, you and this crew, a dead society springs to life!"

Mouse said, "So much to tell."

The captain looked closely at him. "Then tell me, my friend." The captain then stopped. He drew rangefinders from the cockpit rack and focused them on a speck in the sky. "Corporal Hodak!" He yelled.

Hodak was guiding a cargo pallet into the aft hold. He stopped and cupped his ears, yelling back, "Yes, Captain!"

"Present now!" Captain al-Rasheed yelled.

Hodak slung his talwar and firelock, and instead of taking to the gangways caught a transversal and swung out and into the cockpit in a single feat of agility. Landing next to the captain, he sketched a precise salute and stood at what Mouse judged was rigid attention. The captain handed him the rangefinders and pointed into the sky. Hodak looked through them and said, "A sea bird with the sun glinting on its wings?"

Mouse yelled suddenly, "It is a dragon!"

Hodak and the captain looked at him. He could feel the approaching doom. Mouse knew that he had been feeling it for more than a month. That something was in control of him. The multifaceted-solid, or something that held the multifaceted-solid in its sway.

The captain turned to Hodak. "Prepare to slip the lines." He turned and looked to the wind gauge then down into the roadstead. "The current will drive us to the lee of that island

and up on the sandbar. If I order her slipped, it you will be able to float her at dawn tomorrow and leave here."

"Captain, permission to speak?" Hodak said.

"Speak," Captain al-Rasheed said.

"What is a dragon, and what can it do to *Remarker* that would force us to slip lines?" The marine was clearly out of his depth, but holding a brave front, or so Mouse thought.

"In my land it is called *taniyn*," The captain said.

Mouse felt himself blurt out, "*laqad basaq almakhluq alnaar ealaa junud alsalam.*"

Captain al-Rasheed interrupted Hodak's confusion by translating, "The fell being put fire to the dread of the warriors of peace." He looked to the sky again, then added, "No one fires, no one makes a move that I do not order."

Hodak left the cockpit. The captain reached out and touched Mouse's chin. "Now is the time to reveal your secrets, as the dragon approaches and I do not assume he will be simply asking for tea and honey cakes.

The Mouse took out the multifaceted-solid. "The Darkfather calls it a wänd, and says it is a tool of his people." Then he did what he never thought he could do; he handed the multifaceted-solid to his captain.

Captain Javier al-Rasheed took the multifaceted-solid gently in his hand and looked at Mouse with soft eyes. He then looked at the device. It was a multi-sided object, milky-white as a whole on most sides, but with four sides enameled in four pastel colors: green, blue, red, and black. He rolled the object in his hands and Mouse knew what he was feeling. Sounds were more vibrant. Words that were confusing made sense. Memories could be present in the front of his eyes, or suppressed like a horrible thought to live in dreams and passing seconds of ennui. He would feel things, sinister things. The approaching dragon would feel like a pain in his heart that could not be described to anyone, but would take on its own life rattling around his head.

And as he saw the effect settle on the captain, he felt it leaving himself just as fast. Mouse became in a few moments, just Mouse.

"The Darkfather and I will have words on this wänd and the secrecy that he has built around it and his ward, Adjenness. However, you are not at any fault. Where did you find this, if we have the moments to ask," the captain asked.

"At a sailor's store. I just thought it was a die. Twelve sides like any other die. I did not know!" Mouse exclaimed. "But you feel it, the sinister force. The being is trying to control the wänd, control me, I mean, now you."

The captain replied, "But which one of me is it trying to control?"

Mouse looked up and saw the dragon was now clearly visible in the sky, spitting flame. A rider was on its back. They, dragon and rider, plummeted down and then caught air like an albatross over the roads. With the dragon flapping its wings slowly, the rider stood from its perch and yelled with a terrible scream, "*Pripeljite mi ubežnika!*"

Captain al-Rasheed levered himself onto the cockpit top and went to the port forward verge, then yelled in return, "Tell me who you are first, then identify this fugitive. My crew is filled with fugitives."

The creature gesticulated and yelled, "*Tukaj je, čutim jo!*" The dragon was a huge creature of metal, flames, and noise, and if it was terrifying, the rider wore an ungodly suit of metal, giving Mouse a feeling of terror. So much metal, flying in the air. It woke an apostical terror in his spine.

He was woken from his reverie-of-fear by the captain saying in a calm voice, barely hearable in the racket of the monstrous dragon. "Mouse, up here."

Mouse sprang to action, monkey-climbing the side of the cockpit and crashing to a stop at the captain's side. "Captain."

"Get at that cockle on the shore, we are getting this thing away from *Remarker*."

The Mouse grabbed a transverse line and used it to light on the pier, releasing it early and nearly banging himself up. He forgot that the wänd had an effect on his agility. It was like learning to walk all over again. He ran down the pier and to the beach where a ship's cockle stood beached. He released its anchor stone, unshipped its oars, and pushed it into the water. Behind him, he heard the captain speak in the strange tongue of the fiery creature, "*Jaz ti bom ona.*"

"*Zdaj,*" the creature yelled in its alien voice. "*Nepoškodovan in zvezan.*"

"Land at the island across the road!" The captain demanded. "*Zemljišče na otoku čez zaliv,*" he added in the fell tongue.

The rider levered his head toward the small island across the road and screamed again, "*Zdaj!*" But he settled back into the saddle of his fell mount and flew it over for a landing on the far island's beach.

The captain calmly quit the cockpit top and was met by Gordon Hodak and several other crew. There seemed to Mouse to be a soundless argument, but it was soon over, and the captain appeared, girding a falchion on his belt, his uniform stripped to the waist. He came down the plank that stretched from the aft well to the pier with exacerbated, precise movements. His shoulders looked like they carried the weight of Ocean on them. He paced down the pier, then took the stairs they had built to the beach. When he reached the cockle he splashed through the surf and expertly mounted the little boat.

"Let us go face a dragon, Ahar," he said as Mouse pushed off into the stream of the roadstead.

The Mouse marveled. In common, his name was alfar. In the older tongue, he had been told by Salvador Longongo that his name was actually Ahar. Alfar was a weak thing, something despised. It was more of an insult than a name, but it was all Mouse had. Ahar though, he knew, was the name of a legendary scholar who once ruled the lands of Kemaya, birthplace of the captain's wife's family. Altabib Ahar Hakim.

It still meant mouse, but not your common household pest. It meant the wise friend of children who taught cleverness to dominars and patience to the wise. Mouse guided the cockle through the waves, noting how quiet the captain was, how little he seemed to be noticing the flaming, horrible creature of metal flame he was slowly moving toward. "He wants me, Captain," Mouse finally said.

"No, he wants all of us, my loyal friend. Point of fact, the young woman Darkfather brought to us is who I think this abomination seeks, but it does not matter," the captain said again, "It does not matter."

Then he looked at Mouse who looked back at him. "Someday, my friend, you will be a great captain sailing greater oceans than I have ever seen, and you will command a crew that will do anything for you. They will sacrifice themselves to protect your ship and you. They will toil to the bone, drink bad water, eat meager rations, and suffer away from their loved ones. But they will do so knowing that you also are on the tip of the boarding pike. It does not matter who you are in the end."

"But why, Captain?" the Mouse asked.

"Because we are a crew, and to each of us the chalice passes. Now, the drink is in my hand, and I cannot betray the crew. I may not have wanted this Adjeness on my ship, but she is on it, and a crew member in every way. So just as each marine stands before the mast, as each top sailor clambers into the wind-swept sails to keep our drivers biting in, as each person works to see the ship forward, so I as captain am no different, and my time comes. If this creature burns our ship, then we may not be able to build another. The charts and tools in *Remarker* will not be left to salvage. Even if the tools can be made whole and the ship built from felled trees using hand tools of uncertain providence, we may not be able to feel our five score before any escape can be made." Mouse guided the cockle into the shore and watched as the captain stepped off. "Now shove off, Mouse, and let us see what can be done about a demen-of-the-air when a *Remarker* faces them with true steel!"

Chapter XV

The Queen of Darkness

Major Standish, Commander Nine, and Quartermaine Darkfather stood before Queen Nazira, at their feet were chests of silver, rare tea, perfumes from the southern islands, samples of ink, fine tiles of glass and tempera, incense cones, and yards of fine silk. It was a tradition of traders to show a sample of their wares to a reigning monarch, proof of their valor and good sense, but these great treasures were like ashes clinging to loaves shoveled from a stove by the bread maker. They were wealth to pay the great debts she had created for their new nation, the reason she had dispatched the *Remarker* into the currents of Ocean, yet the great victory of their winning such treasure tasted foul in her mouth. It was as if she had won a victory of sadness.

She turned to her council. Amina d' Canus Cragia was dark and saturnine, her sister raised away from her side but now reunited. Leina, called an orphan, but the daughter of the Mistress Silence and Samedi Darkfather sat next to her, now operating the fiscal accounts of the land with cunning and tenacity. The assassin, Regnal Bish al-Biejus, was their policeman, no longer hidden in the shadows of his trade but a part of the Dominion's forces for law. Her friend Gullen, now first minister of state, stood next to her, a gray book in her hand. Nazira looked at them and saw her woe reflected on their faces. *Enough,* she thought. *I am the Dominar.*

"I have fought and killed Kemayans who were partisan to my father, Guisarmes who would take my child and dash me to the rocks of the qabr, pirates who would strangle our nation in its crib, and criminal gangs who would run wild through our lands, knives dripping red with the blood or my people, these people. I am making a nation. Tell me, friends, where is my husband, is he not your leader? Should he not stand with you in this glory?" She asked for the record. A small, crying crewman had visited her first, made a doleful report where he was to blame. Yet it was these people's responsibility to tell her themselves.

Leina said, "Dominar, the loss is fresh. Do not say today what cannot be unsaid tomorrow." Nazira nodded. Good advice. Not that she would take it.

Amina spoke up as well. "Indeed, sister, do not speak in haste."

Nazira turned away from her brethren and said, "Darkfather. In the darkest night when all of our enemies turned their hands against us, you said that strange forces lurk on the Halo. Tell me, what happened to my husband?"

"I did say as you claim," He admitted, his face hidden behind his great beard. "Yet I cannot say what happened to him as I was not present."

He was lying, or hiding the truth. Nazira could feel it. "Who was?" She felt her wrath boiling to high dudgeon. "Who saw the fate of my husband, Captain Javier al-Rasheed.

Sunstar Nine stepped forward and bowed. "I did not see his fall, but of the twenty and one who did, I spoke with each one."

"Fall!" Nazira yelled. "To a storm, or disease, or a pirate's sword? I hear it was none of these."

Sunstar stood back up straight and said, "We had reached the last land as your uncle of Kemaya paid us and had spread across the island to carefully select a cargo of items, both of value, and as your husband ordered, items of history. I led one group, the Major a second, the Quartermaine the third, and our team master the fourth. And we had indeed carefully recorded the wonders of the lost land, sampled its treasures, took its writings and some it its art, and prepared thousands of kilos of tea for the voyage. Yet near the last day, a fire burst in the sky, and we all heard a fell beast screaming in a foreign tongue, and the captain answering back.

"My husband and father of the heir of this dominion," Nazira said. He was standing against some beast?"

"A dragon, a fiery creature ridden by a man of metal. It demanded things the captain refused, then the captain demanded it leave the side of the ship and he would discuss the matter on another shore, away from *Remarker*," she replied.

The Dominar rested her chin on her arms and closed her eyes. In the darkness of her thoughts she could see her gallant husband. Sincere, broken, reforged, brave, intelligent, and doughty. She could see him decide he was the only one who could confront an evil beast. "So my husband sought to fight a dragon."

"You are right, my Dominar," Sunstar conceded. "Our captain ordered these senior crew persons on the *Remarker* to attempt to save all of the crew ashore, no matter what happened to him. He took a cockle, oared by only one crew person, and had that crew person drop him off to negotiate with the creature."

"And you left him?" Nazira asked.

"No, my Dominar," Sunstar replied. "I disobeyed the order prepared for me. You see, we were sure he was dead, but some thought they had seen something."

"What?" Nazira asked.

Sunstar wiped her bald head with her hand, then said, "As the crew present watched, the captain approached the metal man and his mount, sword in hand, screaming words in a tongue that no one could know. And the dragon breathed fire on the captain. Fire so hot we were sure he would be dead. But he appeared from the other side, his clothing mostly burned away, one hand clutching a sword, the other holding what appeared from the position of *Remarker* to be a bright star. He charged the creature and they fell into melee. It was a terrible battle we heard, and the fire was seen across the entire island. Then the dragon leaped into the air with the armored creature on its back and the captain still swinging his sword. It arose into the air, then a massive fireball engulfed them all, and when it faded nothing was left but ash and soot. We prepared a rescue for him, hoping he had fallen to the beach. Twenty of us, armed with the largest of our weapons, were ready to take to the water and fight the beast as well within an hour. But nothing was found. No trace of our captain survived the battle." Sunstar Nine, not taken to maudlin fancy, then broke down. "My Dominar, our captain died saving us all!"

Silence filled the presence chamber like a wave crashing on a beach. Even the First Guards seemed to shift in their place, adjusting their firelocks and polearms against the wave of strife-colored nothing that seemed to flow across from them. She wanted to hate Nine. She wanted to hate them all, to lash out in anger, ordering her Last Guards to cut them to pieces. Then Sunstar Nine said, "He said you would understand that his role has always been that of being a sacrifice."

Nazira turned and buried her head in her hands. In her heart she felt a strike of lightning and pain. "All, leave me," she said. Then she started to cry.

Yet not all left her. Nazira looked up to see the Darkfather and the woman he had 'rescued' standing next to him. "Do you have something to say?" she asked.

"Javier al-Rasheed still lives," The Darkfather replied.

Book Club Questions

1. How does Javier al-Rasheed face his crew after the events of the last two books?

2. How does the crew react to Javier al-Rasheed?

3. What motivations exist for the crew to seek the unusual tea?

4. What is the relationship between Angela Standish and Javier al-Rasheed?

5. How does the Mouse grow in the book?

6. How does the ship *Remarker* become a character in the book?

7. What secrets are revealed in the book about the nature of Halo?

8. Who do you think Adjeness is?

9. What is her relationship with Darkfather?

10. What is magick?

About the
Author

Nelson McKeeby is a native of Iowa, born near Spirit Lake to a Navy Officer and his teacher wife. Placed in classes for slow learners at a young age, he was never able to make education work and left school by age sixteen. He immediately landed a job as one of the country's youngest live-air television directors and professional television writers, a career he has maintained since then. Nelson is neurodiverse with both autism and severe epilepsy. A long-time hitchhiker who often uses his experiences in his writing, he has also served with the Department of Justice and as a deputy sheriff.

Nelson is known for non-fiction writing about insider politics, law enforcement, the entertainment industry, and the Quaker faith. He splits his time between La Habra, California and Iowa, living with a Brazilian doctor of biology and nurse, and four cats in a multilingual household.

Discover more at
4HorsemenPublications.com

10% off using HORSEMEN10